May 31, 2017

To Eliza!
Say "yes!" to the
wild ride.

Karen McSaldrick

RINGS
of FIRE

RINGS
of FIRE

KAREN MCGOLDRICK

Deeds Publishing | Atlanta

Published by Deeds Publishing in Athens, GA
www.deedspublishing.com

Printed in The United States of America

Cover photo by Alicia Frese; cover design by Mark Babcock
Back cover photo by Claire Elise Photography

Text layout by Mark Babcock

Library of Congress Cataloging-in-Publications data is available upon request.

ISBN 978-1-944193-78-2
EISBN 978-1-944193-79-9

Books are available in quantity for promotional or premium use. For information, email info@deedspublishing.com.

First Edition, 2017

10 9 8 7 6 5 4 3 2 1

This book is dedicated to my husband Lawrence, the love of my life.

At this writing we have been happily married 37 years. Over the course of those years he has had to jump shoulder-to-shoulder alongside me through many a ring of fire. And so far, we have landed safely together on the other side.

"Riding a horse is not a gentle hobby, to be picked up and laid down like a game of solitaire. It is a grand passion. It seizes a person whole and once it has done so, he/she will have to accept that his life will be radically changed."

— Ralph Waldo Emerson

A note to my readers

Lizzy's life has been "radically changed," since book one when she first pulled into Equus Paradiso Farm in Wellington, Florida "for the winter season." It has "seized her whole." She stayed, following the farm back to their home farm in Peapack, New Jersey, and her story continued.

One of the problems of writing her story was capturing all the "moving parts" of a training stable, especially ones like Equus Paradiso that are engaged in breeding and selling in addition to training and showing. The characters in the daily routine included multiple horses and riders, stable hands, dogs, cats, the farrier and the vet, and more. It is a well-ordered chaos, with plenty of built in "drama."

In my own barn, I remember when my non-riding father stepped into my barn aisle one busy morning when we had horses lined up in the cross ties. He looked around and retreated, exclaiming, "It's a factory in here!" He instantly grasped that a factory floor is not a safe place for a neophyte! This explains why most busy barns are neat as pins with etiquette sternly enforced to minimize injuries. We aren't necessarily snobs (okay some of the time we are), but we demand order for good reasons.

I have tried to be realistic, while keeping my storytelling "neat as pins" and uncluttered. I hope I didn't lose anyone along the way trying to keep a score card on all the "players." I am also a stickler for correct terminology. But, I hope my non-dressage rider/readers will be able to enjoy the story without getting hung up on dressage-speak. I trust that readers understand they don't have to know the "aids" for half-pass zigzags (although Lizzy must!) in order to enjoy the story and can forgive me.

If you've been along for the entire ride, thank you. If you are one of those readers who likes to start with the last book in a series, decide if you like it, and then back up to the beginning, I welcome you too, but add this "cheat-sheet" to help you jump in without too much confusion.

Primary Players in Book Four:

Main character and narrator, working student, Lizzy and her Hanoverian mare, Winsome.

Dressage trainer and Coach Margot Fanning and Equus Paradiso Farm's top four-year-old, Hotstuff.

Equus Paradiso Farm owners, Francesca and Frank Cavelli, owners of Wild Child, Lovey, Papa, Johnny Cash, and all the young horses and broodmares.

Their son, Chess (Anthony) Cavelli, CPA, musician, who is allergic to horses, dogs, and especially cats.

Deb, EPF young horse trainer, show rider for Wild Child.

Natalie, assistant young horse trainer and budding artist of metal sculptures.

Ryder Anderson, working student, talented and ambitious advanced young rider, riding EPF's Paparazzi Z (Papa)

Emma, Margot's protégé' and former farm manager and "mini-me," riding Grand Prix stallion, Fable. Emma currently works in Texas.

Dennis Walker, longtime (ex) friend of the Cavelli's who jilted Margot for EPF's working student, Sophie. Owner of Word Perfect, Grand Prix mare.

Sophie, prior working student at EPF, ex-girlfriend of Dennis Walker, and prior rider of Word Perfect.

Francesca's dogs, Chopper (rough coated) and Snapper (smooth coated) Jack Russell terrier-ists, belonging to Francesca.

Wheezer, flame-point Siamese kitten given to Lizzy by Francesca.

Writing is a lonely process, where I set down my words on a blank page and send them out into the world like a message in a bottle. Unless I hear back from you, I don't know if the bottle was discovered. So, please, leave a review on Amazon, contact me via Deeds Publishing or social media, and tell a friend.

Thank you.

—Karen

1. Pipe-Openers

There is nothing like sleeping in your own bed with your own precious kitten purring in your ear. I was exhausted in a special sort of post-horse show exhaustion, but this time was about as bad as I ever remembered. My limbs felt like someone had tied weights on them and my calves actually seized up on me in the middle of the night, waking me up. I pulled my toes up and the cramps slowly faded with a few twinges. I blamed it on twelve hours of captivity, a lot of junk food, and drinking too little water.

Natalie and I had made the twelve-hour drive on a Monday, our day off. I just could not jump back into the routine of work today. When I saw Margot in the morning I told her of my almost desperate need for a day off and she took one look at me and agreed. To be honest, Margot didn't look so hot either. She told me that she planned on only teaching Deb on Wild Child and Ryder on Papa. Francesca had agreed to ride Lovey on her own. After Ryder's lesson, Margot was going to get a massage then go home and turn off her cell phone.

Nat however, went right back to her normal routine up at Deb's, eager to get back on Boingo, and to get back to her almost-completed sculpture, although she wasn't sure what to do with it. It had become too big for Chess' apartment. She hoped the shop that sold her rabbit figurines would put it out front and sell it for her.

Thankfully, Francesca assigned the trailer unloading and clean-up to Ryder. The trailer was a total mess because of the rain and the mud, as was the truck. Alfonso had the duty of washing the mud-splattered truck and trailer. Even the cab smelled of junk food and mud. I had been astounded to discover a line of ants marching around inside the truck next to the door frame. Crushed Jelly Bellies appeared to have been the culprit. I almost felt bad smashing ants that had traveled all the way from Illinois to New Jersey, gorging on smashed jelly beans. But, I smashed them anyway, wrinkling my nose at the metallic smell of dead ants. I read somewhere that the smell of smashed ant bodies alerted ants back at the mound of danger. But, these guys were hundreds of miles away from the mound. These ants might as well have been put on a rocket to the moon. Would the Illinois ants be wondering about their brethren, vanished without a trace? Would they make up a story to explain the mystery? It must have been an alien abduction, yeah, that was it. I laughed to myself at the crazed direction of my thoughts.

I was tired, but not too tired to do what I knew would make me feel better. It was a beautiful day, a perfect day to take Winsome out on the hill. I clipped my gate clicker on my belt and put her tack on in record time because the need to get away felt pressing. I did not give her my signature grooming. Heck, I didn't even comb out her tail. Instead, she got "a lick and a promise" for a spa treatment another day. Today I had an almost frantic need to get away from the barn and the arena, and even, if I was honest, Margot.

I was exhausted, yes, but the distress I felt was also due to the fact that my heart ached at the idea of selling Hotstuff. I had no stomach for the mercenary business world I had never paid attention to or cared about. This was about standard operating procedures. My fatigue prevented me from processing what it meant to me and to my future as a horse trainer.

But perhaps this experience would be a winnowing, a burning away, and a clarifying, of what truly mattered. I climbed on at the mounting block and pointed my little mare's small elegant ears toward the electric gate and pushed the clicker. All by herself she walked through the gates, alert and cautious but without incident. I made the right turn and let her walk at her own speed right down the middle of the road.

When we left the road and passed through the old gate hanging crazily open on its hinges, she turned left on her own and picked up a trot. I gathered my reins and just let her go her own way, getting up into my jumping position and listening to her breath fluttering through her nostrils in lovely soft puffs, a soothing mantra that allowed me to not think. I only had to nudge her lightly to break into a canter, and then a gallop. Her hind legs began to work in concert, kicking hard against the turf in a true gallop. I let her rip, and like most bursts of speed, it didn't last long, but it was exhilarating while it lasted.

She wound herself down without me asking, loping along the last big rise and then breaking to a trot. We stopped at the crest of the hill, as we always did, and I let her stand and pant while she surveyed the field and woods with alert pricked ears, her heart pounding between my knees. And there on the top of the hill, with no one to see me, I allowed myself to sob noisily for a few seconds before gathering myself and wiping my tears off my face with the back of my crochet-backed deerskin gloves, true work gloves, not one of the fancy imported brands that were sold at the vendor tents at the horse show.

Winsome and I both seemed to benefit from our pipe-opener. I felt at peace for the first time in days and my mare walked back around the field with her neck low, grabbing at tall weeds and making a sloppy mess of her bridle while she was at it. When we got to the electric gate I opened it with the clicker from a comfortable distance. Winsome passed through in her cautious manner. I smiled at my careful mare who I believed would never be spook-free, but whose world was still expanding regardless, as was mine.

I had put up Winsome when I heard an obnoxiously loud engine sound coming from our parking lot. It wasn't the familiar deep rumble-rumble of a diesel truck, either.

Dennis Walker came walking down the barn aisle. He was wearing motorcycle gear; all black leather. The tough guy look was totally out of character for an older gray haired guy. It was a surprise to see him here. I felt like we had been nice to a stray dog in Illinois and it had somehow managed to follow us home.

He looked pleased to see me, greeting me like we were old friends, "Hi, Lizzy."

Guilt over my initial reaction made me force a friendly tone, "Hi, Dennis. What brings you here?"

He pulled off his jacket and started to look more like himself with a nice golf shirt underneath. "Margot didn't tell you? Word Perfect arrives from Kentucky sometime this week. I flew her back from Europe and she's been at the quarantine station waiting for me to figure out where to put her. It took a bit of convincing, but Margot has agreed to ride her for me."

I think my mouth gaped and it took me a moment to gather myself. "Wow, Dennis. That's great."

He bubbled with happiness. "I'm having Margot over to my place for dinner so we can begin to make some plans for the two of them."

I guess this meant that Margot had somehow forgiven him enough to allow him and his horse back in her barn. Well, it *was* a good horse.

I said politely. "I'm sure Margot will do a great job with your mare."

He tipped his head toward the exit to the arena. "Is Margot here?"

I answered. "She's teaching Deb on Wild Child."

He looked pleased. "Oh, I am lucky then. I still regret letting that horse get away. But, I know it's a great deal for Deb, it gives her the experience in the big arena she could never afford herself. The Cavellis are sweethearts."

I started to have a deeply uneasy feeling listening to Dennis enthuse about the Cavellis, even though what he was saying was true; he was just laying it on a bit too thick. Dennis seemed ready to grovel his way back into the Cavellis' favor. I made an effort to sound friendly. "You go enjoy watching Wild Child. I know Deb won't mind."

"I'll do that, and I'm hoping to convince Margot to get on the back of my new bike and go to lunch with me, too. I even bought her a helmet."

Now that was an improbable picture. I smiled, "Margot on a motorcycle?"

He grinned. "I'm better riding a steel horse than the kind made of flesh and blood, although Margot did try and teach me once. I used to sit on Rave, and he toted me around like a sack of flour, but I could hardly walk the day after our lessons."

He waved good-bye and walked toward the arena. I walked to the parking lot for a look at his "iron horse," an enormous motorcycle made for comfort with lots of padding in the seat and back supports. Two helmets hung on the backrest. One of them was pink and although I could easily picture Emma wearing that pink helmet, somehow I couldn't imagine Margot on the back of that bike; pink helmet or no pink helmet.

I had just settled in for a nap with Wheezer when Chess called. I almost didn't pick up, but then felt guilty and rolled over to reach for the phone.

It did feel good to hear Chess' voice. "Hi, Lizzy."

I sighed and stretched, displacing Wheezer who squeaked in disapproval. I picked her up and tucked her against my heart and put the phone against my ear with my right hand.

"Hi, Chess."

"I woke you up?"

"No, just cuddling with Wheezer and dozing."

"I'm making us dinner tonight at my place, remember?"

"Oh, okay. I don't have to dress up do I?"

"Of course not. I don't care if you come in pajamas."

"Chess Cavelli, that sounds kind of forward, don't you think?"

"Hmmmm. Maybe."

I laughed. "Even if I came in pajamas you would be disappointed, I promise you. I am so tired I can't even describe it. I'll be lucky not to fall face first in my dinner, snoring."

There was a silence, the kind where I suspect he had things he would have liked to say, but decided not to say. On my end I smiled to myself, enjoying knowing that what Chess most likely wanted to say would be quite ungentlemanly. Instead he said, "I'm going to feed you a good meal and pour you a glass of good wine and even make another pa-na-cotta for dessert. It's the only dessert I know how to make, but it's so good I have never felt the need to make anything else."

Suddenly it all sounded wonderful and comforting. "Chess, you are a sweetheart." I smiled to myself as I echoed Dennis, thinking of those "sweetheart" Cavellis.

Chess said, "See you at seven sharp. No one likes overcooked pasta."

It was a different experience this time, knocking on Chess' front door, although I was still strangely nervous. I carried a bottle of wine, although I knew nothing about wine and never drank it myself. I did not want to arrive empty-handed, and let the store clerk pick out something telling him I expected we were having spaghetti.

Chess opened the door. He wore the same apron with the Cavelli logo on it. "Hi, Lizzy. Come on in."

For some reason, he looked different tonight. I felt like I had forgotten what he looked like. But, he looked good to me; open and healthy and real in a way that felt reassuring and oh so welcome. I closed the door behind me and followed him into the kitchen. It smelled fragrant with spices that were both savory and sweet.

I inhaled deeply. "Chess, it smells wonderful." Then I thrust the wine bottle at him, "Here." I handed it to him almost apologetically. "I know nothing about wine. I let the clerk pick it out. I hope it goes with the meal. I told him we were having spaghetti. It was a guess."

Chess took the bottle and examined the label. "You did just fine, Lizzy. This will go well with the Brazhul, Nonna Cavelli's Sunday dinner specialty."

I looked a little sheepish. "So, not spaghetti?"

He smiled. "I am guessing you have never had Brazhul. I am also guessing your exposure to real Italian cooking is fairly limited."

I nodded. "I know that spaghetti and pizza are yummy, and last time you made some awesome pesto. Do I need to know more?"

Chess pondered my question for a moment. "My family's business was successful in part because of my Nonna and Nonno, Dad's mom and dad, my grandparents. My Nonna was a wonderful cook from the old school and the family grocery store only imported foods that she approved of and used."

He gestured to the pans of food on the stovetop. "Take this meal here; the meat and the fresh herbs are from the local grocer, but all the rest comes from Cavelli Foods. The pine nuts and the garlic and the best imported tomato paste and, of course, our own label of the highest quality olive oil; the best you can find in the world. But the most important thing is the time and love and care that go into the preparation. My Nonna taught me all of this. Sunday dinner at her home was a six hour ritual that I looked forward to every week."

My emotions were still crazily close to the surface and weirdly he was somehow tapping into them. It must have been the reference to his Nonna, who he clearly had loved. I tried to lighten the mood, and smiled, "So, Italian grandmas that show their love with food are not a thing of fiction?"

Chess shook his head, "No one could invent my Nonna Cavelli."

I was curious. "So, what is Brazhul anyway?"

Fortunately, Chess missed my fragility and launched into an explanation. "It's a traditional Italian dish, spelled B-r-a-c-i-o-l-a, but pronounced, Brazhul. You take flank steak and you pound it as thin as you can get it and spread a mixture of cheese and herbs and raisins and pine nuts over it. Roll it up and tie it with string, braise it in olive oil, and then cook it in tomato sauce for hours. We then slice it into medallions, snipping off the string of course, and serve it over pasta with the cooked sauce poured over the top."

It sounded like a lot of trouble. "You did that for me?"

He didn't answer me, but instead opened the wine and turned to me. "Let's let it breathe, shall we?"

There was a flicker of a glance, and when our eyes met it was so intense that I immediately broke the eye contact. Every word we were saying to each other felt suggestive. I pulled my handbag off my shoulder and left the room to go set it in the living room. And then I shrieked in recognition, "Oh, my God. Natalie!"

There, next to his sofa, was a statue of a horse in welded iron, about two feet high. This piece looked more whimsical than the rabbits or the large horse sculpture that I had seen. It was standing with one front hoof raised as if to strike out at something, its neck arched like a stallion, but it had a bushy forelock, mane and tail made from some kind of fine springs. I realized in about two seconds that it was based on Boingo! It was fabulous, and required a closer examination, since many parts of the horse were taken from something else, bottle caps and gears and clips and wires, all welded together, with something bright and glassy set into the metal for the eyes.

Chess walked out to join me. "Nat brought that out today. I thought you had seen it."

I giggled as I reached out to touch it. "It's Boingo. I recognize the bushy mane and forelock and the jaunty set of his neck. That girl constantly surprises me. She's amazing in so many ways."

8

Chess stepped closer to the sculpture. "I have to admit, I am blown away. I had no idea. I mean, her sketches were almost photographic in detail, but this is unique."

I nodded, "You're right. Deb and I think one day she'll be famous. Of course, I don't know how that happens in the art world."

Chess looked thoughtful. I added, "She's been doing pretty well on her own selling her stuff at that little artsy-craftsy store down the road. She just finished a bigger piece that ought to bring in a pretty penny."

He smiled. "I have a feeling that Natalie can take care of herself."

I agreed, "Yes, true. But, wouldn't it be nice to see one of the good guys get ahead? If I could help her I would. I could say I knew her when…"

I sat down on the sofa. It felt good to sit. I looked up at Chess, still making me smile standing there in his apron. This time he didn't have any spoon-thingy in his hand, but he did have some tomato sauce or something smeared on the front of it. The apron was practical, I suppose, for someone who actually did cook.

I patted the seat next to me, hoping to lean against Chess and have a good long chat. I said, "There is so much I want to tell you about the past weekend. There was a lot of drama, and Nat and me, and Margot, and of course your mother, we handled it. Yeah, we handled it, but I missed your dad."

Chess held up a finger. "Hold that thought, Lizzy. I need to test the pasta."

He ran into the kitchen. And I yelled after him. "Do you need any help?" Although I hoped that I didn't have to move.

"No, you sit." came from the kitchen. So, I sat and thought about what I did and did not want to discuss with Chess.

Chess had taken off the apron when he came out with a wooden salad bowl and a long narrow basket of garlic bread, placing them on the table while I watched from the sofa. Then he came out with the wine and poured our glasses. He motioned me to stay seated. Then after a few more moments, he came out carrying a large platter, a beautiful platter worthy of the cover of a book on Italian cookery. So beautiful that I pulled out my smart phone and took a picture. I almost posted it on my Facebook, but then thought better of it. This meal was done for me. Just for me. I decided to keep it jealously just for me.

I put my hand on Chess' arm and said with complete sincerity, "This is the most beautiful meal anyone has ever made for me."

His dark brown eyes looked earnestly down into mine, releasing a flock of butterflies in my stomach. "I'm hoping that there will be many more, Lizzy."

I had to break eye contact or that beautiful meal would never be eaten. As soon as I did, Chess pulled a chair out for me.

I couldn't believe how wonderful the food tasted. I had never tasted anything like it before; the flavors were complex and rich. Every time I looked at Chess he looked pleased. He said, "I like that you enjoy your food. I never understood people who pick at their food. Food and family are meant to be loved with near abandon. That's the Italian way."

I laughed again to deflect the intensity of hearing the words love and abandon in the same sentence, because the quiet voice in the back of my head had connected the dots and wondered just what that "Italian" experience would be like. I did my best to silence that voice and make innocent conversation. "I've always had a healthy appetite, but I have to confess I just spent twelve hours in the truck with Natalie eating junk food." Then I turned the talk back to the weekend.

As I expected, Chess expressed the most interest in the potential buyers for Hotstuff. He said, "I understand, and realize it's tough for Margot and the rest of you who get so attached. But I'm preparing to go into an audit with an IRS agent who says that our deductions, which between you and me, are bordering on the absurd, should be disallowed as we are merely a hobby and not a real business." He held his finger up, knowing I was about to object. "If I can at least show income from a substantial sale, well, maybe they will not laugh me out of the room."

I didn't say anything. We had moved from a pleasant conversation about Italian cuisine to this. It had been effective at one thing; my ardor had cooled, and I was back to feeling sentimental about the horses. Chess sensed my mood shift.

"Lizzy." His voice was gentle. "I know you love your world of horses, the world of horses you know. But there's another side of it. The horses are assets. The riders are the means to increase value and showcase those assets; assets whose values are only proven by their sale. And if you didn't know it, the IRS hates horse businesses, they are always presumed to be sham businesses for tax write-offs. Now they've set their sights on Mother and Dad."

His practical assessment of the business side of horses made me sad, but I listened dutifully.

Chess sensed that the romance of the evening was toast. He closed his eyes a moment, looking regretful "I'm sorry, Lizzy, I didn't mean to spoil the evening."

I said, "No, no, don't apologize. I'm glad you wanted to talk with me about it."

"I also need your help."

I didn't understand. "Help?"

He nodded. "Yes, that's the reason I've been so open with you about what's going on. And I know you'll keep a confidence, too."

I nodded.

He continued. "I need someone on the inside who can let me know what really is going on with the farm. Mother is holding something back and not forthcoming about details. Mother is an experienced business woman, but her record keeping is oddly incoherent. I get the feeling that there may be a second set of books somewhere. Dad seems appreciative and trusting that I will work a miracle, At the same time, he says what really matters is what he's doing to help the new owners at Cavelli Foods."

He must have noticed my lack of enthusiasm. I was sure I was frowning.

He said, "I don't mean spying or anything like that."

I sat up straighter and said, "That's exactly what you mean, Chess."

He sighed, "Only the things that you think might help me win this IRS reconsideration hearing. If I have to depend on Mother and Dad, well, I've got next to nothing."

Chess Cavelli was pumping me for information; feeding me his Nonna Cavelli's rich food, pouring wine, and worse still, gazing at me with his mesmerizing dark brown eyes. I was no spy. Never would be. But, I was not immune to spreading gossip, if gossip was worth something to Chess. What was the harm? I gave him fair warning though, I knew nothing of substance, but if I could have another helping of Brazhul, I was ready to divulge any and all details, large and small.

I began to spill, adding my editorial opinions along the way.

"Well, for one thing, Dennis Walker is back on the scene as he's putting his horse in full training with Margot out at the farm."

He looked pleased, nodding encouragement. "That's good. More revenues."

I added, "And Emma will be here next week with her horse Fable, paying board and training while they prepare for Dressage at Devon."

He repeated the nod. "Yeah, I heard. All good for the black ink in the ledger."

I looked for some reaction to the name 'Emma,' but didn't see any.

I went over all the drama of the horse show, the ups and downs, the rain and the rein, and of course the judging. I did keep Francesca's secret about Johnny Cash. I might be a terrible spy, but I wasn't going to break my word to my boss over her secret horse purchase.

Finally, I ran out of steam and asked, "And what about Cavelli Foods?"

"Do you mean, what about the guys that bought Cavelli Foods?"

"Yes."

He grimaced again. "They can't pay Dad what they owe him, and Dad didn't get enough money up front. So, Dad's back working like a dog trying to help them back into the black ink so he can get his money. He's acting as a consultant. I can see that it's taking its toll. But, on the upside, once he gets the company back on track, he can walk away with full compensation. If he didn't get back in, they'd just go belly up and he'd never see the money, and all those folks who have given their working life to Cavelli Foods, well, they'd all be screwed. This is not just about us, y'know? Dad feels responsible to a whole lot of folks, some alive and some dead and gone for years. He takes care of people. That's who he is."

That was sobering. "Frank's stuck then? What does your mother say?"

Chess shook his head again with a stern look. "I am glad not to be privy to that."

Chess wouldn't let me help clear the table or do dishes, but instead brought out his Nonna's pana-cotta and small cups of decaf coffee.

We then moved to the couch where we continued talking, sitting so close that finally our legs were touching and Chess quite naturally rested his hand on my knee. Those brown eyes were looking down into mine in a way that, regardless of the innocence of our words, had my heart pounding. I knew he was just waiting for a signal from me and there I sat, frozen. The words stopped flowing and we just sat silently.

Finally he took my hand and spoke gently. "You okay?"

I had to think about that because I wasn't sure what the answer was. I sighed deeply and bit my lip to keep from having another outburst like the brief one I had turned loose at the top of the hill on Winsome earlier. I struggled to put it into words. "I am very tempted, Chess, but then things just come apart."

His eyes and voice were gentle. "Who says it has to come apart?"

"Every good thing comes to an end." I answered grimly.

He smiled sweetly. "Nothing ventured, nothing gained."

I shook my head no, "Nothing ventured, nothing lost."

Chess grinned. "Lizzy, you do not strike me as someone afraid to 'venture'."

I nodded. "Yes, you're right, of course. I never wanted what would be considered an ordinary life. I wanted a life with horses; and I wanted it to be an extraordinary life with horses. But I think I understand horses way better than I do people."

His grin turned into a laugh. "Hell, Lizzy, no one really understands people. We're all pretty much a mess when you think about it. I could spend my whole life trying to understand my mother and dad. Or, I could admire the things they've achieved, appreciate the gifts, be grateful for the love and all they have done for me, and in return consider the weird tics and temperaments that surround me as part of life's great mystery."

I laughed in return and said, "You sound very wise. It's not just your parents that have tics and temperaments. As a group I think we're a pretty eccentric bunch."

Chess quoted back in a serious tone, "The whole world is mad, except for thee and me... and thee I am not so sure about."

Despite myself I started to giggle and soon the giggling turned into full robust laughter. It was good to laugh. It left me feeling much better than the earlier bout of cathartic boo-hooing. It was right then and there that I decided he was right. I was going to embrace all the good stuff.

Chess said, "Feel better?"

I nodded.

Then he leaned in, taking my head in both his hands, kissing me long and deep. It was like an electric charge that ran down my spine and curled my toes. Wow. So, this was the "Italian" way.

2. Love Tokens

That "load" that had weighed on my shoulders did lighten. Nothing was different at the farm, and yet everything was different. I found myself spending almost every evening with Chess. We avoided talking about money, about the meeting coming up with the IRS auditor, the selling of Hotstuff, or any subject that included his mother or dad. At least for now, it was working.

I tried to stay in the moment, to allow myself to experience the almost electric response that began when his lips touched mine. I was happy each time I answered my door to find him there, usually bearing food. He had truly been accepted as part of our group, in a way as part of me. At our last dinner up at Deb's, the two of them together had produced the meal. Nat had stepped aside in her role as co-cook so that she could use the time out back, welding mask in place, working on her latest masterpiece, while Chess and Deb chatted amiably. It was a space of only two weeks that had passed, but they were two weeks of bliss for Chess and for me. We were still of this time and place with all of its troubles, but it passed in a hazy golden glow, capped off by precious moments when we were alone and my heart would thud heavy in my chest against his chest.

Deb and Emma would be showing at the next CDI at the horse

park in New Jersey the week before Devon, and then they would go on to Devon to compete in the Grand Prix and the Grand Prix freestyle. It would be an intense two weeks of showing. I had never been to Devon, an old and very prestigious show, and I looked forward to seeing the famous "Dixon Oval."

I still rode Winsome each morning in a lesson with Margot, working alongside a perpetually grumpy Ryder. In the afternoons, I helped Francesca with Johnny Cash. I soon learned that the couple who had expressed interest in Hotstuff at the young horse championships were indeed coming with their daughter and trainer to ride him. I had not talked to Margot about it, but knew it had to be hanging like a black cloud above her. Francesca had said to me that she had put an enormous price tag on the horse, but they were coming regardless. She had researched them to be sure that they had the means to pay it. They were not "tire kickers."

Each day at lunchtime, Dennis rumbled into the farm to take Margot away on the back of his gigantic motorcycle. I think his attention to Margot had been a tonic, whatever the baggage he brought with him. He distracted her from the worry of losing her best horse. And then there was the fact that she would be getting a new ride on Word Perfect, albeit a ride with problems. Word Perfect had a stall ready for her as soon as the shippers could get her here.

But the thing that I was eagerly looking forward to was the arrival of Emma and Fable. Emma may have had her own flavor of "tics and temperament" but I had missed her. As Margot's "mini-me" she had been my mentor and friend, helping me find my feet when I first arrived at Equus Paradiso. I also was eager to see her ride Fable. He was the reason she had left, and Margot said he was Emma's "horse-of-a-lifetime."

Emma's homecoming had been orchestrated by Margot to replicate the arrival of nobility. Artist Nat had created a banner across the front of the barn that said "Welcome Home Emma," and we had double bedded Fable's stall and hung another smaller banner that said, "Welcome Fable" on his stall door. I remembered well how Margot had given Emma a firm shove to get her to leave the nest of Equus Paradiso Farm, but she continued to demonstrate to Emma that she was family, and this would always be home.

Getting the ride on Fable, and a well-funded sponsorship, was something most riders could only dream about. At the time though, Emma had resisted. I understood why Margot was making a fuss at Emma's visit. Emma would expect it for one thing, and for another, it was further proof that the nudge from the nest had been for the noblest of motivations. Margot loved Emma, of that I felt certain. But I also knew that Emma worshipped Margot and probably still would rather live here than in Texas. My guess is that Emma would never lose her snobbish attitude toward her Texas redneck patrons, their barn of quarter horses and their cattle fields that Emma claimed drew terrible flies and churned the fields into stinky mud.

It was a long drive from Texas, but they had stopped overnight at a farm along the way, and Emma had a driver to help. Emma hadn't quite reached the movie-star status of flying to her destinations while the grooms drove the horse... but, knowing Emma, I felt sure she planned on getting there eventually.

At least Emma planned to arrive at the sensible hour of four p.m., and although I should have been with Francesca, helping her with Johnny Cash at that time, Margot had announced that she wanted everyone there to welcome Emma and Fable. Francesca didn't protest, she was planning on being there, too. Ryder seemed indifferent.

The way we were instructed to be there reminded me of one of those English dramas where the "staff" lined up alongside the driveway to curtsy and bob when the lords and ladies arrived. Margot even called me on the cell to tell me they had pulled off the main road and would be there in five minutes. So, there we were, ready to curtsy. But, to be honest, I was incredibly excited.

Emma's equipage did not disappoint. I spotted them coming down the dirt road before they pulled up to the gates. Emma's rig was impressive, glossy black, the giant dually tricked out with lots of chrome and extra running lights everywhere, including around the license plate. The trailer was similar to ours, a four horse head-to-head, but shiny-black with fiberglass siding; a giant blown up photo mash-up of a reining horse doing a sliding stop and horror of horrors, Emma on Fable in extended trot. It was a good enough photo of her, but embarrassing, and I'm sure Emma didn't like having her photo combined with some cowboy on display as they rolled down the interstate. I bet Emma thought it in poor taste, but I knew in Texas they liked things big and showy. The farm name was emblazoned under the photos, "Roustabout Ranch, Midland, Texas."

We blessedly had not lined up, but instead stood in a clump, Margot, Ryder, Deb, Nat, Francesca, and me. I was surprised that Frank couldn't make it because he and Emma had been close and this was a moment that seemed tailor-made for the kind of display that Frank adored. Margot reached over and took my hand and gave it a squeeze as the truck and trailer pulled through the gates, pulled up to the front of the barn, and stopped. I was amused to find that Margot was just as excited as I was, if not more so. She was beaming. The passenger door opened before the driver cut the engine.

Emma came bounding out with a squeal and ran to Margot. They had just recently seen each other in Texas when Margot had been there coaching her, but you wouldn't have known it. Emma hugged Margot around the neck with one arm, practically strangling her, while her Chihuahua, "Uno," was gripped tightly with her other arm. Emma looked as beautiful as ever, her long straight blonde hair hanging down her back, sunglasses on top of her head. Stylish as ever, Emma was wearing jeans that sported a sharp knife pleat, and a scoop necked tee in hot pink while Uno wore a beaded collar. Even coming off the road, she seemed cool and clean and bright. I was guessing that there would not be a line of ants and loose jelly beans rolling around in that truck.

Emma continued to bubble over with happiness, "Eeeeeeeee!!! I am so glad to be home. Oh look, a banner! Oh I want to kiss the ground! Oh, thank you for helping to arrange this." Then she stepped to me and continued her squealing. "Eeeee! Oh Lizzy, you look great. Margot has kept me updated on all the drama and goings-on. I can't wait to kick back and talk."

I had to gently pull her off me. "I look forward to that."

Then she gave Francesca another one-armed python hug. The girl genuinely was happy to be back in New Jersey. She greeted Ryder and Nat, and then she and Deb had another long one-armed hug that included a little tear wiping from Emma.

Deb said, "Good to see you again, Blondie."

And Emma answered, "You too, Hippy-Dippy."

That put a smile on my face. Those two couldn't have been more different, yet there was a warmth to their greetings.

Then we all turned our attention to the person who had emerged from the truck. He was an image to give one pause; a handsome young man in a tee-shirt and jeans and cowboy boots. I did a double-take when I realized it was the same cowboy featured next to Emma on the side of the trailer. It was odd to see both Emma and this guy standing side-by-side in the flesh while larger than life side-by-side on the trailer. His dark hair was short under a well-worn cowboy hat. He had bulging arm muscles with a tattoo just visible under the left sleeve of his tee-shirt that I couldn't quite make out. No one was looking at Emma anymore. We were practically rendered speechless. Thankfully, Margot found her voice.

She said, "Tank, you are such a dear to drive."

Then she turned to Emma, "Emma darling, where are your manners? Introduce Tank to all your friends."

Emma had turned around, looking startled to find that some of Texas had followed her home. "This is Tank. He trains for Billy and Lu-Ann on the Quarter Horse side of the business. He shows both reiners and cutting horses. He'll fly back home tomorrow."

Tank tipped his hat towards us, and said in a soft drawl, "Good to see you, Margot. I wouldn't have wanted Emma to make that long drive by herself. Besides, it's kind of nice to have some time away from the ranch."

I thought to myself, with amusement, that Tank was a genuine cowboy.

Margot made introductions and she and Francesca did their best to play the part of hostesses. I caught a few glances pass between Margot and Francesca. I wasn't the only one admiring the cowboy. But it was time to get Fable off the trailer and settled into his cushy digs.

Tank took over and managed it all. He pulled out the ramp and set up the sides of the ramp, then walked into the trailer as Fable's beautiful chiseled bay face became visible. Fable bobbed his head up and down, eager to be off the trailer.

Emma stood next to Margot. Margot linked her arm through Emma's and they just watched, clearly pleased to be together. No two women could look happier to be in each other's company.

I heard Tank talking to the horse inside the open trailer in a deep voice. "Whoa, son. Whoa."

And then, "Okay, son, you're good to go." Then Tank led Fable carefully down the ramp in short controlled steps and stopped in front of us. The horse was stunning, looking alert yet calm. Wild Child always had to put on a display wherever he went. Not this stallion. He was not going to show off; instead he made a calm and thoughtful assessment. As soon as he had a good look around, he gave a tug on the lead rope toward the barn aisle.

Tank looked at Francesca. "Ma'am, if you'll direct me to his stall, I'd be much obliged. I know this horse would like to relieve himself. He don't like to go in the trailer."

I stepped forward, "Right this way, Tank." I led him to the stall, thinking it was only right that a horse of Emma's wouldn't relieve himself in the trailer but had to find the correct "facilities."

Tank put the horse away, taking off the halter and giving the horse a friendly slap on his butt before leaving the stall. "Son, you stay on your best behavior now for these ladies."

He handed me the halter and I hung it on the stall front. Our entourage stood and peered through the stall front at the beautiful animal as he stretched out and had a pee that seemed to go on forever, and when it seemed done, he moaned and managed to squeeze out a few more spurts.

Tank had turned his back, as if to give the horse privacy. That little action by Tank was kind of cute. In fact, Texas cowboy or not, Tank was more than just kind of cute. In short, he was a hunk. I'll bet he had a slew of cowgirl admirers back in Midland, Texas. I turned my attention back to consider Fable.

Fable was lighter and more elegant than Wild Child, more leggy and trim; like Hotstuff. His face, not masculine like Wild Child's "tomcat" cheeks, was shaped like a kite, broad between the eyes but fine in the muzzle, with small ears. His full tail was also similar to Hotstuff's. And like Hotstuff, there wasn't a bit of white on him. He was what would be called a plain bay, but I knew that when he moved there would be nothing plain about him. Margot had said so.

I turned to Emma. "Oh, Emma, he is everything I imagined from your descriptions. What a horse!"

She was grinning, but it was Tank that answered. "I don't know much about dressage horses, but before Emma arrived I was riding Fable for LuAnn. Even though I'm not giving up reining just yet, I can tell you that this horse here is something special. Of course when Emma rides him, he moves like nothing I've ever seen before."

He smiled and shook his head, "Then Emma came and started showing me how it's done. Well, I don't mind sayin' she's taught me a lot."

I looked at Emma; her cheeks had pinked up.

Margot broke in. "Tank, I hope you can join us tonight for dinner. Frank is taking us all to his favorite Italian restaurant."

He drawled back in an accent that almost couldn't be real. "Yes, ma'am, that would be real nice. I got to get myself to the airport real early though." He suddenly looked concerned. "And I didn't bring any nice clothes with me."

Francesca said, "I can take care of that. You just wear one of Frank's sport coats over your jeans, and you'll be fine."

Tank looked embarrassed when he said, "I'm not an easy fit I'm afraid, being an old football player."

He continued to look embarrassed while we eyeballed his large biceps. But Francesca was reassuring, "Don't worry, Tank, my husband is not a small man. We'll have a driver pick you up from the hotel."

Tank nodded. "Much obliged."

Tank started unloading the trailer while Emma directed. Hay and grain and supplements went into the feed room that still had labels over all the bins in Emma's neat block printing.

When Emma got to the tack room though, she hesitated. Emma had always had the primo spots for her tack. Ryder had moved Papa's saddle to the lower rack, peeling off the labels for Chipotle's saddle and bridle and replacing it with her own. Emma placed her finger on what had always been her rack and stood silent. Tank came in with a saddle over his arm, a bridle over his shoulder, and a big tote bag hooked over his wrist.

"Emma?"

She turned. "Uh sorry. I suppose just any empty rack will do, Tank, and you can leave the rest of the stuff in the trailer, I know you need a hot shower and some rest. You've earned it."

Tank plunked the stuff down on the nearest empty racks and then smiled. "Why don't you stay and visit? If you can spare the truck, I'll go park the trailer and check us into the hotel."

Emma caught my eye but didn't crack a smile. "That would be lovely. Go ahead then, I'm sure Lizzy will drop me off." And he turned and walked away, with both Emma and me having too long a look at the backside of his jeans.

When I was sure he was gone I said with a grin, "Oh man, is he for real?"

Emma put her hand on her forehead and leaned into it for a moment. "Lizzy, you have no idea. It's like being dropped into that old TV show, The Beverly Hillbillies, and at first I thought for sure that Tank was Jethro. But he's actually pretty sharp. And he's good with horses."

I poked her, "He's into you, too!"

She shook her head vigorously. "No, no, no, Lizzy, no. Margot's been driving me crazy over this, so I don't want to hear about it from you, too; even if he is a good rider. Even if he is nice. And none of this 'you could do worse' stuff either. Tank is just too Texas."

I nodded obediently, but I was thinking, "The lady doth protest too much." Instead I asked, "At least you could tell me more about him."

She shrugged, then said, "He used to play football on the team that Billy and Lu Ann co-owned. But since he grew up riding Quarter Horses they hired him once he couldn't play anymore. He's won a bunch of money for them with the Quarter Horses, doing the cutting and the reining shows."

I was stunned. "These folks owned a pro football team?"

She looked back at me like it was no big deal. "They co-owned, but they sold it."

I blew out my cheeks, "Emma, they must be really, really rich!"

She still wasn't impressed. "Yeah, well, they talk just like Tank." Emma was still the same snob she always was.

"But are they as nice as Tank?"

She tipped her head as if she had to think about that one. Then she answered slowly. "Yes. Yes, they are very nice, and they are good to me, too. But I miss home so much. If I can do well enough at Devon, I'm hoping I can stay with you guys until we ship directly to Florida. Lizzy, Texas may be a big state, but the ranch isn't even in the great metropolis of Midland, it's in the middle of nowhere. I can't wait to go into the city for a night out. Heck, I'm excited to eat lunch at my fav Jewish deli, maybe get some first rate sushi."

***

We all converged at Frank's favorite Italian restaurant at the same time, hailing each other in the parking lot. As a group we were ushered into a private banquet style room at the back of the restaurant. Frank and Francesca were standing when we arrived and welcomed us as if it were their home. Frank pulled out chairs and seated us. Chess had come, and Margot surprised me by bringing Dennis. Considering his history with both the Cavellis and with Emma, it seemed an awkward move. But, Dennis and Frank were chumming with each other when I arrived as if all had been forgiven. I wondered if Dennis had pressed Margot for the invite. He was persistent if nothing else in his efforts to work his way back in. On the other hand, Dennis was being clever. Having a stranger at the table meant that no old sore spots would be exposed. One was always on best behavior when a stranger was present.

Frank then sat down at one end of the long table, and Francesca at the other end, like the Momma and Poppa at a family dinner. Emma was placed directly on Frank's right where he continually kept placing his hand over hers. He had truly missed her.

Emma looked stunning. I had forgotten just how blonde her hair was, and how white her teeth were, her complexion peachy-perfect. She came in looking like a New York glamour girl with high heels and a short skirt and a ruffled blouse and not an ounce of body fat. Her nails were long with a French manicure. I don't know how anyone who rides could keep nails like that, but if anyone could, it was Emma, who always seemed made of Teflon; no dirt ever sticking to her.

I suddenly got self-conscious and glanced down to check mine. I gave Winsome so many scratchies on her withers that my nails constantly had dirt under them, even after a shower. Luckily, only one looked bad, so I cleaned it out with my thumbnail under the table, but it probably didn't matter because everyone seemed to be focusing on Emma, who glowed with happiness. She was the center of all of our attention at the moment and she infused the evening with her happy vibes as she bubbled about life in Texas.

Her cheeks were pink as Frank refilled her wine glass. She said, "The whole town is about oil; oil and cows. And it's hot there. Really hot. Billy and Lu Ann have a huge covered arena with lots of those "big-assed" fans constantly turning in the ceiling of the arena and in the barns. It's a good set-up and makes it bearable. And I have the cutest apartment over the barn. It has a gourmet kitchen and a huge entertainment room. I couldn't ask for nicer digs, really."

Tank had ordered a beer and had skipped the wine. He leaned back in his chair and seemed to be studying Emma as he sipped at his frosted glass. He had cleaned up nicely, wearing a collared shirt and jacket that must have been Frank's. Tank filled it out almost to bursting. I looked over at Frank and then Chess, and then Dennis. Emma had their full attention. She had entranced all the men in the room. What a glamour couple they would make.

I asked Tank, "Do you live on the ranch, too?"

Tank said with a smile, "Well, Emma there got me evicted. But Lu Ann put me up a mobile home that suits me fine for now."

Emma exclaimed, "It's not one of those icky mobile homes."

And Tank said, "Trade?"

Emma looked horrified, and Tank laughed. "Don't worry, Emma, I wouldn't dare. Besides, when I had that apartment over the barn no one ever called it 'cute.'"

Francesca finally broke the focus of the awed worshippers. "So, Emma, what's going on with Romp? Any prospects? Chess tells me we need to get him off the books."

I thought I noticed Em's cheeks get a shade pinker. But she was saved by a procession of waiters coming into the room with trays held aloft, and Frank putting on his reading glasses to inspect a bottle of wine being presented to him. Pretty soon we were having our plates loaded up with all sorts of Italian specialties, including Osso Bucca, soon to become one of my new Italian favorites. I wondered how this version would compare to one made by Chess. Conversations broke into smaller groups as we began to eat in earnest, but Frank continued to chat up "Blondie" and Tank continued to watch her quietly, even while Margot engaged him in polite conversation.

Tank explained that he spent a lot of time on the road with the Quarter Horses, but that he most enjoyed his time home on the ranch training. Billy and Lu Ann had more horses than he could possibly ride, so he had assistant trainers who did a lot of the riding and training, too. Unlike dressage showing, his horses earned prize money, so there was a lot of pressure to hit the big money events. He did say he was intrigued with Fable though, and what Emma did with the horse.

I noted the sweetness in Margot's voice. "You are a such a darling to take time away from your own horses to help Emma." It occurred to me then that Margot had taken a shine to Tank, and because of that perhaps Emma's fate was sealed.

Deb was chatting up Emma in a friendly way. "Blondie, did you ever think you and I would be competing against each other at a CDI at Grand Prix?"

Emma almost squealed her reply. "Not in a million years. No, I expected to be grooming for Margot riding Wild Child at the CDI's. No offense, you know I love you Hippy-Dippy, honest. But, in a way, I wish that's what I was here to do."

Deb shook her head. "No offense taken. It's kind of a "pinch-me" time in my life, but whatever happens from here on out, I'm going to savor it. May not happen again for me, y'know. I'm not as young as you, Blondie."

Emma should have corrected her. But, she didn't. Instead Ryder spoke up. "Margot, Papa is sound and feeling good these days. When do I get to get back to showing, do you think?"

Margot turned to Ryder. "Darling, as soon as we get this next CDI and Devon behind us. I have made a schedule, at least up here" ...and she tapped her head..."I have you and Lizzy showing at Regionals and if all works out, Nationals. After Devon, Wild Child can skip Regionals and if the fates allow, both he and Fable will go to Florida for short-list training sessions for the high-performance league."

Ryder had somehow turned the night's celebration away from Emma's homecoming. Now Margot was the center of attention. All eyes turned toward Margot who felt obliged to have an impromptu barn meeting to brief us on the training and showing for each horse and rider in the barn.

Dennis broke into the conversation as if to remind us all that he and his horse were now to be considered in that show schedule in Margot's head. Dennis said, "And don't forget Margot, you'll need to make plans to get Wordy out in the world. She needs to establish a show record here in the States."

I saw Margot clench her jaw briefly, even though her facial expression stayed pleasant.

"Now Dennis, It takes time to get two strong females to work in concert."

Dennis began buttering up Margot by bragging about her to the table. "I don't think it's going to take any time at all. I wish you guys could have seen Margot sit on my mare at the Herm Martin clinic; within minutes she had that mare looking like a world-beater."

Margot had a go at trying to stem his enthusiasm. "Dennis, no one makes a world beater in one ride: No one. That mare has a lot of defenses, and I surprised her and got the best of her that day. That doesn't mean the next day she wouldn't be better prepared and get the better of me."

Dennis looked skeptical, and answered, "That's what Sophie said, too, but I don't believe it for a moment."

Natalie, who had been happily stuffing herself while surely taking in every word of at least three different conversations, sounded quite innocent as she asked, "Dennis, so who is this Sophie person?"

Dennis looked startled. So much for my assumption that 'company manners' would prevail while Tank was here. Natalie was being naughty. She knew damn well who Sophie was and frankly, I thought she was punishing Dennis for inserting himself into our party.

Dennis fumbled around. "Well, she's my, my, well sort of my ex. We never married though."

Francesca's lips curved upward, and she took another sip of wine, silent but clearly enjoying Dennis' discomfort. Natalie was not the only one with a naughty streak.

Natalie probed deeper, "Was Word Perfect her horse?"

Dennis harrumphed. "Well, frankly, that was a point of contention.

But the mare belongs to me; I always was the owner of record. I suppose these disputes are common when couples split. I had to take back the horse and the Range Rover and trailer. Sophie never liked the horse anyway."

Amongst the several conversations going on at once there was a beat of silence, but Frank took that moment to tap his wine glass and rise to his feet. Wise Frank was stopping this line of talk in its tracks. I noticed his face was pinker than earlier, and I wondered how many glasses of wine he had consumed. Frank always drank a lot, but he never appeared drunk, only jolly. But as he began to speak, he uncharacteristically slurred his words.

"My heartfelt gratitude to Tank," he drew a deep breath and held his glass up in their direction, "for bringing our Emma safely back to us, even for a brief visit." We all chanted "hear-hear" and took a sip. Then he turned to Francesca and his voice deepened with emotion, "and to my lovely, lovely Francesca. I still don't understand how a street urchin like me ended up with a beauty queen. For her embrace I would give a hundred horses, and a hundred dogs, and a thousand acres of green, green New Jersey countryside. All this, my friends, the horses, the acres, the dogs, everything you all enjoy, are just my love tokens to my lovely Francesca, and though they seem generous, they can never equal what she has given to me."

He raised his glass high. "To Francesca!"

Margot pulled back her chair, and Chess followed, and soon we were all standing, glasses held high, repeating Frank, "To Francesca!"

Francesca looked absolutely stunned. Frank's eyes were shining bright. He was drunk, utterly and completely, slightly swaying on his feet. Yet his words were achingly honest and I had to fight to hold back my own tears. I glanced over at his son, Chess. And I saw concern on his face.

3. Gravity

I was grooming Wild Child for Deb when Emma and Natalie came down the barn aisle. Natalie had been given the job of Emma's groom during her stay. They would make one heck of an odd couple if you asked me.

Emma had Uno held in her left hand, tucked against her body, and a latte in her right hand. She came directly over to inspect Wild Child. "Good morning, Lizzy. Is Wild Child still a terror?"

She ran her eyes over every inch of his body. She knew better than to reach out and pet him, but she finished her inspection by looking straight into his eyes. He didn't snarl at her, but instead met her gaze levelly, looking back at her with interest.

I said, "Nope. We have an understanding." I smiled, first looking at Emma and then at Wild Child as they studied each other. I remarked, "Hey Em, I think he remembers you."

She nodded. "He definitely recognizes me, but he's your horse now, yours and Deb's. I never would have guessed that Deb would be interested in showing him. She's always been a free spirit and not much interested in conforming to anyone's standards, let alone FEI judges."

Natalie was listening with interest. I expected her to rise to defend Deb, but she didn't. I think it was because Emma was close to the truth.

Deb rode to her own standards, and fortunately they were exceptional. The awards came as a natural course because of what she produced, but if they did not come, I'm not sure it would matter to Deb.

When I walked into the tack room to get Wild Child's tack, Emma followed. My back was to her as I pulled his saddle off the rack, and I knew without turning around that she was inspecting "her" tack room, just as she had just inspected "her" horse.

I turned around with loaded down arms to find her looking a bit sad. I said, "Are you okay?"

She took a deep breath. "I'm fine. Everything looks just like how I left it. I'm glad to see you haven't messed with my set-up. It's odd, how it feels like I just stepped away for a minute, and everything looks the same, but it's not the same. Those stairs across the hall go to my home upstairs. But, I am staying at the Residence Hotel where we used to put up Margot's students who came in for training. It's all so weird."

I felt the same. I took in the image of Emma, tall and thin as a rail with a dancer's erect posture, blonde hair pulled neatly back into a bun, skin like peaches and cream, make-up perfect, a pink sleeveless blouse and mocha and tan High Horse Couture breeches that were crisp and tailored. She looked the same as the tall thin blonde who was the first to greet me at Equus Paradiso Farm down in Florida.

But she wasn't the same to me. The Emma I first met down in Florida was intimidating and remote and so far above me in skill level that I could only trail after her in adoration and obedience. It was amusing to think of it now.

In the process of learning who Emma was, I no longer saw the same girl I had met that first day. She was indeed a real person with fears and foibles and not a few eccentricities. Of course all those things only made me fonder of her; but to have her here as a client was indeed weird, and she was clearly uncomfortable in her new role. I almost would have preferred Emma find fault with how I was doing my job and make some not so gentle corrections, because if she had we could slip back into the old roles.

I had the place looking neat as a pin, without having changed anything, and she was clearly at a loss for words, or simply conscientious of her proper place in the new order. In the past she had gently ridiculed my hair, my clothes, and my horsemanship and not always guided me with patience. Yet I couldn't dislike her. I had never disliked her. Because, behind her practiced perfection, was a heart that was loyal and true and also fragile in a way that made me want to treat her gently, kindly. The essential Emma was still the same as ever, and the essential Lizzy was the same as ever, but so much had changed around us, and I guess we were simply more "seasoned." I thought of Chess' words about embracing what was in front of you, despite the flaws. It made me want to embrace Em.

I meant it when I said, "I've missed you, Emma."

She looked back at me seriously, looked over her shoulder and then whispered. "Margot told me about what happened with Wild Child at Gladstone." Hearing Emma bring that sordid business up froze me in my tracks. But then Emma continued, "He got cast in the stall and put you in the hospital? She said you put yourself at risk to save the horse. That was awfully brave of you, Lizzy; risky, but brave."

I must have looked shocked. I was surprised if that was all that Margot had told Emma. But, then again, it was the story that we had all agreed to. I had no intention of saying more about it, not to Emma, and not to anyone else. Emma was looking at me sympathetically, but also in a knowing way that suggested she may know more.

I hedged, "It was basic instinct, pure and simple, but that seems like a lifetime ago."

I then deflected, turning the conversation back to the big changes in her life. "But, look at you, showing that incredible stallion in the high-performance Grand Prixes. I bet you could never have imagined yourself where you are now. I remember your first Grand Prix on Chip. You were so nervous."

She kindly followed my deflection, chuckling. "Oh my God, yes, and I fell off mounting and Chip ran around all the barns and I had to catch him and practically run to the arenas. I will never forget it, never."

I laughed, too. "I'll never forget Margot's face when we finally got you on and headed to the arenas."

Emma was still laughing. "Poor Margot saw me through my crazy teenage years, and then all the way to the Grand Prix arena. Somehow we've both survived."

I added, "You're getting all you ever wanted, Emma. It's great to see."

She shook her head and said, "All I ever really wanted was to do the job you are doing. You're doing it well. I'm glad for you."

I smiled, "I knew if I screwed it up, I'd still have you to answer to. I'm trying to do the job just like you taught me."

We stared at each other for a beat before she added, "My God, you *are* the new Emma after all. You didn't think you were ready, and frankly, at the time I agreed, but you seem to be keeping the barn and horses in good shape without me."

I smiled back. "Look at you; winning CDI's. You didn't think you were ready either, remember? You fought Margot tooth-and-nail on the move to Texas. But, Margot was right. You *are* the new Margot."

She wasn't going to agree, not totally. "Lizzy, that's silly. I am not the new Margot. Margot is not done yet, and anyway, I have a long way to go to be comfortable at this level. Margot is smart, I'll give her that, but remember it's always easy to be wise for someone else."

I asked breezily, "And what's that supposed to mean?"

She answered just as breezily, "Well, for one thing, you shouldn't wear those purple socks with that green shirt. Don't you ever look in a mirror?"

That got me laughing. I said, "I guess my fashion sense disqualifies me as the "new" Emma."

Emma, in a serious tone, said, "Some things cannot be trained."

She walked over to the bridles and took Wild Child's off the wall. "Where's Miss Hippy-Dippy anyway?"

We headed back to finish dressing Wild Child for "Miss Hippy-Dippy," who soon arrived and gave as good as she got in good natured reparte' with "Blondie."

Francesca showed up earlier than usual and soon it felt like a party. Ryder was put in charge of the CD player for Deb to run through her musical freestyle. Deb had Wild Child full of power and enjoyed showing him off to Emma. Then Margot showed off how great Hotstuff was going. Ryder was allowed to show off, too, by stepping up the intensity level with Papa, and Winsome got to demonstrate her half steps and tempi changes. Francesca even did a good job on Lovey, earning praise from Emma. Emma said all the right things, admiring everyone's progress.

The piece de resistance was finally getting to see Fable and Emma work through the Grand Prix exercises for the first time. Fable's gaits were light and airy. His way of going was a bit like Hotstuff's, but of course, developed to the Grand Prix level.

His weakness was an extended walk that did not show the shoulder freedom or reach with the front leg in the same way as Wild Child and Hotstuff's walk. I think Fable's limited freedom in the reach of his forearm had something to do with the very high action in his front leg that naturally lifted more up than forward from the knee and forearm. It was similar to the horse that beat Hotstuff at Young Horse Finals. Fable could cover more ground and stretch out with his lower leg in his extensions, however, flattening his knee, unlike the horse that beat Hotstuff.

All these differences in movement gave each horse a distinctive style. I think it reflected the very real changes in breeding for dressage sport. Horses were more and more bred to be specialists for dressage rather than simply bred to be "sport horses" and the highlight of these specialists seemed to be a trot with a very high knee. As much as I enjoyed a flashy trot, I admit to having mixed feelings about that trot that Natalie called a Hackney trot.

Like Deb, Emma and Fable were entered in the freestyle at both the New Jersey CDI and Devon, but Emma didn't want to practice her freestyle on her first day back in New Jersey, so we all had to wait to hear her music. After the long haul she was trying to make the first day an easy one for Fable. Music or not, Fable and Emma showed us a jaw-dropping ride.

Every one of us finished the training day feeling buoyant and hopeful for the upcoming shows. It made for a happy energy in the barn. Even Ryder couldn't dampen our spirits. She had begun to think about her next competitions and it had wiped the grim expression from her face.

Emma and Deb had this week and then half of next week to finish their preparations. Things looked better than good.

I met Francesca over at Claire Winston's for our Johnny ride. We were both still buoyed with the morning's optimism. Our optimism channeled to the horse, making Johnny appear joyful, too. Johnny was good from the first step of warm up. I could tell Francesca recognized the good feeling in Johnny as soon as she got on.

I sat on the mounting block and watched quietly for a few minutes before saying, "Francesca, what do you think about running through the test? Easy-like, for fun."

Without any acknowledgment, she simply turned down centerline and "played" her way through the test. I had never seen her look so relaxed and I said so, encouraging her even when she made mistakes by saying, "It doesn't matter, just keep going."

It was the best she had ever done. After her final salute she dropped the reins and walked around the arena, for once looking at peace with her performance. I said, "Do you still want to enter a show?" She looked back at me surprised. "Lizzy, you who doubted me, even you are suggesting I should enter a show? Frankly, you surprise me."

I smiled back. "And you surprise me, too. You should get back out there again pretty soon if you're going to do it at all. If you're going to take another swing at it, it's better to do it here than down in Florida. Of course, you're going to have to figure out how to slip away undetected. Margot's not going to Texas anytime soon. If you can figure out how to do it, I would love to take Winsome along so I can show, too."

I expected her to snap back at me. Instead, she looked thoughtful. She had not said no. The fact that she hadn't cut me off was a wonder in itself. But, I could also tell she considered the conversation done because she pulled Johnny up and dismounted. I would not get an answer today.

Francesca handed me the reins, and walked to Johnny's head, taking his large white and pink nose between her gloved hands. Johnny got his lipstick kiss on his pink nose, and then Francesca said, "Lizzy, Frank is bringing over some new decor for our horse show tack room this afternoon. We have new flower boxes with artificial boxwood shrubbery to set off the tack room curtains. They have the farm logo on them and look quite sharp. There are a few other things as well. Please store them in the farm trailer." With that, Francesca strode back to her Benz, dismissing me with a backward wave.

I put Johnny up then drove the short trip back to the farm, my head preoccupied with the anticipation of seeing Chess. When I pulled up Ryder was still pushing the feed cart through the aisle, and I felt happy to join her and help finish the barn chores.

I jumped out of the truck talking. "Hey, Ryder. What's left to do?"

Ryder was still more chipper than usual. She said, "I'm done. I'm meeting up with Suzette and some of her friends for dinner and this new serious golf place we've been going to. It's like a really nice driving range on steroids."

I laughed, "Golf, really? Ryder, you golfing... not something I would have guessed in a million years."

She laughed. "I know, right? Turns out, I kill at golf. I have a really long drive, and am pretty accurate, too. Suzette found some nice dudes who like to pull off their ties after work and go hit golf balls. They're so cute, y'know, like they work out. We have a good time and they pay for everything."

Ryder was actually chattering happily away to me and I was glad to let her. She pushed the feed cart into the feed room and flicked off the lights. We stomped briskly up the stairs and I stayed out of her way while she showered and primped. In a half hour she was heading out, looking more like a runway model than a golfer. She had a way of doing her makeup that took her from a teenager to thirty after only a few short minutes in front of the bathroom mirror. I hoped she had golf shoes in her car.

I was happy to not be going anywhere, but had Chess coming here tonight. I showered and pulled on clean jeans, twisting my wet hair up on top of my head and securing it with a plastic clip. Chess texted that he was on his way, but stuck in commuter traffic. I remembered that Frank was supposed to come by so I headed back down to the barn, figuring I could take Winsome out for some grass and wait for Frank.

I started to get Winsome out, then heard a car's engine running in our parking lot. Frank must be here and probably could use my help bringing stuff in.

I walked out and there was his pretty little moss-green classic Jag, engine idling, Frank behind the wheel. His head was down, perhaps on a cell phone call. I didn't want to interrupt so I hung back for a minute, but then realized he wasn't on the phone. He was just sitting there.

I walked up and tapped on the window. "Hey Frank, do you need help?"

He still didn't move. Frank was slumped in his seat, chin on his chest. My heart dropped and I began wildly beating on the window, my voice rising in panic as I repeatedly called his name. "Frank! Frank! Frank! Frank!"

I pulled at the door handle; locked, damn it. I again beat on his window. "Frank, open the door. Frank!"

I kept yanking on the door handle, thinking that somehow I could will it to open. Nothing. I wildly looked around, but no one else seemed to be in the vicinity.

Then I heard a strange voice that wailed like a high-pitched siren, finishing in a child-like scream. I realized with shock that the frightful noise was coming from me. I continued to beat frantically on the window. I had to get a grip and think, but I just kept yelling. "Frank, open the door, Frank, Frank! Oh my God, Frank just open the door!"

I ran around to the passenger side and pulled at another locked door, my heart pounding. But, then I saw him move and froze, uncertain at what I had seen; a small movement of his head. Frank was alive. I pressed my face against the window and watched carefully. My eyesight seemed to have sharpened, like Superman x-ray vision; looking through the closed windows was like looking through high-powered binoculars. Frank's right hand was moving across his lap weakly, feebly reaching for the handle of the door, but definitely moving, he was going to get the door unlocked, yes, yes, yes.

I ran back around to the driver's door and flung it open. Frank was now holding his left bicep with his right hand. He breathed in short gasps. He looked at me, his eyes pleading for help, but he was unable to speak. I knew of course, I knew, I knew, I knew.

Heart attack.

I was still yelling at him, "Frank, I'm calling an ambulance, don't move. Don't move, Frank." What a stupid thing to yell at poor Frank. He couldn't possibly move; he had barely been able to open the car door.

I squatted down next to the open door and dialed 911, placing one hand on Frank's knee as soon as I could. I gave the dispatcher all the pertinent information, and even before I hung up it occurred to me that we had that giant bottle of aspirin in the feed room. I had read somewhere to chew an aspirin if you were having a heart attack. I yelled back at Frank, "Don't move!"

I ran for the aspirin, my heart pumping wildly. It was just where I had left it; a large dusty jar. I snatched it off the shelf and ran back to Frank. My hands shook as I squatted down again next to the low-slung Jag and twisted off the cap, shaking out a fistful of aspirin, many little white chalky pills spilling out into the parking lot.

"Open your mouth, Frank." And like a little bird in a nest, his mouth opened, and I put two tablets in his mouth. "Chew, Frank, chew!" I was still needlessly yelling. Frank chewed, leaning his head back against the headrest and closing his eyes.

I then called Deb, yelling into the phone that Frank was having a heart attack. I then decided to stop making phone calls, and just be with Frank and let others make the rest of the phone calls while I waited for the ambulance. If these were Frank's last minutes of life, well, it was too hard to think of, but I did think of it, and I wanted to do my best by Frank.

I continued to squat next to the car, keeping my right hand on Frank's knee and talking to him in as reassuring tones as I could muster. My panic was soon replaced with clearer thinking, but also with fear as I wiped away tears. I did not want Frank to die. I was afraid that Frank would die right here. I was not prepared to see Frank die.

Gradually, Frank's face relaxed. He placed his right hand over my hand that rested on his knee. His hand was clammy, yet comforting, and without tension. Frank was trying to comfort me. Frank could be no one other than Frank, even while having a heart attack. That small gesture both calmed me and made me sorry that I could not do more for him. That small gesture gave me the strength, though, to stop crying and find a small moment of peace. If Frank could be brave and calm, then I could, too.

His lips were trying to form words and I leaned over to hear what he was trying to say to me.

"Ouch," he said, voice weak.

I started laughing and crying simultaneously.

Thankfully, Deb and Nat soon joined me, Deb taking charge, undoing the seat belt,

loosening Frank's collar and belt and generally being reassuring. She told us in soothing

tones that the new ambulances were as well equipped as the emergency rooms, and that the EMTs were going to take great care of Frank. She complimented my having already given Frank the aspirin. In short, Deb was the "adult in the room."

Nat went to stand at the farm gate to let the EMTs in; she opened the gate as soon as she heard the siren coming down our road. Deb stood by my side, talking to Frank, and keeping one hand on my shoulder.

The EMTs pulled next to the Jag and took over with blinding speed, getting Frank out of the car and onto a gurney. They gave me praise for getting the aspirin into him, and then they turned and asked, "Any of you relatives?"

Without missing a beat, Deb put her hand up, telling a fib, "Daughter." She hopped into the ambulance before anyone could question her. She called out to me before the doors closed. "I called Margot. I'm letting her deal with Francesca." Before they could drive away, I got the name of the hospital where they were taking Frank.

Things were unearthly quiet once they were gone, like the air had turned to cotton balls; as if there were now some kind of soft padding between me and the world around me. I briefly wondered if the dull feeling was shock as I turned to Natalie. "Are you going?"

She shook her head 'no,' and then squinted at me. "You did good, Lizzy. One of those EMTs told me that the aspirins may have saved his life. But, Frank's got a bad time ahead of him."

I felt myself float crazily, as if I'd been drinking or something, and asked the dreaded question. "Do you think he's going to make it?"

She blinked before answering. "Sure, Lizzy. Sure I do."

I caught my breath. "I'd better go."

Nat shook her head. "You're not fit to drive. In fact, I'm thinking you need to sit down before you fall down."

Chess' car pulled up to the farm gates. I had forgotten all about Chess. But, as he pulled into a parking place and got out, he was grim faced. He somehow knew. How could he know? I walked up to him and took his hand.

He looked into my eyes and said, "I passed the ambulance."

Then he pointed to the Jag, sitting there with a door still open, his face contorted for a split moment, and then became composed and he stated as a matter of fact, "Dad's had a heart attack."

I nodded, unable to say anything more, dead on my feet. Natalie was right. I was not fit to drive. Natalie told him what hospital, and Chess and I got into his car. And what I knew was going to be a very long night began with a very stressful car trip, where Chess asked questions, and I gave answers the best I could, my body no longer floating, but sitting heavily into the car seat, gravity reasserting itself.

Chess and I sat on cold hard plastic chairs in the ER waiting room. Frank and Deb had been taken to the back before we arrived. Within minutes Margot and Francesca arrived and were taken right to the back as well. Then Deb and Margot returned to the waiting room, Margot taking a seat next to me, but Deb standing.

Deb gave us a report. "Frank's stabilized. But, he's going right now for an angiogram. They won't let him go until he's had a full work up, and maybe a procedure or surgery to repair the blockage."

Margot breathed out a sigh of relief. "He's lucky to be alive."

Then she sat down next to me and put a hand on my knee. "Lizzy, your quick thinking probably saved his life."

My lower lip wobbled, and Chess put his hand on my other knee.

He said, "It was a train wreck we all knew was coming. Shit, Dad knew it was coming, too." He leaned back and put his hands on either side of his head, looking at the ceiling. Clearly, he was angry and frustrated at his dad.

Margot exhaled. "Please don't be angry. Change is hard, Chess."

Chess put his hands down and slumped in his chair. Then he sat back up. "I should see how Mother is doing." He went to the front desk and then was escorted to the back to sit with Francesca.

We sat for a few moments in silent misery. Someone needed to call Ryder. Emma would want to know, too, and would be upset if no one called her. But at the moment, after all the adrenaline had drained from my body, I was consumed by fatigue and too tired to deliver grim news to anyone.

I looked at Margot and noticed in the florescent waiting room lights that she was not so young anymore, noticing the fine wrinkles on her neck, the shadows under her eyes, and the creases in their outer corners. She was still a beautiful woman... elegant, sophisticated, well groomed, and immaculately dressed at all times. But not young anymore; no, not young, and she looked so very tired.

I looked into those tired eyes and said, "He's going to get through this, right?" Despite my best efforts I started to cry again.

She sighed, "Lizzy darling, I certainly won't make promises I can't keep. But, remember what I told you my darling... nothing is ever settled until they pack the dirt over your grave."

I stopped crying and sat silent for a moment, trying to consider what Frank's heart attack meant for all of us, for the farm, and the precarious financial situation it was in. Was it cold of me to have such thoughts?

I leaned toward Margot and whispered. "Margot, I have to tell you something."

Margot reached out and pulled me closer. "Sweet Lizzy, you don't need to tell me anything, darling. You've had a heavy burden to carry, haven't you; with all the secrets you were asked to keep? You shouldn't have been asked to do that. That was wrong of Francesca. I have been unfair in other ways. But I've admired how you have conducted yourself."

I was stunned and could barely manage to formulate a reply. Margot knew I'd been asked to keep secrets by Francesca. How much did Margot know? She spoke to me in an unguarded way, as if I were her equal. I was not, and never would be her equal.

I met her eyes, sadly, honestly. I said, in a flat tone, "But Frank was going to save us, and if Frank can't save us, then who can?"

She frowned and shook her head. "Francesca has been terribly foolish, hasn't she?"

I stated the obvious. "You know about Johnny Cash."

"Darling, of course I knew about Johnny Cash. I had told her not to buy him, that it was not a suitable horse for her. Not that he isn't an excellent horse, but certainly the wrong horse and with the cost well into six figures it seemed a lavish purchase for her needs. Frank had been working incredibly long hours consulting for the new owners of Cavelli Foods, and I could see things were tight, so the timing also seemed all wrong. I thought Francesca had discarded the idea. She was determined, I suppose, to prove me, and everyone else, wrong. After I learned that she bought him anyway, I hoped she could pull it off without me. If you two could pull it off, well, I knew it would have pleased her beyond all measure. I would have been the first to congratulate her, and you as well, and then this whole silly charade could come to a happy conclusion."

My shoulders sagged, whispering to Margot. "How did you...?" Then I said, "Ryder?"

Margot whispered back, "Oh, Ryder tried to rat you out, as they say, but I stopped her flat. She's quite the tattletale, isn't she? I already knew before she did. Doc did Johnny Cash's Coggin's test the same day he did our horses. He called me to ask why the horse was over at Claire Winston's barn. Doc thought perhaps there was some medical issue that was causing Johnny Cash to be away from the other horses, sort of a quarantine or some such. Good old Doc and I go such a long way back. We agreed to keep it between us and watch it play out. I knew Chess was fighting for our business status with the IRS and would be re-presenting to an auditor in some kind of scheduled reconsideration hearing. I've wondered if she was hiding the horse from Chess, and Frank too, until that was settled business. I still don't know where she found the money to buy the horse on the sly."

I whispered, "I do."

Margot leaned a little closer. I said, "She borrowed it from her High Horse Couture business account. She told me she intends to pay it back when she sells Johnny Cash." I added in an even lower voice. "Please don't tell Chess. He asked me if I knew of a second set of books. He suspects something, and I am in the middle of it all."

Margot pressed her lips in a hard line and sat perfectly still before exhaling and saying. "Unbelievably reckless. But I see now what is going on. She'll sell Hotstuff to pay back the account. Yes. That's another reason I've been kept in the dark. I lose; Francesca wins. It's her money after all. The horses belong to her, and not to me. It's her right to manage them as she sees fit. No matter how many years we work together, that fact remains."

Deb had listened silently, taking it all in. But she was now shaking her head, looking disgusted. She leaned closer and we three made up a small close knot. Deb whispered, "She's gambled everything on a whim. For crying out loud, it's not like the woman is going to the Olympics. Why spend all that money on a Grand Prix horse?"

Margot tipped her head, motioning to the door. We rose and stepped outside to continue the conversation. We stepped around the corner, disturbing someone who was sneaking a cigarette. They stubbed it out on the ground and nodded at us as they returned to the waiting room.

Deb and Margot looked at me expectantly. I said, "Francesca wants her USDF rider Gold medal. She wants to be able to say she rides Grand Prix. When people look her up on Centerline Scores, she wants the heading to read 'Grand Prix Rider.' She wanted to pull it off and then she would come clean after it was all a done deal. It was something she had to prove to herself, and to you too, Margot. But, I don't think she fully understood the seriousness of the farm finances and the scrutiny of the IRS, or for that matter, the scrutiny of her son. Frank tends to downplay problems; at least that's what Chess says. And Margot, she always intended to sell Johnny Cash once she had met her goal. She was going to sell him and pay back the money from the sale."

Deb looked at Margot and said, "The woman hasn't changed, she's the same nut-job she's always been."

Margot said, "Deb, please."

Deb leaned forward toward Margot, saying, "Let's hope Frank pulls through this, because if the unthinkable happens, we lose the only reason she's bearable."

We three stood speechless for a moment. Deb's cheeks were slack. There was no look of a pixie about her today. She was almost speaking to herself when she finally said, "No matter what happens, Margot, it's been a good ride, and we'll land on our feet. It will be okay. There's always another wealthy person out there with horses that needs someone who can ride and train. As much as I love Frank, just think what it will be like not to have to deal with Francesca anymore."

Margot looked like she pitied Deb. "Darling, aren't we being selfish thinking about ourselves when Frank's life is in peril?"

Deb shook her head, "Frank is the linchpin that holds this whole thing together. He's like King Frank. Long live the king is why I'm bringing it up, Margot. I want him to recover, too. But, I know that the chips may not fall that way."

Margot reached over and took the end of Deb's braid in her hand and gave it a gentle tug, then said, "I am not worried about that, not now, and you shouldn't be either. Besides, should the worst happen, you and Lizzy can move on easily, adapt to new situations, new owners, new locations, new homes. I'm getting too old for all those major life changes, besides, I could stop riding right now, today, it's enough for me."

I spoke in normal tones, but it felt like yelling. "That's crazy talk. Riding is like breathing for you... you stop and you'll just die, Margot, you'll die."

Margot looked startled. She smiled and patted my shoulder. "Darling, I'm sorry. I didn't mean to upset you. My point was just to tell you not to worry about me. Anyway, we are talking as if Frank is not going to survive. Let's be more optimistic than that. Don't forget that I've been in just this situation before. As angry as I am at Francesca, I don't wish my fate upon her. I hope she'll be spared. I hope Frank will be spared."

Deb looked mortified. She said, "I was there too, Margot. I remember. Maybe that's why I'm so scared."

Then the three of us once again, dropped into silence. It had not occurred to me once, not once, that Margot had lost her husband Walter to a heart attack. Quietly I reached over and took Deb's hand, and then reached over and took Margot's, too. Then Deb and Margot joined hands. The three of us stood there for a moment making a circle. It did occur to me then that we were just one small circle. The Cavellis would need to make their own circle, and the best we could do would be to draw our circle protectively around theirs.

Chess came out to say that Frank would be having bypass surgery as soon as the surgical team could assemble, and that all of us should go home and rest. He would leave his mother here for now, and return later to sit with her.

***

It must have been the middle of the night when I became aware of Chess and Wheezer curled around me. I don't care what Ryder said, Wheezer still smelled like baby powder and something else that I found essentially pleasing that just could not still be flea powder from the pet store. Whatever it was, it settled me like a tranquilizer. Slowly, I left my happy baby powder kitten-scented stupor as reality woke me up and filled me with heavy dread. I thought about what Frank had gone through last night. I wondered if Francesca had gone home, or was still sitting at the hospital. She would be beyond exhausted.

Chess was currently out cold and I didn't bother him as I quietly got up and dressed. I watched as Wheezer stretched and yawned and then repositioned herself against Chess. I knew as soon as he was awake, he'd be heading back to the hospital.

Ryder and Emma and Natalie were standing in the barn, a barn that was being cleaned by Alfonso and the others, but with grooming stalls standing empty. Ryder spoke up as soon as she saw me. "Hey Lizzy, I was just getting Emma up to speed. No training rides today."

Emma looked shaken. She said, "I'm going to ask Natalie to hand graze Fable, and leave my baby Uno in his crate with his teddy while I go over to the hospital. Do you think I can see Frank today?"

I shrugged my shoulders. "He had a bypass last night. He'll be in the cardiac intensive care unit. Even if you can't see Frank, I think we need to give Francesca moral support. So, I want to go, too. We'll take Francesca a few things, like maybe a cold drink and some snacks, maybe stop at the bakery on the way."

I turned to Ryder. "You coming?"

She shook her head firmly. "I don't see what I can do. He can't even have visitors yet.

Besides, I hate hospitals. They give me the creeps."

Natalie said dryly, "Yeah. They're full of sick, injured, and dying people. Who'd want to go into one of those places?"

The irony seemed to go right over Ryder's head, but I caught it and smiled slyly at Nat.

I looked at Ryder. "Ryder, Francesca might benefit from your company right now. Why don't you sit with her for awhile?"

Ryder looked as if she were decoding my words. She nodded. "I read you loud and clear. Yeah. You and Emma go now, and then if Francesca is still there when you come back, I'll go sit with her. There's stuff she and I can talk about. Maybe I can take her mind off of Frank for a few minutes. I'll go by her house and get the housekeeper to give me some fresh clothes for her. She hates not looking her best."

Well, well, Ryder was going to step up. I was surprised. I said, "That's a really good idea, Ryder, very thoughtful. You should do that."

Then, as if my approval was something she needed to dispel, she added, "Good thing you were around to once again play the hero, Lizzy."

Emma picked up on Ryder's tone; she narrowed her eyes and said, "Ryder, it could have just as easily been you, or any of us. If Frank had arrived a few minutes earlier, you would have been the one to find him. Would you have remembered the aspirin?"

I had to admit, Ryder, the know-it-all, would most likely have done the same thing. But she just shrugged her shoulders. "Actually, I did pass Frank on our road on my way out. You can't miss that classic Jag. He waved at me, he looked normal."

Emma studied Ryder, clearly searching for some way to take her down a peg. But instead she turned to me and said, "C'mon, Lizzy, let's go buy some things for Francesca and go sit with her for an hour or two."

I nodded, but then with perverse satisfaction gave Ryder final instructions before leaving. I said, "Ryder, Chess is sleeping upstairs. Let him sleep as long as he can, and when he comes down, please tell him that Em and I went to the hospital to sit with his mother."

Ryder lifted her eyebrows without a hint of a smile. "Yeah, sure Lizzy. Will do."

Emma and I were not allowed to see Frank. He was to be in the Cardiac Intensive Care Unit for two days and only family members were allowed. After two days he would have another five to seven days in a regular hospital room and we could see him then. The important news was that he was expected to survive. That heavy black cloud lifted from our shoulders. Frank would live. Margot's wish had been granted; Francesca was not to suffer Margot's fate of being widowed by a heart attack.

Margot was in the waiting room, and to my surprise, Doc was there, too. He stood as we came in. "Hey there, ladies. I just stopped in for a couple of minutes between calls, Margot called to let me know about Frank. So, let me know if I can do anything, okay?" He and Margot hugged and he left us.

Francesca was still back with Frank but she did come out to see us when we asked a nurse sitting behind a desk to fetch her so we could give her our care package. Emma had been smart in selecting our purchases, not only putting in bakery items, but also sport drinks and even one of those meal replacement drinks. We also let her know that Ryder was coming with fresh clothes.

As we expected, Francesca looked like she was ready to faint. She sat down in one of the hard plastic scoop chairs set out in a little alcove waiting area outside the ICU, and Emma and I sat down next to her.

Emma unzipped the vinyl cooler and pulled out a meal replacement drink. "Here, drink this, Francesca."

Francesca lifted it to her nose and gave it a suspicious sniff. "Smells disgustingly sweet, like maple syrup." She tried to read the label but did not have her reading glasses. "What is this, one of those drinks for people trying to lose weight?"

Emma didn't flinch. "It's not. It's for people who need more calories, not people who need to diet. Lizzy and I were worried you hadn't eaten anything. Have you?"

Francesca sniffed and then took a swig from the bottle. Then she took another and lifted one corner of her mouth. "Not bad, actually. It reminds me of pralines. I haven't eaten a praline since I was a kid. Down on the shore in summer."

Francesca's voice sounded different; tired, but also just different. She sounded less polished, and frankly, more "New Jersey" than I'd ever heard her.

Emma looked pleased. "I'm glad you like it. I had a hard time deciding which flavor to buy."

Francesca furrowed her brow. "Frank was spending all that time trying to help those boys put Cavelli Foods back together again after they wrecked our company. Throw the bums out I said. We have the legal right to throw them out, they've defaulted. But Frank, he wants to do right by those fools, just because he knew their father in the old days. Frank is too damn good and now it's just about killed him."

Emma narrowed her eyes. "We all love Frank. But, he needs to lose weight and y'know, probably cut back on the drinking, Francesca.

And we all know he sneaks those giant cigars of his. That can't be helping."

I saw Francesca visibly stiffen. Emma saw it, too, and immediately apologized. "I'm sorry, Francesca. I was shocked to see Frank looking so unwell at our dinner. You know I love Frank."

Francesca sat up very tall in her chair. "Frank Cavelli has never been sick a day in his life. I know what Frank has got to do. He and I will take our company back, and he'll be back in his element, right as rain, running things the way they need to be run. Cavelli Foods has always turned a good profit and every year we expanded and grew, until we sold to those idiots. Since then it's headed straight into the toilet and that is what has almost killed my Frank. Chess will have to step in for now, of course. Chess was always the child with the backbone and the business sense. Chess will do it. Chess has to do it while Frank recovers. Of course, I can't say anything to Frank until he's strong enough. But Chess will listen to me. He's so much like me." She was rambling, as if in conversation with herself.

Emma and I looked at each other, and I wondered if she was thinking what I was thinking.

Francesca was totally deranged.

4. Hail Mary Pass

We started the next day as if everything was the same. But of course, nothing was the same and probably never would be again.

I got Wild Child ready for Deb, and waited...and waited. Finally Margot came down the aisle, coffee in one hand, a large mailing envelope in the other. Ryder was grooming Hotstuff in the next grooming stall.

Margot leaned toward me and whispered. "I downloaded everything from that horse show entry website, including the numbers for Johnny Cash so you can find his file, and Francesca's numbers, even her password and Paypal info are in here. Should be everything you need to do her entries, including her online signature page...here."

And she handed me the file. "Please go ahead and enter them in the next Hill and Dale show... and Winsome, too; put it all on Francesca's Paypal account. Keep this stuff safe somewhere. You can tell Francesca later... maybe wait a week or two. She can't cope with anything right now, but she needs to do this soon or it may never happen at all."

I took the envelope, looking into Margot's very tired eyes. "You sure you don't want to tell her you know about Johnny Cash?"

Margot shook her head. "No. Look darling, this is something you can do for Francesca that I cannot. Do your best to make this dream of hers come true. You and I both think that horse will soon be a memory for her. Let it be a good memory, without regrets."

Margot took me by the wrist and gave it a squeeze. I felt my eyes grow hot, and my nostrils flared and ached for a moment. And then she turned away, speaking in normal tones. "Good morning, Ryder. How is my big black Labrador puppy this morning?"

Ryder's voice was flat, matter-of-fact, "His normal weird self."

Margot tried to sound upbeat. "I think I'll go ahead and ride him first today, but lightly. Deb and I will need time today to go through Wild Child's freestyle. After that, Emma has to show us what she's got for her freestyle. I haven't a clue what she has to show us. I've never even heard her music. It will be a long training day, I'm afraid. Ryder, I want you to take over the ride on Lovey for the time being, until Francesca is back in the saddle, both literally and figuratively."

Ryder paused before replying, and then sounded whiney. "Why not have Lizzy take the ride on Lovey? She never gets to sit on any of the FEI horses." She quickly added in a more positive tone, "It'd be a treat for her."

Margot's voice turned chilly. She drew her words out slowly, carefully; "Ryder, weren't you recently complaining you weren't getting enough riding time?"

Ryder didn't sound a bit contrite when she answered. "I'm not complaining. I just thought I could help out more by tuning up Johnny Cash for Francesca. Especially if Francesca's going to try a 'hail-Mary pass' for her medal. If I tuned him up, and then did the warm up for her at the show, all she'd have to do is keep the horse together for the duration of the test. It might give her a fighting chance."

Ryder evidently was not going to even pretend in front of Margot that she didn't know about Johnny Cash, or Francesca's effort to win her USDF Gold rider medal. Not only that, she was insinuating that I wasn't up to the task.

Not that I was confident that I was.

I could see by Margot's furrowed brow that she was astounded at Ryder's impertinence. But, she answered in her usual measured tone. "Now Ryder, this is a tough time for all of us, most of all Francesca. Francesca decided who she wanted helping her with Johnny Cash, and she chose Lizzy. I intend to honor her wishes. In addition, she was not sharing that horse or her efforts with that horse with anyone other than Lizzy. That's a fact we all could spend time pondering, but what's the use? In the meantime, while Francesca is occupied with nursing Frank back to health, we need to keep things running smoothly and carry on the best we can. We each of us have important duties to perform. One of them will be that *you* keep Lovey in good shape until Francesca can once again ride him. If you like, I could give you a lesson on him. Would you like that?"

Ryder once again answered flatly. "That's okay. I'll keep the old man going for Francesca. I know you're going to be busy with Emma and Deb." Ryder now made it sound as if she was doing Margot a great favor.

Margot curtly nodded. "Good, that's settled then; get the tack on Hotstuff. He's only getting a twenty-minute stretch ride today and then a good long turn out. He's had more than enough stress in his life lately. I'll go make a phone call in the office, give you say, ten minutes? When Deb gets here, do get her up to speed on the schedule."

Ryder just nodded. And then Margot shot me a meaningful glance, before turning and going to the office. Poor Margot, poor me, Ryder was treading on both our nerves.

Margot was barely outside of hearing distance when Ryder turned to me. "Good luck pulling off that medal. At least you'll have the fun of sitting on Johnny Cash. Suzette and I took turns riding him while you guys were at Young Horse. He's a piece of cake to ride."

I shook my head in dismay. "Damn. You just couldn't stand it, could you?"

Ryder's voice had a sarcastic edge to it. "Uh, pot's calling the kettle black, don't you think? You told me Deb let you sit on Wild Child first chance you got with Margot off in Texas."

Of course she was right. Touché for Ryder.

She was not finished. "Johnny Cash is the perfect horse for me. I could do the Under 25 Grand Prix on that horse tomorrow and win it. Your trip to Chicago gave me a great opportunity for an extended test ride. I simply took advantage of the opportunity to try him out without stressing anybody out about it. It was nice and quiet over there. No prying eyes."

My eyes narrowed. "What are you saying, Ryder? Francesca's not going to give you that horse."

Ryder huffed a disgusted huff. "No shit, Sherlock. I'm clearly not getting any favors from either Margot or Francesca. The thing is, Lizzy, the Cavelli ship is going down, from what I can observe. It's been pretty clear for a while now. You probably know it better than the rest of us because I'm guessing your boyfriend has shown you the numbers. That horse will need to go; most likely all the horses, this farm, the farm in Florida, all of it. But, the only thing I care about is that horse."

I was narrowing my eyes and scowling, my stomach churning. But, I couldn't really disagree about how dire things were looking. Margot had said essentially the same sort of thing, but in much kinder and more generous words with genuine sadness in her voice. Ryder sounded angry, as if Margot and Francesca had owed her the best of everything that they had, and somehow she was being cheated. She was out of line.

But, I didn't want to fight with Ryder. We had spent a lot of time in a passive-aggressive war, and I was not proud of some of my behavior around her. I didn't want, in this delicate emotional place I was in, to get pulled back into that hopeless cycle. I didn't trust myself to stay in control of my mouth or my actions.

We would never be friends.

We weren't even allies.

She was not interested in being on my team; on our team, the Equus Paradiso Farm team. I did not like her. I could not like her it seemed. Tolerance was even tough now, but it didn't really matter in the end, did it? She would never like me either. But, still, I was curious. I cautiously probed. "Ryder, how will you raise the money to buy Johnny Cash? He won't be cheap, even in a fire sale."

Ryder crossed her arms over her chest. I sensed I had gotten closer to a target. I continued, "That's it, isn't it? You're waiting for a distress sale? Even still, you'll need money. And a lot of it."

Ryder turned and went into the tack room, leaving me leaning on Wild Child and pulling at his mane in a way he enjoyed and gave me time to breathe, calm myself, and absorb Ryder's words. I knew Ryder well enough to know her words were not idle dreaming. She must have a plan; she always had a plan. She came out and quietly put on the saddle pad, the fleece half pad, the saddle, the girth, saying nothing.

Finally, I breathed out her name, "Ryder?"

Tersely she answered, "What?"

"The money?"

She shook her head at me, "You don't think I've thought about that little detail? Well, I do have a plan and when the moment is right, I'll execute it." She shrugged casually, "But, in life, like in riding, timing is critical."

I was shaking my head again. "Does Margot know about this?"

Ryder was short in her answer. "Oh hell, no. But I'll tell her soon enough, unless you go running to Mommy and tell her first."

I shook my head and answered sadly, calmly, "No, Ryder, I won't do that. It's your job to give notice if that's what you have planned. I won't say a word, not to anyone, until you give notice. But you owe Margot and Francesca two weeks notice. That's considered standard practice for any job."

"Lizzy, don't worry about me. You better look out for yourself. I don't think Dennis is interested in keeping the current system of working students in place."

Now I was really puzzled. "Dennis? Dennis Walker?"

Ryder rolled her eyes at me like I was an insufferable idiot. But our conversation was done. Margot had composed herself and was striding down the barn aisle pulling on her gloves, spurs on her boots. She was ready to ride Hotstuff. Deb walked into the barn at the same moment, game face on, all business.

The thought that entered my head with despair was a single word.

Horses.

It was a word, one word that bubbled up into my consciousness, forcing me to examine what I was doing in the horse business. It was a word now burdened with layers of frustration, anxiety, and some deep emotional ache. The sound of it no longer elicited the surge of joy as it once had. Horses were creatures that I loved, but now so much more than that.

Horses were not widgets. Each horse was an individual. That is what I had told Chess the day I tried to explain that they were not just... what had he called them? Oh yeah, livestock. What a strange and almost offensive sound that word seemed to my ears. They were not "stock" the way that reams of paper on a shelf were stock, or the way an online store had something; widgets, "in stock" or "out of stock."

They weren't cattle, and they weren't pets either, like Wheezer. Her lot in life was a simple one. She batted and played with anything that moved in the apartment, which would presumably include her official job of scaring away mice and bugs, while really doing not much but being my companion; the small heartbeat against my heartbeat. I already loved her and we two could stare unblinking into each other's eyes; a glimmer of understanding between such dissimilar beings. It was presumed to be a lifetime bond.

But horses, at least the horses in the dressage world, had much bigger expectations placed upon them. They were bred as part of a business to produce athletes for a specific sport, dressage. They were athletes expected to fulfill amorphous dreams that we had for them – and ourselves - of grace and beauty and temperament; our companions, our partners. Partnerships, in order to work, needed cooperation, trust, and understanding.

But it was not necessarily a lifetime partnership.

Cooperation, trust, and understanding only came through time and sweat and strain in order to form a bond. How coldly calculating, how shallow and unfeeling, to betray that trust you worked so hard to establish by selling out your partner for money. And of course, no horse ever had a say in that sale. They were our mute partners.

Reality demanded that we do just that; sell our partners. Why? For money; egos; human desires; all things that should never be attached to the intimate relationship between horse and rider. But, without those things, no one would pay us to ride them, to breed them, to train them, to compete them in a sport that we invented to showcase what we had produced. Betrayal was built into the relationship that we initiated from our very first touch.

So perhaps I was half-correct, and Chess was also half-correct. It was a bond, a partnership, but it was also a commodity business. The impurity of that reality saddened me.

I watched Deb and Wild Child work through their freestyle, my stomach in turmoil, trying to keep my outer face composed; as did Margot, as did Deb. They were workmanlike; professional. Wild Child, too, seemed calmer and more workmanlike, catching the mood of his rider. But today the happy swing dance music seemed flat and routine. Maybe I had heard it too many times.

The bright spot of our workday was watching Emma ride Fable. Natalie had the music cued up and hooked up to our arena speakers.

Emma did her warm up routine on Fable and then stopped, smiling sheepishly before speaking.

"Margot, you need to know, the music was NOT my idea. I had no choice. Lu Ann insisted, and she pays the bills."

Margot grinned back at her. "Darling, I can hardly wait."

Natalie rolled her eyes. "Margot don't listen to her, it's fantastic, don't apologize. I heard it already. Emma, get out there and put your arm up when you're ready and I'll hit 'play'. Then rock the house."

My spirits lifted, my stomach settled, and I leaned back in my chair. I was going to do my best to enjoy this. Emma picked up her reins, and turned Fable around and began to put him back to work. She did a few passage to piaffe transitions and then halted, signaling to Natalie with a raised arm.

Music swelled and Emma picked up the passage and turned down centerline. Her entrance music was only vaguely familiar but had the distinctive twang of country music. After her salute she picked up the canter, and this piece I did recognize: *The Yellow Rose of Texas.* It matched the striding of the canter perfectly. The rest of the freestyle had lots of different country music pieces done as a medley, all with Texas themes. There was *Deep in the Heart of Texas* with clapping, and *Luckenbach Texas* for the walk section, *Blue Eyes Cryin' in the Rain* and some others I didn't recognize.

Natalie was right; it was fantastic, even if not exactly Emma's taste in music. No one watching would doubt from whence this horse and rider had hailed. I am sure she would be the only one at the New Jersey CDI and at the Devon horse show with a Texas themed freestyle.

Margot was grinning at the final salute and leaned forward clapping her hands, clearly delighted. "Emma darling, that was sensational. I don't want to change a single step of it. Whoever did your music and choreography was very talented." She looked at us, conspiratorially. "Ladies, would you like to know a deep dark secret?"

We were all ears.

Margot leaned back and smiled, looking into the distance. "One of my Walter's secret vices was country music. He loved country music, thought it told such wonderful stories. When we were on the road together he used to play country music cassettes, and would sing *Blue Eyes Cryin' in the Rain* as loud as he could. And do you want to know something else?"

Head nods from all.

"Walter's skills and talents were with horses. He was one of the worst singers I ever heard in my life." She started to giggle and the rest of us joined in, our laughs echoing in the arena.

When things were quiet again, Emma dropped her reins and rubbed Fable on the withers. "LuAnn spent a fortune on it. She had it recorded in Austin with studio musicians. It's very professionally done; I'll give her that. I helped with the choreography. So you really liked it?"

Margot bobbed her head. "I do. Don't change a note. It's perfect. It's distinctive, memorable. But in a good way."

Emma looked skeptical. "Honest?"

Natalie interjected. "Aw for God's sake. We all love it, Emma. You're just being a snob about the country music. If the judges don't like it because of the music, then they're snobs, too. Piss on 'em."

Margot barely suppressed a laugh. And then Emma laughed and said, "Natalie, tell us how you really feel, please, don't hold back or anything." And we all laughed again. It felt good.

I asked Margot if it was alright to ride on my own today, and she didn't try to talk me out of it. I knew she had put a lot of energy into helping Deb and Emma. Margot looked exhausted and I knew she would also be traveling back to the hospital to spell Francesca. There was no need to make her stay and coach me. Ryder had Papa and Lovey to get ridden, and I had Winsome and Johnny. We could do all that without Margot.

I put some music on in the arena, some nice instrumentals a long way from the heart of Texas, and turned it up loud enough that I wouldn't feel tempted to speak to Ryder. I got on Winsome and drew the curtain around Winsome and myself and entered my quiet place. I let the music calm me and center me and put my focus on my horse.

I allowed Winsome to begin her work a bit under tempo, at half power, riding lots of long leg-yields, finding the bounce and swing. I sat relaxed and let myself just ride simple bending lines, deciding to forego rising the trot, and just sitting, because it felt right. I asked little of my mare. This was a ride for relaxation and suppleness, not power. This was a ride to let go of stress and strain, and not a ride were I wanted to tempt either of those two evils to interject themselves.

I had so little control over what was happening around me and what was at stake. But, I had this. I owned Winsome and we were in this together. I had all the responsibility for her, and I would not let her down. That meant that while I sat on her I owed her my focus and I owed her the ability to detach myself from the human problems that had nothing to do with her. That was important. Not easy. But important.

I could do that now better than I thought I could, even with Ryder in the arena. She had chosen to ride Papa first of her two rides, and I only noticed her peripherally. I wondered how easy it would be for her to discard Papa, to leave him behind for what? To be sold? Papa had been her ticket to Gladstone, and to the NAJYRC. I guess mentally Ryder had moved on and was simply biding her time. Today she rode as if simply checking off her 'to-do' boxes. She had Papa done in thirty minutes. Then he was put away in a flash and it was on to Lovey. She was still on Lovey when I had put Winsome away and closed the driver's side door in my truck to head over to Claire Winston's for my Johnny ride. I watched Ryder's profile canter by above the kickboards before putting my truck into reverse. It was time to turn my attention to my next ride, a ride that had its own pressures.

I had a job to do, but riding Johnny Cash was not a box I could easily check off for the day. I had to prepare Johnny Cash for Francesca to show at Grand Prix. I had to do what Ryder clearly thought she should be doing and that I was not capable of doing. No, according to Ryder, I should be thrilled to be allowed to just sit on Lovey. I did have a challenge. I did not have Ryder's FEI experience. But, I needed to do this not only for Francesca, but also for Margot.

Ryder had said that Johnny Cash was "a piece of cake" to ride, and at the same time inferred that I was not up to the task of preparing the horse for Francesca. So, where did that mean Ryder ranked my riding skills? Not very high.

I drove over to the Winstons', feeling my resentment of Ryder festering and defending myself in an imaginary conversation in my head against her unspoken assessment of my ability. What a waste of my mental energies. I needed to be thinking about the difficulty of the Grand Prix test and the need to have Johnny Cash one hundred percent committed to going forward on whatever line of travel his rider requested, no matter if it was a line of shadows, or if metal chairs were noisily tumbling to the concrete floor. The distractions of sights, sounds, smells, touch, could all be interpreted by Johnny Cash, a flighty creature, as dangers. But between my boots and reins he must find safety and courage, whether I led with my reins or drove the horse with my legs. It was obedience, yes, that too, but obedience trained through repetition and earned because the horse found he could trust my judgment. My technique may not yet be as skilled and trained as Ryder's, but Francesca had chosen me over Ryder for a reason. Francesca had chosen the right girl for the job. Trust; it was the same for both horse and human. No one in their right mind would place their trust in Ryder.

I pulled into my parking spot at the Winstons' without even seeing my surroundings. I seemed to float through the process of gathering Johnny's tack and bridle. I stroked his big wide blaze-face, his long chin whiskers tickling my ungloved palm as I fed him a peppermint and slipped on his halter. Such a big bright red horse, tricked out with so many flashy white markings; but just a horse who had no way of knowing that he was now a desired object of two different riders' ambitions. Both riders were intensely focused and driven, and I wondered how this craziness would play itself out.

I was assigned to be the one who provided a happy memory. It was a tall order that I could not promise to fulfill. I put my back into the currycomb. Johnny enjoyed it, and it felt good to work my arms. I had nowhere else I had to be, and no Ryder or Francesca to come and disrupt my solitude. So, I took my time, making no promises to myself of anything exceptional happening in my ride. Just to do what I could do today; to take the crazy pressure away for this ride, this moment.

So, I walked an extra long time to think about the test, and after the warm up, walked again, choosing a couple of exercises from the test on which to focus. Not the piaffe and passage, not the canter pirouettes, and not the dreaded zigzags. No, I chose the trot half passes, the rein back, and the collected canter to trot transition, that and to ride well-executed corners. Johnny didn't spook the entire ride, and just as I had felt with my Winsome ride, I was refreshed.

I had gone to that special place of inner calm, of motion and stillness. In that strange land of thinking and not thinking was a feeling I identified as happiness, a happiness in the midst of such unhappiness. My two rides were gifts, as if tiny frayed edges of cloth that bound up my hurts, so recently unraveling, were being knit back together through the act of riding. These large animals that could not know my frailties, my hurts, and sorrows. Animals that were silent and solid were somehow powerful healers. I'm not sure how or why, but did it matter? I thanked Johnny with a hot shower and a handful of treats, and left him contentedly enjoying his timothy hay.

Back at the apartment I had my own hot shower, and then my exhaustion caught up with me. Ryder had eaten a salad in silence in front of the TV and then gone to her bedroom and shut the door. I stretched out on the now empty sofa and watched TV. Wheezer climbed up on my chest, her ice blue eyes focused on mine. She chatted me up, and then kneaded my shirt with her peachy colored paws, purring loudly. She turned circles and settled on my chest, licking my chin a few times with her scratchy tongue. I closed my eyes and sank into a deep and dreamless sleep.

I'm not sure what time it was when I drifted into consciousness, but I sensed I was being kissed on my forehead. The television was turned off, and a soft throw blanket had been spread over me. Wheezer was gone too, but I heard her meowing from somewhere near the kitchen.

Chess spoke softly. "Hey there sleeping beauty."

My head felt too heavy to lift, my contacts stuck to my dry eyes, my left arm gone all pins and needles crammed against the back of the sofa.

I croaked a reply. "Hey." I stretched and sighed and finally sat up, rubbing my arm that felt dead, hardly part of my body.

Chess shook his head. "Been a rough patch for all of us. You doing okay?"

I nodded, "Sure. I'll be fine. How's your dad?"

"He's hurting. But, the doctors seem satisfied. Mother's the one that I'm worried about now."

I wasn't sure how to reply, because frankly when I last saw Francesca she had seemed off her rocker.

Thankfully, Chess changed the subject. "I brought us dinner. I put it in the oven when I saw you were out cold. I saw Ryder briefly and offered to share, but she said she'd already eaten. She's gone on to bed; shut her door. I was thinking you were going to sleep through the night and miss eating dinner, but I waited anyway. It's almost ten."

That astounded me. "Wow. You shouldn't have waited. I guess I almost did miss dinner. But, now that you mention it, I'm starved."

So Chess pulled the pizza out of the oven and poured us sodas. The two of us ate the entire pizza. Wheezer kept us entertained by crawling up my leg to beg for pizza. I put her on the floor, and then she simply crawled up Chess' leg instead. She gave us reason to laugh as she meowed in bitter complaint after being put yet again back on the floor.

Clean up was easy. All we had to do was stuff the folded cardboard box in the trash.

I felt much better. I put my hand over his. "Thanks. You want to stay?" I motioned over to the sofa, leading him by the hand.

He hesitated, and then examined me for a moment. "No. I think I'll let Wheezer take care of you tonight. I need to go into the city early tomorrow, and it's a shorter drive from my condo."

I examined his fine features. He was so much like Francesca and so unlike his dad in appearance. He did look weary. "Chess, Francesca was talking to me about you stepping in and taking over the old company. Is that for real?"

Chess looked down and ran his fingers through his hair. "Yeah, she's said the same thing to me, too." He yawned. "She's already talking to corporate attorneys, and now is not the time to pick a fight with her. But it's not what I want. I never have. I'm more than happy to clean up the books, make a business plan, and to fight like hell with the IRS. That meeting's coming up soon, by the way. But my brother Bobby and I both decided long ago we didn't want to run Cavelli Foods. That's why Dad sold it. But now Mother feels she's been cheated, she's pissed, those buyers have broken some unwritten code. She sees this now like it's a blood feud."

I winced. "She's blaming Frank's heart attack on them, too."

Chess did not look happy. "That woman has a will of iron. She still thinks we're in the old country, even though it's been two generations since our people were over there, and that some sort of honor code has been breached. These guys who took over are children of their pals from the 'hood. According to Mother, their family should just "remove" them. For God's sake, you'd think she was in the Mafia. I just want Dad to get the money he's owed. I don't wish anyone any ill and I certainly don't want to be tied to Cavelli Foods for the rest of my life."

Chess looked genuinely anguished. I answered softly, sitting down on the sofa and patting the seat next to me, "I don't want that for you either, Chess. Not if that's not what you want."

Chess sat down and took my hand. "I promised to take care of this IRS audit. I can only focus on that right now. You can help me out. I got to make this thing fly. What's happening on selling Hotstuff?"

I swallowed hard. "Does that really have to happen, Chess?"

He nodded. "That, and much more, Lizzy. The auditor thinks we've been fudging and we will owe lots of money and penalties if it sticks. I've got to show them we can make money at this, even if it takes years to fully realize it. I've got to show them a plan for future profitability and some progress. They hate horse businesses. They see them as a tax dodge. We've got to trim the fat and make plans. We've got to sell some of our assets, and we cannot afford to turn away anyone with cash in hand offering a reasonable price. I know this is hard for you, but that's the reality."

My face must have changed expression; he squeezed my hand, sounding truly apologetic. "I'm so sorry. Life is hard, but it could get even harder. I don't want to screw this up. The folks could use some good news."

I nodded, "I'm sure Francesca has the contact information of the people in Chicago who expressed interest. But Margot will need to be the one to ride the horse and show him to the daughter. Margot will be the one you need to talk to."

He looked thoughtful for a moment. "I can get the contact information from Mother. But then I'm going to give it to you and let you and Margot take it from there. Other than giving out her bank routing numbers, Mother doesn't need to be part of this. She's been glued to Dad's side. I can barely get her to eat or rest."

I sighed. "Okay."

He continued. "I want to ask you to look over some numbers with me. I can't cut expenses if I don't understand what they are for, although I have a clue. I saw Emma at the hospital and we discussed the horse we have out there with her in Texas to be sold. She said he was going to be a difficult sell. I told her to cut his price. We're losing money on his upkeep that we'll never recover, regardless of his sale price."

I gasped. "Oh, Chess, are you sure? I mean, is Francesca going to have a fit when she finds out?"

He frowned and shook his head. "I already told her. She agreed. In fact, I think she's relieved to let me make some decisions for her right now. It won't last. Like I said, I'm just planning to get through this IRS thing and then step back out of it."

He gave me a sweet kiss. I marveled at the burden he had taken on. Clearly this was not by choice, but he was kind, and he was willing, and he was motivated by a genuine love and concern for his parents. Chess Cavelli was a good man. I snuggled up next to him, and he put his arm over my shoulder and drew me close.

I thought of Chess at that club in Greenwich Village, singing into the mike and playing the piano with such soul. I said, "Sing me *Moon River*." That brought out a smile.

His voice was low and soft, this was a song just for me. But his voice was clear and pure.

"Moon River, wider than a mile, I'm crossing you in style someday.

You dream -maker, you heart-breaker, where ever you're going, I'm going your way. Two Drifters, off to see the world, there's such a lot of world to see.

We're after the same rainbow's end, my Huckleberry friend,

Moon River and me."

I had tucked myself under his arm and enjoyed every note. Now I turned my face up to look at him directly. "I love that song. It makes me think of Mark Twain, and the novel *Huckleberry Finn*. You know, rafting down the Mississippi River, runaways, both of them. I was an English major, y'know. I loved American Lit."

Chess smiled. "I never thought about it that way. It's from the movie *Breakfast at Tiffany's* and in that story the main character, Holly Golightly, is also a runaway of sorts. Pretty sweet analysis of the song, Lizzy."

I nodded. "It's sad and evocative. I want to sing it, too. Sing it again and let me try."

Chess smiled. "Okay, you start, that way you can pick the key. I'll join in."

I made one false start, but then found the range that felt comfortable. Chess and I sang *Moon River* together, and, being the expert he was, he made it sound amazing. I felt like we had violins backing us up. I had tears in my eyes when we finished the last note.

I tucked myself back under his arm, speaking with my face pressed into him. "Chess, what if everything falls apart? I don't have a back-up plan. I'm not ambitious like Ryder, or famous like Margot. I don't have a track record like Deb; no other marketable talents like Natalie. Being Margot's working student was a dream come true for me. I'm not ready to leave."

He sighed. "I can't see the future, Lizzy. Wish I could. I'm probably as anxious as you are. Right now, I need you to be strong and pull shoulder to shoulder with me. Don't look too far ahead. Can you do that for us?"

I nodded. "I can. I've got a horse and a cat. It makes it hard to be a drifter like Huckleberry Finn.

Chess stood up and kissed me on the top of my head, and left.

5. Tiny Cog in a Turning Wheel

The morning began with my phone buzzing. Chess.

He said, "Hey. You looked beat last night. Did you get enough rest?"

The barn was already in full swing, with horses being led out to paddocks. I took my phone into the feed room, and pulled the door behind me. "I'm not sure rested is going to happen anytime soon, Chess."

I flipped the lid up on the big grain bin and started measuring out the evening grain. I no longer even looked at the feed board, I knew it by heart. Tucking the phone under my chin, I began scooping and dumping measured amounts into individual buckets, each marked with the name of the horse whose dinner it would hold.

Chess continued. "I spoke to the Reynolds. I hope you aren't angry at me for taking the initiative. Mother asked me to, and actually I was eager to get things going."

I picked up the tub of supplement for joints and peeled off the lid, but then froze. "Am I supposed to know what you're talking about?"

There was a beat of silence. Then, "The people interested in buying Hotstuff. Mother is relieved to let me take care of this for her and I'm happy to help."

I put down the tub of supplement. In fact, I leaned against the wall. This was really happening. I think I just said, "Oh."

Chess kept speaking. "Good thing I called. They found another horse, but since I called, they want to fly out tomorrow and let their daughter try him before making a commitment on the other one. They assumed we had decided not to sell, something about crying grooms."

Now he was teasing me. I could hear it in his voice. But still I said, "I don't think they said that."

He answered softly, "Well, it was something like that. I apologized, and explained that Dad had suffered a heart attack and Mother had been at his bedside and everything else has had to be put on the back burner, hence, the delay in getting back to them. Anyway, I said that of course they could come tomorrow. I know this is short notice to spring on you and Margot. They'll arrive in the afternoon. That way if they like Hotstuff, they can stay overnight and ride him a second time the next morning. I'm sorry to spring this on you, but I didn't want to tell them "no" and let a live prospect get away. I don't know the business, and won't know how to answer their questions. But I can't imagine that there are too many people with that kind of money to spend on a dressage horse. Mother shared the asking price with me."

I slid down the wall and sat on the floor. "Chess?" All I heard was some sort of hum sound, letting me know he was waiting for my question. "Chess, you want me to set this up with Margot? I can't do anything about Hotstuff without Margot, and this is going to break her heart. You're asking me to break her heart."

There was another long beat of silence. Then he was speaking softly, tenderly, yet at the same time, with resolve. "I tried to call Margot and it went to voicemail. I didn't feel right leaving her a text. But, you can get her to call me, or if you want, we can do a conference call. I could use your support; remember, shoulder-to-shoulder you and I are going to pull off this IRS problem. This is about more than the sale of just one horse. I can make a phone call, but I can't show Hotstuff to his potential new owners. For that I need you and Margot. I can take it if you and

Margot need to curse me and cry together. But at the end of the day, I'm placing a higher value on my family, on people that I love and want to protect, than I am on Hotstuff. And I hope everyone understands and forgives me."

I was already quietly tearing up, but I nodded into the phone, not trusting my voice. Chess knew I had agreed to forgive him. Somehow he knew. He said, "Good then. I'll text you all the information so you can hand it to Margot. I'm hoping you guys will move heaven and earth to make this happen. And Lizzy, they may not want the horse after all. They've already picked out another one; so don't spend energy crying just yet. We may have that horse a long time. Just give it your best shot, and regardless of the outcome, I will be grateful."

I sniffled a little, and then sighed, "Okay. But, I hate this."

And Chess said, "I know you do. Just don't hate me."

Which made me gasp into the phone; "Oh my God, of course not. I don't hate you, Chess, I..."

And I couldn't say it.

I felt terrible that I couldn't say those three little words that I should have been able to say. I couldn't say it because I was still unsure if it was true. So the silence hung out there. He said nothing to fill that silence either, and it hung there stretching from awkward into humiliating. Chess had asked that I not look too much to the future, but to simply pull shoulder-to-shoulder with him now. So, that was what I was going to do. To say too much right now would be to look too far forward, but forward to what?

And so finally, mercifully, Chess said, "It's alright, Lizzy. I'll have my phone close at hand and will take your call no matter what."

I simply said, "Okay," and we left it there, but "there" did not feel good. In fact, I felt crummy, like I was no one's friend at all. Not, Chess', not Margot's, not Hotstuff's. I was a tiny cog in a wheel that was turning in a direction I did not want to go.

I grimly finished making up the evening feed, and did it slowly, mindlessly checking the feed board to go over the supplements and see if I had given them to the right horses, although I knew for a certainty that I had. Then I took the whisk broom and dustpan to tidy up to delay being finished, because when I finished I had to step out into the barn aisle, and then Ryder and I would groom and tack up Hotstuff and Wild Child. Margot would arrive. And I would have to take her aside, head into the office and call Chess, and then watch as we broke her heart.

When I saw Margot coming down the barn aisle I wanted to blurt it out to her, but I didn't. For one thing, Ryder was there, and I instinctively knew that her presence would make things worse. For another thing, Margot needed to ride Hotstuff, and I knew that she did not need to be emotionally in turmoil before her ride. I made a quick decision. I said nothing, but carried the tension and sadness in my stomach, while trying to keep my composure.

Deb arrived, and again, I wanted desperately to unload on Deb. But, that would be wrong, too. I did not want to poison the atmosphere for everyone, spoiling their rides in the process. So, I waited. Hotstuff and Margot returned from their workout looking relaxed and refreshed. She handed him off to me and returned to the arena to coach Deb. Then Emma and Natalie arrived to get Fable ready for their session. The day was rolling and I had not discharged my very important duty.

I had just put Hotstuff away, and Deb returned with Wild Child, also clearly satisfied with her ride. She handed him off to Ryder and left to go help Natalie with the Bambinos.

Ryder was finishing up bathing Wild Child when Dennis came roaring in on his gigantic motorcycle. Even though he cut it off in the parking lot, it was still loud enough to startle the horses and annoy the rest of us. He came down the barn aisle with a slight swagger. My stomach tied itself into a tighter knot when I envisioned him looking around the farm, imagining it as his. Dennis called down the aisle as he walked toward us. "Good morning, ladies!"

I had to admit, I could see why women might find him attractive. His face was handsome, with even features and an open honest look about him, his grey hair cut short, his face slightly sun or wind-burned, and his demeanor relaxed and happy. But I remembered what Ryder had said. And, when I looked over at Emma, she had an angry expression, her eyebrows drawn together, the corner of her lips turned down. She turned her back to Dennis, as if she needed to attend to Fable's saddle pad or girth, but I knew Natalie had put on the tack perfectly and already had snugged up his girth. Emma was composing herself. When she turned back around she was back to her usual businesslike manner. She simply nodded at Dennis.

Dennis looked toward the arena. "Is Margot riding?"

I answered him. "She's only got Hotstuff to ride these days and she's done him already. She's just sitting in the arena, waiting for Emma." In my mind I was thinking that this was the moment, I needed to ask for a few words alone with Margot in the office. It seemed too dramatic, definitely not my style. I didn't want her to think that Frank had died or something equally devastating.

Dennis was smiling broadly. "Fantastic. I can't wait to tell her, but I'll share it with you ladies first; Wordy is out of quarantine and on her way home. It won't be long now before Margot has another horse to ride. I know Margot is going to make her famous. Word Perfect should arrive late tonight. I plan to be here to greet her and hope Margot will come too, and of course you all are invited to welcome Wordy to the farm. I know it's a tough time, but there's nothing like a good horse in the barn to turn things around."

I tried to sound happy, but Ryder's words were still settling in my head and making me wary. "That's exciting, Dennis. I know it's a relief for you to get her back."

Emma was not going to congratulate him, instead she answered dryly, "Dennis, we already have a barn full of good horses. What we need is Frank back to good health."

Dennis did not get defensive, but instead seemed genuinely concerned. "Of course, Emma. You know, Frank and Francesca have been my dear friends for such a long time. I'm just as concerned as anyone."

Ryder chimed in and actually I was glad that she did, because Emma's expression may have looked neutral, but I could tell it was hardened, pitiless for any discomfort she may have caused Dennis, and frankly the whole scene was making me uncomfortable. Ryder said, "Dennis, I've heard your mare is a knockout. Maybe if I'm lucky you'll let me sit on her."

Dennis laughed. "Ryder, you'll have to finagle that one with Margot. Wordy can be a total bitch and very selective about who she allows control of her reins. She knows her own worth, and she rates her worth very high indeed."

Ryder cut her eyes at me briefly, and then turned her attention back to Dennis. "Let's go share the good news with Margot."

And the two of them strolled off toward the indoor. As soon as they were out of earshot Emma stage whispered to me. "I can't believe that weasel is back."

Natalie led Fable up to the mounting block and said to Emma, "Emma, don't go there. Not now, and not here. I don't want you getting your knickers in a twist when you need to focus on Fable here."

Emma put her helmet on, her lips pressed together tightly, her eyes narrowed, but she was silent. She had heard Natalie. She patted at her bun, and then pulled on her gloves, almost looking like she was impersonating Margot. We passed a couple meaningful glances at each other. But before she mounted she whispered again to me, "And I don't like that Ryder person either. I don't know how you've put up with her, she's insufferable." I loved that Emma called her 'that Ryder person.'

Once Emma was up on Fable, I looked up into her face and shook my head, finally smiling at something. "Em, I didn't realize how much I've missed you until this very moment."

She nodded curtly. "You and I, we need to go have a drink. Or two."

I answered softly, still smiling. "I don't really drink. Remember?"

Her answer: "We'll go out, and I'll happily drink for both of us."

Emma would now have her session on Fable, and afterwards Ryder and I would once again just work on our own, me on Winsome and her on Papa and then Ryder would work Lovey on her own while I headed over to ride Johnny. We had all agreed that we could do without Margot's coaching until after the CDI in New Jersey.

That meant that Margot would be leaving after Emma's session was over. My opportunities were vanishing. I had to do it. I walked into the office to get a scrap of paper and write down the contact information that Chess had texted me. It was an odd feeling to step inside, to see Francesca's desk stacked with papers, but no Francesca, and no wiggling terriers to greet me. There were some fabric samples on the desktop, too, and invoices. I pulled out Francesca's chair and sat down. Wow, it was incredibly comfy, probably one of those ergonomic designs. I rolled the chair a little forward and back, then put my elbows on the arms of the chair and leaned back to just have a look around for a moment.

What would it be like to call this office mine? I reached forward and ran my hand over the dark wood and leather set into the top, then traced the scrollwork edging with my finger, lifting the brass pull on the drawer and letting it drop with a substantial thud. I admired the polished wood floor and the large red Oriental rug. I looked up at the upholstered chairs with little embroidered cushions that faced the desk and imagined myself sitting in one of them. The walls were covered with photos of horses. I appreciated those of dear Rave, and of Papa, and Lovey, and of course the newly hung photo of Hotstuff from the awards ceremony in Chicago.

There were also some amazing photos of foals, some still wet in the straw. This room was a marvel and represented years of work; Margot's wisdom and talent, paired with Francesca and Frank's money and drive. But, there was such a lot to manage, and clearly it had gotten away from them, maybe so far away that it could not be managed back into shape. This fancy chair, this massive desk, the oriental on the floor, well, this seat was not really very comfortable after all. I pulled out the desk drawer and grabbed one of those little sticky pads and pulled up the text on my phone. I found a pen and copied out the information for Margot, stuffing the little pad of paper into my pocket, putting the pen back, and closing the drawer.

I'm not sure I wanted to be in that office with Margot, looking up at the photo of Hotstuff while I made the call to Chess. I almost tiptoed out the door.

***

I hung out at the wash stalls and waited for Margot. When Natalie and Emma came in they were leading Fable and still analyzing the ride. Natalie said, "What I don't get is why you guys aren't letting this one open his throttle to kick up some of that footing. He can do more in those canter extensions. You know he can."

Emma was quietly answering. I let them file into the wash stall.

Ryder ambled in after and nodded my way. "It's you and me, Lizzy, the arena's all ours."

I nodded back at her. "Yeah. I'll be there in a minute."

I gave Fable a pat on his wet neck as Natalie lowered the bits out of his mouth. "He's an awesome animal, Emma. Margot was right to send you out to Texas for this ride. Chance of a lifetime."

Emma pulled off her helmet and looked puzzled as she and I made eye contact. "Uh, yeah, of course. I've made peace with that a long time ago, Lizzy. It looks like Texas will be my home for now. I'll never be a Texan, though."

Natalie rolled her eyes, but then nodded. "Damn straight about that, cupcake."

I huffed a small laugh, but then put up my finger to interrupt. "Emma, Margot's heading out, but if you aren't busy, can you watch Winsome and me go? I'd love your help."

Emma looked pleased, and that pleased me. "Of course! I'd love to, Lizzy."

"Great! I'll tack up Winsome. I really want to show you how far she's come. I'm kind of proud of her actually, but I need to speak to Margot, where the heck is she?"

Natalie said, "Sitting in the indoor talking to Dennis."

When I stepped into the indoor, it was empty! I had a moment of panic, but then heard the noise of Dennis' motorcycle being revved, so I sprinted to the front of the barn.

They were on the bike, Dennis in front and Margot seated behind him, her pink helmet on. It was an odd sight to see Margot behind Dennis, her hands loosely holding on to his leather jacket. I waved at Margot and she waved back at me, as if I was waving them off to their lunch or whatever. But, Dennis got the drift, and put his feet back down on the ground as I approached closer. It was now or never, and never was not an option. I had told Chess that I would do a conference call, let him explain, but that plan evaporated. I pulled the little sticky pad out of my breeches pocket, handing the whole thing to Margot. I could see her eyebrows lift, disappearing under the brim of her helmet.

"Lizzy, what's this?"

I bit my lip before speaking. "Francesca, well, Chess actually…"

I stopped. Nothing was working out as I planned. For one thing,

Dennis was there, and both of them were now staring at me, their helmeted heads swiveled toward me as they sat astride that huge piece of machinery. It seemed stupid to ask her to get off the bike and come to the office. I was struck dumb, searching for words while Margot patiently waited for me to spit out an explanation. "Chess spoke to those people for Francesca, the ones who are interested in Hotstuff. The thing is, they're coming into town tomorrow and they want to try him."

Margot's eyes got wide then narrowed. "Tomorrow?"

I nodded back. Margot forced a grim smile. "You'd think someone would have had the courtesy to put me in the loop on this, I had no idea."

I began a feeble excuse. "I think with Frank's heart attack…"

Dennis put his hand on her knee, speaking over his shoulder. "Margot, let the horse go. He's a good horse, but he doesn't have the sparkle of my mare or of Wild Child."

That pissed me off, and it had to piss off Margot, too. What could that dolt know about Hotstuff? He didn't even ride. I added, "Chess says the rush is due to the fact that they've already found another horse, but they don't want to commit to it until the daughter sits on Hotstuff. Maybe he won't sell."

Margot shook her head firmly. She spoke through narrowed lips, "I've ridden a lot of horses in my time and, Dennis, Hotstuff may not sparkle like Word Perfect, but he's wonderful to ride. Any good rider will recognize his quality."

Then she poked Dennis in the back and took a lighter tone. "Darling, sometimes that thing that sparkles, it's just rhinestones. Hotstuff is a genuine black diamond. If those people pass him up then they're fools. It will nearly kill me to see him go."

My eyes began to burn. "Margot, I'm so sorry. Chess wanted to tell you himself, for Francesca, but now I've blurted it out. Was I wrong?"

She reassured me. "No, darling, no. It's kind of Chess to help Francesca, but there's no need, you did fine to tell me. I won't shoot the messenger. I absolutely need to be here to see that the girl rides him properly so I'll call and coordinate the times." Then she sighed, "We are having a rough patch though aren't we?"

Dennis said, "I promise when you see Word Perfect tonight, it will be a balm to your soul. Lizzy, she'll be here around ten. You'll come help settle her in?"

I nodded. "Sure, I'll be there; Ryder, too."

And he picked up his feet, and began to back up the behemoth of a bike. Margot shocked me by putting her arms around his waist, and off they roared. The sight made me clench my jaw.

***

Emma watched me ride Winsome while Ryder made short work of her ride on Papa, putting him through a simple warm up and then leaving the arena. Emma and I had actually been chatting and laughing when she left. I was lapping up Emma's praise over-eagerly, the same way Wheezer lapped up a dish of cream. Her words seemed sincere, and they meant so much to me. When Ryder exited the arena after only about twenty minutes, we said nothing. We didn't need to. We both knew that our friendship was an irritation to Ryder. And I thought to myself that Emma's stellar riding and training with Fable just may have been intimidating to Ryder, although I knew she would never have admitted it. Emma, the superstar to be, was my friend, and not impressed with Ryder.

I suppose the arrival of Word Perfect should have been a cause for excitement. But it was not. The horse belonged to Dennis Walker, not to the Cavellis. As friendly as Dennis was around the barn, he was not,

and never would be a "team player." No, I had figured out that he wanted his own team, and he wanted Margot to be his star player.

I would have loved to skip the ceremony of it all, but my presence was required. Ryder intended to be there, too. One of us would be
"Wordy's" groom. When Emma heard about Wordy's arrival, well, she
said she wanted to be there too, because, "I wouldn't want to miss it."

The people who were clearly missing in our welcome party were
Frank and Francesca.

It seemed like only yesterday that Wild Child had arrived in Florida. Emma and Frank had orchestrated the purchase and delivery, and it
had been done to thwart Dennis Walker from purchasing Wild Child
for Sophie. Wild Child had been a sort of consolation prize to Margot
after Dennis had dumped her for the buxom working student Sophie.
Although no one ever hinted at such a thing, I got it.

Here I stood, once again at Emma's side, waiting for the others to
arrive to greet the trailer with Dennis Walker's horse. Thinking back to
the "snatch" of buying Wild Child as a sort of coup and nose thumbing
at Dennis, it seemed that things hadn't worked out exactly as Emma
had hoped. And it appeared now that Dennis had come back to Margot
after realizing what a bad deal he had made with Sophie. If I found the
entire scenario galling, clearly it was killing Emma.

Emma motioned to me. "Hey, come chat with me while I check on
Fable."

I nodded and trailed after her. I had just done bed check and was
wearing my sweatpants and a baggy shirt, my hair still damp from the
shower, but pulled into a ponytail. In fact, this was the get-up that
served as my pajamas. I had slipped into my clogs, neglecting to put on
socks. I would have preferred to be reading in bed.

All the barn lights were on, and Word Perfect's stall door was open,
the bedding fresh and fluffy, and her hay bag stuffed full. She was sta-
bled next to Winsome in the "girls' dorm." The geldings acted as buff-

ers between the stallions and mares. No matter though, I knew all the horses would be excited by a new resident.

Emma slid open Fable's door and walked right in. He was a totally different stallion than Wild Child. He was sweet. Emma was able to wrap her arms around his neck and lean into him, inhaling his clean and shiny coat. She dug a treat out of her jeans pocket and he made a charming begging face, ears pricked, neck arched as he tried to focus on the treat.

Emma cooed to him. "How's my man? Sorry to keep you up so late." Then she squatted down and ran her hands over each of his legs, nodding, clearly satisfied. She looked up at me and gave a sad little smile. "I fricken love this horse."

I nodded back. "He's a dream, Emma. And you ride him beautifully."

Her voice got serious. "I've never seen Word Perfect, and Dennis is clueless. Actually, he's worse than clueless because he thinks he knows something. But you I trust. Tell me about the mare."

I nodded. "I've only seen her that one time, at the Herm Martin clinic."

She nodded again, silently encouraging me to continue.

"By Weltmeyer, I think the dam side was Bolero, but I'm not sure about that. She's really tall, and jet-black. She was hotter than a two-dollar pistol though. Sophie only pissed her off. Remember I told you that Herm put Margot up on her in the clinic."

Emma smiled a wicked little smile. "Herm's a bad boy, isn't he? God, I wish I could have seen that."

I smiled back at her. "It was amazing."

Emma said, "Of course, Margot is amazing."

My smile faded. "Margot's shirt was soaked with sweat when she got off. And that mare is more like Wild Child than your sweet Fable there. I don't think Word Perfect is going to make herself agreeable to Margot or any of us."

Emma stood up and moved closer to me. Fable went back to his hay bag, clearly understanding that Emma was all out of treats. I marveled a bit at what a laid back guy he was. Wild Child would have tried to chase me out of his space by now. Emma whispered. "So, what the hell is that back-stabber up to? Why did he come crawling back here, hat-in-hand? That is not his style."

I was silent for a moment. Emma sure didn't mince words. I inhaled and exhaled and waited a beat. Then I laid it out there, because Emma knew the players better than anyone, and Emma's love for Margot was unconditional and real. "He just showed up, Em. You heard him at dinner. He dumped Sophie and decided to 'come home.'"

Emma snorted. "She probably dumped him. Then he got mad and tried to get even because that's just the kind of sweetheart he is, a vindictive son-of-a-bitch."

I shrugged. "Well, he has to do something with the mare. He certainly can't ride her, not many could, but he knows Margot can. He's formed Walker Sport Horses and given money to the foundation, too."

Emma stared off into the distance, mumbling, "Doubling down on his stupidity."

The humid summer air hung heavy between us. I said, "He seems to want back in. He says he wants the Cavellis' friendship back, and it seems he wants Margot back."

She narrowed her eyes. "Do you think he'll be satisfied to stop there?"

Emma was no dummy. I said, "Ryder has said something that makes me think the answer to that is no."

Emma waited. I continued. "The farm is stressed right now."

"Frank's health?"

I shook my head no, but then nodded yes. "Frank, plus an IRS audit, plus Cavelli Foods has been, uh, in decline. The money's disappearing, Emma."

She looked like she was going to burst into tears. Then she closed her eyes and leaned her forehead against the stall, lightly banging her head and moaning, "Frank, Frank, Frank, Frank." Then she pressed her lips together and said, "Dennis is a scumbag opportunist."

I felt myself deflate as I broke more news that I knew would disturb her. "Margot's been going out with Dennis, riding on the back of his monster motorcycle, her arms around his waist. Emma, this is not looking good."

And at that we exited the stall, our shoulders slumped and our steps heavy in the beautiful and historic barn aisle; walking out to the security lights where the biggest BMW sedan I had ever seen had pulled in. It was Dennis and Margot. Emma and I exchanged glances; our faces wiped clean of expression as Dennis got out of his car, and opened the door for Margot, like she was royalty.

I looked at Emma again. Her gaze was on Dennis, and although her face was impassive, I could almost feel the temperature drop, sending shivers down my arms. I waved at Margot and Dennis and they both waved back. Emma whispered behind my back. "For God's sake, Margot, stop encouraging him."

Margot couldn't have heard Emma, but I almost saw her shake her head at Em, before a welcoming smile creased her face. Dennis looked over our shoulders, which made us both turn. There stood Ryder. I wondered how long she had been standing there. Sneaky little thing.

Dennis walked directly to her. "Ryder, I can't wait for you to see Word Perfect. Then he turned to Emma. "You too, Emma. Lizzy and Margot have already made her acquaintance."

Ryder made a thin smile, more like a smirk. "Her reputation precedes her."

He nodded back but then we all turned because headlights lit the road beyond our gates. She was almost here. A gooseneck truck and trailer came down the road and made the tight turn into our driveway, swinging wide across the road to make the turn. It was a long trailer, even longer than ours, and I could see that the trailer tires had cut into Francesca's flower beds slightly. I'm sure tomorrow I would find smashed flowers and dark mulch dragged across the paver stones. That would be work for Alfonso or one of his guys to tidy back up, and of course Francesca would notice.

Then I felt a pain in my nose, a prick, which was palpable sadness. Who knew when Francesca would be back at the farm, able to fuss over things like her flowerbeds? Crazy to say, but there was no doubt, I wanted her back at the farm, fussing over the flowers and the mulch, and even fussing at me. I wanted Dennis to go away, and for Frank to come back down the barn aisle, laughing and joking and bringing us donuts or steaks or nothing but his jolly self.

The trailer pulled up in front of us, not so differently than when Tank had pulled Emma's trailer up just a week prior. Except this time, there was no Frank or Francesca to greet this trailer. Instead, Margot stood beside Dennis, who grinned in happy expectation. He reached over to Margot and took her hand, tucking it into the bend of his elbow.

The driver got out with a sheaf of papers which Dennis signed while they exchanged pleasantries. The trailer began to rock slightly. There was the distinctive rhythmical tap-tap-tap-tap of a pawing horse. Then the tapping stopped, and was replaced with a loud metallic "wham!"

I saw Margot lift her eyebrows. She was thinking what all of us were thinking. The driver twisted his lips into a sarcastic smirk. "Yeah. That would be yours. Glad to get her off my rig."

He took his papers, and then went back to the trailer to fetch a small plastic trunk that had a wire tag on it. "This here goes with the mare."

Margot said pleasantly, "Just set it down. The girls will get it put up properly."

The driver went to get the mare off the trailer. She came down a center ramp just like we had on the four-horse. There were two other horses on the trailer that I could see. The mare pinned her ears flat back at each of them as she exited the trailer, bringing her ears quickly forward to examine her footing carefully on the ramp.

She stepped daintily down the ramp, neck arched, nostrils expanded. When she got to level ground she froze, and cast her eyes around in the dark, nostrils flared, deeply inhaling. She smelled her own kind, even though she couldn't see any other horses, and I hoped that she found the green grass and horse smell of New Jersey comforting.

She was beautiful and feminine yet statuesque, reminding me of an exotic runway model. Word Perfect was jet black, but something about the slope of her hip, the elegance of her head, the amazing arched neck, instantly reminded me of Wild Child. I hadn't noticed that before now. Then it hit me, they were both Weltmeyers. They were half sibs. We had three horses on the farm now with "W" names: Wild Child, Winsome, and now Word Perfect, although Winsome was not a first generation Weltmeyer (he was in her pedigree).

She let out a huge deep-throated whinny that shook her entire body... and then of course, every horse on the farm seemed to welcome her with return whinnies. We stood there struck dumb. But, Ryder broke the spell by stepping forward. "I'll take her."

Ryder took charge. She led the mare briskly into the barn, Emma and I following behind like ducklings. Dennis and Margot stayed with the driver to finish business while Ryder turned Word Perfect loose in the box stall, stepping out and sliding the door shut.

The mare peed, and then rolled, and then sniffed every inch of the stall. Then she went to the back of the stall, pinned her ears and shook her head at us. Since we didn't do her bidding and depart, she charged the front of the stall with her mouth wide open. She then swiveled around and gave a small buck that lightly tapped the front wall with two steel clad hind feet.

The three of us reflexively stepped back. Emma and I exchanged meaningful glances. I asked, "Are all the Weltmeyers like this?"

Emma frowned. "He was named "Sire of the Century" so I'm thinking, no."

I grinned. "So, with two Weltmeyers in the barn like that, we just got lucky?"

She nodded. "Appears that way. Lucky us."

Ryder crossed her arms. "The great ones are rarely easy."

Emma laughed. "Y'know Ryder, I have heard that quote all my life. Sometimes I think someone made that up so we would hang on to our crazy ones. The truth is that great ones may seldom be easy, but sometimes average ones aren't easy, either. I'm sure every now and then an easy one turns out to be great and a hell of a lot easier to love."

I fingered a peppermint in my pocket, pulling it out and crinkling the plastic, watching the mare's face. She had turned her butt to us, but she picked up her head at the noise, and swiveled her ears back to listen.

Margot and Dennis strolled up arm in arm. Emma turned to look at them, but immediately turned her head back to look at Word Perfect. Margot walked to the stall front, letting go of Dennis' arm and lining up with us. She looked at the mare intently, no doubt assessing her. Then she spoke softly. "She reminds me so of Wild Child."

We three agreed. The mare turned and came to the front of the stall, sticking her head out tentatively. I offered her the peppermint, and she spent a long time sniffing it, refusing to take it. I had never had a horse refuse a peppermint. Dennis said, "Sophie didn't approve of treats. She thought it would make the mare bite."

Margot shook her head. "Dennis, I'm guessing that mare already bites, and kicks, and crowds."

As we watched, the mare backed up and charged the stall front with her teeth bared. We all stepped back again, including Margot who spoke through gritted teeth. "Lovely. Can't wait to ride her."

Dennis, clueless Dennis, stared at his horse with adoration. "I know she's difficult. Sophie hated her as much as the mare hated Sophie, but ladies, you are looking at a Grand Prix horse that is exciting to watch. Margot's right, she does look like Wild Child and I do love Wild Child. Weltmeyer has made a lot of Grand Prix horses, and Wild Child and Word Perfect are two good examples of his get. I'm telling you, Margot is going to wow 'em on this one."

While his admiration of Weltmeyer bloodlines was shared by many, his assumptions about his horse seemed unrealistic. Margot took him gently by the arm. "Let's let the girls get some rest, including Word Perfect. Things always seem better after a good night's rest."

But Dennis was reluctant to leave. He answered somewhat dreamily, "I think things look damn good right now. Damn good."

We said our good nights. Emma looked angrier than ever. I briefly grabbed her by the hand, giving it a good squeeze that she returned, and then followed Ryder up the stairs. Wheezer was waiting right inside the door and practically tripped me as I entered, winding herself around my ankles, meowing in her full sentences and looking up into my face with her ice-blue eyes and pink nose. I scooped her up. She and I were not going straight to dreamland. We had a date in another time and place. This one was a classic, *Gone with the Wind*. I had never read it. It was an old heavy hardback copy that Nat had picked up at a thrift store. But, I was hooked. There was incredible comfort in living in someone else's stress instead of my own. I would not be getting a lot of rest tonight.

6. Betrayal in the Bond

Before the training day got rolling, Margot pulled me aside. Her face was serious. "Did you get the entries in?"

Luckily, I had, and even though the closing date had passed, the show had accepted the entries. I said, "Yes, yes I did. But, you realize it's the weekend before we go to Devon?"

Margot nodded. "She's not ready. I can guess that. But, it's now or never, Lizzy. Do your best to make it happen. Just give it your best shot."

Margot glanced down at her left hand, examining her nails. I knew what she had been doing; she had been chewing on her cuticles. I had seen her do it before when she was stressed. In fact, I could see some rough bits of skin alongside her usually manicured nails. She was just about to put a nail in her mouth, when she became aware that I was aware, and her hand instead made a fist, her thumb rubbing the rough spot along the edge of the nail on her index finger. She said, somewhat breezily, "We better start riding."

I had to pose a delicate question. "Do you still want to ride Hotstuff this morning, y'know, since you'll be riding him again, um, later?"

For a moment her face was blank. Surely she knew exactly what I meant. Then her lips pressed together into a thin hard line and she muttered. "Yes. I might as well have one more ride where I can have him all to myself."

She was fatalistic. In her mind it was over and done with already. I went and joined Ryder in the grooming stalls, and we quietly did our work without any chit-chat. When Margot came for Hotstuff, she had put back on her usual friendly and composed face, patting her tight little blonde bun and calling us both "darlings" as she pulled on her brown suede gloves. But I knew it was costing her something today.

It occurred to me then that Margot was looking even more stylish than usual. She always was well dressed, with hair and make-up perfect. But, I could tell she had put thought into her outfit. She was dressed in a pair of High Horse Couture breeches that I had never seen before, with the company logo embroidered on a wide belt loop in the middle of the back of the waistband, and her brown gloves had a blue and gold plaid backing that coordinated with her blue sleeveless blouse. She wore a finely woven leather bracelet with little blue and gold stones threaded into the laces. Natalie had created something finer, more delicate and sophisticated, just for Margot. It touched me that Margot would wear it. I should have complimented her, but I was speechless as I handed Margot the reins, and watched her lead Hotstuff toward the arena. I couldn't help it, I teared up.

But then I turned back to Ryder, who was finished tacking up Wild Child. She was putting the halter back on over his bridle, leaving his girth loosened until Deb made it down from the mare barn to ride him. She said, "When do you think Margot will start giving us our lessons again? I mean, that's our pay."

I had just wiped away a tear. But leave it to Ryder to turn my sadness to barely repressed anger. "Ryder, you don't really want a lesson right now, do you? I mean, we are not out of the woods yet with Frank, and Margot still has to focus on Deb and Emma and the CDI, and then those people are coming to try Hotstuff tonight."

She shrugged. "Yeah, I get what you mean. I'd rather go over to the Winstons' with you anyway and help you with Johnny Cash. At least that would be interesting. It feels sort of pointless around here. Anyone could move Lovey and Papa around. At least if you and I traded horses we could have some fun. I could help you with Winsome, too."

I was glad she had moved on from Johnny to suggesting she "help" me with Winsome, as presumptuous as I found both her suggestions, because there was no way was she getting on Johnny Cash if I could help it. And there was no way I was taking instruction from Ryder with Winsome. I brushed her off politely. "Thanks, Ryder. Emma has offered to watch me go on Winsome. She's been really helpful, and I'm planning on working with her while she's here. I know you don't really know Emma, but she's made her own Grand Prix horse from the very start. Emma's an incredible instructor and she and Margot are totally on the same vibe since Emma trained with Margot for eight years."

She just shrugged and said. "Suit yourself."

Deb arrived and we had a whispered conversation. She said, "Margot's on Hotstuff? People still coming tonight?"

I whispered back, "She wants a little time alone with him, sort of a good-bye. She acts as if he's already sold."

Deb was stone-faced. "She's trying to prepare herself. I get it."

She tipped her head at Ryder, who had been listening to our whispers.

Deb sighed, and now nodded toward Wild Child. "I guess I'll take that ginger-cat now."

Ryder shook her head and said, "So, today he's a cat."

Deb dimpled up briefly. It was good to see those dimples. She said, "Yeah, Ryder, he's a ginger-cat, or if you prefer, a big sexy jungle-cat. Yeah. Hand me that jungle-cat."

The big sexy jungle/ginger cat swished his tail, perked up his ears, and seemed to eagerly leave the grip of Ryder and follow his girl Deb out toward the arena.

After my session with Emma on Winsome, I had to book it over to the Winstons' barn to squeeze in my Johnny session. I did not want to be one minute late when the Reynolds came to try Hotstuff. I had promised Margot to have him braided when they arrived. Margot had asked me not to put the tack on. She wanted them to see him first without his tack. Regardless, I would need to keep the Johnny session short and sweet.

I loved the fact that no one was ever at the Winston barn. It was so quiet there in the afternoons that there were often swarms of little black birds with iridescent rainbow colors like spilled gasoline on wet pavement shining on their throats. I have no idea what kind of bird they were. They spread across the green manicured lawns and paddocks of the farm. When I led Johnny out of the barn toward the arena, they rose like a black cloud, their wings moving the air in a sound like an exclamation, their chirps coming in a chorus.

Today when we startled them, Johnny and I both stopped to watch as the cloud rose and twisted and reformed itself, first flat then rising and round, and then flat again looping back on itself like a length of ribbon. Something about it was marvelous and mystical and beautiful and gave me a feeling of peace. I took it as some kind of sign, its meaning unclear but soothing.

My ride on Johnny was also restorative. I went to a place of no worry, not even about getting Francesca through a Grand Prix test. I just allowed myself to have no goals with the horse other than to focus on what he felt like; to memorize his gaits and how he could quickly and easily gather himself to turn a canter pirouette, how he could sit down and piaffe under me and then bounce out of it into passage. When would I ever get to sit on a Grand Prix horse like this again? Would I ever? No matter how many plans and goals I made, I was dependent on others to see them through. Except, of course, with my Winsome, but would she make Grand Prix? Nothing was a certainty. What was certain is that I was sitting right now, here, on a wonderful Grand Prix horse, and I needed to savor every moment.

I finished my ride and hopped off, loosening the girth and giving Johnny a sugar cube. And then I smiled to myself and cupped his big chin in my two palms, lifting his nose toward mine and placing a kiss right between his nostrils on his slightly sweaty pink nose. It made me giggle. But as I wore no lipstick, I didn't leave evidence behind like Francesca, but I had taken on her role as kisser of Prince Johnny.

I was almost halfway up the path when I saw Francesca leaning on the front of her little black Mercedes. She had her arms crossed across her chest and I wondered how long she had been standing there. She was not wearing breeches today but instead had on a pair of pressed khaki slacks and some sort of lightweight bright white blouse with long sleeves. The collar was open to reveal a chunky silver necklace. She had sunglasses on that looked overly large for her fine features. It was not an outfit that anyone would wear to the barn. Instead, I think Francesca had been somewhere else, and I felt cheered by the idea that she just couldn't stay away. She had missed her Johnny time.

I waved at her and she uncrossed her arms and headed my way. Once she got closer I was struck by how thin she was. Of course, Francesca was always thin, and perhaps I noticed it today because I hadn't seen her outside of a hospital room in a week or so. I think the stress of the last week had used up whatever small reserves she might have had.

I waited for Francesca to catch up with me. I didn't dare give her a hug, she was pristinely clean and I was sweaty and dirty from a day in the barn. Plus, I didn't think it would be welcomed. But I tried to carry warmth in my greeting. "Hey, Francesca. It's good to see you out and about. How is Frank?"

She nodded back, her voice flat. "He just got back home and I have Marta at the house looking after him so I can at least get some fresh air."

I was confused. "Marta?"

We strolled side by side into the barn, and Francesca pulled her sunglasses up on the top of her head. "Of course you don't know Marta, our housekeeper. She's pretty good at handling Frank."

That comment puzzled me, but I said nothing. The Frank I knew didn't need to be 'handled' by anyone. Francesca, of course, was another story. I changed the subject. "Well, now that Frank's home and on the mend, I hope you'll start riding Johnny again."

Francesca reached out and touched Johnny lightly on his neck. "Ah. Well, things are so uncertain right now."

I led Johnny into the grooming stall, unbuckled his throat latch and his noseband, unhooked the curb chain, and placed my hand on his nose to gently lower the bits out of his mouth. He was sweet the way he opened wide, as if I had said, "Say aaah." I hung up the dirty bridle on a hook and slipped on his halter, clipping him into the cross-ties and then handing him another peppermint. I saw Francesca watching silently.

I had been thinking about how to best approach Francesca about the show without enduring a lecture or worse. I said in a matter-of-fact tone, "There's another Hill and Dale show the weekend before we go to Devon."

Francesca looked disinterested. "Hmmm."

So, I kept going. "I thought I'd take Winsome, get some more mileage."

Still no response, her eyes were unfocused and flat. I pushed further. "If you want to put your superstar horse in my rust-bucket of a trailer again, well, I could use some company."

That did it. She looked at me and the faintest twist of a smile appeared. She had to respond to that. "Lizzy, wouldn't that old thing collapse under the weight of two horses?"

I grinned. "Francesca, Winsome and Rave rode in that trailer together and the floor held just fine. Besides, I think Johnny would love the company. I'll bet it would settle him." She said nothing, but was at least focusing on me. Francesca was considering it. I could tell.

Then she said. "I'm sure the closing date has long since passed."

I had to think about how to finesse this one. I said, "I know, right? But for you, they would take our entries. If it's just me I'll be told to try again next time, but if I enter us both, well, they'll take the entries when they see your name. I'm sure of it." I was impressed with my strategy, one that had just come to me in the spur of the moment.

Francesca shook her head as if she were going to say no. But she didn't. I waited a beat. I had just lied to my boss. It made me a little queasy. I never could lie convincingly and I wasn't sure she was buying it.

She really focused on me now, narrowing her eyes and tipping her head. I think she was on to me and it made me break back into the sweat I had worked up while riding. I turned my back to her and pulled off Johnny's tack so I could avoid her laser beams.

I put the tack away and when I returned she shook her head "no' again. She said, "I can't imagine dealing with a horse show right now, Lizzy. But thank you for thinking of it. I could use a little bit of . . . normal again."

My shoulders sagged. This wasn't going to be a slam dunk. I said, "Just let me enter us both so I can go. I'll take care of the paperwork, and if you don't feel up to it we'll just scratch Johnny. But honestly, Francesca, I think this horse is a tonic for you, and the show at least will give your rides some structure and a goal to work toward. It's the best thing you can do for yourself right now."

Francesca gave me an odd look that was almost angry but wasn't. She seemed puzzled and suspicious, sensing I was up to no good at her expense. I braced myself for a wicked dressing down, but instead she said, "My password is the farm address, and my Paypal password is our town and zip code. Don't be upset if I can't do it though, it will all depend on how Frank is doing. But, I'll go ahead and pay for your little mare, too."

I'm sure I was beaming, but not for the reason Francesca thought. I had pulled off my little deception. Normal people would at this point accept a hug as a thank you, but again, this was Francesca, and if she were a porcupine her quills would be up warning me to keep a safe distance.

She said, "I'm heading back to sit with Frank, he really cannot be left alone for a minute right now. He's heavily medicated. I trust you and Margot to do a good job presenting Hotstuff to the Reynolds family this afternoon. I expect an honest effort. Don't scare them away, understood?"

I simply nodded, "Of course, Francesca."

She said, "I plan to be here to ride Johnny tomorrow afternoon. If I'm late, just go ahead and get him warmed up for me. If I don't make it, just finish the ride."

I resisted doing a happy dance or pumping my fist, instead I answered in my best secretarial voice. "I'll take care of everything and see you tomorrow."

She touched Johnny on the neck again, like touching a talisman, one more time, before turning to leave.

***

I didn't start crying until I was half way through braiding Hotstuff; pulling up and wrapping into knots the tight little pigtails in his mane. Each one had a final braid-ette black rubber band secured around the base. They were neat and tight; as good looking as the day of his final ride in Chicago. My big goofy horse friend enjoyed having his hair done, oblivious to what it meant. I hadn't seen Margot yet, but Deb and Nat had come down to the barn to chat me up. Deb was being brave, and Natalie sang and joked and tried to keep the atmosphere light, which was working for a time.

Ryder showed up, and then Emma. It was a crowd. And things got solemn. Suddenly I felt sorry for this girl who was coming to try our baby boy. I would have felt intimidated to be trying any USEF national reserve champion four-year-old, but Hotstuff's extended family vetting her riding ability was almost too high a bar for anyone. I mean, this was a young rider, not Olympic gold medalist Charlotte Dujardin coming to test ride him.

I wondered what Margot would say to us. Would she send us all away? In Florida we could hide in the lounge or apartment and look into the arena, but here you had to go into the indoor and sit on the platform to watch. I hoped Margot would not banish us. The fact was I *did* want to vet this girl's riding ability. No way was she getting our horse if she wasn't a good rider.

Margot arrived, and we stood chatting around Hotstuff who perked up momentarily, his giant ears pointing at our little group. He lifted up a front hoof and let it dangle in the air, begging for a treat. But, although Margot stroked his neck, no treat was forthcoming. As we chatted amongst ourselves he gave up, grew bored, and began to droop his head and drift off, his lids half closing, one hind leg resting on the toe with a dropped hip. Hotstuff went to sleep in the middle of his little herd of humans, feeling safe, even as we all were thinking of his departure.

Then the spell was broken. A car with rental plates pulled through the gates. It was really happening.

Car doors opened and closed as we stood as a group in complete silence. No one had on a happy face. Margot's shoulders sagged, her face impassive. That is, until the Reynolds family came into full view. There they were, the people we met in Chicago. And there was Becca, dressed in breeches, and pulling a rolling boot bag down the barn aisle behind her. Margot had pulled herself up while the rest of us shrunk backwards, moving even closer to our horse. She met them halfway, hand extended, smile plastered on her face. Saying, "Finally, we get to meet Becca. Hello, I'm Margot."

They did all have names. There was Hank the Dad, Penny the Mom, and the very lucky and clearly adored daughter, Becca.

I just couldn't make myself dislike Becca. She was soft-voiced, thin and blonde, with small features, but very tall, probably six feet in height. Hotstuff would be tall enough for her, but not too heavy or wide. She was young, probably out of the young rider ranks, but most likely still in her twenties. The first thing Becca did was speak softly and sweetly to Hotstuff, then stand next to him and stroke his neck. As usual, Hotstuff swung his huge ears around, turning to get a good look at her and brushing her gently with his long nose whiskers. They literally were "feeling each other out." It was a tactile, "how-do-you-do?"

Margot introduced all of us, and when she got to Deb she explained, "Deb is a very special person in Hotstuff's life. You see, Hotstuff's mother was Deb's Grand Prix horse. And Deb was the first person to lay a human hand on his still wet coat. Deb was the first person to sit on his back. So much of what you see in his character was formed by his wonderful dam, and this woman right here."

Deb smiled her great dimpled smile, and pinked up a bit in her cheeks. Penny Reynolds looked moved by Margot's eloquence. The father Hank nodded enthusiastically. "You see, Becca? You could see by this horse's attitude that he's had good handling all his days. And I didn't even know about the dam. Do you still have her?"

Deb answered sadly. "We lost her, I'm sorry to say. But we have more of her babies still to raise and train. In fact, Hotstuff's full brother just got started under saddle."

Penny looked moist-eyed now, saying, "Oh Deb, I am sorry to hear about the mare."

Becca's eyes showed interest. "A full sibling going under saddle? Wow, is that one for sale, too?"

Margot broke in, "If you'd rather look at him, you could, he's a year younger than Hotstuff. I'm hoping to do the FEI young horse next year with him. His name is Habenero."

I briefly thought that there was no happy ending in this. If she preferred Habenero, then Deb's heart would break instead of Margot's. But, no. Becca looked at Margot's eyes, intent and sincere, and said, "Only if Mom and Dad would let me have more than one! I've watched your rides on this guy from the championships over and over and over again, imagining what he must feel like. I really like the other young horse we tried recently though. Mom and Dad are willing for me to buy one young horse right now, not two. I'd take two or three or a dozen if they'd let me!"

And we all laughed because all of us, when it came to horses like Hotstuff, well, we would take a dozen of them if we had the income and 'staff' to support them.

Margot asked me to pull Hotstuff out of the grooming stall and stand him up so the Reynolds could look him over carefully. Then she had me walk him up and back from our little cluster of people; down the barn aisle, then repeat it in trot, just like in an FEI jog. It seemed unnecessary to me, but it was still good practice for our boy, who I hoped would perform many more FEI jogs in his life.

The Reynolds seemed pleased enough. I snapped him back into the grooming stall and Margot asked me to tack him up. As I fetched his tack, Margot gave a running narrative. "Lizzy has been his groom for some time now, of course the other girls help too, and we are all terribly attached to him. Emma was my working student and barn manager for eight years, so she knew him from the very start, too. He's really part of the family."

Becca asked, "Was he easy to start?"

Deb nodded. "All of Regina's foals are easy to start and easy to ride. Regina was all business, and I think the new filly will be like her mama. But the boys are clowns. They love to work, but they have a sense of humor and they are very interactive with their people. Of course, they've never known anything but good handling and riding; love and kindness and top care all their days."

And then, as if on cue, Hotstuff demonstrated his yoga moves, complete with the front leg scratching performance. I only half expected him to do his routine as he had been standing around so long, and had already been ridden that morning. But putting on his saddle seemed to trigger it.

Everyone laughed, even those of us who had seen it many times before. It lightened the atmosphere. Deb dimpled up. "Yeah. Well. That'll do, Hotstuff, they get the idea."

Hank the Dad was grinning. "See what I mean, Becca? You will never be bored with that guy in the barn. He'll keep us all laughing."

Penny the Mom stepped forward and let Hotstuff smell her hand, as if she were approaching a dog. She must have had on perfume or hand lotion because Hotstuff inhaled deeply and then showed us all the "flehmen response" which delighted Penny enough to get a giggle out of her.

I wished that Hotstuff would stop being so charming.

Margot offered to get on and warm him up for Becca, which was standard procedure when trying out horses, but Becca surprised me. She said, "Do you mind just talking me through his warm up and routine work? I've watched your video a million times. I love the way he goes. What matters to me now is the way he feels, and if I think he is "my" sort of ride. I'm picky about that. That's why I don't let anyone choose my rides for me. Sven, my coach, will just have to deal with what I pick out for myself, and then of course, the judges will have to agree that it's a good match."

Hank the Dad, chimed in, "Of course, Margot, if you feel you need to ride him first you tell us."

Margot pressed her lips together. I saw her finger her cuticle on her left hand with her thumb. But she sounded almost relieved when she answered, "There's no need. I gave him a very light ride this morning, but it wasn't to ride him down for you. No. He's a delight every day, from the first step into the arena. Of course, he's more horse the first day at the shows, he is a baby still."

I finished the last touches on his bridle, handing him a peppermint as I tightened the girth another hole. Then I fluffed out his big heavy tail, his one fully developed feature in an as yet unfinished body. Then I pulled him out of the grooming stall and walked him to the indoor with the crowd following.

When we got inside, Becca unzipped her boot bag, and sitting down on the viewing deck began to put on her boots, strapping on some small "Prince of Wales" type spurs. I led Hotstuff around and marveled at the confidence that Becca seemed to have. She knew what she wanted from a trial ride and she didn't seem at all nervous. When I had lapped the arena, Becca was waiting, helmet and gloves on, ready to ride. Margot was giving her instructions about the kind of warm up that Hotstuff was used to getting.

I had pulled down the stirrups and Becca measured them against her arm length, putting them down and adjusting the length for her long legs and then coming to the 'off' side and adjusting the other one. Then she mounted from the ground while I held the 'off' side to steady the saddle. Even before she picked up the reins, I could tell that this young woman was the real deal. I don't know how, but I could tell she was going to sit well and ride with elegance. It was just apparent. Off they went on a loose rein, Hotstuff showcasing his wonderful walk. Unlike Ryder, Becca had the demeanor of someone who did not need to prove anything.

Margot remained standing, hands behind her back, leaning against the kickboards in the corner of the arena. The rest of us took our places on the viewing stand. No one spoke at all. It was more silent than a church. I noticed Becca's mom and dad sitting together; they held hands and gazed adoringly at their daughter. What a lucky girl Becca was. What would it be like to have parents as sponsors like that?

Becca walked around each way and then gathered the reins. She did some simple turns on the forehand, a little leg yielding at walk, and a couple walk/halt transitions. I knew she was testing his reactions. Did he stop on a light aid? Did he go forward on a light aid? How easily did he move sideways? How easily did he answer the request for a flexion in the poll, left and right? Did he yield slightly to both reins, the "squeezing of the sponge" action, even offering her a rein back, but going smartly forward when she applied both legs?

Hotstuff went through all of Becca's tests like the well-schooled horse he was. He was a teacher's pet. Each time she made a request he practically jumped into the correct response, like a child blurting out the answers before the teacher finished asking the questions.

Then she went to rising trot and did all the usual loosening exercises, Hotstuff's regular routine. Becca was a cool customer with all of our eyes on her, judging her. And yet, I could tell she was in her own world. She had developed that skill that was part showman, part introvert, of delivering the goods without being self-conscious. She had gone to the place where only two beings existed; and none of us were included in that world.

Margot said nothing, but she and I were probably thinking the same thing; the girl seemed to know what she was doing. You couldn't fault the girl's riding. This was probably going to work out in Becca's favor.

Becca finished her warm up and let Hotstuff walk on a loose rein. I saw Margot push herself away from the kickboards and dust off her backside before looking up at Becca.

Becca turned Hotstuff in a circle in front of Margot. Becca didn't enthuse the way I thought she should have, but she was at least positive. "He's lovely and absolutely correct. That's the great thing. I wouldn't have to go back to fix anything in his training. The other horse is very flashy, but I am not thrilled about how he's been started."

Margot nodded. "I think you will find that Hotstuff is very straightforward and eager. If he has to go, well, it's important to me that he go to someone who protects his eagerness because physically he is quite unfinished and soft in his joints. He's a baby and has a lot more growing left to do. Soft horses like Hotstuff can be easily destroyed by an overly ambitious trainer. In addition to the physical aspects of training, he will need to be corrected gently so that he never loses his desire to please. I worry that such a horse as Hotstuff would get pushed too hard too soon. I want his soundness, physical and mental, to be cultivated carefully and left undamaged in the training process. I want a long and healthy career for him."

Becca was listening intently and answered, "I hear you."

Margot said, "Go ahead and put him together. He does a forward version of everything, so you certainly can get an idea of his future. Just don't take him to the point of fatigue. Reward approximations. That is how I teach and how I train. Build their confidence each day a little bit as you shape them toward your ultimate goals."

Becca listened to her words with a serious expression. Margot leaned against the kickboards again, and this time crossed her arms and pressed her lips together. Becca took up the reins and made a few trot to walk to trot transitions, starting with several walk steps, and finally leaving out the walk steps, just like a Margot lesson.

She then rode him forward and back in trot, making some smaller sized circles and short bits of shoulder in. I grudgingly admitted to myself that they looked great. She rode some leg yields across the full diagonal and then did them again in an easy half pass bend.

Becca then made a transition from trot to the canter; she rode the transitions forward and back, then did some smaller sized circles. She then tried a bit of counter canter and then surprisingly made a flying change each way. They were green but clean. Hotstuff did them big and bold with a bit of a buck after the first one. He clearly thought that it was exciting.

I looked over at Margot because I was pretty sure that Margot had not started counter canter or flying changes with Hotstuff yet. She never looked my way. She only had eyes for her horse. Becca rewarded Hotstuff with soft praise and a stroke on his neck and then stretched him forward and downward on the big circle in a forward rising trot. When she walked, Becca finally smiled. "I certainly see why you would hate to see him go."

Hank spoke next. "Bec, which one? You and I have a deal; one young horse to bring up the levels; one trained horse. You have to choose."

There was a stretch of silence. It was long enough to give me hope. In that tiny blip of time my mind held one thought: that the other horse she was looking at had to be a hell of a guy for her to hesitate on our boy.

But then she broke the silence. "Let's see how this one vets. See if you can hold off the other seller for another day or two."

There was a collective exhalation from team Equus Paradiso. Margot suddenly needed to examine that cuticle of hers.

Penny nodded, oblivious to our collective moment of mourning. "Oh yes, we can't let the other get away and then discover we can't buy this one because of the vetting."

Margot's head snapped up. We all turned to look at Penny, who seemed to recognize that just maybe she had insulted us. "I'm sorry, that came out all wrong. It's just that our vet is so picky and we've had to turn down horses before that we thought were just perfect, you know? I don't really understand all this mind you; goodness it's a tricky business."

Margot walked over to Hotstuff to take a rein while Becca hopped down and ran up her stirrups and loosened the girth. Margot turned to look at Penny and Hank, composed and friendly. "Oh, no offense taken. I understand. We bred him and raised him and I never remember taking any radiographs, so I have no clue what they will look like. But, I know Hotstuff's always been a sound horse."

The Reynolds family hung out for a bit by the grooming stalls, and then watched me give Hotstuff his shower, which he dearly loved. Margot stayed right by their side chatting.

Penny said, "We are so sorry to hear about Mr. Cavelli's health problems. I was looking forward to meeting him, and I had hoped they would be able to join us for dinner tonight."

Margot replied, "Frank loves to entertain, and he has a favorite Italian restaurant where I'm sure he would have loved to take you. I can give you the name and how to get there. It really is good."

Hank joined the conversation. "May we at least take you, Margot? Since you know the horse so well I know Becca would love to hear about his riding and training and management from you."

There was a beat of silence, and then Margot smiled. "Thank you, Hank. I accept."

Becca remained silent, but she had been staying close to Hotstuff, watching him in a relaxed and friendly way, making some idle chit-chat with me about his adorable personality. But we were both listening to her parents and Margot.

Penny said, "Oh Margot, I'm so glad. Becca works with Hubert Otterbein whenever we can bring him over, and she did a month in Germany with him last year, and now we have dear Sven who was his, oh what do you call it Becca, when someone works under the head trainer?"

Becca said, " Bereiter, mom, it's called a Bereiter."

Penny continued, "That's it, Sven was his Bereiter, but he's not much older than Becca. We take Becca to clinics when it's someone of note, but, if you want to come down to North Carolina and help her get off to a good start with Hotstuff, we would love to have you."

I wasn't so sure Becca was excited about that idea, and Margot appeared hesitant. Penny, for all her good will and innocence, was once again stepping over the lines of proper etiquette to suggest such a thing without first conferring with her daughter.

Becca, who did not appear ruffled said, "Actually, Margot, I've always admired your riding. And if you would come down I could probably fill a clinic for you from my small barn. We live in a beautiful area of North Carolina. You would approve, I think, of the facilities we could provide Hotstuff. He would have great views from his paddock and stall, for what it's worth."

Hank winked and smiled at Margot. "Did I mention we live on top of a mountain?"

And Margot smiled back. "I want to hear all about it at dinner."

Penny said, "Can we trouble you to help us arrange this vetting? I have a list of locals, but you need to tell us who you recommend. Who's the best for a pre-purchase exam?"

Margot blinked. Penny just didn't know when to stop. It was standard practice to NOT use the horse's normal vet for a pre-purchase since that would put the vet in an uncomfortable position of potentially ruining a deal for his own client.

But even if Penny did not want to hire Doc, it is also fairly certain that Margot would know the area vets and who would be the toughest, nervously rejecting a high dollar horse for every little abnormality to reduce his own liability if the horse went lame soon after a deal. Margot would also know which vets tended to be more relaxed and "real-world" about what is a deal-stopper and what can be lived with.

Hotstuff was an expensive and competitive horse that was being purchased to go all the way to Grand Prix. The pre-purchase bar he had to clear was high; he had to appear suitable physically to withstand the demands of the highest level of dressage. No one has a crystal ball, and it was always a gamble, even if he had great radiographs and worked sound at his tender age of four. Even so, I suspected Margot would be tempted to choose a vet from Penny's list who was a nervous-Nelly type, eager to protect himself by noting every little wart on Hotstuff and how it would make him unsuitable as a Grand Prix prospect. Francesca was not around to stop Margot. I was guessing Margot was hoping for a miracle so she could keep her horse.

Margot said, "of course" in the most pleasant and friendly tones. "Come to the office and I'll see what I can help you arrange."

Becca chimed in. "If someone can come tomorrow, it would be best. I want to be here if possible. Daddy, I want you to record it, too." Hank agreed.

Becca asked if she could feed Hotstuff a treat. I brought out a carrot and he lifted his leg and held it there, begging. This delighted Hank and Penny, and I suspect Becca, too. He was terribly endearing.

Then they went to the office to arrange the vetting. I couldn't imagine anyone would even take the call, let alone come tomorrow on such short notice. The only one I knew who would do such a thing for Margot was Doc.

7. Cloud Variations

*Ryder had rolled the morning feed cart around, and mixed up the din-*ner feeding by the time I made it down. She was ahead of me. It meant that I could have a second cup of coffee and relax. So, after checking with her, I headed back upstairs. Wheezer was bumping against my an-kles as soon as I stepped inside. I scooped her up while I got the coffee machine set up. Then I looked through the window down into the barn aisle while Wheezer purred and vigorously rubbed her chin against my chin. It made my chin itch, so I distracted her with scratchies behind her ears. She was almost deliriously happy about that.

I listened while my coffee machine brewed. It whirred and hummed and then the stream of coffee trickled into the pot, filling the air with an enticing aroma. As much as I loved my coffee, it always smelled better than it would ever taste. That's why it got doctored with sweet flavored cream. Today's cream was dulche de leche. I poured it in and gave it a stir, balancing my purring kitten on my shoulder or tucking her under my arm. That first sip was always the best and I savored it. Then I sidled back over to the window to sip coffee and watch the morning chores begin as the horses finished their grain and the guys started turn out and mucking.

But I didn't get settled because Doc came into view with Ryder standing by his side, which was a wake-up call. Wheezer got a kiss on her head and then a gentle toss to the middle of the room so I could get out of the apartment without squishing her in the door. I was anxious now to get down to the barn to figure out what was going on. Was someone hurt or colicking? I knew, of course I knew, but still did not want to acknowledge why Doc was here.

Doc stood in the middle of the barn aisle, hands on hips, deep in conversation with Ryder. I didn't wait for a pause to interrupt. "Hey, Doc." Then turning to Ryder. "Is someone sick?"

Ryder looked at me like I was the village idiot. "Lizzy, he's here to vet Hotstuff."

My stomach did a flip, and then I felt very heavy, like the barn aisle had turned to quicksand and I was sinking down into it. Even my cheeks felt heavy and droopy. Ryder and Doc noticed. I never could hide my feelings. Doc took pity on me. "Lizzy, no one was more surprised than I was to get that call last night. I expect all of you ladies love that horse, especially Margot. But I got the call and rearranged my schedule to do this, so I'd better get started."

Ryder was all business. "I'll get him for you, Doc. I'm sure it will be okay for you to start the passive exam before they all get here."

Once Ryder had left us, Doc put his warm and gentle hand on my shoulder, speaking gently. "Tough situation. I'm so sorry about Hotstuff, Lizzy. I know it's been a rough stretch for you. I heard you were the one to keep Frank alive 'til the EMTs arrived. You did well, young lady."

He continued his lecture in a fatherly tone, "Now, I know that you and these horses get bonded, and that's not a bad thing, not at all. But you will have many good horses over your lifetime. Margot needs to remember that, too. This is not the end. There will be others. The Reynolds sound like they will be good owners. Margot says the daughter can really ride and they have the money to keep Hotstuff in the style to which he has become accustomed."

Doc looked up the barn aisle toward an approaching Ryder leading Hotstuff, then back at me. He was a good guy, our Doc, and I instinctively knew he was not going to say anything more about it in front of Ryder. But I had taken note that Doc had talked as if Hotstuff was a goner.

I wondered why the Reynolds had hired Doc to do the pre-purchase exam. Why had Doc agreed? Wasn't this the "conflict of interest" situation that was supposed to be a non-starter? Or was I being unrealistic in trying to come up with ways to delay?

Ryder clipped Hotstuff into the cross-ties and Doc began by taking his vital signs; pulse, temperature, and respiration. He then put the stethoscope up to Hotstuff's chest and listened to his heart. He ran his hands down each leg, palpating as he went. He lifted each hoof, and then looked at the horse from front and back and from each side, running his hands over Hotstuff's spine, too. He lifted Hotstuff's lips, pulled his tongue to the side and examined his teeth. He next pulled out a little light and examined each eye as I quietly watched. As soon as he finished I tentatively asked. "Doc, I'm just wondering something?"

He hummed back at me and then asked for Hotstuff's Coggins and passport. Ryder turned and headed for the office to retrieve them. Doc flipped open the top of a metal box-style clipboard, pulled out paperwork from the box, then closed it with a snap. He secured the papers under the clamp on the clipboard and began scribbling away. He looked up and made eye contact.

"Go on, shoot."

I sighed, slightly embarrassed. "I thought buyers weren't supposed to do a pre-purchase exam with the farm's vet."

He nodded back at me, his eyes thoughtful. "That it was a conflict of interest?"

I nodded back.

He said, "Well, the Reynolds have their own vet back in North

Carolina. She and I actually know each other from some veterinary conferences. We agreed to video the flexions and I'll email her those and the digital x-rays we take today, along with a copy of my report. Francesca has also generously agreed to share anything in our records with these folks. That's over four years of vet records, starting with his birth. There's nothing to hide on that boy, anyway. I think Margot's praying that we find something, but the truth is that she would be devastated if we found something that would limit his career. Margot's too much of a horsewoman to wish this horse ill out of some sort of possessiveness." Doc turned back to his clipboard, scribbling down his initial exam findings.

I watched for a moment and then heard car doors closing. The Reynolds were here. A second car door shutting meant that Margot had probably arrived, too. The show was about to begin. It was happening too fast for me to take in.

Margot and the Reynolds were chatting like old friends as they approached us. But when Margot drew up alongside me, we exchanged a knowing glance. I was still rooted to the same spot, and Margot put her arm around my shoulders and gave me a brief hug. I read a lot in that hug. I couldn't remember when Margot had done that before, but that hug spoke volumes to me. It was reassuring. It said, "It's going to be okay."

And suddenly I felt a bit lighter, less melted into the floor. I could move again. In fact, I picked up a currycomb and went into the grooming stall and began giving Hotstuff his usual currying, although it raised the dander on his coat, making him look dirtier rather than cleaner. But it felt good to both of us.

I had left the little knot of people in the aisle chatting and retreated to be with Hotstuff. But I was still listening. In my peripheral vision I watched as morning greetings were exchanged. Doc shook hands, and then began a little lecture about what his normal routine pre-purchase included, what he had already done, and that he would make no recommendations regarding purchase, but simply give his findings both orally and in a written report. His written report would include his examinations of the radiographs.

He asked if they wanted him to fill out an insurance form and a health certificate for shipping. They said yes to both. I know Doc was just being business-like. Those items were not expensive, but both would be required if the horse were purchased and needed to ship out and cross state lines. But to me, it made it seem like a done deal. Everyone was assuming that Hotstuff would pass the physical examination.

I grabbed the flicker brush and gave Hotstuff a good once-over. Hotstuff then amused the crowd with his morning yoga routine. I said nothing, but Ryder explained that this was his normal routine. Hotstuff crossed his legs and rubbed his shins while everyone laughed, including Doc. Penny even used her camera to catch the moment, saying, "Can you make him do that again?"

Ryder explained in a dry tone, "It's not a trick. He's just a weird horse. Does it every morning when we tack up."

It occurred to me then that any of us, including and maybe especially Ryder, would love to own this "weird horse."

Penny enthused. "Well, I just think it's charming. Don't you, Becca?"

Becca smiled a shy smile. "Yes, Mom. It's cute. He's cute."

I chimed in. "It's part of who he is and why he's special. Hotstuff is a one of a kind horse."

My voice didn't sound like my own. Both Doc and Margot gave me a warning look. It was a look that said, "Pull yourself together."

I quickly grabbed the special "no tears" kiddy hairbrush we used and composed myself by brushing out his glorious tail. Then I brushed his mane. Ryder had appeared with the headstall of his bridle, reins removed. She looked impatient for me to finish grooming. I quickly spritzed him with fly spray and ran a towel over his coat. I felt that I should have been the one to handle him for the flexion tests and the longing, but Margot had instead assigned those jobs to Ryder.

So I joined the Reynolds on the viewing platform. Doc first watched a few moments of Hotstuff longing in walk, trot, and then canter. Then Doc began the flexion tests, all videoed for the Reynolds vet. Penny manned the video on her cell phone while Hank watched the procedure while standing at her elbow, making sure Penny wouldn't miss the important moment when Doc counted down to Ryder the ninety second flexion test, after which Hotstuff would be asked to trot off.

Doc instructed Ryder, "Okay, Ryder, I'll count it down from ten." Doc had Hotstuff's right hind leg cocked up tightly against the horse's belly, creating a tight flexion of the hock joint, while he stared at the sweep second hand on his watch.

"...five, four, three, two, one, go." Margot clapped and clucked and Hotstuff jumped forward. Ryder and Hotstuff trotted off in a straight line, made a turn, and trotted straight back to Doc and Margot.

This test was repeated on all four legs. And then Hotstuff was put back on the longe line to walk and trot and canter on circles, both large and then small. It didn't take long for Doc to look satisfied, but he made no comments on the results.

Hotstuff appeared to me to have done just fine.

We returned to the barn, where Deb was quietly grooming Wild Child. She looked grim as she greeted us. Margot and Deb said nothing to each other in front of the Reynolds, but when Deb pulled Wild Child out of the grooming stall, tacked up and ready to ride, Margot politely excused herself to the Reynolds and to Doc by saying. "I don't think you will need me for the radiographs. But of course I'll be right there if you do." And she pointed back at the indoor.

Penny and Hank and Becca all made the correct noises. Then Hank added, "Margot, you will be the first one I call as soon as my vet has a look at this. I just want to add that we enjoyed our time with you last night. It was an evening that we won't soon forget. You have been incredibly gracious."

And with that he surprised Margot with a bear hug that I could see almost dissolved her composure. She managed a "Thank you" and then patted her little bun as if to pull herself together and gave a small wave. She and Deb had a flash of eye contact, and then they were gone, clip-clopping in a slow dirge out of the barn and to the arena.

It took a long time and a lot of patience to complete the radiographs. Hotstuff was getting bored. But with some treats and patience we got it done.

And then they were gone.

I took Hotstuff from Ryder and for once she had nothing snide to say. He was happy to go back and have a lie-down in his fresh bedding, filling his big fluffy tail with shavings, and when he rose he rolled his eyeballs back in his head and gave a full body shake. Then he yawned and looked at me as if to say, "Go on, leave; naptime." I dug out a peppermint, gave his withers a brief scratching, and then let Ryder know I had to take a break and ride later. It was weird, but I was exhausted again, my legs feeling heavy as I dragged myself back up the stairs. I almost fell over Wheezer as I dragged myself to my bed. I fell face down into my pillow, not even taking off my barn clogs.

***

I found myself back in the old nightmare. My head pounded and I had the sense that I had been hit across the back of my head and fallen face first into the shavings of a dark stall. I was aware this was a dream but it was still serious business. With some urgency I knew I had to rise and be prepared to fight.

I rolled over and crawled to the front of the stall, peering into a dark barn aisle that I recognized as Equus Paradiso, but at the same time not Equus Paradiso. I got to my feet and wobbled a few steps, passing an open stall door. I stared into the stall, my eyes adjusting to the darkness enough to know the stall was empty.

I staggered to the next stall. Empty. Stall by stall, not a horse in sight, until I crossed the almost imperceptible end of the barn aisle, where I knew I should be looking at the parking area. And there against a dark sky was an even darker outline of a horse van, not our trailer, with a slender form of someone soundlessly leading a horse up the ramp, a horse I knew was Lovey. The van was full. I knew that, too. And the shadow figure; it had to be Ryder. This of course could not be, but also must not be. I opened my mouth to scream in anger at the shadow Ryder. No sound emerged. All the shadow shapes, the things that were but were not, those images that were torturing my rest, they dissolved into darkness. I think I had angrily willed them to dissolve and after I had willed that, then came sweet oblivion.

No one came to wake me up and so I didn't. And when I finally did it was with a slow dawning that something was not quite normal. I checked my watch; I had slept right through any opportunity to ride Winsome. Drat. And in fact, I needed to get my buns over to the Winstons' or I would be late if Francesca showed up. I had to jump start from a dead standstill, but my limbs were still leaden. What was wrong with me?

I had left drool on my bedspread, my contacts were glued to my eyeballs, and I had creases across my face. One clog had fallen off my foot, and when I poked around with my foot trying to locate it, I accidentally pushed it under the bed, which meant I had to crawl on my hands and knees to retrieve it. I looked like someone *had* clocked me one on the back of my head, knocking me flat. I could pass for a victim of a mugging. Only my faithful kitten had looked after me. When I had regained consciousness I had found her curled up in my ponytail, purring; my faithful little Wheezer!

When I got down to the barn, everyone had cleared out. I thought for sure Ryder would still be riding, but she had managed to ride her two in record time these days, so I shouldn't have been surprised.

I changed into my boots, grabbed my spurs and helmet and gloves, and walked out to my truck. But as I did I glanced over to the indoor, and a big black shape crossed my line of sight through the windows above the kickboards. I glanced at my watch. I really needed to get moving, but this was too enticing.

It was Ryder and she was longing Word Perfect. The mare sensed my presence immediately, raising her head and arching her tail. She lifted her knees and strutted her stuff, looking a bit wild in her eyes. Ryder shortened the line, regaining control of the mare on a smaller circle. I went ahead and walked into the arena and took a seat, my legs stretched out in front of me, my gloves and spurs and helmet in hand.

I greeted Ryder. "Sorry to surprise you two." After a moment I said, "She's really beautiful, isn't she?"

Ryder shrugged. "Yeah, I guess so."

I said, "I wish you had woken me up. I missed riding Winsome. And I wanted to watch Emma and Fable go, too."

Ryder glanced at me. "Margot said to leave you alone. She probably thought you were up there bawling over Hotstuff."

My cheeks got hot. There was nothing to say to that. It certainly could have been true.

I changed the subject. "Why isn't Margot riding Word Perfect?"

Another noncommittal shrug. "She told me to longe her, so I'm longing her."

I nodded again, and then stood up. "Okay. Well, I'm going over to the Winstons'."

Ryder simply said in a flat tone, "Have fun."

I thought about our two "black beauties," Hotstuff who was big and goofy, elastic as a rubber band, easy-going like a Labrador Retriever and this new girl, Word Perfect. Hotstuff was easy on the body, with very little concussive impact on the spine or hips of the rider. Word Perfect was sensitive and defensive, cranky and opinionated, with a tendency to explode. I had no idea what she would feel like to sit on, but I expected she was never going to be easy.

Margot had thought she was done with that sort of horse. She had given away the ride on Wild Child to Deb for all those reasons. She had given away a Grand Prix ride, preferring a FEI four-year-old; a First level horse. Fate was dragging her back to the exact same spot from which she had just extricated herself. This mare was going to be a pain in the ass, the kind of ride requiring nerve and timing and stubborn persistence to arrive at a place of cooperation and trust. It was going to take energy and commitment. I sighed. I knew that Margot had all the tools she needed to ride Word Perfect. But it did not mean that she would look forward to it, or would have volunteered for it given different circumstances. Training and riding and showing Word Perfect would take fortitude.

I had my own challenges focusing on Johnny Cash and Francesca, and Winsome, too. I needed to be sure Winsome was prepared to compete. It had been a while since I had run through those Third Level tests. Test Three was a complicated test, even if it wasn't FEI level. It was challenging enough for my Winsome.

My heart skipped a beat when I pulled in to the Winston barn to find Francesca's Mercedes sitting in the parking area. Francesca was sitting in the driver's seat, her head down on the steering wheel. I flashbacked to seeing Frank in just that position. My heart started to race. But as I scurried up to her door she rolled down her window and scowled at me. "Running a bit late, aren't you?"

It might have been inappropriate, but I started to laugh. Francesca was taken aback. "I fail to see any humor here. Would you care to explain?"

I sighed and composed myself. "Francesca, I must be suffering from PTSD or something because I saw you with your head down and thought maybe I would be calling the EMTs again. When I saw you were okay, well, it made me laugh... in relief I guess. I didn't mean anything by it."

Francesca made a little harrumph, and her face softened. "I see. Well ..." her voice trailed off a second, then was all business again. She nodded and swung her legs out of the car. "As you can see, I'm quite fine. But, it appears that now that I'm ready to ride my horse, my groom seems to find herself in a state of un-readiness."

Now I had nervous energy but was glad to have a job to do, glad to finally have a chance to get my project, Francesca's project, back on track. I was going to salvage this very weird day.

I put my back into grooming Johnny Cash while Francesca fetched a boot brush from Claire's tack room and buffed her boots. Francesca's boots were professionally polished at a shoe shop, so they always looked great, but by the time I had Johnny tacked up she had them gleaming. I asked how Frank was doing, but Francesca dodged the question. I tried again, and this time she shut me down, saying, "Lizzy, I know that you mean well, but I am simply exhausted. Frank has his days and nights mixed up. I need this time to focus on my riding as a mental health break. So, if you don't mind, let's do just that, shall we?"

I nodded, giving up on chit-chat. I snapped the plastic buckle on my helmet, tightened the girth one more hole, and then led Johnny down the path to the indoor.

The pleasant summer afternoon offered a mild breeze that pushed us gently down the slope to the arena. The arena was full of slanting shadows and funny iridescent speckled birds. Johnny and I were used to them, but Francesca swore at them and they took flight. The shimmer of rainbow colors on their necks reflected in the late afternoon sun that slanted through the large windows of the indoor.

Francesca muttered, "Filthy things leave their droppings everywhere."

My voice sounded weak. "I think they're beautiful. And when a bunch of them fly around they form a cloud and do the most amazing dance. They make a cloud dance."

Francesca turned and stared at me. It was a long stare, but not unkind, it was instead a thoughtful look as if she was seeing me differently somehow.

Then she said, "The 'corps de ballet' only made up of starlings. Still, I wish they wouldn't nest in the bluebird boxes or be quite so dirty. But it is a dance that they do, isn't it? Artists and photographers are forever taking movement and freezing it, but I prefer my art to move. I see we are the same in that regard, Lizzy. Perhaps someday Frank and I will have you and Chess join us at the ballet."

I almost shook my head in disbelief. Never before had Francesca ever compared the two of us in any favorable way. I could hardly believe my ears. I might have answered too enthusiastically. "Oh I would love that."

And then she shooed me off to 'get on with it' and warm up her horse.

I had not ridden Winsome today, and I only got about ten minutes into my ride on Johnny Cash when Francesca called me over. She stood on the mounting block, gloves on.

I should have been happy about this. It was what I wanted and needed for Francesca to do to prepare for her horse show. But, of course it had been a downer of a day and I had just started to ride Johnny. Sharing him again with Francesca felt like I was being cheated out of my riding time. But that was selfish; he was not for me. I was not like Ryder. I got her stirrups set, got her aboard and off they went. I sulked a few minutes on the mounting block before I could do my job. This would not be a day to bother Francesca with corrections or feedback. She needed to find her groove, or at least what passed for her "groove." I tried my best to step outside myself and look at them both without prejudice.

And what did I see? I saw a big flashy dressage horse, the kind who you could take to any arena and be proud to ride. He had the right "look." And there on his back was an older lady, thin, but looking the part with her custom black dress mirror-shine boots, posh helmet, and tailored clothes. She was clearly not a professional rider; she didn't look like a poser either. This was the best I could hope for Francesca.

I called out across the arena, "You look really good today, Francesca. It must feel good to be back in the saddle."

Francesca made a small nod, but then rode past me, ignoring me. The look on her face made me smile. Francesca was absorbed in her riding, her face not so different from the face that Margot made, and probably the face that I made, too. It might be misconstrued by someone else as aloof or even angry or intense, but I knew it was not anger. It was simply the expression of a person absorbed and focused and intense. Francesca would not be drawn away from the moment or distracted by externals.

I studied what she was doing, and I was amazed. She wasn't stopping and starting anymore. She wasn't even trying to do the test patterns. She was doing different things, changing it up, adding transitions, adding lateral exercises, freshening the gaits forward, and even adding a rein back to trot, and then a walk pirouette to trot. She was experimenting in an attempt to bring Johnny into better balance with the right kind of power, and what she was doing made total sense.

Then it hit me, oh my God, the thought surprised the heck out of me; Francesca was really riding. She was riding in a thoughtful way. The little break away from the daily struggle to master riding Johnny Cash had not hurt her riding, but instead she had somehow gained something. What was it? Francesca was different today. The weird day had gotten even weirder. I couldn't react. I needed to let this weirdness steep in my mind and hopefully at some level at some point in time, I would understand what was happening. She finished her ride with an air of satisfaction, leaving Johnny with the first lipstick stain he had received in a long time. Francesca and I made our date for the next day and I enjoyed putting him up and heading back home where I knew I had the behemoth *Gone With the Wind* to dive back into.

When I got home, Chess' car was in front of the barn. As I passed Francesca's office, the door was ajar and the lights were on. I didn't hesitate or knock but just walked right in. Chess sat in his mother's chair, talking on the phone, a laptop open in front of him, a lined yellow legal pad next to it. Instead of his usual contact lenses he wore glasses, making him look older. He smiled at me, but he was clearly having a serious conversation. I headed for one of the upholstered chairs and sat down, feeling sad without seeing a little rascally terrier ready to jump up into my lap. I really had missed seeing those little devils.

Chess hung up and then leaned back into his chair. He began tapping his ink pen against the yellow pad in a rhythmic beat. His fidgeting, which I initially thought was a sign of pure nerves, I now recognized was musical.

When I'd started to pay attention, I noticed his fidgets were always rhythmic. True, it was still a form of fidgeting; but I knew now that it served multiple purposes for Chess. Music was always with him, and served both as center stage in his thoughts and as a backdrop to whatever was going on. It was as if he was scoring and performing the soundtrack of his life in every waking moment.

I was just learning the customs and the language of this stranger, and I knew he felt the same about me. Would we ever be able to see the world through each other's eyes? I don't think that was possible. But, there was a growing appreciation, wonderment in our discoveries.

Chess removed his glasses, rubbed his eyes, and turned to look at me. He sighed, "Well, I'm in this deep now." I nodded to encourage him to continue. Instead he shut down his laptop and slipped it into a case, changing the subject, "You hungry?"

I smiled. "Always, if you're cooking." He put his glasses back on and I followed him out of the office as he switched off the light and closed the door. And then he started walking toward his car. I had to walk fast to keep up with him. He locked his computer bag in the trunk. "Okay, off duty now," he said. We walked to the apartment in silence. I could tell he was still thinking through whatever the call was about, still not quite 'off-duty.'"

My mind was now on food, whether he was cooking or if he had brought pizza from the "Little Napoli" place. I said hopefully, "Pizza?"

When he opened my apartment door I was hit by an amazing aroma. Chess clearly had cooked at "my place." What a surprise. I bent down and scooped up Wheezer at the same time that I said, "Wow!" Then I noticed the table was set with three place settings. Always the gentleman, Chess was including Ryder. I tried not to look disappointed.

He noticed that I noticed. He said, "Ryder was interested in the menu, and I have plenty to share. I know you'd like to have a hot shower, and I can finish up here by myself. If you don't mind; let Ryder know that all I have left to do is to toss the salad and it's ready." Chess then shooed me away.

I did as I was told, while my stomach grumbled about having to wait even a few minutes. I gave Ryder the message and then I took the speediest shower ever. Ryder and Chess were chatting amiably when I joined the party, Ryder leaning against the counter, casual and relaxed and even, if it was possible, happy. Ryder and I were invited to sit down and relax and allow Chess to treat us to deluxe service.

Chess Cavelli was an amazing cook. That's all there was to it. I had never tasted anything like it, and even though he had cooked for me multiple times, he had never repeated the main course. Tonight was chicken like I had never tasted, flat little medallions dipped in something and crispy, served with capers and artichokes in a light cream sauce over Orzo.

I raved, "What the heck is this?"

Chess smiled and shook his head. "You've never had Piccata?"

Ryder who had been fairly quiet broke in. "I have. But this is different from what I've had. It's better actually."

Chess nodded, satisfied. "Thank you, Ryder."

Even Ryder recognized that this was a distinctive dish. Chess was a multi-talented guy, a veritable renaissance man. I had a notion this was another one of his Nonna's dishes. So I asked. "It's really exceptional, Chess. Is it one of your Nonna's recipes?"

Ryder interrupted, "Can you give me the recipe?"

Chess smiled but shook his head firmly. "Ryder, sorry, can't. And yes, Lizzy, this is from my Nonna, and I was specifically bequeathed Nonna's black book of specialties in her will. I will guard it with my life. It has to stay in the family. But her legacy for me goes beyond the recipes in that little black book, which is mostly in Italian anyway. What matters is that I stood by her side and learned all the tiny little things she did that made a difference. A lot of that stuff you won't find in any book." He bit his lower lip and I actually thought he might tear up.

Ryder said, "Seems a shame that so few will be able to enjoy it. I'll bet you could make some serious money with a restaurant serving this. But anyway, I'm glad you included me tonight. Thanks, Chess."

Chess smiled, regaining his composure. I'm glad you like it, Ryder. I have some warm panna cotta on the counter for after."

I changed the subject so I could ask Chess about Frank.

I said, "How's your dad doing?"

A shadow passed over Chess' face. He said, "I've never seen Dad like this before. He's having a hard time bouncing back from this surgery. And his spirits are really down. Not like him."

Ryder added, "Dennis said the same thing. He's been to visit him a couple times and they've had some long talks. I know Dennis is trying to help out any way he can. He's known Frank a long time, and he's a little freaked out over it."

I sat back in my chair, taking a long pause from my almost empty plate. I felt terribly guilty. I had not been to seen Frank. I had never been inside the Cavellis' home and, to be honest, had never felt a visit there would be welcome. But, now I had Chess at my side and surely that changed the dynamic. I needed to go. I looked at Chess and asked, "Can you take me to go see him? I feel terrible that I haven't seen him."

Again, Ryder broke in. "I went to see him once with Dennis. When I got there Margot was just leaving, and Frank was already really tired, so I just spent about five minutes with him and then I sat and chatted with Francesca while Dennis sat with Frank. I had assumed you'd have gone by now, Lizzy."

That made me feel even worse.

Chess ran his hands through his hair once, a sign I had come to know that he was thinking of the best way to say something. "Lizzy, don't feel bad. Dad is weak and very emotional right now. I would have taken you to see him, but I know he'll start crying when he sees you, and then you would start crying, and no one needs that right now. I think you should wait."

Though I felt slighted, I instantly proved Chess right because my lower lip started to wobble and I had a hard time getting out the right words. I said, "That doesn't sound like Frank to me. Frank is the one who lightens up every situation. Frank is a rock."

Chess smiled. "Yep, that's my dad. But the rock is teetering a little bit right now and we have to be careful." He looked at me, then at Ryder, and said, "Who wants coffee?"

It was the right thing to say. I stiffened my resolve, quieted my wobbly lower lip, and turned my attention to Ryder, "So, Dennis has visited twice, huh?"

Ryder simply nodded, then added, "Lizzy, I don't know why you don't like Dennis. He's a nice guy, and easy to be around. He and Margot seem to be hitting it off, too. He wants to learn everything about high performance dressage and is very supportive of my goals. And he's rich; very, very rich."

Ryder was doing it again, poking me where she knew she could get a response. I refused to let her get my dander up. So, I said softly, "Ryder, you say the word 'rich' like it's a virtue."

Ryder smiled. She loved this game. She said, "Don't knock it till you've tried it." Of course she was right. I'd never had money, but couldn't say that I'd never fantasized about what it would be like to be rich.

Chess cleared our plates then turned to me and said, "I've known Dennis a long time, casually, and always found him very nice to be around. But then there was the business with Sophie, which soured things to the point that I thought Mom and Dad would never welcome him back. Shows how much I know."

Ryder added, "If Margot has done the 'forgive and forget,' then why should anyone hold a grudge for her?"

Chess and I exchanged a glance. It seemed to me that someone had been giving her "talking points." Chess added, "That's a valid point, Ryder. In any case, Dennis is once again a client of Mother and Dad's business, with Margot clearly enjoying his company. He's paying good money to have his mare in full training with Margot, which helps our monthly cash flow. And he's talking about participating in the breeding program as well, which I'm still trying to figure out money-wise. As far as I'm concerned, he's part of the Equus Paradiso farm family again."

Ryder offered to do the dishes, which was polite but meant I had no chance to privately unload on Chess what I was thinking out of her earshot. It also meant I had no chance to ask him what he had meant by his off-hand comment of being "in deep." He left after dinner with apologies that he had to get up early to go to the city. I didn't feel like I had been able to thank him properly for all the spoiling, and instead we only shared a chaste sort of kiss goodnight.

I unloaded the dishwasher and wiped off the table and counters while Ryder rinsed and loaded. We had little to say to each other. Ryder seemed disinterested in hearing about Francesca's ride on Johnny Cash, even though I truly was enthusiastic about what I had seen that day.

By the time I curled up with Wheezer in my bed, the feeling that I should, no, I *needed*, to see Frank had grown to a sense of real urgency. Tomorrow I would ask Chess to take me, and promise to control my emotions. I would be brave. I had to see Frank.

8. Lose, Win, And Draw

I woke up resolved to somehow see Frank before the day was done, though I had a feeling that both Chess and Francesca would stop me from going if I mentioned it. I had never been to Frank and Francesca's home. Emma had been there and would be my best bet as someone to support a quiet and unannounced visit and hopefully go with me. But first I had to get through my workday.

Ryder and I started our usual routine, and after the horses had eaten, I got Hotstuff out to groom and tack up for Margot, as usual. The guys had on their Mexican radio station and fun mariachi music drifted down the barn aisle, which lifted my spirits. I gave Hotstuff a good grooming while I danced around and then put on his saddle, leaving the girth loose until Margot was ready to ride.

To my happy surprise, Snapper and Chopper came tearing down the barn aisle, nails scrabbling on the concrete. Hotstuff raised his head in alarm. He still wasn't completely over the little accident the terriers had caused while he was being shod. Horses had amazing memories for negative experiences. So I walked out of the grooming stall and knelt down so I could greet the terriers a little distance from Hotstuff so he wouldn't worry. The terriers came skidding to a stop when they saw me, they were squealing, actually sort of shrieking. They slammed into my knees and began licking me all over my face.

I sang back to them in the high-pitched voice reserved for animals and babies, "Snapper, Chopper, my little buddies, I missed you, too; I did, I really did, I promise I did."

They were hopping on their hind legs and continued making weird screeching noises, scratching at my breeches and frantically licking me. They had lots to tell me, stopping the frenzy for split seconds to stare intently at me, whining with black button eyes shining, then resuming scratching at my legs and licking me all over my face. Snapper, the smooth coated one, climbed into my lap, still crying, and then he put his chin over my shoulder like a baby, hind legs pedaling. He felt like he was going to climb on top of my head or something, so I wrapped one free arm around him and hugged him tight.

Chopper then climbed up too, so I finally just sat fully down on the barn floor and wrapped my other arm around Chopper and squeezed him tightly. They did their best to hug me, and I hugged them back. They had never shown me this much affection. Perhaps in their own way they had been traumatized by Frank's heart attack. Or maybe they were just nuts from being cooped up. Perhaps it was a combination of the two. But regardless, they needed the hugs and after only a few seconds of full body to body contact, their frenzy began to abate, and the screeching turned to whines, and finally into panting. They were settling down. I used my best soothing voice, dropping it to lower tones. "That's better. You guys are okay. It's all going to be okay now. You're okay, you're okay."

I realized just about then that both Ryder and Francesca were standing over me. I looked up to see Francesca looking down, gently shaking her head, slightly amused. Ryder rolled her eyes; I think as usual she found me ridiculous.

Ryder spoke over my head to Francesca. "You riding Lovey today?"

Francesca ignored her. Instead she looked down at me again and said in her droll way, "I hope those aren't High Horse Couture breeches you're grinding into the concrete. You will cause the fabric to pill."

There was not the hint of a smile on Francesca's face, but I laughed out loud, pulled myself up off the floor and smiled at Francesca. "Francesca, your little guys needed a hug, and they weren't going to settle for anything less than full body contact. For that I had to sit."

Francesca tipped her head to consider me, and then said, "I have no doubt you treat all the animals well, Lizzy, but your treatment of inanimate objects borders on torture."

Now Ryder guffawed. "Yeah, you've got her pegged all right. You should see her books when she's done with them. I'm surprised the pages don't all fall out."

I resisted taking the bait, and Francesca wasn't done anyway. She lifted her finger and weakly pointed at Ryder. "I *am* ready to ride my horse again, Ryder. I hope you have kept him tuned up for me."

Ryder's face was impassive, she laid it on thick. I knew it was bull. "I hope you'll feel some improvement in the level of his engagement. I worked on it for you."

And Francesca replied, "Good, I expect to be impressed."

Right then Margot joined us, coffee in hand, looking slightly uneasy. She looked at Francesca without saying "Good morning" or calling Ryder or me "Darling." Instead, she dropped her gaze, then examined her left hand, turning her fist so she could inspect her fingernails. She was probably dying to chew on them. But she caught herself and looked back at Francesca, taking a deep breath. She curtly nodded and said, "Well?" Then pressed her lips together in a hard, thin line and waited.

We three stood like statues for a long cold moment, all looking at Francesca. But, it was probably only a second or two. Francesca simply said, "They wired the money this morning as soon as the bank opened. Van will pick him up tomorrow."

Margot dropped her head, then turned and looked at Hotstuff, all tacked up and ready to ride. She said softly, "Well then." Margot drew herself up, and her voice was now businesslike. "Lizzy, please untack him and put him away. "

Then she lifted her chin and looked at Ryder. "Go ahead and tack up Word Perfect. Use my saddle, and shim it up with the pocket half pad to sit level. Be sure and look at it both from the side and from the rear. Stand on the mounting block to check from behind. I won't use that dreadful saddle that came with her. I don't care how much Dennis paid for it."

She and Francesca turned together and walked back to the office. Whatever was to be said now would not be said in front of Ryder or me.

It was over.

I felt numb. I lectured myself that Hotstuff had been sold, not sent to the slaughter like a 4-H project. But it still felt like he had been sacrificed. I pulled off his saddle, gave him a peppermint, then handed him over to Alfonso who would take him out to the paddock for an extra long turn out today. Alfonso gave him several pats on the neck and called him a good horse. He also gave me a sympathetic nod.

I watched Ryder clip Word Perfect into the grooming stalls. The mare followed her like a lamb. But that did not last long. When Ryder went to pick up her foot, the mare snatched her hoof out of Ryder's hand and stomped it down hard, barely missing Ryder's toes. When Ryder asked again for her to pick up her hoof, Word Perfect refused, instead putting all her weight on it and wrinkling her nostrils. This was not a green horse. This was a Grand Prix horse. Word Perfect knew how to pick up her feet to be cleaned out. This was simple defiance.

Ryder was just getting started with the grooming process and the mare was spoiling for a fight. I watched as Ryder matter-of-factly turned and walked away, going into the tack room. The mare perked up, watching Ryder walk away. She looked happy; ears up, eyes bright and shining, thinking she had won round one.

Her expression changed the instant Ryder walked back into the barn aisle holding a long dressage whip. The mare pinned her ears and lunged forward in the cross-ties, mouth open and lips pulled back to show her teeth. Word Perfect rose to the fight. I caught the mare's eye, sending her a telepathic message that she had made a bad decision. I pursed my lips, thinking that the mare did not know who she was dealing with. But then, this could be very interesting. Word Perfect and Ryder seemed to have a lot of similar personality traits. It would be a battle of wills.

I braced myself for the coming conflict. I should have been helping or giving Ryder some privacy to sort things out between them, but I couldn't help myself. I knew better than to ask Ryder if she needed help. I would have gotten my head bitten off. And of course, I was not going to miss the show. I was relieved that Margot had assigned this one to Ryder and not me. Ryder could have her.

Ryder put her hand on the mare's leg again, asking her to pick up her hoof for cleaning. Not only did Word Perfect pin her ears, but she pushed her shoulder into Ryder, bumping her off balance. Ryder stepped away a foot or so, then snapped her fingers and pointed her index finger at her barking, "Get over now, you big cow."

Instead, Word Perfect did a tiny rear.

The whip instantly came whistling through the air, meeting Wordy's flesh fully on her shoulder; three hard blows in quick succession: "Whisst, whisst, whisst!"

The mare sort of cantered on the place, straining against the cross-ties, taking her licking, but she didn't pull back or panic. After the third blow, Ryder put her arm down and stepped back. The mare stood still and tall, head high and twisting her neck to take a long hard look at Ryder. She snorted once. The two looked long and hard at each other. Then Ryder looked at me and said, "I'll let her think about it a few minutes and calm down." Ryder handed me the whip.

I scored that round for Word Perfect.

Ryder walked away, back to the tack room to gather all of Wordy's tack, and pads, bringing an armload that included our special lamb's wool half pad that had little pockets in it. We had "shims," made of felt, that we could slide into the pockets to balance a saddle that didn't fit perfectly. It was a stopgap measure of course, and wasn't the same as having the saddle adjusted by the saddle fitter. Horses, like people, needed all their equipment to fit properly if we intended to ask them to be athletic. Margot had clearly not been impressed with Word Perfect's saddle. I was amazed that she could remember so much from that one ride she had on Wordy at the Herm Martin clinic so long ago.

I shouldn't have continued to stare as Ryder tacked up Word Perfect. She was going to be a very tough horse to deal with, and a tough horse to ride, but there was no denying that she was stunning to look at. Someone in Germany was able to stick it out all the way to Grand Prix. Someone had shown her enough to get decent scores. It almost did not seem possible, but clearly it was. Sophie had not been up to the task, but I knew Margot had the training and the feel and the timing to bring this mare around. I had faith.

By the time Ryder was ready for Round Two, Word Perfect had settled. Her head had come down, and her eye had halfway closed. She actually looked relaxed in a weird way. Ryder stepped to her off side, and this time she didn't even touch the mare's leg. Instead she pointed at her right front hoof and snapped her fingers.

The mare picked up her foot. Ryder didn't even look at me when I said, "Damn." I added, "I didn't think she'd come around that easily." Ryder took a firm hold of the hoof, and in a brisk and business-like way, got down to business, going 'round to hoof number two, and three and four.

Round Two to Ryder.

Word Perfect stood perfectly still, but sharply swished her tail around toward Ryder. She only managed to spank Ryder's knee, in a statement of irritation. Each hoof was obediently picked up by the mare from the snap of Ryder's fingers. The mare's eyes stayed half closed, her ears at half-mast, a couple wrinkles behind each nostril. She was enduring the process with certain indignation. The long dressage whip stayed loosely gripped in my hands. Word Perfect saw it there, and Ryder had shown she was not opposed to using it with force. This mare was smart as well as aggressive, and I guessed she would look for her next opportunity to assert herself. This must be what is famously known in the horse world as an "Alpha" mare. She was ready to let us other "fillies" know who ruled the roost. There were certainly more battles in store. Poor Margot. Poor us.

We had little pieces of cut felt that slipped into the pockets of the fleece correction half pad to play with to get Margot's saddle to work on the back of Word Perfect. Ryder and I had pulled the mounting block into the grooming stall to stand directly behind Wordy while we fussed over the fit. Everyone knows horses have a blind spot directly behind and in front of them and every person has heard the dire warning never to stand directly behind a horse. But, that was usually so that you didn't trigger a lethal kick that was delivered out of a startle reflex. Word Perfect was in no way startled by us as we positioned the mounting block behind her. We did it in a slow way, letting her see us carry it around her side and placing a hand on her rump to position it. Still, I did not like the look in her narrowed eyes. She wasn't worried or frightened. She was thinking, and I could tell they were not nice thoughts.

Word Perfect seemed to already be thinking about Round Three.

When Ryder placed the saddle on her back, Wordy pinned her ears and her mouth pulled tight into the corners. Ryder pulled the saddle pads lightly into the gullet of the saddle, and then buckled the girth on the off side, walking around to buckle it on the near side. I was still standing in front of Word Perfect, dressage whip in my hand. When Ryder reached under the mare to grab the hanging girth, "Wordy" swung a hind leg up and under her belly. I swear she was aiming at Ryder's hand, but Ryder was quick to protect herself, grabbing the girth and turning her body so that her body and her hand were beyond the arc of the swing of Wordy's hind leg.

Ryder yelled, "Bitch!" Then yelled at me, "Lizzy, for God's sake, I handed you that whip for a reason."

I had been so busy watching that I had not even moved the whip. I swished it a bit in the air. Word Perfect swiveled her ears toward me, but otherwise looked unimpressed. I had the distinct impression that she was toying with us. Ryder put the girth on loosely and then proceeded to lecture me. "I don't trust this bitch, and one of us has to climb up on that mounting block and check the saddle fit. If I do it, you've got to let her know that it will cost her some hide if she dares pick up a foot. So, which one of us is going to deliver the beating and who is going to check the saddle fit?"

It didn't take me more than a split second to answer her. I sure as heck didn't want to be behind the mare if she was going to kick. "I'll hold the whip."

Ryder growled at me. "Yeah, I thought that would be your answer. Look, you tell me to get out of the way if she so much as wrinkles her nose, and then let her have it." And with that she grabbed the mare's lead rope and snapped it back onto the halter. Ryder jerked the rope three times and snarled, "Mare, you try to hurt me and I'll make sure you hurt more."

Then Word Perfect did the most amazing thing. She picked up a hind hoof and tapped the mounting block lightly with her hind toe three times, as if she was considering the distance and force it would take her to knock the thing out from under Ryder. Ryder and I looked at each other with disbelief then we cracked up laughing. I said, "Ryder, she's making war plans. And letting us know she's doing it."

Ryder said, "We are so screwed."

I shook my head. "I'll unhook her from the cross-ties and lead her far enough forward that you're out of range. Then I'll run a chain over her nose and carry the whip."

Ryder nodded. "Yeah, and we need to do it out in the barn aisle where she can't run backward and trap me in the back of the grooming stall."

So, we did, and the mare was completely passive, maybe even bored. But I knew that she simply recognized that her opportunity had passed. Ryder and Margot and I would have to stay on our toes with this one.

When Margot showed up, Ryder and I gave her a blow-by-blow. Margot listened, staring unwaveringly at her new project.

When we finished our story of Battle: Day One, Margot placed a hand on the side of the mare's beautiful full bridle. It too was the latest in fashion, the noseband made of shiny patent leather, the brow band set with Bavarian crystals that sparkled and winked even in the dim barn light. It had the new ergonomic design with a cut out on the noseband and behind the ears, a bit of elastic set under the brow band. Sophie had clearly enjoyed shopping with Dennis' money.

Margot spoke to Word Perfect. "Now look here, my new friend, you have some big shoes to fill. I know you didn't ask to come into my barn. I know you're an angry girl right now, resentful at how your life has been turned upside down. But, even though you don't know it yet, I'm your new best friend. It won't be today or tomorrow, but someday you are going to love me and look to me to take care of you. But, first we have to establish some ground rules. Do you hear my voice? Do you read me?"

The mare didn't pin her ears or wrinkle her nose. But she didn't look happy either.

Margot turned to me. "Lizzy, come to the arena with me please. I'm putting on my sharp spurs and I want you to hand me the long whip off the arena wall and hold her while I get on. I also think you should close the arena doors. I've dealt with other Word Perfects, but it has been a few years."

Ryder crossed her arms and said, "This ought to be good."

Margot shrugged. "Darlings, I'm glad that Dennis won't be here for this first ride, since he would not understand the process. And I'll depend on both of you for your discretion, of course. With a strong-minded horse like this one, you never know. It's like what they tell middle school teachers; your first job is to establish a productive environment for learning and sometimes that requires not smiling until Christmas."

Then she turned to Ryder. "Darling, please get Wild Child ready for Deb, and tell her not to get on until I finish with the mare. I'm certain there will be drama enough without adding Wild Child's sex appeal to the equation."

Word Perfect stood like a good soldier for Margot to mount. She also walked like a lamb into the arena. I closed the arena doors, just like Margot asked.

Wordy looked tight over her top line. It's something that is not easy to see, but even I could see it. When Margot first touched her side with her legs, I could see the skin twitch. But I also marveled for a moment at how beautiful the horse was, and how good Margot looked sitting on top of her. Margot simply walked her around on a loose rein, frowning and shaking her head. Then she looked at herself in the mirror. The mare had a chiseled face, a long and arched neck that smoothly joined her body. Her hipline was long, as were her legs. She was made for the sport, at least in her looks. But Margot walked and walked and walked silently around the arena, with an intense look on her face.

I finally asked, "What do you think?"

I had broken some sort of trance. Margot looked surprised to see me. "Lizzy, darling, do you have any sugar or peppermints?"

Of course I did. Margot walked over to me as I unwrapped a peppermint, Margot watched and then nodded at me to give it to the mare.

I reached out to give it to Wordy, who looked surprised. She simply blew at it repeatedly with her ears pricked, clearly interested in the smell, but it rolled off my hand into the arena footing.

I looked up at Margot, who said, "Put it in her mouth this time."

I shoved it in the side of her mouth behind the bits. The horse instantly opened her mouth and spit it out.

I said, "How weird. Most horses are crazy about peppermints."

Margot said, "Lizzy, this mare's a survivor, and she's bright. She doesn't know us or trust us, and intends to defend herself from us. I have to say, I feel the same way about her. We'll have to sugar her up every chance we get, and at the same time watch her every move and demand that she color between the lines. She could hurt me. I respect that. On the other hand, I have to make this work. For my own good, and ultimately for hers, I have to make this work. I need all of my focus and skills, and without Dennis watching, or Francesca interfering."

She could see that I did not fully understand her meaning. "Part of me resents the very fact that at my stage of life I still have to take on the problem child while giving away my perfect child. I know what this project is going to cost me, in a lot of ways. When I was your age, darling, I would only see the beauty of this horse and underestimate the personal cost of my time and potential risk to my body and the sheer exhaustion, both physical and mental, that I know is coming. Now, I see much, much more."

I shook my head in disagreement. "But Margot, you have the experience of lots and lots of horses. Wordy doesn't know you yet. You just may turn this one around in record time."

Margot drew a deep breath. "Perhaps. I will just have to summon the courage to find out." And with that, Margot asked for the long whip off the wall. And the battle commenced. There was no way that Word Perfect was not going to test Margot, and once the testing began, Margot could not stop until she felt the mare reach some state of submission.

I understood then why Margot had walked around the arena, round and around and around. It was just as Deb had explained to me at the horse show. Margot was on that metaphorical high dive standing on the edge and looking down. She had to summon her courage. She had been quaking in her boots, imagining all sorts of dreadful outcomes, rehearsing her failure. But, when the moment came, she just gathered herself and jumped. And then she couldn't think anymore, instead she had to focus and react by feel; it was the training that took over. And I was the privileged one to have a front row seat to see it happen. She sat tall in the saddle, looking unconcerned with the theatrics that took place underneath her, and there was no shortage of theatrics. I clenched my fists and my jaw and braced myself, as if by flexing my muscles I could help in some small way.

The mare pinned her ears at the first step of trot, taking tight small steps, snorting a few hard snorts that pulled at the reins. Margot sat quietly, but her jaw was firm and her torso unmoved. I noticed that Margot did not bother to rise the trot as we would normally do at the beginning of a ride. She sat instead and sweetly asked for simple figures. Wordy was clearly behind the leg and tight over her back, but Margot did not address it. I could see from Margot's face that she was fully concentrating on the mare as she rode simple circles. Wordy in return was also turned inward, but holding herself like a little ticking time bomb; looking for a way to release the anger that was building under the saddle.

It came with a flitting of a house sparrow in front of her nose. The mare flung a front leg up in the air and grunted. Then she stood up on her hind legs in a tall rear, followed by throwing her head down and humping her back in a series of hopping bucks.

The whip came whistling through the air like an incoming missile as Margot leaned back in the saddle like a rodeo rider, grabbing the saddle with one hand. I caught my breath sharply because for a moment I saw daylight under Margot's seat. Her timing was perfect though because instead of throwing another buck or spinning, Word Perfect took off in a canter, her head now flung up in the air. Margot let her go and in fact I heard her say, "Go on, that's right. Go, go on, mare, work it out."

I noticed that Margot still held the front of the saddle with her outside hand, which meant that Wordy could not pull Margot's butt out of the tack or get away from the reins, because Margot's outside rein was like a side-rein on a longing surcingle and she had used her hand to pull her seat bones to the front of the tack, deep and forward, while her back stayed ramrod straight. No matter what Word Perfect tried, that rein length was going nowhere, and Margot was going nowhere.

Margot used the whip again, but lightly this time, clucking at the mare to keep her going in the canter. Instead, the mare broke to the trot, but Margot clucked and gave her another smack with the whip. And off they went again, lapping the arena in canter. They cantered and cantered until Word Perfect was finally tired, coming into the contact in a reasonable and steady way. Margot praised her and the picture transformed before my eyes to a picture of steadiness. It appeared that all was forgiven and forgotten. Margot then went back to trot, once again riding sweetly, and did shoulder in and haunches in, beautiful long half passes, then finally passage and medium trots. She was full of praise, giving Word Perfect tiny micro-breaks but never letting her down completely. She even did a few steps of piaffe at the end. Then she jumped off and loosened the girth quickly, before I could get to her.

I could see her hands were shaking as she undid the girth. But she smiled at me, and she said, "Darling, I'm exhausted, but so glad that is done. It's like eating a frog for breakfast; the rest of the day just has to go down easier."

I replied with a finger in the air, drawing a number one. "Score one for Margot, zero for Word Perfect."

Wordy then turned her head to get a good look at Margot, breathing hard, her sides rising and falling. The mare seemed to study Margot long and hard, her ears hung slightly to the side before both coming forward in an alert expression. Margot pulled off her gloves, and reached her cupped hand out to meet the mare's nose, as if she had a treat, but she didn't. The mare did the most amazing thing. After taking in Margot's smell in short quick breaths, she began to lick. She licked and licked and licked while Margot stayed stock still, silently turning her hands over while Word Perfect continued to lick.

I had no idea what was going on, and I'm not sure Margot did either, but the mare had a weird soft look in her eye.

I spoke almost in a whisper. "She looks like she's cleaning off her foal."

Margot was deep in thought and she didn't respond, but we continue to stand and watch. Then Margot said, "Hand me that peppermint."

And I did, and this time when Margot offered it, Word Perfect took the mint, taking a long time to work it back to her molars and crunch it up.

Margot and I walked side by side with Word Perfect back to the wash stall. People asked how it went, and Margot barely answered them. Instead Margot and I discussed stress hormones and we discussed memory. Did Word Perfect lick her because of stress hormones rising and falling? Did Word Perfect recognize and remember Margot after the ride when she smelled her? Would the rides go better now? Why was the mare so difficult and defensive? Would we ever know the real history of the horse? Could you ever really 'know' such a defensive horse?

Margot and I were absorbed with the intricate puzzle that was Word Perfect. And as I watched her walk away from me I had a clear realization: Margot, with all her reluctance to take on this project, was hooked: Totally.

***

Deb took Wild Child to the arena, and Emma and Natalie arrived to groom and tack up Fable. The week was getting off to an interesting start and would end with the CDI just up the road. The pressure was on Deb and Emma. If it went well, then we could go to Devon feeling hopeful. We needed good news; we needed hope. It had to go well.

I wanted to ask Emma to go with me to visit Frank, but I didn't want to distract her from her ride, so I waited to speak to her. I was sitting in a director's chair untangling a wad of polo wraps fresh out of the dryer and chatting with Emma and Natalie when Dennis arrived. He couldn't exactly sneak in since he always drove his noisy motorcycle. As he passed the office, Francesca opened the door and released the terriers, who made a fuss barking. Dennis gave them a butt-scratching, causing Chopper to thump his hind leg and then throw himself on the ground for a belly scratch. It seemed that's all that was needed to win over the terriers. Dennis chatted up Francesca for a few minutes in a jovial way. They walked down the barn aisle together, where he spotted his wet horse standing in the cross-ties, the fan on to help dry her off.

Dennis slapped the side of his leg, "Oh, shoot, I missed seeing my Wordy have her first ride."

"You've forgotten, Dennis, Margot always rides her horse first in the line up."

He tssk-tssked. "She knows I can't make it here that early, but I'm glad to hear that she considers Wordy her own. Still, I think the owner should get to see the ride."

Francesca shrugged. "You have to learn to pick your battles, Dennis. I have learned over the years that Margot has her reasons. She may not want to tell you what they are, but she has good reasons nonetheless."

Dennis refocused on Wordy, looking over to Ryder before speaking. "She's a knockout, isn't she?"

Everyone understood he meant the horse and not Margot.

Ryder replied with uncharacteristic enthusiasm, "I'd take her!"

Emma and I traded looks but said nothing. Francesca sniffed and said, "Margot would say 'pretty is as pretty does'." Somehow Francesca already knew that Wordy's behavior had not been 'pretty'.

Dennis dug around in his pockets and pulled out a peppermint, which he unwrapped and handed to Word Perfect, who took it right away without hesitation. Interesting. Dennis winked at me. "I only fed her treats when Sophie wasn't around."

He stepped into the tack room and came back out with a big handful, which he proceeded to feed Wordy one after the other, crooning to her like a baby. He and Francesca stepped away to go to the arena to watch Deb finish her ride and damn if the mare didn't softly whinny to him.

I was dumbfounded. I wanted to go tell Margot, but of course I couldn't. Ryder simply said, "Bitch knows her Sugar-Daddy, doesn't she? But she doesn't respect Dennis, nope; she just thinks he's her personal Pez dispenser."

I said, "That mare is going to keep us all on our toes."

Ryder answered, "Mare just needs the right rider."

And I couldn't help myself. "That would be why she's here for *Margot*." I said, knowing full well that Ryder was not thinking of Margot.

I was fortunate that by the time Emma and Fable were finished, Dennis had lost interest and left. Margot was ready to get back to teaching me on Winsome and I didn't want that man comparing Winsome to Word Perfect.

We were back on the old schedule, at least until we loaded up for the CDI on Thursday. It was a good thing, too, because I needed to get back into show mode and run through test three of the Third level. I had already qualified for regional finals, but needed to begin polishing the test, and riding it without a whip under the rules of regional and national championships.

As usual, test riding felt awful. My inner metronome was set too high, and Margot told me I was running Winsome off her feet. Everything was too hectic, the corners coming up too fast, the test pattern too much in my thoughts, fearful that I would go off course. Margot soothed me with "darlings" and a slow and low voice. By the time we finished, Ryder had been walking around on Papa, waiting her turn, looking bored and annoyed. My tee-shirt was soaked through with sweat, and I felt like I had just demonstrated my inferiority in front of Ryder.

Emma was playing with Uno and the terriers in the aisle when I returned. Chopper had a hold of some grungy stuffed rat and Uno had the other end. They both growled like killers. Sweetly, Chopper would drop it to let Uno enjoy shaking it around while he watched and panted. Then Snapper would take a turn. The two terriers looked like they were baby-sitting Emma's Chihuahua. I wondered if they remembered him.

Natalie was hand grazing Fable out in the sun to dry off from his bath. I began untacking while I spoke. "Hey Em, I have a favor to ask."

Emma scooped up Uno, throwing the stuffed rat down the aisle and watching Chopper and Snapper go for it. "Shoot."

"I want to go see Frank tonight after I finish up. Want to come with me?"

She smiled. "Great idea. Maybe we could take him something? But not food, I think he's on a serious medical diet."

I said, "I don't want to tell anyone we're going because I have a feeling if we asked we'd be told to wait."

That stopped Emma. She stared at me, but I could tell the wheels were turning. "You mean that Francesca would stop you?"

I nodded. "But it wouldn't be fair for us to wait, since Dennis and Ryder have gone to see him."

Her eyes widened and she drew out the word. "Realllllllly? That stinks. I just know that Dennis is up to something. I just don't understand why Margot is riding his horse and sitting on the back of his obnoxious motorcycle. It's pissing me off, and I can imagine that it's giving Francesca an ulcer. Plus that Ryder is a self-serving thing that thinks way too highly of herself, and she and Dennis are getting chummy. I don't like it."

I whispered, "You and Frank are like this though." And I held up two fingers crossed together. "I just think he needs to see his real friends right now, you know?"

Emma frowned and shook her head. "Lizzy, Frank is a really sick guy right now. We need to tread lightly, and not burden him. We need to be smart."

I nodded. "I agree, I totally agree, but my gut tells me that we need to at least go see him. It's just wrong to have Frank out of the picture totally. He's always been the real heart and soul of Equus Paradiso. I mean, in a way he's the only sane one among us."

She shook her head again. "Don't forget Chess. Chess is ..." And she stopped herself.

My stomach did a flip, making me hesitant to urge her to finish her thought. Emma not only knew Frank and Francesca, but also Chess. Hadn't Francesca insinuated something? I couldn't quite put my finger on it, but for just an instant, I felt awkward. I changed the subject to practicalities, like what time we would "stop by," and what we would bring as a gift.

9. Roller Coaster Ride

We came bearing gifts. Natalie had given me one of her little rabbit sculptures to present as a gift to Frank, and Emma and I had stopped at the bakery to buy a bag of his favorite lemon squares, although we weren't sure he would be allowed to eat them.

Although Frank and Francesca lived only a few miles away, I had never been invited over and had never seen their home. When they entertained us, it had always been at Frank's favorite Italian restaurants.

We pulled up to electric gates similar to those at the farm. Emma put her window down and entered a code. I looked over at her. "You know the house code?"

She winked at me. "Easy, it's always been the same as both barns. That way Francesca only had to learn one code. Of course, she'd hate it that I told you or anyone else that little tidbit of info."

The gates whirred open and we pulled Emma's big truck through and then drove uphill on a long and curved driveway framed by an alley of mature, leafy trees. The front of the property was densely wooded, but soon we saw lawn and house. I could almost feel the air cool as we drove. A green manicured lawn stretched in front of a sprawling house. The center part of the home looked old; made from stone. White framed wings stretched on either side; surely additions. In a way it was not as grand a home as I had imagined, but it fit in beautifully for the area. This was, after all, where the American Revolution was fought. I imagined the central part of the home being a place where George Washington actually could have slept.

We parked the truck on the side of the home where paver stones made an apron. The large detached garage sat slightly back with a covered walkway to the rear door. The garage doors were open and I spotted Frank's moss green Jag and his bigger Mercedes sedan, with a little red compact parked directly behind it that must belong to the formidable Marta. Francesca's Mercedes convertible was missing from the third spot in the garage. What a relief.

I stared out the truck window at the view of the backyard. The pool had one of those self-cleaning gizmos floating around in it and a small Jacuzzi alcove built into the side. Around the pool were abundant mounds of flowerbeds and a seating area under a vine covered pergola. I only hoped Francesca wouldn't show up while we were here.

Emma turned off the engine and unbuckled, put her hand on the door, and raised her eyebrows. "Let's roll."

I nodded back and unbuckled and we simultaneously opened the truck doors, women on a mission. We rang the bell and nervously shifted back and forth on our feet. I could hear a commotion of frantic barking right before the door opened, and then the door only opened about a foot. Chopper and Snapper were cramming their heads into the gap, happy to recognize us, and quieting down from their wild barking into excited whining.

I don't know what I was expecting, but even turned sideways and pressed into the small space I could see Marta was a squat woman with bandy legs, her face a web of wrinkles, her hair gray, her eyes squinty. She was probably in her seventies. Marta wasn't wearing any kind of maid's uniform, but instead wore what I would call "comfort pants." She had on a bright tee-shirt, orthopedic style shoes, and a pair of reading glasses hung around her neck on a colorful beaded lanyard. Francesca's maid was all about comfort and utility. That must grate on Francesca's fashion nerves.

Emma put on a bright tone. "Hi, Marta. It's Emma."

Marta narrowed her eyes. Emma tried again. "From the barn. Lizzy and I are here to see Frank."

At least Marta's face softened a bit. She even smiled when she said, "Oh, yeah, Emma, nice to see you again. Francesca said you moved to Texas."

Emma patted her blonde bun and then smoothed the front of her blouse, actions that always struck me as an imitation of Margot. "I'm in New Jersey on a visit and I wanted to visit Frank. I know he's supposed to rest, so Lizzy and I won't stay long, but we would love to see him."

Marta stood her ground, and the door, although it opened a tiny bit more, was still not open very wide. We had yet to be invited in. Marta shook her head sadly. "Francesca told me no visitors for Frank. You know how she is."

From behind her came a low and husky voice. "Marta, who's there?" It was hardly recognizable as Frank.

The door opened a bit more as Marta yelled back over her shoulder. "What's it to you? You're supposed to be resting."

Emma quite boldly called over Marta. "Just Lizzy and me, Frank. We won't stay long."

Marta closed her eyes and said, "Francesca's gonna kill me."

Frank called out again, just much more weakly. "Well, then let them in. You trying to air condition the great outdoors?"

Marta bellowed over her shoulder, "Suit yourself. But you gotta answer to the Mrs." Marta swung the door open, while simultaneously using her foot to push Chopper and Snapper back.

Emma and I stepped into a beautiful wide central hallway with polished hardwood floors and Orientals. A striking large painting of three ballerinas hung over a hall table. An elegant staircase to our right curved up and to the left, forming a landing before rising again to the top floor.

Marta waved at us to follow her as she turned left under an arched opening. "Watch your step." She pointed down. The additions were on a slightly lower grade than the old central part of the house. We stepped down into a long narrow office/library space where Frank sat in the far front corner of the room, nested into a large chair with reading glasses perched on the end of his nose, a closed book in his lap with his finger still holding the place. Chopper and Snapper bounced up into his chair, each tucking into a flanking position, wedging themselves between the outside of Frank's thighs and the arms of the chair, his bodyguards.

Frank had a view of the front lawn and drive, and I wondered if he had seen us coming up the hill. I scanned the room. It had that old-money look, with book-covered walls and an enormous desk with carved legs and an embossed leather top. A thin TV set was mounted into the wall amongst the shelves of books directly across from Frank's chair. Frank's feet were propped up on an ottoman and crossed at the ankles. He was wearing those little footies with treads on the bottoms. His slippers sat on the floor. I had never seen Frank in sweat pants before, but there he sat, wearing sweat pants and a tee-shirt, with stubble on his face. He also looked smaller, somehow shrunken in that big chair.

Marta pointed at his feet, scowling. "What do you think you're doing?"

Frank looked puzzled. "What?"

Marta crossed her arms and shook her head. "The doctor said you're not allowed to cross your legs."

Frank said, "Aw, hell. I forgot." He uncrossed his ankles and placed his feet on the floor.

Marta sighed, "Elevate your feet, Frank."

Then he whined. "My knees get stiff." Marta glared at him like a teacher at a misbehaving student. Frank obediently raised his legs up onto the ottoman while Marta stuffed two small throw pillows under his knees.

Then Marta marched out of the room.

I stood silently, waiting for someone to say something. Emma, God bless her, went over to Frank without saying a word and grabbed his hand, leaning over to kiss his cheek. A bit of the old Frank came to life.

He smiled, but his voice was weak. "Hello, Em. I wish that kiss could turn this old toad back into a prince."

Emma smiled down on him and whispered. "I'm so glad we got past the sentry. Marta almost didn't let us in."

Frank leaned forward conspiratorially. "She's Francesca's pit bull. Very efficient, though." He looked up at me and smiled. "Come here, you." I went and embraced him, conscious of not wanting to hug him too hard.

We all smiled. Then Frank said in a weak voice, "Emma baby, I'm so glad we got you settled out there in Texas. Margot was right about that, even though you kicked like hell at the idea. You gotta confess, she was right."

Emma and I stood there, nodding and smiling.

I offered Frank a shopping bag containing the little rabbit sculpture. "Look what Natalie made for you."

Frank put the book on the side table, losing his place, then took the little sculpture in his hand, turning it around and peering through his readers to examine all the incredible details. He said, "Well, I'll be damned. That little girl is something. What talent. What does she want to do with these?"

I said, "I think down deep she would love to have these out for sale in galleries, gift shops."

Frank nodded in approval. "That would be terrific. But the art world is a hard place to make a living. It's all about knowing the right people.

It can be a tough place to get any notice. The question is whether she's getting to see the right people to promote her work."

I agreed. "Chess has someone he says he's talking to about her."

Frank replied, "Can't hide your light under a bushel. I'll say something to Francesca. We do know some people in that field."

Then he got quiet and set the little rabbit on his side table, seeming to deflate again. Emma sensed the mood change and said, her voice a loud stage whisper, "So, how are they treating you here in the big house?" Frank chuckled. It was wheezy, but still the Frank laugh that I treasured. His voice went to a matching loud stage whisper. "I'm being held hostage. No cigars, no alcohol, and no food that tastes like food, and my chest hurts like hell. This is not life, I can tell you that." His second laugh morphed into a wheeze and he grabbed a small pillow that was wedged in the corner of the chair behind a terrier and pressed it tightly to his chest. The weird wheezy cough ended in clearing his throat with his eyes closed. He was grimacing as if in pain, becoming an old man in mere seconds.

Emma and I glanced at each other, stunned, while the terriers licked his arms.

Marta marched in with a full size pillow. She barked at Frank. "Elevate your feet, Frank." Frank silently obeyed, and Marta fluffed up the pillow, removed the much smaller throw pillows, and wedged it under his knees. Then she pointed at him. "No crossed legs." Frank nodded obediently. She crossed her arms and glared at Chopper and Snapper, then uncrossed her arms and pointed at the floor and with a snap of her fingers they jumped down.

Marta turned to us. "I'll get you girls some lemonade." Before we could answer she marched back out.

Emma took Frank's hand again. "Frank, this will pass. You'll feel better again."

Our jovial moment with him had passed. He looked straight ahead with weirdly unfocused eyes and spoke in that same weak whisper, but we both heard what he said. "If I had died, the insurance pay-off would have been huge."

I gasped and Emma shot me a look. She tried again. "Frank, this isn't about money."

Frank spoke into the air, speaking about things that seem unrelated to our visit or his recent health crises. Emma and I stayed quiet and let him talk. He said, "Money is not always about what you can buy; sometimes it's about what it can keep you from. That has always lived with us, with Franny and me."

Frank patted Emma's hand as if to reassure her and then let it go. He closed his eyes and seemed to doze. Emma and I exchanged looks, but then his eyes opened again. Frank's eyes were watery but he wasn't crying so much as he just looked weary. He continued in his hoarse whisper. "At twenty we were married and having kids and we focused on building the business to hand down to our kids. We did it for the kids as much as for ourselves. Those boys running the company are good boys; they're just not *our* boys. That's what is killing her. I won't kick them out. Why would I? Besides it would rupture age old friendships."

Marta's footfall was so heavy that we heard her before seeing her. Frank clammed up and he picked up the bakery bag. Marta handed us our lemonades and then Frank said, "Put these on a plate so the girls can have some. I hope you'll let me at least have a taste."

Marta took the bag and opened it to peer in. She sighed deeply. "If I let you have a sliver you gotta behave with the salt tonight."

Frank crossed his heart, and Marta left.

Frank turned and looked up at me, his voice hoarse but urgent. "My opinion is that Cavelli Foods has to grow or it will simply fade away while the go-getters steal our market-share. I can't take it back to the way it was back in the day. Francesca doesn't understand; if we do that, the company will simply wither away. The new boys have some good ideas, but they need help in the execution. I've been working my tail off consulting with them. They need to understand the heart and soul of the company. You shouldn't lose sight of what made the company great while upgrading and expanding. I know it will take the younger set to recognize what direction to grow. I can provide history and context and support. The world has changed. Francesca and I need to step aside; we sold the company after all. But the boys are in default and things are a muddle now because I'm useless. I hate to go to plan B, but I don't know. I'm tired. The way I am now is useless to everyone." He seemed to sag further into his chair.

Marta was back, handing us each a small plate with a lemon square and a napkin. Frank literally got his sliver along with a half glass of watery looking milk. Marta pulled a wooden chair out from behind the desk and a small, upholstered chair up for us to sit. Emma and I thanked her. We silently ate our lemon squares and sipped our lemonade. It was a lot of lemon in one sitting and I didn't enjoy it, but we bit and sipped and chewed and made appreciative noises while Marta fussed around and we three waited for her to leave. She asked Frank if he needed anything, and he shook his head. Finally, she left the room.

I felt for a moment that I did not know this man. Frank, the jovial, Frank the fixer, Frank the larger than life anchor to all the crazy barn drama, was shrinking. He was a worried shadow of the man I knew, a man who had just uncharacteristically shared his business worries with us.

My brain started working, the ideas churning in my head and flying out of my mouth before I could fully vet them, but my intent and tone meant to reassure. "Frank, you just let Chess take care of things. He's got it well in hand. He's full of good ideas. He's confident about meeting this IRS auditor next week, and then he'll take the next step. He spoke well of the young men who are running Cavelli Foods, and I got the feeling that he gets along with them, although he wasn't happy about the contract you had with them for buying you out. But that's all history now. Now it's about making a new plan, right? Chess can be your spokesman while you are recovering. Look what he's done already on the IRS problem. I think you are going to be really proud of him. All you need to focus on is getting your strength back and recovering from your surgery."

Frank turned to look at me, seeming to see me for the first time. His eyes widened. He still looked weak and old and sick, but he managed a small smile and said, "You kidding me?"

I replied in my best New Jersey, "I would not kid you. Your heart attack gave him a jolt, but he's stepping up."

And once again he hoarsely whispered almost to himself, "Well, I'll be damned. That is good news." He closed his eyes, and then said, "I think I'll go lie down; I'm really tired."

I swallowed hard, thinking I had just over promised.

Marta walked back in and jerked her head toward the door. "I'd high-tail it if I were you two. I just got a text message. Francesca's on her way back home."

Emma and I got back in the truck and down the driveway and through the gates in record time, relieved to get away clean with no run-ins with Francesca. We had put a good mile under the tires before Emma turned to me, surprise in her voice, "Chess is going to go to work at Cavelli Foods?"

I slunk down in the truck seat and grimaced. "Sort of. Well, maybe."

Emma gave me a sharp glance. "You were winging it, weren't you?"

I looked out the window. "Well, maybe not totally. Francesca's been on a crazy rampage about sending him in, and calling lawyers and taking the company back, kind of like a foreclosure or repossessing a car. Chess doesn't want to, but I think he's considering stepping in as way to calm her down. Maybe do a deal with the new owners or something."

Emma was silent for a full minute, and then asked, "And what's this about the IRS? What's that about?"

I turned back around in my seat and unloaded on Emma. Emma was all ears, and I could see her wheels turning. She listened silently all the way through. Then she had a few pointed questions that pretty much covered everything and everyone; Ryder, Johnny Cash, Hotstuff, Deb and Wild Child, and a few questions about Natalie. Then I got grilled about Chess.

I sat up straighter as we whizzed pass the turn-off to the farm. I turned in my seat, "Hey. You missed the turn."

Emma sat like a queen behind the wheel, her posture perfect, her small pert nose turned upward. She said, "I would never miss the turn. I lived at that barn for eight years."

I said, "Okay Emma, I'll bite. Where are we going?"

She spread her fingers, displaying perfectly clean and manicured nails with French tips, before re-gripping the wheel, and then said, "We need to talk to Margot. Now."

Emma was focused on the curvy road and going just a tad bit too fast. I grabbed the little loop handle that hung down inside the door. Its real purpose was for getting in and out of the truck, but it felt steadying to hold onto as we whizzed around yet another curve.

Emma now felt the same urgency to see Margot that I had felt earlier to see Frank. She said, "Margot must be worried sick, but she keeps things to herself. She's worked so hard to keep Francesca happy all these years, and that hasn't been easy. Francesca can try the patience of a saint. Frank has had to jump in a few times to smooth the waters, and he's always come through. But now, I don't know. This is different. I didn't understand all that stuff he was saying back there, it was as if we weren't even there. He was rambling, like he had to tell us his last wishes or something." She was silent for a moment, and then said, "I think he's given up." I thought I saw the beginnings of a tear in her eye.

Emma put her blinker on. We were turning into a subdivision of town homes. I had no idea where we were. I said, "I've never been to Margot's."

Emma shrugged. "Don't feel bad. She never has anyone over. It was years before I stepped over the threshold. She's kind of a hermit, actually. Margot's idea of a good time is to go home to an empty house and read in bed with a glass of white wine. I'm not sure she even owns a TV. The one time I got her to go to dinner and a movie with me, she fell asleep during the movie." Emma turned and grinned, "It was an action flick!"

We curved around the maze of streets with Emma examining the street signs, then tapping the steering wheel, "There's our turn, Buttercup Lane."

The homes were bland and modern, not at all fitting for such an elegant and historic area. I quietly remarked, "These aren't at all what I would have pictured for Margot."

Emma defended her, "Her place at least backs up to undeveloped and heavily wooded acres. She's the last one on the end. It's private and she could afford it."

We got to the end of the row, and Emma hit the brakes and put the truck in reverse. She backed up fast and I didn't have to ask why. I had seen it, too. That damn gigantic motorcycle was sitting in Margot's driveway, right next to her little Beemer. Emma backed up into a driveway and turned her behemoth of a truck around. At the stop sign at the end of Buttercup Lane we stared at each other. Emma said, "Shit. Any suggestions?"

I felt a little nauseated, maybe from all those curves taken too fast, maybe from following that up by zooming backwards. I always hated roller coasters, and especially the kind that went backwards. Maybe it had just been too long and stressful a day. "Emma, I don't think we can count on Margot here. I think she's already given up, and is making a new plan with Dennis."

Emma looked furious. "No way. No way. Lizzy, that is not possible. Dennis is a worm. We can't let her get back with that worm."

I touched her wrist lightly. "Let's get out of here. They might come by and see us. Besides, I don't feel so good."

We both drew deep breaths simultaneously. Emma got the wheels rolling again, this time a lot slower, thank goodness. I leaned back in the seat and was able to let my arms just rest naturally in my lap while I looked out the window at a dusky sky. It was getting late, and I was hungry. Emma pulled through the farm gates and dropped me at the front of the barn. Before I got out I said, "Look, Emma, I think it's time we had a council of war."

Emma nodded. "We need Deb and Chess and you and me, and we need to get it all out on the table."

I added. "We need Natalie in, too."

Emma looked skeptical. "Why? I mean, she's so new, she can't really know the players."

I smiled. "You don't know her yet. She's a survivor and smart as hell, and for sure as last one hired in, she'll be the first one to lose her job. We need her smarts. Just trust me on this one."

Emma tipped her head and smiled. "Okay. Natalie is in."

I nodded again and said, "Let's meet at Chess' place tomorrow night for dinner."

Emma said, "Yeah, makes sense to meet off the farm so Ryder doesn't catch on."

I opened the truck door, hung one leg out, and said, "Good point. Mostly I was thinking about eating some authentic Italian. Chess is a great cook."

I stepped out and as I was about to close the door she said, "Yes. I know that."

Perhaps a bit of Frank's depression had rubbed off, not only because of Frank, and Margot and Dennis, and the uncertain future of the farm and my job security, but also my uneasy feeling over Emma's occasional comments about Chess. Paired with some things Francesca had hinted at in the past, well, there had clearly been some sort of 'thing' between Emma and Chess. Did it matter now? Of course not; it was stupid of me to dwell on it. But, here I was, dwelling on it.

Ryder sat at the table eating her dinner alone, computer open in front of her. She had a tray of sushi in front of her and was eating it with chopsticks, raw ginger and wasabi paste on the side. For some reason I found it repulsive. I looked around for Wheezer and was puzzled. I said, "Ryder, where's Wheezer?"

She looked up and said, "Shut her in your bedroom. She wouldn't shut up, plus she was using the sofa as a scratching post."

"Oh. I'm going to let her out. I'll watch her."

Ryder had just popped a sushi roll into her mouth, and so she raised her chopsticks in a salute of acknowledgement. I went and got my kitten, holding her meowing little self against my body, I walked into the kitchen and opened the freezer, rummaging through my stack of frozen dinners while mulling over Chess and Emma and imagining what may have been, then mentally getting my mind back to the present. I would need to call Chess right away to ask if we could have dinner at his place tomorrow night. It had been presumptuous of me to volunteer Chess and his apartment and his cooking. If he agreed, I needed to alert Deb and Nat, and do it all quietly so that Ryder didn't hear. I did all this while clinging to my kitten, who began to purr and reach up to pat my cheek. Wheezer and Winsome, they were my rocks. Everything else in my life felt insecure. Ryder shutting my kitten in the bedroom was the least of my worries, but it had added a feeling of resentment against Ryder. I let it smolder, repressing what I knew would be absurdly overblown if I said something.

I picked out a rigatoni dinner with sausage, wishing I was eating the real deal from Chess' kitchen. I popped it in the microwave and went to my bedroom to call Chess. Chess picked up almost instantly.

"Hey, Chess. I have a confession," I said quietly.

"Lizzy. I was just about to call you. What confession?"

I braced myself for his reaction. "Emma and I went to visit your dad."

There was a long pause. "I hope it didn't upset you. Dad's been really depressed, and he says things I don't think he really means. I've been telling him not to make any decisions while he's in this shape. That's why Mother and I thought you should wait. He's on medication for depression and on pain meds, that and being post-op; he's not himself right now."

I barely let him finish his sentence, my voice a whisper. "Chess, can you have me and Deb and Emma and Natalie to dinner tomorrow? We need to talk about all of this. Maybe we can help."

Chess sounded short-tempered. "Lizzy, don't you think this is more of a Cavelli family problem? Mother is a very private person. She's finally opening up to me, and I think I can begin to talk her off the ledge, if you know what I mean. She was ready to call lawyers and sue the buyers and take back Cavelli Foods and ruin some very old friendships in the process. And if Mother and Dad take back the company, how will that work? The company was pretty much Dad, and right now Dad can't be involved. But, he is devoted to Mother, and he'll defer to her judgment, especially when it comes to the horse business."

I sounded equally terse. "Chess, don't you want to hear what your dad said to me today, because it concerns you?"

There was another silence, which I filled. "This business stuff impacts all of us, it impacts me and Deb and Natalie and Margot, too, and the guys in the barn, and all the animals. We've already lost Hotstuff. Are we going to lose all of them?"

Chess said, "I kind of wish you and Emma hadn't gone over to the house today. This is exactly what I was afraid would happen. I can hear how upset you are."

I said, "Emma and I both love your dad."

Chess' voice softened. "I know you do. And I know Deb and Margot care, too. Look, I'm doing what I can. I can't make any promises though. No one can see the future, and what Dad said about turning around the company being like turning around a battleship is true."

I said, "Chess, please don't shut me out. Don't shut out all of us. Feed us tomorrow night and talk to us."

He waited a second and said, "Why not include Margot?"

I waited a beat before I answered in low tones, "Because, I'm not sure we want to hear what she has to say. Dennis being back has made things . . . complicated."

Chess gave me what I wanted, promising to feed us another one of Nonna Cavelli's specialties. I quickly dialed Deb to get them lined up. We would go in separate cars to be sure Ryder's antennae didn't pick up on being left out of something.

I went to reheat my now cold microwaveable dinner and sat back down with Wheezer sitting on my lap. It was terrible, and of course it didn't help that I had heated it twice. I chewed on the rubbery rigatoni noodles and the dry and leathery slices of sausage. And I heard in my head the distinctive voice of Frank Cavelli, not the sick and weak Frank, no, it was the loud and boisterous Frank and he spoke clear as day, "Goddam it, this food is awful. Cavelli Foods could do this much better."

And it came to me like a flash,

"Nonna Cavelli's Special Recipes."

An entire line of frozen dinners.

10. Dodging Bullets

It was the last day to school horses at home before shipping out to the CDI. It was also the morning that Chess had his meeting with the IRS agent to reconsider the farm's business designation. If the finding of the initial audit was reversed, it would save the farm a large sum of money in taxes, penalties, and interest, which the Cavellis presently had no way to pay. I also knew that the IRS had the power to seize property to settle such debts. I tried not to dwell on it.

I trusted Deb and Emma, and Margot, to pull off solid performances at the CDI. And I trusted Chess to move heaven and earth to make a convincing case to the IRS agent. If anyone fell short, it would not be for lack of preparation. If I had learned anything working with horses it was this; preparation is indeed everything, but I had also learned that sometimes shit just happens. Even in my head, I was sounding more and more like Natalie these days. At least I hadn't burst out in song.

Ryder and I tacked up Word Perfect together again. Two against one kept the odds in our favor. Ryder practically dragged the suspicious and reluctant mare from her stall to the cross-ties. Wordy looked sullen, dragging her feet, and stopping to scratch her nose on her knee; a few steps later she stopped to bite at an invisible fly on her side. I almost laughed at her. I swear the mare was procrastinating getting tacked up.

Ryder turned her into the grooming stall and clipped her into the cross-ties. I put a chain over her nose, and got a small bucket that I had filled with chopped pieces of carrots. Ryder ducked into the tack room and came out with a whip. We looked ready to tame a tiger. Word Perfect took note. She took a deep breath and then proceeded to blow her nose all over the two of us.

I looked at Ryder who was scowling. She looked at me and said, "Bitch did that on purpose!" Ryder's shirt was covered in raindrop size speckles of green horse slobber, which showed up pretty badly on her tan collared sleeveless shirt.

Even the sound of Ryder's voice made Wordy pin her ears and shake her head in Ryder's direction. The mare did not like Ryder calling her names. Silly, but that is exactly the thought that came to me.

I said, "Ryder, she wants to be treated like a princess, so I'm not going to call her names. I know she's got problems, but you and I saw how she mooned over Dennis."

Ryder shook her head. "Lizzy, I thought you were finally over the fantasy thing."

I counted to ten before answering in a tone that didn't sound defensive. "Ryder, I'm just watching the horse is all. She's already showed us some interesting things, okay? This girl is very smart. Willful and cranky, yeah maybe worse than just cranky, but she's not stupid. She knows when you call her names. Not the names themselves, but she senses the tone."

Ryder was thoughtful for a moment, and then said, "You're right about one thing. She's smart for sure, but remember she doesn't care if you live or die, and if she has to hurt you to make her point, she's going to do it. So, don't get all woo-woo about her."

I picked up the chain to show Ryder. "I am not woo-woo, I've got the chain over her nose, but I want to offer her something positive, too." I picked up the bucket of chopped carrots off the floor where I had set it aside. Word Perfect took note.

Ryder shrugged. "Suit yourself." But I noticed she drew Wordy's attention back to her with a swish of the whip. And there it was; we had presented Wordy with the classic choice, she could take the carrots or feel the whip. It would be her choice.

Wordy did not repeat any of yesterday's tricks. Instead she pulled new ones. As soon as Ryder tried to snug up the girth, Wordy threw herself into Ryder, almost squishing her into the wall. Ryder gave her quite a slice with the whip for it, too. Wordy flew to the other side of the stall, and stood erect with the girth half done up, one buckle hanging free with the other one halfway buckled into a lower hole. The skin on her side was crawling and twitching. She was not pinning her ears now. Instead she was tipping her head to look again at Ryder who was still calling her a bitch.

But I got to play the good cop. I did sound like a complete amateur as I cooed to the mare. "Calm down, Wordy, let's just calm down; you need to get your girth on and you need to be polite about it. You're not allowed to squish Ryder against the wall like a pesky bug."

We both stared at the mare and I shook my head. "You can't touch that girth until she relaxes. Look at her sides. The skin is still twitching. It pinched when you pulled it up. She needs to deflate. I'll walk her around before you try again."

Ryder looked pissed. She said, "Whatever. She didn't do that yesterday, but okay. I'll go get her bridle."

And while Ryder ducked into the tack room, I held the bucket in front of the mare. At first she blew into the bucket, rejecting my offer. I dropped the chain and reached up to touch her forelock. She jerked her head back at my touch, but then allowed my hand to settle there. I said in a chatty tone, "My Winsome loves her forelock gently pulled; she also loves her ears massaged. I think someday you might like it, too." Word Perfect dropped her head into the bucket and started on a carrot piece. I let my hand slide down her face, pushing her forelock to the side then lightly tracing the whorl in the center of her forehead. She was taking normal breaths again; the skin had relaxed around the girth. Wordy picked her head out of the bucket and pinned her ears hard, shaking her nose. I looked over my shoulder to see Ryder standing there with her bridle.

After she was bridled I walked her around the indoor arena and slowly took the girth up one hole at a time. By the time Margot came to get on her, Wordy was so relaxed she looked sleepy.

I was leading a mellow Word Perfect away from the gate when she suddenly stopped and turned her head around to peer behind her. She made a low "woof-woof-woof" whinny that surprised me; but then didn't. Standing in the doorway was Dennis. Margot wouldn't get her privacy today when she rode Wordy.

I greeted him cheerfully. "Hi, Dennis. Your horse spotted you before I did."

Dennis patted his pockets and removed a sugar cube. His eyes were shining, looking at his mare. He strode over to her, and literally threw his arms around her neck and gave her a hug. He said, "Hello, gorgeous!"

The mare never pinned her ears or wrinkled her nose, or resisted. Instead she wiggled her top lip on the back of his shirt. Word Perfect was clearly her Daddy's darling, spoiled rotten, short-tempered, and willful. I also got the feeling she fell short on work ethic, and was basically lazy. She was a girl of extreme feeling and behavior. She loved what she loved, and she hated what she hated. Anything in between was not worth her time or attention. In some ways Word Perfect reminded me of Ryder.

I wasn't just flattering Dennis when I told him, "Dennis, she really has a thing for you."

Dennis laughed. "You know how parents overcompensate by lavishing attention on the child who has problems? Yeah, that's me. Sophie was so mean to her; the two of them fought like hell, and I always felt like I had to compensate by feeding her treats and taking her out for hand grazing. Then the mare bonded to me, and that upset Soph even more. I often think things would have been different if we'd gotten Wild Child." Sophie really wanted that horse. Wordy wasn't her first choice, plus, well, I think the dynamics would have been different with a stallion.

I had the urge to set this idiot straight about Wild Child, but Margot walked in. Dennis looked at Margot just like he was previously looking at Wordy. I could tell right then that spelled trouble. Wordy gave him the most gentle of nips, and then pulled back a step with the whites showing in her eyes. I couldn't help myself. I laughed. I said, "Um Dennis, I think that the mare is jealous."

Margot tipped her head and look amused. She said, "Lizzy is doing what we are all told not to do."

Dennis said, "What is that?"

She grinned, "Anthropomorphizing. But frankly, I don't blame her. Word Perfect does seem to be attached to you, and right now she's pretty unhappy with the rest of us. She's probably glad to see a familiar face, especially one that feeds her treats and never asks anything of her in the way of work. But, Dennis darling, I do need her to begin to focus and bond with me, and I don't want her to be distracted by her daddy sitting in the classroom."

Dennis grinned. "Would that be, what did you just call it, anthropomorphizing?"

Margot nodded. "The children only stop crying at pre-school after Mommy and Daddy are out of sight."

He said, "Duly noted. I'll leave you three ladies then, but damn it, I want to watch my horse go. I think I'll get Lizzy here to video some of it with her phone, and she can send it to me. It's killing me."

I suggested, "It might be easier to just use your phone recorder, if you want to leave it with me."

"No!" The sharpness of his response surprised me, but he quickly smoothed it over. "I need to make a few calls. So just send the videos to me." He gave me both his cell number and his email.

Dennis exited, and Margot waited until he was well away before speaking. "Lizzy darling, please don't video until the very end; five minutes at the most. He doesn't need to see the fight that's coming. That mare finally gave in yesterday, but she's had all night to sulk about it and decide not to let that happen again."

I said, "Margot, look how relaxed she is today! I think you may be surprised."

"I hope you're right, but in my experience the second ride is always the worst."

I was wrong, and Margot was right. Wordy stood quietly while Margot mounted, but as soon as Margot put her leg on, the ears went flat and Wordy made a lazy kick at her leg. Margot clucked and tapped her with the whip, and Wordy started backing up. When Margot gave her a harder tap with the whip, she slapped her tail down hard between her hind legs and backed up faster and faster and faster until her butt was up against the kickboards. I knew she was threatening to rear, trying to intimidate Margot. The whip came singing through the air, meeting flesh like a bolt of lightning. The mare took the whip stoically, gathering herself for an impressive rear that would make good on her threat. I was still in the arena, and instinctively I ran at Wordy's hindquarters clapping my hands and growling, "Get going, mare!"

Wordy launched herself off of bent haunches, gracefully leaping like a gazelle. I gasped as I saw daylight under Margot's seat, but I also noticed with relief she had grabbed the front of the saddle again. The mare was now trotting, her back was tight, and her gait was more passage than working trot, and she was blowing like a dragon, surprised and indignant, but she was going. Her ears were still back and her mouth tight. Wordy was thinking through her options; I could see it in her face. Margot stopped the mare. Both the mare and Margot were breathing hard. The mare began to paw. Margot asked me to hand her the long whip.

I walked over to the wall and grabbed the long whip. As I walked back I noticed that the mare noticed me, and the whip I carried. Word Perfect's legs quickly began to buckle, folding carefully under her body. She was going to lie down with Margot! Margot realized what was happening and nailed her with the spurs at the same time that I sprinted at them with the long whip. Thankfully the mare righted herself with a leap and a kick, and then she and Margot were off again in a bolt. Margot was not going to let the mare stop going forward now; instead she let the whip sing again and drove her on.

Each time Word Perfect passed me holding the long whip she tucked her tail a bit and increased her speed. This girl was clearly well acquainted with the whip. Once the mare slowed down, Margot added turns and then tested the obedience to the driving aids down the long sides and across the diagonals. It didn't take long before Word Perfect's black coat had lather under the reins. Margot was not giving her any breaks. I knew what Margot was waiting for, that feeling of release and acceptance. She wasn't there yet.

After a few minutes Margot called out as she passed by, "You can film now."

I picked up my phone and hit record. Wordy was now in a steady tempo in trot, and Margot smoothly went through all the trot movements, including a few steps of piaffe. There was still too much tension, and a judge would say the neck was too short, the poll not always the highest point. However, the half passes floated and had scope and reach, the extensions were dramatic, and the mare lowered her croup and had power in the passage. She was a genuine Grand Prix horse, despite being a total temperamental bitch and nut job. Whoever had trained Word Perfect to that level deserved a medal.

Margot pulled her up in front of me, and slid to the ground. Again, her hands were shaking. But she loosened the girth and gave the mare a sugar cube, which Wordy took without hesitation. I heard the crunch as Wordy worked it back to her molars, even over the rapid panting of the mare. And when Wordy finished her cube, she proceeded to lick Margot with dreamy half-closed eyes, just as she had the day before. It reminded me of the handshake at the net following a tennis match where two opponents had just gone at it with everything they had.

Margot stood and let the mare lick her in that weird Zen-like way she had done the day before. Margot whispered to me, "Tomorrow will be better." Margot continued to whisper while watching the mare. "Darling, you were splendid in your reactions, thank you. But, please, let's keep this between us, okay? I hate aggressive riding, but when you are up against the wall like that, literally and figuratively, you have to react instantly as life really can hang in the balance. You quite possibly saved me from getting badly hurt."

I didn't really believe that, but I drew an imaginary zipper across my lips, which got a chuckle from Margot. Then Margot said, "You walk her around, then send the video to Dennis. We can watch the film together while you sneak her into the wash stall and give her a warm shower. I don't even want him to see her all sweaty and exhausted. She'll be happy and relaxed after she's had her shower. And I have a feeling, given the right time and enough privacy, this one will come around and be my pet. That is, if Dennis doesn't ruin everything that is."

Before I walked Wordy I forwarded the videos to Dennis. Ryder was putting the finishing touches on Wild Child, snugging up his girth and giving him a spritz of fly spray. I had finished giving Word Perfect her shower, but had left her in the wash stall with the fan blowing on her. She was one tired girl. Her head hung low, she rested one hind leg, her hip dropped so low she was practically resting on the front of her pastern rather than the toe of her hoof. When Wild Child tried to gently court her attention with low rumbling noises, she did not even bother to pin her ears at him. He just wasn't worth the energy.

Ryder had a smug smile on her face. She asked, "Did the mare get a butt-kicking?"

I hedged, "Margot did her usual great job."

Ryder smiled, "Whatever. Dennis was bummed that Margot kicked him out of the arena. He and I hung out and talked."

I cringed, but refrained from my knee-jerk desire to defend Margot. Instead I asked, "Did you and Dennis have a nice time chatting?"

Ryder leaned against the side of the grooming stall, both hands behind her back, studying me. I could tell she wanted to tell me something, but was holding back. It seemed like a good time to probe. Carefully, that is.

I tried to sound playful, "Did you get him to buy you Johnny Cash yet?"

I noticed she tensed up. It was slight, and she was playing it cool, but yeah, she had reacted physically in a way that was spontaneous. I had hit a nerve.

I let her off the hook by taking it a different direction. "Dennis still thinks that Wild Child is an easy ride. Isn't that funny?"

She seemed relieved that I had changed the subject, and said, "Wild Child's not so difficult. He's more lazy than crazy, if you ask me."

Again, I had to stop myself from correcting her. I went back in to probe close to the nerve I had hit. "So, is Dennis still going to buy the farm and kick out the working students?"

She looked serious, and for once she answered me without her usual sarcastic edge. "Yesterday, while you were over at the Winstons' and I was the only one here, a real estate appraiser was out here walking the property with Dennis. Dennis asked me to get him a list of all the horses owned by the Cavellis. I put Johnny Cash on the list. I know I'm not supposed to be sharing that, but it's only fair to let you know what I saw. You deserve a heads up to start looking around for another job."

My stomach tightened down, my cheeks felt slack and hot, and all I could say was, "Oh. Well, thanks, I guess." My first thought was that someone had told Dennis what time the place was dead quiet, so he could snoop around unobserved. My second thought was why would Ryder want to do *me* any favors?

Ryder picked up on my skepticism saying, "Don't let on I said anything. I'm just trying to do the decent thing. You squeal, and I'll say you're lying."

I thought about the Florida property and the fact that Deb and Emma had both planned to be there for the big CDIs during the winter season and if they were invited, the USEF High Performance training sessions. So I asked, "What about the Florida farm?"

Ryder shrugged, indifferent. "If the Cavellis are getting 'out' of the horse business, then why would they keep that place?"

Why indeed. I would have probed more, but Deb came in and Ryder immediately clammed up. Soon, Dennis and Margot joined us, and then came Emma and Natalie and little Uno. The conversation turned to the planning for the upcoming weekend. It would have been happy talk under usual circumstances; getting ready for a big show meant beauty-parlor time for the horses and planning for packing and stabling and setting up the tack room. It was hard to engage in happy talk as I looked at Deb and Wild Child, on the cusp of what could be a long and happy career together.

Or not.

It seemed we would still have our usual picnic at our stalls after the FEI jog on Thursday night. This was usually provided by Frank and Francesca, predictably Dennis volunteered to play the role and be in charge of food and drink. He seemed happy to be a part of the group with a role to play, probably practicing for his imagined future. I wanted to share all my new information with Deb and Emma, but it would have to wait until tonight. Meanwhile our training day was now in full swing.

Ryder was back to a full lesson on Papa, and she went through the motions, although I knew that mentally she had moved on to Johnny Cash. I had my lesson on Winsome, and managed to go through my test in a lackluster but accurate way. I couldn't seem to find my groove. Ryder had gotten Lovey ready for Francesca, but she sent a text for Ryder to go on and ride him; she wasn't going to make it out. That couldn't be good.

Francesca also said that Ryder and I would need to meet the driver sometime tonight who would be picking up Hotstuff. I wondered if I would even make the dinner tonight. For some reason though, shippers always tended to arrive late at night. I think it was to avoid traffic and heat.

The driver would call either Ryder or me about thirty minutes prior to pick up. All Hotstuff's papers were on Francesca's desk in a manila envelope, and the only thing shipping with Hotstuff was his leather halter, his shipping boots, and a leather and chain lead shank.

Ryder passed the information on to me in a business-like voice. Even though I thought I was ready for the news, it still made me weak in the knees. I had known this was going to happen today, but I had somehow forgotten. How was that possible?

Hotstuff was about to simply disappear from our lives, and no one had spoken about it since Margot had taken him off the training list. He had been lounging in the paddock for half the day, swatting at flies with his huge tail and trimming the tall grass that grew along the fence line that was in need of weed-whacking. I saw him kneeling down to reach under the low board to use his rubbery lips to pull the grass toward his teeth. My nose burned and my eyes teared up just pulling the image up in my mind. He was our happy boy, and I would miss him terribly. I prayed he would always be a happy boy, and lead a happy life. I kept telling myself that Becca and her family seemed like fine people who would take good care of him.

I only half expected to see Francesca at the Winstons' farm to ride Johnny. But she came. She was quiet and workmanlike. Today she tackled the test movements. Like my ride on Winsome, her efforts were lackluster, going through the motions. Johnny still got his lipstick kiss, and Francesca promised to see me the next day. Neither one of us mentioned Hotstuff, but I sensed that Francesca was in mourning just like me. It was a dark cloud that cast everything in shadow. Hotstuff was the best horse she had ever produced.

When I thought of what Ryder had said about Dennis marching around the farm with an appraiser, well, Francesca was perhaps about to lose more than her best young horse. My potential losses were small compared to hers; she quite possibly was losing everything, throwing everything overboard in an effort to keep herself and Frank afloat.

The thought made me want to go home and dive back into *Gone with the Wind* where at least I knew Scarlett was going to survive, even if it was alone in her mansion with Mammy. We all knew Rhett would be drawn back eventually, like a fly back into the spider's web. Scarlett always had another trick up her sleeve, even if she had to wait until tomorrow to figure out what it was. Scarlett would never give up. There were a lot of things to hate about Scarlett O'Hara, but one thing the reader could count on: Scarlett would survive to see that tomorrow. It was, after all, another day.

I had no time to catch up on Scarlett and her troubles. I had a dinner date at Chess' place and a lot to share with not only Chess, but Emma and Deb and Natalie, too. And Ryder couldn't know any of it.

Ryder was making herself something for dinner with an ear bud sticking in her left ear, her smart phone hanging in a holster on her jeans. She took note that I had my purse slung over my shoulder.

She pulled the earpiece out of her ear. "You going out?'

I nodded. "Over to eat at Chess's. Just text me if you hear from the shipper and I'll come back to help."

Ryder grinned. Wondering why, I asked, "What's so funny?"

Ryder was not unkind sounding when she answered. "How things turned out with you and Chess. I saw it a mile away while you were busy talking him down. Thing is, you guys are perfect for each other."

I felt guilty. Had I really talked that badly about Chess? Ryder was the one who thought he was such a prize, wasn't she? What I remembered is that she had seen him as a gravy-train. I unkindly thought that now that Frank and Francesca were having financial problems, Ryder was happy to concede Chess to me. I then felt guilty about how much I had read into what sounded like a nice comment. I managed to say, "Thank you" before I did my usual routine of kissing Wheezer, baby-talking to her that "Mommy" would be back later, and then doing the "kitten-toss" to prevent squishing her in the closing door as I made my get-away.

***

I was the last one to arrive at Chess's, and let myself in without knocking. Everyone sat in the living room; appetizers were spread across the glass coffee table, along with glasses of wine. I admired Natalie's sculpture before pulling up a chair to join the circle. Chess handed me a glass of sparkling water with a twist of lime, along with a peck on my cheek.

He said, "I've been discussing this IRS situation with everyone, along with my business plan. Selling Hotstuff has really helped. Since we have his full brother in the barn we might be able to repeat this in a year or two. Then of course, if Deb continues to do well with Wild Child, we need to start breeding him. All in all, I think I've come up with a realistic plan, along with some hard cash. I'm feeling good about it."

I broke in, "Hotstuff leaves tonight. I may have to run if I get a text."

There was a moment of silence, then a collective sigh. Chess was the only one excited about the sale. He looked pained looking around at our faces. He frowned, "I'm sorry guys. I know you hate losing the horse."

Natalie slapped his knee. "Chess my man, you are doing your job. It sucks that Hotstuff was sacrificed to save the ship, but we get it, really we do. It's not like he's going somewhere bad. Looked to me like a great home. We need to be happy that the horse is going to be valued and cared for and ridden well. We need to get over it." Natalie looked directly at me when she said the last sentence.

I looked back at Nat, and thought about the tough times she had gone through and how she had found a home among us. If this thing happened, if Dennis' plan actually happened, what would happen to Natalie? My thoughts tumbled out of my mouth with urgency and enthusiasm, so fast I could barely make sense of them. "Nat, Francesca said something, and Frank said something, and well, I thought of something, and it's all about you and your sculptures, and the bottom line is, can you make your sculpture move?"

Natalie literally scratched her head, and I looked around the room at blank faces. Chess said, "Shall I put on the pasta? It's angel hair, so we'll eat in minutes if you're ready."

Deb stood up. "You want help in the kitchen?"

And Chess said, "Always." while giving me an odd look. They all thought I was just changing the subject away from Hotstuff. They thought I was talking nonsense. But actually, I had some unformed thoughts about Nat's artwork that I needed to think through out loud. I just wasn't sure what they were. Emma excused herself to refill her wine glass, but Natalie leaned forward in her chair. At least she was taking me seriously.

She put her elbows on her knees. "What are you trying to say, Lizzy?"

I leaned toward her. "Francesca and I were talking about how the starlings fly in a cloud formation that changes shapes and how beautiful it was, like a dance. She said that most art was too static, and that she preferred her art to move. Well, all of us that are obsessed with dressage are like that, aren't we? We prefer our art to move. Francesca asked me to go to the ballet one day with her."

"Uh, probably to drive her there."

"No, to watch the performance. She's a ballet freak if you didn't know it. Anyway, I kept thinking of you and your sculptures. And then when I gave Frank your gift, he mentioned that they 'know' people in the art world. So, I thought what if Natalie could make her art move? I think Francesca might put some of her energy into being your... what do you call it?"

Natalie nodded, "Patron. Patron of the arts."

I beamed, "Yes! Exactly. Am I crazy?"

"No, you are not crazy." Natalie nodded, thinking through the idea. "I've seen some amazing kinetic sculpture. It takes a lot of engineering. But, I bet the guy at my shop class could help me out. I'm willing to try. Thanks for the idea, Lizzy. It's a real good idea."

I repeated, "Kinetic sculpture?"

Natalie nodded, "Look it up on the internet. Amazing stuff."

I wondered if Natalie was just being indulgent, and felt that our discussion was unfinished, but Emma came in carrying a salad bowl, and then Deb came in with a bread basket. Chess called for everyone to refill drinks and find a seat, and Deb and Emma went back into the kitchen, but not before Deb instructed Natalie and me to sit down.

They came back out with individual pasta bowls filled with aromatic steam rising off them, set them down in front of Natalie and me, and then went back for their own bowls. I inhaled deeply and my mouth watered. Chess called out from the kitchen, "Hey Lizzy, can you start the salad around?"

When we all were seated, I looked up at Chess and asked, "Nonna Cavelli's?"

He smiled, and said, "Start eating while it's hot. This is her Chicken Marsala with sautéed mushrooms."

We dove in. Of course it was divine. But, my brain was still on speed. I chattered too fast again, half the time with food still in my mouth, but I couldn't find the brakes. "Chess, could you do something like this as a frozen food?"

Chess looked pained. "Frozen food? Are you kidding me? This," he gestured at all of the plates of food. "This is art. This is spirit. Frozen food is, is -"

"Frozen?" Natalie interjected. We all laughed.

I persisted. "I'm serious. What about starting a line of frozen entrees based on Nonna Cavelli's recipes? I eat frozen dinners every night, and I'm telling you, on behalf of bone tired and hungry people across the country, we need Cavelli Foods to share Nonna's cooking. You could do it without releasing the recipes. It would honor your Nonna and maybe help the company expand into a new market. Your dad said that companies need to expand and grow, or they get stale and lose market share. Gourmet frozen foods. Maybe make it healthy and nutritious."

Everyone stared at me. Then Chess said, "Dad said that? Dad actually said that to you?"

Emma interrupted. "He did, Chess. I was there." She lifted her wine glass and took a sip, studying Chess. Then she added. "I'll tell you what else, Chess, your dad is very down right now, you know that. He's not the same guy. He seems to have given up, and in part I think he's depressed because what he and your mother spent their lives building is not staying in the Cavelli family. At least, that's what he said to us. He needs you to be the voice of Cavelli. I suppose it depends on whether the guys running the company now would welcome you, but if they would, would you consider taking a bigger role at Cavelli Foods? They had been open to your dad getting back involved though, so I don't see why they wouldn't welcome another Cavelli to Cavelli Foods. You're diplomatic too, like your dad."

Chess said, "Actually, I'm way more diplomatic than my dad." He leaned back in his chair, his lips pressed into a line that made me see his mother's face in his. He began to twirl the stem of his wineglass. There was a connection between them that bypassed all of us and made me feel small and young. I would never have dared say what Emma had said because Chess and I were still too new with each other, unwilling to stretch our good feelings for each other. Emma had no such stake in his good opinions. But she spoke freely as someone who did indeed "know" Chess Cavelli.

Emma wasn't done. She said, "Look, I know, this is old territory and I remember the fights. But a lot of time has passed, Chess. Lots of water under the bridge. If something doesn't change, I don't know what will happen to your dad."

Chess looked up and locked eyes with Emma. "This feels like a trap, Em."

I had seldom heard anyone call her the informal "Em", and expected her to bristle, but she did not. Instead she flipped back her blond hair with a manicured nail and said, "I'm resettled in Texas, Chess. For the time being, my future is secure. This is not about me, and it's not even about you. I'm here tonight because I love all these people and this is war, and this is a war council."

Now Deb jumped in. "Whoa. Will someone fill me in? The depression is a typical side effect of open-heart surgery, and it's usually temporary. The prescriptions contribute to it as well. As far as Cavelli Foods, Frank told me things would turn around in time. Chess, you were here to help with the books and the IRS thing. I thought it was all going to work out."

Emma frowned at Deb. "The moment I saw Dennis hanging around I knew the Cavellis were in big trouble. Dennis must have heard through the grapevine about the money troubles. Frank usually wouldn't be so vulnerable, except that he saw Dennis as a potential source of cash, and Francesca would never have let Dennis back in the barn unless she thought she might need him and his money. There is no love there anymore; Dennis broke that bond when he ran off with Sophie. Dennis is a con artist. Sophie's probably waiting somewhere in the wings to show up like a bad penny and steal the whole kit and caboodle once Dennis has the warranty deed."

I thought her conclusions were off. "Sophie? Emma, I don't think so. You heard how he trashed Sophie at dinner."

Chess now held up his hands in surrender. "I have no idea what you guys are talking about. I knew you had seen Dad and was upset at his condition, and I guessed you all knew about the IRS meeting on Friday, but Hotstuff's sale has helped on that front. We now have a cash inflow and a transaction to show the IRS that the farm is a bona fide business. All this other stuff has my head spinning."

I joined in, still speaking too fast. "Let me share what Ryder told me, but of course she swore me to secrecy. She said that yesterday Dennis was out in the afternoon walking the farm with a real estate appraiser. He also asked her for a list of all the horses owned by the Cavellis."

I saw everyone visibly sag in their seats, except for Chess, who sat rigid, his face stony. Mouths opened and shut and there was dead air that lasted so long that I heard someone's cell phone make a notification ping. Finally Chess spoke. "A real estate appraiser? Who the hell gave him permission to do that? Mother never said anything to me."

I said, "I don't think your parents were aware of it. Dennis timed it for when no one would be there but Ryder, and Ryder is playing her own game in all of this. Ryder thinks she can get something out of it."

Chess pondered that. "Lizzy, this is a lot of important information that I'm not processing. I'm sorry if I'm lost here, but can you please slow waaay down and give me the version for dummies?"

Deb added. "Chess, I'm with you. This sounds like those conspiracy theories you read on the internet."

Nat piped up, "Deb, I think Lizzy and Emma are on to something. They may have some of the details wrong, but I agree that Dennis is making plans of some sort. It makes sense that he would use Ryder, too. That girl is only about herself. Dennis picked up on that real quick. He's probably promised her something for sleuthing for him."

I took a sip of wine and said, "Natalie's right. It's Johnny Cash. Ryder rode him while we were in Chicago to try him out without anyone knowing. She thinks she can do the under 25 Grand Prix with him. I think in her mind that horse is already hers."

Chess looked frustrated again although his voice was low. "Would you all please hit the reset button and take it from the top?"

I took a deep breath, organized my thoughts, and drew an imaginary chart on the tabletop. I reminded Chess that Dennis had been Margot's boyfriend before he broke her heart by running off with Sophie, the working student. Emma had then worked with Frank to buy Wild Child, the fabulous Grand Prix stallion that Dennis had promised Sophie. When the purchase of Wild Child was thwarted, Dennis had then purchased Word Perfect. Sophie had not been able to ride the mare, and she and Dennis had broken up. Sophie had, in fact, been caught stepping out on Dennis, or so he said. Dennis was getting even with Sophie by insisting that Margot ride the mare. Even more stunning was his renewed courtship of Margot, and what was puzzling was that Margot seemed to be welcoming his attention.

Chess nodded, taking in the information and occasionally asking a question.

Emma took up the narrative. She said, "I guess Margot is trying to protect all of you guys as best as she can. And I think Margot knows Dennis is not to be trusted. But, Chess, let me add, and I don't intend to be mean, but your mother has been a hard woman to work for. Margot always said we could find ourselves on the street any day. Keeping Francesca happy has been no small feat. Keeping Dennis happy, well, Margot's used to walking that tightrope. She's been walking it since the day Walter died."

Deb added, "If it wasn't for Margot, and Frank, well, I almost did end up a homeless person."

Emma added, "Margot was the center of my world when I had no one else."

I said, "This business part of this, the insecurity of it all, well, it's too hard. I never understood before."

Emma said, "That's why we have to fight, fight, fight. Lizzy, who says it's a done deal? If Chess can be successful in the audit meeting, if he can get the money tap turned back on at Cavelli Foods, if Frank can get back to being Frank, then there is no sale. If there is no sale, then maybe we can get rid of that nasty man, and life can be good again."

I added, "What about Margot? What about Word Perfect? She's putting everything she's got into the mare."

Emma narrowed her eyes. "But is the mare worth it?"

I nodded. "Margot has put herself at risk to get through to the mare. There is almost something desperate about it. But, when the mare finally gives in, it's impressive. When she is done trying to kill Margot, that is. It's pretty rough out there."

Natalie looked over to Emma. "You think this Sophie chick is still in play?"

Emma thought for a moment before answering. "If Dennis is going to get the Cavelli farm and the horses, primarily Wild Child, I'm guessing she'll turn back up. Oh, Sophie won't want the mare back after she's made such a fuss about how bad a horse it was. But I'll tell you what, she sure as hell won't want to see Margot out there successful on a horse that she has told the world was un-rideable."

I piped up, "Yeah, I heard her say the mare must have been drugged when they tried it."

Nat smiled, "Hey. I have an idea."

I laughed. "The super-spy has an idea. We should be scared."

Natalie wagged her finger. "I don't want to make any promises, okay? I'll do a little research and get back to you guys if I find out anything."

Chess sighed and stood up. "What kind of a world do you guys live in? Give me a keyboard, or a line of numbers to add up, or a well-stocked kitchen." He picked up his plate and mine and began to clear the table. I stood up too, and when Deb began to pull her chair back I shook my head at her. Everyone got it. I went into the kitchen where Chess had started running hot water. He was rinsing off and stacking the bowls, the dirty baking dish filling with hot water in the bottom of the sink. I set the other bowls down on the counter.

I said, "I know, it sounds crazy."

He shook his head again and rinsed another bowl, speaking softly. "Damn straight it does. I forgot how much Emma gets into this kind of drama. Of course, Mother always fed into it. There's a vindictive streak in both of them that I find unattractive."

I continued. "Chess, I'm not vindictive. I just love my home. I love my job. Is it crazy to fight for what you love?"

And then he turned and suddenly, almost violently encircled me in his arms and kissed me with real passion. And I let some of my crazy energy meet his and I was afraid we were going to end up on the kitchen floor because my knees went to jelly and we traveled from the sink to the opposite counter in his galley-style kitchen. Instead, we pulled apart, breathing heavily and letting the hot water tap run at full power, steam rising over the baking pan that was overflowing in the sink.

I turned to find Emma standing in the doorway with her bowl in one hand and a stack of salad bowls in another. Her face was carefully blank. She said, "Did you make your Nonna's panna cotta?"

I studied the tile flooring while Chess answered, "I bought gelato. I thought maybe Lizzy was tired of the panna cotta."

11. Marching Onward Through The Fog

*No one seemed to want to leave. We ate our dessert and drank our cof-*fees. Then we watched Chess clean the kitchen, all of us leaning on counters and doorframes while he kindly refused our help in the tight space. Deb and Chess listened as Emma characterized Dennis and Sophie as schemers and backstabbers. Natalie listened intently but said little.

I kept my cell phone close at hand, expecting a text from Ryder as the night progressed, but heard nothing.

Finally, Deb declared we all needed to leave, that the next day would be a long one as we packed and set up at the show grounds. I hadn't realized the lateness of the hour. We were all fired up; anxiety and a bit of crystal ball gazing had lent the gathering an intensity that literally had made time fly. I gave Chess a kiss goodnight, a very chaste kiss this time, and got a reassuring squeeze of his hand before I left.

Driving home alone I was overcome by fatigue. The electric buzz that had energized me all night had dissipated, leaving me with a disconnected and foreign feeling. The night was densely cloudy and moonless.

Once I had turned off the four lane onto the back roads, the only thing I could see was what was illuminated in the arc of the headlights.

It gave the odd sensation of driving in a tunnel. I even turned off the radio because its noise made it harder to concentrate on the road ahead. I knew where I was, but I did not recognize where I was. It was a relief to see the lights flickering on top of the farm gates. I hit my remote and could barely make out the black iron gates, but could clearly hear the whirr of the motor. The security light made a pool of yellow light in front of the barn, which thankfully provided my bearings like one of those maps at the mall: "you are here."

I was about to take my foot off of the brake pedal when I was transfixed. There beyond the yellow circle of light at the front of the barn I could barely make out the bulky outlines of a horse van. The only reason I could see it at all was the faint glow of the interior dome lights. That feeling of 'deja vu' pressed upon me. I had seen that van before. It had the classic lines of the old "Imperator" make of horse van that had populated the shows of my youth. I could see that the ramp was down. Into the milky pool of the security light at the front of the barn appeared Ryder, leading a horse, Hotstuff this time instead of Lovey. This was my bad dream come to life. My heart began to pound in my chest.

I zipped around to the back to park my truck where Francesca made me put it so no one had to look at its faded red paint, back next to the horse trailers and the farm tractor. I needed to hurry if I wanted to say my goodbyes. I cut the engine, turned off my headlights, and jumped out into total darkness, suddenly blinded. Ryder had not turned on the aisle lights.

For one short panicky moment, the line between waking and dreaming had blurred. My judgment of distance and space was lost to me, but I wanted and needed to see Hotstuff one last time, and stupidly walked with purpose right into the side of the barn, fortunate to find it with my fingers instead of my nose. Right then I remembered my cell phone. I fished in my bag, cursing my stupidity. Once I had my phone, the screen illuminated and then I hit my flashlight app to light my way. I was walking up the barn aisle when I heard my name.

"Lizzy... why are you sneaking around?"

It was Ryder. It was an odd relief to hear her voice. I walked briskly toward her, my cell phone held out in front like a lantern, noticing that she no longer was attached to our horse. I rushed past her, to the front of the barn in time to see the van pulling away through the gates. It was over. I had missed it all. I had foolishly parked my truck rather than stopping to say good-bye. My throat began to ache. I croaked plaintively, "He's gone. You never called me."

Ryder said, "Lizzy, I didn't need your help. I had it covered. But, honestly, the driver didn't call until he was at the gate. He woke me up." She glanced at the clock on her cell phone. "You sure stayed out late. Besides, I kept it low key, only turned on the light in the grooming stall to put on his shipping boots. We tiptoed out to the van without disturbing the barn. No drama."

I simply nodded in agreement, even though my throat ached. I hated to admit it, but Ryder was right. I wouldn't have been so relaxed or stoic or businesslike. It was probably better for Hotstuff that Ryder sent him on his way like it was just a trip to another horse show. I hoped he was finding his balance on the van, nibbling on his hay, and then dozing off in the dimly lit box. It would be a long trip to North Carolina.

Ryder led the way up the stairs to our apartment. Wheezer met me at the door and scampered ahead of me into my bedroom. She followed me into the bathroom, chatting me up. I noticed that my little baby's legs and tail both seemed to have been stretched. She was growing. I wanted to read, but instead, pulled Wheezer up under my chin and turned off the light and closed my eyes. Immediately I felt dizzy, my mattress seemed to levitate and turn, giving me a carnival ride in the dark or a ride on Aladdin's magic carpet. I slipped my foot off the mattress and onto the floor, bringing my floating mattress back on its bedsprings and then it took me on a dreamless journey into the dawn of another day.

***

Ryder and I had almost finished tacking up Word Perfect the next day when Margot appeared. She looked better, more rested. I was surprised since I knew she had just walked right past Hotstuff's empty stall, which should have darkened her mood.

She exclaimed, "Darlings, I just got off the phone with Word Perfect's previous trainer. What a lot of good information, what a story!"

Ryder looked puzzled. "How'd you figure out how to do that?"

Margot's tiny smile looked impish. She shrugged her shoulders. "I just asked Dennis who it was, and then asked for the phone number. He found it for me."

"You called Germany?" Ryder asked.

Margot sounded matter-of-fact. "Yes. I do have an international cell phone and speak German, if you didn't know, Ryder. I lived there for a number of years. I still have friends there. But this fellow, Werner, spoke quite good English. He sells a lot of horses to Americans."

I was getting impatient. I said, "So, what did he say about Word Perfect?"

"Well, here's the most amazing story. He was only able to keep her so long and get her to Grand Prix because he couldn't sell her since she was terribly difficult to work with. But the longer he kept her, the more attached he became and the better the mare worked for him. Once he got her training finished to Grand Prix, she started to get some very good scores at the local shows. He decided he would keep her and show her because she was turning out to be a much better horse than he had ever imagined. But, just listen to this, he and Wordy got so bonded that his wife got jealous. Can you imagine? One day his wife decided to ride Wordy with the idea that *she* should show the mare. Werner didn't object, since he said his wife is a very good rider who cares more about that sort of thing than he does. Wordy had other ideas."

I was grinning and shaking my head. I said, "Yeah, I can guess what happened."

Margot nodded, and then continued, "His wife fought and fought with the mare until Wordy threw herself down on the arena floor in a temper tantrum! Werner climbed back on to correct the mare, and his wife really wanted him to punish Word Perfect, except when Werner climbed on, the mare was, well, perfect."

Ryder said, "That mare shoved it in her face, didn't she?"

Margot raised her eyebrows at that and said, "His wife flew into a rage and told him to get that bitch out of the barn. Werner said it was going to be a problem if he did not do as he was told. His wife was serious. He told me he still misses the mare, but he thought that the lady who tried her, meaning Sophie, looked very good on Word Perfect and he had thought it was going to work. Besides, they paid him good money for her, and according to Werner, his home life has improved dramatically. Funny story isn't it?"

I shook my head in wonder, funny wasn't really the right word for the story. Wordy wanted her old rider back, her male rider. That seemed the point of the story to me. Margot, being a woman, sure had her work cut out for her. But I remained upbeat. "It sure is. I hope Werner knows that Wordy has a rider now that can handle her and appreciate her."

Margot nodded. "I tried to reassure him that the mare, although angry when she arrived, was beginning to settle in here."

Ryder looked very serious, but said nothing. She finished putting on the bridle and led Word Perfect out of the grooming stall. Margot pulled on her gloves in a way that told me she was eager to ride. Word Perfect and her "story" had lit a fire in Margot. Talking to Werner had helped her make the leap. She appeared committed to the formidable task ahead of her. As she took the mare from Ryder she addressed us.

"Darlings, I've made a plan for the day. Lizzy, after I ride Wordy, I'll teach you on Winsome, and then together we'll work Lovey and Papa. Ryder, you, my dear, are the barn manager for the horse show. You are in charge of Deb and Wild Child. Natalie will take care of Emma. I'll depend on you to get them packed up and moved over to the horse park this morning. Deb can drive the trailer and you can follow in your car. With just the one horse I told Alfonso you could manage. Call me when the girls are ready to ride and I'll be over to coach Deb and Emma. The jog is at four so we need to have the horses bathed and braided in time for that. We can't tarry."

I thought Ryder would protest at losing her ride and lesson on Papa, but I was wrong. She must have liked being put in charge, and also in her own mind, she had moved on from Papa to riding Johnny Cash and was simply biding her time.

Margot motioned for me to follow her to the arena. She made one last comment to Ryder over her shoulder. "Darling, if Dennis arrives, please entertain him. He's dying to watch, but I need a couple more rides on my own without an audience. Use your charms to keep him away from the arena, please."

I almost giggled on her last comment. Ryder's charms were non-existent. Margot flashed me a naughty grin that I hoped Ryder did not notice. I was feeling happy to see Margot happy. This pain-in-the-ass mare, Word Perfect, was restoring Margot in some mysterious way.

Margot swung up on the mare and then pulled a sugar cube out of her pocket. Word Perfect did not hesitate to swing her neck around and carefully lip the cube into her mouth. Margot gave the mare a little pat and addressed her. "I talked to your former daddy this morning. He told me that underneath that uncouth exterior lays an insecure soul seeking to harness her power behind a strong leader. You do not respect most women because like you, they are too emotional. You loved your Werner because he never got emotional, and he respected you and you knew that. He was always calm and secure, while at the same time only accepting your complete obedience. Werner said that you needed things black and white, and that you understood the concept of fairness. That you are one of the most intelligent horses he has ever known." Margot looked over at me. "Isn't that something?"

I nodded. Then Margot said, "You can sit down to watch today. I don't think I will need to even carry a whip. I just have a feeling."

So, I sat and stretched out my legs in front of me. Margot walked around on the buckle for a lap or two. Then she picked up the reins and without delay, she and Wordy were off in a brisk working trot. They lengthened across the diagonal twice, Margot testing the gas pedal. After only a couple of minutes Margot sat the trot and went to work.

It was so quiet in the arena that all I heard was the chirping of the birds and Wordy's rhythmic breathing. Margot's face had the look of deep focus so typical of her. The mare's face was also free of expression. Word Perfect was not exactly relaxed. It was just that the anger was gone.

Wordy's opinion of Margot appeared to be in flux. She had decided not to fight, but she was not exactly submissive yet. I thought that Word Perfect still missed her old rider and that if Werner showed up this minute, that Wordy would put Margot in the dirt and run to him. This mare felt things intensely, of that I was sure. Wordy had bonded with her old 'knight in shining armor' Werner, only after he had stormed her castle and impressed her with his courage. He had become her "hero" only through a display of strength, yet it was a strength coupled with his sensitivity to what the horse wanted from the relationship. Once she had been impressed and accepted him, he reciprocated with affection toward the mare, and a bond was formed. That thought was an epiphany to me. It was a funny thing, the way my mind worked. I'm sure a real naturalist would scoff at me and tell me I was being ridiculous. Heck, Ryder would tell me I was ridiculous.

Margot would not. She had gained an understanding of this horse because of what she had just learned from Werner. As humans, we had to put things we felt into words, and perhaps words were insufficient to explain the complexities of the myriad emotions and traits that make up personality, both in humans and in animals. I suspected that the differences between human and animals were not as vast in that regard as we liked to think. Both human and animal males had been working hard from the dawn of time to impress females in order to "win" their love. Maybe this was what had gone on between Word Perfect and Werner. The wife "got it." That's why Word Perfect had to go.

Word Perfect would now have to learn to bond with a woman. I expect that it would be a slightly different kind of relationship; but one that could be strong regardless. Luckily for Wordy, Margot was no ordinary woman and I suspected that when they did manage to bond, a horse as fiercely loyal as Word Perfect would make an amazing partner, shoulder-to-shoulder with you pulling as a team as she and Margot faced whatever challenges came their way. Shoulder-to-shoulder was what Chess had said. His words were gaining a deeper meaning all the time.

Margot put Word Perfect up all by herself while I tacked up Winsome. Dennis was nowhere to be found, so Ryder had not had to utilize her "charms" after all. I don't think I'd ever seen Margot put her own horse away before. She hosed Wordy off in the wash stall, fed her carrots, and rubbed her face off with a towel, all while maintaining a steady monologue. The mare wasn't whinnying to Margot like she did for Dennis, but I could tell her defenses were softening. Margot even took Wordy out to hand graze in the sun to dry. As she passed me tacking up Winsome she said, "Go ahead and start, I'll be there in a few minutes."

Ryder was schlepping stuff out to the trailer. She stopped briefly to watch Margot lead the mare out to the grass, and then said, "I'm guessing someone had a good ride. I've never seen Margot hand graze a horse."

I knew Ryder had no clue what a dangerous nut-job the mare had been before today, so I nodded non-committedly. Ryder picked up the rolling hay bag and returned to the job of loading the trailer. The show was going to be pretty light duty for Ryder with only one horse to pack, but I still didn't envy her. I was going to get to ride Lovey after Winsome today. I never had, and expected it to be a treat. On top of that I would have Margot to myself.

Winsome felt light and forward in our ride. It seemed Margot had sprinkled magic fairy dust over the barn with her positive energy. I wondered if she understood the power she held. Last night for me had been full of fear and quiet desperation. Today, just seeing Margot happy calmed my fears. Margot saw a future somehow, and the way she had sent Ryder on to the show and kept me by her side meant something, didn't it? Margot helped me run through my test and for the first time in ages I felt competent and relaxed. It went smoothly.

After Winsome was put up we tacked up Lovey and Papa side by side in the grooming stalls. Margot was chatty in the adjoining bay. Deb and Ryder had driven off with Wild Child, and Emma and Natalie had also left with Fable just as I had had come in from my lesson on Winsome. The barn was empty except for the two of us.

Margot said, "I am so glad to not be showing this weekend. And I can't remember the last time I sat on Papa. This will be fun."

I added, "And I've never ridden Lovey."

Margot smiled. "I guess that's true. He's a peach, and as comfortable as an easy chair."

We led the horses to the arena and it felt good. Papa towered over little Lovey, but they walked relaxed and amiably at our sides like the good and solid geldings that they were.

I smiled as soon as I began rising trot on Lovey. He was a nice compact "package." It wasn't long before I shifted into sitting trot. Wow, he was easy to sit. I picked up the canter and it, too, was easy, not scopey but balanced with a rocking horse quality. I looked in the mirror and admired his sweet and pretty face and arched neck. He had large eyes like a deer, and small pointed ears. I did not look too large on him either. He had a good enough engine without feeling overly sensitive. I did have to give quite a few half-halts to keep him sitting and off the shoulders, but when I found the right feeling he was good to stay back in his bodyweight from the upright position of my firm torso. It occurred to me that Francesca was sending him too much into the reins with her tight hips and thighs. I gave him a break and was about to share my thoughts with Margot but she was totally absorbed in Papa. I strolled around on a loose rein and enjoyed seeing her back on her "boy." Papa looked relaxed and happy, too. It took me back to my very first days as a working student, when Papa was still Margot's up and coming star. I wondered if it made her sad to sit on him, but she didn't look sad at all. Finally she took a break.

Margot brightly offered, "Let's switch horses!"

I couldn't believe it. I said, "Really?"

Margot had already jumped down and was leading Papa over to me. She said, "Here." We traded horses and I took Margot's stirrups up a hole while she took mine down. Even walking on Papa was intimidating. He was not only a big horse, but a nervous horse with a sensitivity that felt intimidating. Margot could sense my anxiety.

"Darling, just relax. Take him a bit in hand, but sit up and enjoy him. He has a huge heart that matches his huge engine."

Margot proceeded to coach me around the arena. She generously allowed me to feel his passage and his extended trot. A few times he felt like he might explode, but he didn't. We did the changes down to the two tempis and I had to work to keep him from running away by the end of the line, each change getting a little bit away from me. We avoided piaffe and one-tempis; Papa's bugaboos. It was fun and exhilarating.

Margot then put dear Lovey on the bit and played around for a few minutes. He looked bug-eyed with Margot on his back, but tried his best to perform for her. She dropped her reins and smiled. "Let's go cool out around the field. Then I'm afraid it will be time to go back to work." It was clear that what we just did was not "work" to Margot. The real job lay ahead.

We strolled side by side on the well-worn trail around the paddocks. I was a little nervous on the jittery and hyper-alert Papa, while Margot was relaxed on little Lovey. But we were able to enjoy the sunshine and admire the youngsters turned out in the fields up at Deb's. Margot reached over and patted me on the knee. "Darling, you looked very sharp sitting on Papa."

I wondered what Margot was thinking, but did not have my thoughts organized enough to ask an intelligent question. So I just said, "It was a treat, thank you."

Margot added, "Hmmm." A beat of silence passed between us. Then she said, 'I'll have to make plans, you know. I don't want to lose any more horses. Each horse must pull its weight and it's my job to figure out how. We owe these guys. I owe these guys."

I thought how Francesca had lost interest in Lovey, and Ryder had lost interest in Papa. What would happen to those two horses? I realized then that my ride on Papa and Lovey had been a sort of test. Margot knew they would both need new riders, but she did not want to see them sold away. I blurted out, "We are their guardians."

Margot nodded firmly. "Yes. I knew you understood. But, Lizzy, it's my burden. You have to trust me on this one. I will work it out."

Her words filled me with guilt. There was a lot to be worked out indeed. We had kept Margot out of the loop with our little strategy session. Was that right? I wanted to spill my guts, right then and there. But I didn't because I could still see Margot with her arms wrapped around Dennis' waist on his bike. Emma and I had wanted to confide in Margot, but instead fled her neighborhood after seeing Dennis' motorcycle in her driveway. Had Margot given up on Frank, and expected Dennis to take on the financial burden of keeping her herd together, of keeping her riders together? Yet, I knew that Margot loved Frank as much as I did. I also remembered what Emma had said to me on my first day on the job: We could all be out on the street. I was at a loss for words. We walked on in silence, heading back down the hill toward the barn.

Margot softly added, as if to herself, "Think of how Wordy's life has been disrupted. Think of Hotstuff right now arriving at his new home. What can they be thinking?" Then she frowned and continued, "Maybe they don't exactly think like we do, but for sure they feel, perhaps deeper than we can imagine. We all want to feel safe. We all want to survive, and so we humans plan and plan and try to gain control. But control is mostly an illusion, even over the horses. Still, making plans feels good, feels hopeful, even if it is an illusion."

And there was the answer to the question I had not asked. I broke her trance-like tone by saying, "You don't want to share those plans yet?"

She turned in the saddle to look me in the eye. "It's too soon to say. I couldn't have foreseen the current circumstances, darling. I don't have a crystal ball. And although I know how to ride and train and teach, don't assume that means that I am just as good at other things. I worry as much as the next person, because I've learned that as grim as things may look, they can always get worse."

I must have made a weird face, because Margot actually laughed and said, "Take heart, Lizzy, I can't see the future, but I think we're survivors, the lot of us. Never underestimate a horsewoman."

We stopped in front of the barn and dismounted, running up our stirrups and loosening our girths. Margot changed the subject by saying, "Now, let's put these two gentlemen away so I can go do *my* coaching job and you, my darling, can do *your* coaching job over at the Winstons' barn."

I had almost forgotten about that. "Oh. Yeah."

"We don't need your services at the horse park. Francesca needs every ride she can take before next weekend. Just come afterward for dinner. Dennis is hosting our horse show picnic tonight, and he claims his offerings will rival a Cavelli meal."

I cringed at his name and the suggestion that a Dennis gourmet would even be close to what Frank could offer. Margot appeared oblivious.

***

Francesca was even less chatty that usual. I reminded her of our upcoming horse show and recommended we run through the test. She didn't resist, but she didn't respond either. I plopped down on the mounting block, pulled off my gloves and helmet, and sighed deeply. Then I watched as Francesca made little circles in each corner of the arena, followed by transitions on the long sides.

Was she going to run through the test? I bit my tongue, and thought about how exasperating she was. How much worse could Dennis be as the farm owner? Of course, if Ryder's hints were accurate, I probably wouldn't be around to find out, regardless of what Margot was trying to negotiate. No, if the Cavellis survived these problems, I would be thrilled to be stuck with Francesca. Strangely she had grown on me. Or maybe I had "Stockholm syndrome," where you get emotionally attached to the people holding you hostage.

Francesca dithered around and dithered around, and just when I thought she would finish her ride without practicing the test, she turned down centerline in canter and halted and saluted at X, and began.

It was underpowered, but not terrible. She even managed not to bungle up the canter zigzags too badly. The most impressive thing was that Francesca looked more relaxed than usual. Her knees and thighs were much less grippy, her shoulders were looser. While Francesca would never look "casual" in the saddle, this was, it seemed, part of the "new" Francesca. Her riding on Johnny had lost the greater part of the unrealistic ambition and downright fear that had always been along for the ride. At her final halt and salute I could genuinely compliment her effort.

"Francesca, it's getting better, a lot better. You still need to add impulsion, but technically the entire test looks more correct, and you don't look so..." I hesitated to find the right word.

Francesca was walking on a loose rein. She waited for me to finish the sentence. She finally said, "Don't."

She jumped down and planted the big red lipstick kiss on Johnny's nose. I changed the subject. I said, "You coming to eat with the gang at the show grounds tonight?"

Francesca looked confused. I added, "The CDI at the horse park? Deb and Emma are showing this weekend."

Francesca lifted her chin and replied. "No, no. I had to plan coverage for Frank next weekend so we can have our little adventure. I can't leave him two weekends in a row."

I must have sounded disappointed. I just said, "Oh."

"I still intend to ride in the afternoons. You *are* still able to groom for me?"

It was a statement more than a request, but I nodded eagerly. "Sure. We both need to get in every ride we can before the show."

With that she said, "Same time tomorrow then." She did her backward wave as she walked away. I briefly wondered if she knew that Dennis was providing our dinner tonight. I began to get hungry, and wondered how Dennis could possibly outdo the spreads that Frank and Francesca usually provided. Selfishly, I hurried to finish putting up Johnny so I could go find out.

***

I arrived at the show grounds just as Margot and Dennis started to set out the dinner items. Ryder and Natalie were pulling out braids while Natalie filled water buckets.

Emma and Deb were still dressed sharp from the FEI jog. Margot insisted they sit, and she had poured them each a glass of wine. A little "ping" went off in the tack room, and Dennis emerged with a tray of mini BBQ sliders. He had brought a portable microwave oven. He walked them around so that even Natalie and Ryder managed to pop one in their mouths while they got their charges put up for the night. Dennis was working it.

Someone hit "play" on the CD player and we had piano tunes creating a nice ambiance as a backdrop as Emma and Deb and Margot all described a good day and good rides. Wild Child had been a little too excited in the jog, lifting Deb off her feet at one point, but she said she got his attention back by grabbing the skin on his neck and pinching it while still on her tip-toes, which surprised the heck out of him. After that he kept an eye on Deb instead of the environment and was more respectful.

It was odd that I had no job to do. Instead I got a cold drink and pulled up one of the director chairs with the farm logo on it and ate a slider. Natalie and Ryder were doing the jobs I usually did.

And then Chess arrived, a sight for sore eyes, dressed in a coat and tie with the knot pulled down and the collar button of his shirt undone. He was grinning. "Hello, Equus Paradiso Farm, legitimate equestrian business par excellence!"

I knew right away what he meant, as did Deb and Emma. I squealed, "You did it?" And he nodded back. Then I nearly strangled him with hugs. Deb poured him a glass of wine. Margot finally seemed to "get it."

She stepped forward to give him a much gentler hug. "Darling, that is wonderful news. I am so proud of you, and I know your dad will be, too."

Right about then Deb and Emma and Chess and I exchanged glances. We were no longer in our "council of war," Dennis and Ryder and Margot had taken in our news. We had not been circumspect.

Emma gave Chess a very serious nod, lips pursed. I took Chess by the elbow and led him to the buffet saying, "Let's get you something to eat."

We turned our backs to the aisle and I leaned in close while Chess whispered a short summary of his meeting with the IRS agent. "It looks pretty good. We have some disallowed deductions, which I expected. So that means we will owe additional taxes, plus some penalties and interest, but it's manageable. The agent said he had to pass his recommendation up the chain, but was confident it would be approved. What really swung things our way was the horse sale last week. Even though it wasn't in the audit year, I had something to show the farm revenue and a return."

I gave Chess a one-armed hug around his waist while he looked over the offerings.

He added, "The agent kept looking at the expenses and the numbers and the plan. He said that although the horse business looked like a terrible choice for a business, there was no law against stupid."

I whispered back to Chess the old saw, "The only way to make a small fortune in horses, is to start with a large one."

While Chess loaded his plate and we whispered to each other, Margot had pulled the chairs into a circle. Everyone sat down and Deb and Emma managed to redirect the conversation to the horses and the next day's contest. Natalie added jokes and songs to make us laugh, and we made it a party. Still, I missed Frank's great belly laugh. Our menu was high-end with smoked salmon with capers and sour cream served up on toast points. We had marinated asparagus spears and baby mushrooms. We had miniature wedges of iceberg lettuce with blue cheese dressing and crumbled bacon. For dessert we had iced petit-fours. It was a spread meant to impress someone. I knew for certain I was not that someone.

Emma never looked at Dennis or spoke to him. She barely ate anything, as edgy as one of Deb's feral cats. Dennis was laying it on thick about how he was a fan of Wild Child's and Deb smiled and said all the right things back to him. Margot and Dennis chatted and smiled and seemed to be having a wonderful time while they drank more than they ate. Except for Emma, our cheery performances could have been labeled as "over-compensation." I made a point to thank Dennis and compliment the food. It was only Emma's behavior that bordered on rude.

I offered, "Hey, Dennis, let me do the clean up." Natalie chimed in, "Yeah, I'll help." She tipped her head toward Margot and Dennis. "You crazy kids go on home."

Margot laughed but nodded. Dennis agreed too, saying, "Okay. Ryder, please take the leftover food home tonight and put it in the fridge. I know you guys won't let it go to waste."

Ryder nodded back and thanked him.

Margot quickly went over the next day's schedule with a rundown on preparation times while Chess stood apart, politely listening. Emma was an early draw tomorrow, and Deb had the good fortune to be in the final slot. Margot and I would need to go back to the farm to ride our horses mid-day tomorrow, and I would still have my regular duties in the afternoon with Francesca.

Once Dennis and Margot were well away, Natalie pulled me into the tack room and whispered. "So, I told Deb and Emma already, but..."

And Ryder came in, scowling, but also whispering, "What's Emma's problem? It was embarrassing."

Natalie and Ryder looked at me. I drew a deep breath to give myself some time. I finally just stated the obvious. "I guess she doesn't like Dennis. History."

Ryder hissed back, "Well, she's making herself about as welcome as the plague. Stupid."

I deflected. "Who is doing bed check tonight?"

Ryder frowned. "Me. Natalie does tomorrow. I'm out of here until then. I have a ridiculously early wake-up time. You seem to have gotten a vacation this weekend."

I shrugged. Ryder added, "Emma needs to get a grip. I don't really care if she messes up her show, but she's like toxic or something, and I don't want it affecting Deb's ride."

Ryder pulled her purse out from behind a basket of polo wraps in the corner and was gone. Natalie flipped open the cooler and pulled out a beer. She sat down on the closed cooler, twisted off the lid, and took a long swig.

Chess walked into the tack room and it only took a second for him to register that something was afoot. I whispered to him, "Is she gone?"

Chess poked his head back out of the tack room, looking down the barn aisle, left and right. He started to speak, but I put my finger over my lips and in a low voice whispered that at horse shows the walls "have ears." Emma had taught me that. It was always a dangerous place to tell secrets, since one man's wall was usually another's and you couldn't tell the difference between a lone horse browsing through his hay, and a horse and a girl, silently braiding his mane.

Chess whispered, back, "So what's up?"

Nat's voice was low and husky. "I located Sophie. Surprise, surprise, she's not in Germany with some hunky trainer. She's a "Jersey" girl again, matter of fact. Not only that, her Facebook status is "single.""

I processed that, not quite sure what it meant or if it mattered. Natalie's eyes narrowed and her whisper was barely audible. "I sent her a private message, just to let her know that I had seen *her* mare over at the Cavellis', and also let her know that I had heard the whole kit and caboodle was in the process of being sold to Dennis, and wondered if she had heard."

I was incredulous. "You did what?"

She smiled again. "I deleted it of course after about three minutes. But I hope she saw it first. If she did, then I'm guessing I'll hear from her, or someone will."

And then Natalie gave me a devil of a smile and a wink, and said, "Sophie just may take care of our Dennis problem for us."

12. Apparent Wedges

As soon as I fed the horses their breakfasts, I drove to the show grounds.
The CDI Grand Prix class would be the first class of the day in the covered arena in order to give the advanced horses the coolest time of the day. I fed in the dark, because I didn't want to miss a single ride in the class. Ryder had left the apartment at o-dark-hundred, since she was in charge of the barn and would need to have it spit-spot way ahead of braiding and tacking up.

When I arrived at the stalls, the air had an intensity that was palpable and Emma looked like a caged tiger pacing back and forth. We made small talk and even though she had a watch she asked me every couple of minutes what time it was, and I dutifully answered.

Natalie had just finished braiding Fable. Deb slumped in a chair in the aisle with a ball cap pulled over her eyes, her arms crossed, eyes closed with a set of earphones blocking out the world. I think she may have been sleeping so I tiptoed around her. I didn't see Margot or Ryder. Natalie jerked her head my way and whispered, "Hey, Lizzy. Walk with me to the concessions stand."

I looked at our "hostess table" and noticed... nothing. I frowned and said, "No one made coffee or brought breakfast?"

Natalie shrugged. "Appears that way. I guess the coffee stuff got left in the trailer, and y'know, Dennis must not have gotten the memo about providing breakfast."

I grabbed my purse from the tack room and Nat and I started walking. We didn't start chatting until we were well away from the stalls. We mostly discussed Emma and the chip Emma wore on her shoulder about Dennis, and of course, Emma's self evident show nerves. The bad vibes that had been so obvious last night had not abated, not at all.

The little trailer that served breakfast had quite a line forming, and people sat and ate and chatted at the nearby picnic tables. The arena was being dragged and the ring crew placed potted ferns in the tops of the tall arena letters that were manufactured with indentations made to fit a flowerpot. The rising sun hung low and created long shadows across the footing. The metallic smell of water, so recently sprayed from the shotgun style jets set into the top rail of the fencing, still hung in the air. All this was familiar to me and brought a jittery feeling to my stomach; though I knew that I would not be called on to perform, my body was still tuning-up for action.

Natalie and I joined the end of the line. I studied the offerings listed above the bus style window on the food truck and as we got closer to the front, stared at the grill. Little metal rings had eggs dropped into them to fry, sausages were being turned and hot coffee poured into tall Styrofoam cups. The aromas helped to change the feeling in my stomach from nerves to a different kind of anticipation.

These mundane things absorbed my attention before I noticed that Ryder and Margot were at the front of the line. I had a small twinge of jealousy seeing them chatting and clearly enjoying each other's company. Margot put her hand on Ryder's elbow and they laughed together. I reminded myself that Ryder was just a teenage girl, and Margot her coach. Their relationship shouldn't be any other way than warm, despite their ups and downs. Ryder should have been like a little sister to me, but we basically tolerated each other. Whose fault was that? I suppose it couldn't be one hundred percent Ryder's fault. Life was never simple, never black hats and white hats.

Margot had seen something in Ryder on that first day months ago in Conyers, Georgia and Margot had been able to guide Ryder along in her riding, had in fact made her better in spite of Ryder being a pain-in-the-ass prima donna. I felt sure Margot took pride in that. It had become hard for me to feel anything positive about Ryder. Was I being unfair? To Ryder's credit, she had recognized, and still did recognize, that Margot was an incredible teacher. Ryder had sought out the job with Margot for a reason. Ryder always had a reason, a plan. Ryder was tactical. She had needed Margot. She had needed Papa.

I thought about how Ryder had sported purple hair the first day we met her and that even then she had "attitude" that grated on both Francesca and me. But, Margot had let it pass because she had seen talent, and wanted to provide that talent with an opportunity. Margot had always shown interest in taking on projects, even with plenty of attached "baggage." It was clearly never about the money for Margot.

Margot was the same with her horses, taking on a neurotic Papa, an aggressive and lazy Wild Child, and now an angry, intelligent, and emotional Word Perfect.

Margot had taken on Ryder. Margot had taken on... me. That thought was slightly painful. It rang true, deeply true, and I cringed to think I was one of Margot's projects, while realizing that, of course, it was true. I had been a bundle of insecurities, some I'm sure I still couldn't quite see. Margot, it seemed, liked a challenge. I sighed, and then Natalie poked me in the back to step forward to fill the gap in the line, putting an end to my ruminations.

Margot and Ryder held cups of coffee and little brown paper bags that were beginning to show grease stains as they came toward us. I waved, but Margot had stopped to chat with a tall lady a few feet ahead of me. Ryder stood to the side, but interrupted to ask Margot how many creams and sugars, and then wandered off to fetch them from an adjoining table. After a few pleasantries, Margot turned around, and again I waved, but she walked right past Natalie and me as if we were invisible, her face an expressionless mask. Natalie and I glanced at each other. I said, "Okay, was that weird or what?"

Natalie agreed, "Yeah. Weird."

Ryder saw us and stopped. She said in a monotone voice, "Hey."

I answered with concern in my voice, "Is Margot okay?"

Ryder looked puzzled. "Uh, yeah, she's in a really good mood actually. The horses both schooled great yesterday."

Then I heard my name. "Lizzy?"

The tall woman, the person who Margot had been chatting with, had gotten her food and turned around. Oh God, she was walking right up to Natalie, Ryder, and me. And there she stood right in front of me, a ghost from the past.

I managed to find my voice. "Sophie."

Sophie looked as beautiful as ever. She wore a form fitting short-sleeved shirt with a zipperd front pulled down just enough to display her bronzed cleavage. She sported one of those lanyards around her neck with a card on the end that said "Volunteer." Her hair was just as blonde, her lashes just as thick and long, and her skin smooth and tan. She was all that she ever had been, and her perfection was uncomfortable for me to be near.

I now understood the expression on Margot's face. Sophie's reappearance had rocked the foundation beneath her feet, which had been shaky enough with Frank and Francesca's problems, but then Dennis had pushed his way back in and offered support.

Sophie had returned just as Natalie had told us, and I had a bad feeling about it. Natalie might not be the reason for Sophie being here at the show, but maybe her little Facebook post had brought it about. What would Sophie's presence mean to Margot? What promises had been made in the past by Dennis, only to have been broken on behalf of that towering bit of perfection? Why would Sophie have even bothered to greet Margot? All I knew is that I felt awkward and small and befuddled. I wanted Dennis gone, but this was just another complication.

Margot had said that regardless of how bad things were, they could always be worse. What if there were no Frank and Francesca, and no Dennis either? Equus Paradiso Farm could end up a Paso Fino or Quarter Horse farm or, God forbid, a subdivision. I had failed to consider that possibility.

Sophie spoke to me like an old acquaintance. "Lizzy, you have time to sit and keep me company while I have my breakfast?"

Natalie and I moved to the front of the line and I put Sophie off momentarily with an uplifted finger while we placed our orders. I dug around in my bag and paid for my breakfast, Sophie stepped away to doctor her coffee.

Natalie and I exchanged looks and Nat whispered, "Leave me out of it, okay?" Then she lowered her voice to the point that I had to lean in and could barely make out her words. "But get some intel if you can. Lizzy, you are our perfect spy, quiet and unassuming, she'll never suspect you." Natalie made a little airplane with her hand. "You're flying under the radar, my friend."

I nodded, but thought that no one would be a worse spy and that I had no idea what "intel" I was supposed to dig. Sophie sat at a picnic table and scrolled through her phone, eyes down while she nibbled at her sandwich. Natalie and I got our food, and Nat peeled away.

I hated this.

I doused a ton of those little cups of creamer into my coffee and took my greasy bag and a stack of napkins over to join Sophie. I started to perspire, feeling like I was approaching an unexploded bomb. This would be a delicate procedure. She was going to subtly press me for information, and I would be doing the same, all masked with superficial pleasantries and cautious probing. I did not know Sophie except by reputation, had met her only a handful of times, and spoken to her about the same number of times, yet here I was about to sit and chat her up like an old friend.

I asked an innocent question. "So, you're volunteering?"

Sophie answered, flashing me a blindingly white smile of perfect teeth. "Yes, giving back to the sport and all that."

I said, "Or, so you're not showing?" The game had started. I already knew she wasn't showing.

She said, "Not this time. What about you, dear?"

Dear? Sophie called me dear. She might as well have said darling, except that she would *never* pull that off.

I sipped my coffee and even with all the creamer it was very hot and tasted burned. Although I was careful, it still burned my tongue, so I waited a beat to answer, "Next weekend at Hill and Dale."

Sophie acted as if my answer had some deep meaning, which it didn't. She said knowingly, "Ah, Hill and Dale."

Then I got bolder. I said, "Sorry to hear about you and Dennis."

And she said with conviction, "We are still *very* good friends, of course. He's a dear."

That surprised me, but I simply echoed Sophie and said, "Ah."

I could tell that bothered her, but she brushed it off with a shrug. "I was so relieved to get rid of that mare. Margot did me a favor to take her off my hands. Word Perfect never did suit me."

I took a bite of my sausage and egg and cheese biscuit. My only answer, my mouth full of food was, "Hmmm."

Then she added, "I'm afraid I let that mare come between Dennis and me. It was silly, really. The horse I really wanted, have admired for years, was Ben's horse, the stallion, y'know, Willy."

For a moment I drew a blank, and then I got it. I mumbled, "Wild Child?"

Sophie corrected me, "Ben always called him Willy. His barn name is Willy."

I took another sip. My coffee was just the right temp now. I said, "Funny, he doesn't seem like a 'Willy' to me."

Sophie's voice was condescending. "Well, dear, I suppose you don't know him as well as I do, having followed his career since he was a four-year-old. What a pistol he was as a young horse. Of course you've only known him as a mature, fully trained GP horse. It's such a shame that Ben lost his sponsor, but it's all part of the game. I'm dying to see the horse go again, but it will be strange to see him ridden by Deb."

Margot's 'darling' was unaffected and affectionate, Sophie's 'dear' was completely phony and condescending. If it was meant to get under my skin, it was effective. I couldn't seem to keep the defensive tone out of my voice. "Deb brings out the best in him, though."

At first Sophie seemed to agree. "You know, I get why Margot gave the ride away. He's not a horse for an *older* person. I can see that. But, I was surprised that Deb went for it, her being more of a circus trainer and all that sort of thing."

I smiled the smile of a dog showing their teeth. She had just insulted both Margot and Deb. Even as there was some truth in everything she had said, or maybe because there was truth in her words, it stung. I tried my best to keep a monotone. "I think when you see them go this morning you won't be surprised at all."

She smiled back. "I don't doubt Deb can ride him, but Willy is so tall, and Deb so short, must be odd looking." Then Sophie leaned toward me and gave the table a smack with the flat of her hand to add emphasis to her show of sincerity. "Good for Deb. And good for Margot to give Deb a shot since Deb's worked like a slave in Margot's shadow for so many years."

I sat upright, putting back the distance between us and changed the subject. "So, where are you keeping your horses these days?"

She answered breezily, "I'm only riding client horses at the moment, taking my time to find the right horse for the big arena. I bought Wordy in haste. This time around I'm waiting for the right horse." She sighed dramatically, "Live and learn. Live and learn."

Sophie continued with her own redirection, "So, dear, how are you faring at Equus Paradiso since the Cavellis' bad luck."

I wondered if she was bluffing. How could she know? I suppose that people talk and bad news travels fast. But, I couldn't help but wonder if she had heard it directly from Dennis. She had hit another nerve and my blood was rising. She had gotten to me.

I sounded too enthusiastic, "I am doing well. My mare and I have made progress. It's hard to believe how much I've learned since I arrived. Plus, I've gotten really close to the family; terrific people."

Sophie looked skeptical, one well shaped eyebrow raised, a small smile forming on her glossy lips. She wasn't buying it.

I added with some relish, "Chess Cavelli and I are dating. Life is good."

As I said it, I realized that I was bragging. I was proud to call Chess my boyfriend.

That shut her up. Which felt okay for an instant, except that shutting her up wasn't supposed to be my "mission" as commissioned by Natalie. I shoved the last of my biscuit in my mouth. It was too much and I felt like a hamster with my cheek bulging. Across from me sat a human Barbie doll. I'll bet she never looked like a hamster. My cheeks felt warmer. I half swallowed a reluctant lump of biscuit and took a swig of coffee to give it a push. It went down, albeit painfully. Then I grabbed my coffee and stood up abruptly. I began brushing the crumbs off my jeans with my free hand, managing to drip coffee on my pants in the process.

This spy needed to make her escape. I blurted out, "Well, Sophie, nice to see you again. Hope to see you around."

Sophie remained seated. Her voice was calm and relaxed. I felt sure she was feeling smug. She said, "Be sure and tell Emma and Deb that I said hello, and I hope they both have great rides today. I mean that. I'll be cheering them on in the stands."

I smiled back. "That's nice of you, dear, I'll be sure and let them know." She was already looking down at her phone and missed my use of her new affectation. Whatever she had wanted from our little chat, she appeared to have gotten, and she had moved on.

I walked slowly toward our barn, dropping my Styrofoam coffee cup into a trash can on the way since I had somehow created a crescent shaped leak from a fingernail. I stood at the can, looking down at puppies in a pen set up next to the can at the end of a barn aisle.

A friendly woman chirped at me. "They're ready to go to their new homes!"

They were Jack Russell pups, scruffy little tri-color rough coats. They all stood on their hind legs, paws climbing on the wire of the playpen fencing around them. They were barking and whining, stubby tails wagging, trying to get my attention. I picked one up and held it under my chin, inhaling the distinctive puppy breath as it licked my chin. To me, puppy breath smelled like charcoal.

I lifted a paw and placed it on the tip of my nose and inhaled. The underside of the paw, the pads, were velvety soft and multi-colored and held the aroma of fresh popcorn. No doubt about it. The smell reset me emotionally, taking my brain to the fuzzy feel good emotions of holding countless other puppies. You might as well have hit me with a tranquilizer dart.

I said to the woman, "Popcorn paws and charcoal breath. That's what I smell when I hold a puppy."

The woman smiled and said, "I know what you mean. I think they're called pheromones. Nature knows how to rope you into falling in love with babies."

I smiled back. "Puppy smell is the best."

She smiled back. "Baby anything smell is the best. Cures what ails you."

I put the puppy back down and said, "I can't buy one, but if you don't mind, I may come back later for some more therapy."

She nodded. "You come back and bring your friends. The pheromones are free of charge."

I could think more clearly again. What had I learned from Sophie? I mulled over our short conversation.

One: Sophie had some sort of emotional investment in "Willy." That was worrisome.

Two: Sophie did not want Word Perfect back. That was good.

Three: Sophie knew something about the Cavelli "bad luck." That was not good.

And Four: Sophie had said that she and Dennis were still "very good friends." Whether that was bad, or good, I was not sure. In sum, I hadn't been such a bad spy after all. I would be ready for my de-briefing.

When I returned to the barn, Emma had dressed, Fable was getting tacked up, and Natalie and Emma were arguing. That could not be good.

Natalie was saying, "Suck it up, Buttercup. Fable doesn't care about your drama."

Emma narrowed her eyes. "If I wanted your opinion, I would have asked for it."

Then Nat shrugged her shoulders and said, "Fine."

And Emma said, "Fine."

I went into the tack room and pulled Uno out of his crate where he napped, curled up against his teddy. Today he wore a tiny blue leather collar, hand tooled and painted with daisies. Puppy therapy to the rescue.

I carried him to Em and lied, "Uno seemed upset. You might need to calm him down."

Emma took the bait. "Baby, what's wrong? You come to Mama." Emma cradled her baby and he licked her chin and wiggled, bright eyed and happy.

Margot came out of the tack room and stared at Emma with raised eyebrows. She looked worried. Finally she just said, "Emma" and gestured at her. Emma came right to her. Margot's arm went around Emma's shoulders and Margot guided Emma back into the tack room where their voices were low and unintelligible.

I wondered if Emma had either heard about or seen Sophie. Emma had a job to do. Her first responsibility was to her horse and to her sponsors who had footed the bill. Natalie was right, even though she hadn't been tactful. Whatever Emma was worried about, she needed to suck it up and focus.

We got Emma to the warm up arena, and I waited for Emma to get 'on task.' I knew Emma, and I knew she was always a nervous wreck at shows, even when she had no distractions. But, I also knew she could turn it on when it counted. She was a talented rider who had worked for this tirelessly for most of her life and her time to shine had finally arrived. It was time to jump off that metaphorical diving board and let the training take over. If anyone knew how to advise her on how to do that, it was Margot.

I stood ringside next to Natalie, who held a bucket of supplies. Margot stood on Natalie's other side. The rest of our team had gone to the stands, probably at Margot's request. I'm not sure why I had been given a pass, but Margot had let me stay. I leaned against the fence and heard Margot's soothing voice, low and sweet as she talked into the coaching system.

"Darling, you have time, you have time. You and your horse know the test, and I'm not worried about any particular movement. I just want you to find a deep level of relaxation and focus. Be sure he's in front of the leg and reaching into the contact. Deep breath. Forget everything else. "

I saw Emma turn her head and look right at Margot. Margot mouthed more than said, "Do it for me, darling."

Emma nodded in response.

Things got better, not in a rush but in a controlled uptick. Natalie sighed and shook her head. "That girl's gonna kill me."

Emma ran out of time to do much more than a basic warm up. Margot pulled the coaching system off and Natalie and I removed the polos and bell boots. Then all we could do was give her a drink of water and wipe off her boots. Emma was on her own.

Margot's parting words were, "Darling, if you ask him, he'll put his heart and soul into it. Don't be afraid to ask. This horse loves you."

I watched a bead of sweat trickle from under Emma's helmet, down her temple and fall from her jaw line. And then she trotted into the arena. The bell rang, and Emma halted, piaffed a few steps, and then picked up the canter to enter.

Margot and Natalie and I barely drew a breath. We leaned against the railing, our shoulders hunched, leaning forward and riding every stride right along with Emma. My imaginary spurs pressed into an imaginary horse. Emma was riding too conservatively, with every step precise as could be, but without letting Fable show his incredible range of motion and lightness.

At her final halt, we unclenched our fists that had held imaginary reins and let our shoulders drop, finding our normal breath again and standing up straight. At least there had been no disasters, no real mistakes. Emma had pulled it off with room for improvement. We applauded and Natalie's ear piercing whistle nearly blew out my left ear drum. We turned our eyes to the electronic scoreboard as the collective marks were displayed. It was a board full of Sevens. For most of us, that would be something to celebrate, but Emma and this horse could do better.

As a newcomer to the high performance league, 70% was certainly high enough to draw the attention of the selectors, but not nearly high enough to shake up the establishment.

Natalie looked unsure as she turned to Margot and said, "What do you think?"

Emma was still far enough away from us, getting her bits and spurs checked by the ring steward, so that Margot could speak candidly. Still she whispered, "Give her a chance. Nat. She has to build her confidence. But know this, barring disaster, our Emma and that horse, Fable, they're going to be famous." I was impressed with Margot's conviction. It was real.

Margot turned to go to Emma. Emma looked slightly embarrassed, but Margot was saying. "You did splendidly, darling. It's just the beginning. Very solid."

I looked up into the stands to see our group, including Dennis, sitting and chatting amiably. Then I saw Sophie, two rows down and directly in front of Dennis. He couldn't watch the show without staring right at the back of her very blonde head.

Margot and Natalie trailed Fable back to the barns. Instead of following them I wandered a different direction. I needed more puppy therapy, stat.

After a few quick deep inhalations of free "pheromones" I returned to our stalls. Emma had handed Fable off to Natalie, who quietly untacked him. Em had carefully pulled off her gloves by the fingertips and hung them with a clothespin on a hanger on a bridle hook. She silently pulled off her sweaty jacket and turned it inside out, shaped it with her hands, hanging it up to air dry. Her helmet was turned upside down in its box so the lining, too, would air dry. All had been done with evident care.

Emma pulled her clogs out from under her saddle rack where she had stowed them. Today's clogs were hand tooled baby blue leather. She used a polished wooden shoehorn to put them on. She ran a towel over her boots and lined them carefully against the wall. Emma was still Emma, as meticulous as ever. She would have to put the entire outfit back on for the awards ceremony at lunch break today.

I watched from the oblique angle of the barn aisle, trying to give Emma her space. But, finally I invaded in order to help Natalie by cleaning off Fable's tack and putting it away. Emma had by that time sat down on a trunk and had her cell phone pressed against her ear.

I heard her say, "Tank, I'm so glad I reached you." And then she lowered her voice, her words unintelligible, but her tone evident. Emma was not coping well. I backed out of the tack room to give her some privacy, but I was intrigued. The first person she had wanted to talk to was Tank. I would not have guessed that.

Emma reappeared in the barn aisle a few minutes later with a tiny Uno tucked under her arm. His collar coordinated with Emma's clogs, and she had snapped on a tiny matching leash.

Deb walked in. It was time for round two. Deb nodded to Emma and said, "I will be thrilled if I get your score, Blondie."

Emma's lips turned down as she shook her head with disappointment. "Deb, you know how the world disappears and time slows down when you have a good ride?"

Deb nodded. Emma continued, "Well, it wasn't one of those rides. It felt awful. I kept trying to slow my heart down and focus on each piece of the test. But, I kept seeing Sophie in the stands, every damn time I came past her. It was like passing a bad car wreck. I couldn't look away."

Deb gave Emma a warning look, and Emma looked over her shoulder. "Where's Margot?" Emma asked.

Deb spoke from the side of her mouth. "She's down at the warm up arena. I've got to get on and get down there." Deb lowered her voice even more. "But we aren't sharing this with Ryder, remember? We need to play it cool, okay? Sophie is here because Natalie tipped her off. We know there's going to be a dust up. It's inevitable. But there's no need for you to stress over it. You're safe in Texas. We're the ones who could find ourselves on the street."

Emma's lower lip quivered and she pulled Uno over her heart and hugged him a little tighter. Deb immediately looked remorseful. "Sorry, Blondie."

Emma sagged. Deb tried again. "Emma, c'mon, I didn't mean to hurt your feelings. Look, I've got to get on. Then she looked around her. "Where the hell is Ryder, anyway?"

I offered to get him ready, but Deb waved me away.

Deb slipped the halter on a sour-faced Wild Child. She put him into the cross-ties and he snapped his teeth in the air, barging forward. Deb grabbed the lead shank and gave it a jerk. Wild Child backed up a step but barely gave Deb a glance. Instead he arched his neck and drew himself up big and tall, looking down the barn aisle transfixed on something. It was Ryder, jogging and breathless.

"I'm here. Sorry, Deb, sorry. He's clean and ready for his tack, I'll be fast. Dennis and I were chatting and time got away from me." She swung into action.

Deb never got angry and she wasn't going to start now, but she dropped the lead rope and announced to the air around her. "I'm getting changed and then I intend to go have a time of my life riding that mighty beast. I may score well or I may go down in flames, but I'm going to remember this ride, and I'm going to remember this day." Then she pointed her finger and drew a circle that started with Emma and her tiny dog clutched to her chest, then traveled to Natalie and me and finally pointed to Ryder who looked up at Deb from a crouching position where she had begun putting on shiny white patent leather boots on Wild Child.

Deb's tone was serious. "That includes all of you interesting characters."

Deb grabbed her coat bag and marched off toward the restrooms. Emma smiled and kissed the top of Uno's little tennis ball shaped skull and then stared at me like we had a secret. That smile followed the circle that Deb had made with her finger, from Emma to me to Nat and even worked its way to Ryder, who made her classic smirk that was so embedded into the character of Ryder Anderson.

Deb had just lightened the load. Sophie's appearance suddenly seemed trivial. In that moment, I sensed that Deb was about to have the ride of her life.

***

It was magical, even in the warm up arena. Emma and Natalie and Margot and Ryder and I made a line along the ringside. Quietly, without any announcement, I found Chess standing at my elbow, extending our line. He gave my hand a squeeze, and without speaking we both turned our attention back to Deb. Right from the first step, Deb was in total command. Margot said few words into her coaching microphone and there was no idle chit-chat among us.

Wild Child's summer coat was at its glory, shining iridescent in the sunlight. He had never looked more impressive. It wasn't just his glorious chestnut coat and sinewy muscles. Today he seemed to have upped his game, and was not going to make Deb work for the impulsion. Perhaps he had been influenced by having Fable join our barn. Did he sense competition from the younger stallion?

Margot whispered into her headset, "Beautiful, simply beautiful." I don't think it was meant for Deb, or for anyone. It was just what she felt. It was what we were all feeling.

When it was time, we did our pit crew duties. Deb said nothing while we fluttered around her, but she took one sip of water, borrowed a dirty towel to wipe the sweat from her face, and then walked with purpose to the main arena. There were no parting instructions from Margot. Deb did not need any encouragement or guidance. She had more than the horse "in hand."

I watched Deb's test in an entirely different emotional state than when I had watched Emma's. I wasn't nervous, but I was enthralled. I glanced over at Chess, who seemed absorbed. I wondered if he could enjoy it even more than I did. He could see the beauty of it without seeing the little technical glitches. I was glad he stood next to me, to have him close, and in some small way, it helped me feel connected to Frank, and even Francesca, who should be here to see their prized stallion at his best.

It was funny, but in a way it didn't matter how it went, or what Deb's score would be. The judge's opinions were going to be positive, and even if one of them were stingy, well, it wouldn't change anything for Deb. Deb knew her own worth. Wild Child's exuberance seemed to announce to the audience that he, too, knew his own worth. They made some little mistakes, Wild Child getting a little tight in his neck in a few moments. The zigzags still lacked the light-footedness of the rest of the test. But it didn't matter. Wild Child still wowed them in the piaffe and passage tours.

When Deb finished, we made a ruckus. Emma was at my elbow. She said in a raspy voice. "I need to take lessons from the hippie."

There was a general air of excitement while Deb was having her bit and spur check, and we waited for the scores to appear on the electronic score board. I had hardly noticed the scores as the ride was going, but now my jaw dropped. Wild Child had gotten a nine on gaits, and a nine on impulsion. His final score topped the 74% mark. It was his best score to date. There was no doubt now that he and Deb would be invited to the training sessions in Florida.

I hugged Chess, I hugged Emma, and I hugged Natalie, and Margot, and even felt obliged to hug Ryder. Then it was time to do a quick clean up back at the barn, to watch Natalie tack up Fable for Em, and enjoy the lunchtime award ceremony. After the first day, Deb was first, a Canadian rider was second, and Emma was third. Tomorrow they would do their freestyles and Emma would showcase her Texas music medley. The music selection was a bit risky, but definitely memorable. I hoped for her sake that tomorrow she would loosen up and go for it.

I suddenly wondered where Dennis had gone. I glanced over to the stands where earlier our gang had been sitting. I shouldn't have. Dennis was hurriedly getting up from his seat and turning toward us, walking with a big smile on his face. But no matter how quickly he stepped, how brightly he smiled, I saw who he had left sitting next to him.

We enjoyed the ceremony and our horses behaved. Then it was time for me to get back to my own work. It was just Margot and me back at the farm. We had Word Perfect, Winsome, Papa, and Lovey to ride, and I looked forward to having Margot all to myself again.

I led Wordy to the grooming stall and clipped her in. I had set all her tack, including her special shimmed pad and polo wraps next to her spot. Margot watched me hook her in, and then said, "Go ahead and fetch Winsome. I don't mind tacking her up today."

I shook my head. Margot must not know what she had just volunteered to do. "Margot, tacking her up is an athletic event."

Margot looked amused. "Darling, if I can ride her, surely I can tack her up."

I nodded. "Of course, you're right. But, if you want, I could tack up Wordy and give you Winsome."

Margot shook her head. "Nonsense. Besides, it will be good for our relationship."

I agreed. "That makes sense. But, so far it's taken both Ryder and me to get her to behave, so just ask if you want me to, y'know, enforce the rules."

"I don't think that will be necessary, darling, but thank you."

I went to fetch Winsome and was in her stall when I heard a commotion and Margot's raised voice. "Don't you dare!"

By the time Winsome and I got to the grooming stalls, Margot was emerging from the tack room with a dressage whip. She caught my eye and shook her head. "Darling, you weren't exaggerating. Someone's behavior is rude, and lacks any respect for authority."

I thought about that for a couple of seconds. "I don't think it's that she doesn't respect your authority, I think she doesn't even acknowledge your authority. That's a different problem."

Margot pondered that for a moment. "Interesting insight." She nodded at me approvingly, and then focused on the horse. "You and I are going to reach an understanding." Her tone was like a schoolteacher taking control of a troublesome student.

Wordy's ears were up and she watched Margot as she spoke. When Margot lifted the whip, Wordy lunged forward at her with ears pinned and teeth bared. That mare's glare was so incendiary it would have blistered paint right off the side of a barn. She looked like some kind of serpent-like creature emerging from the depths of hell.

Margot firmly barked out, "NO!" and smacked the mare hard across the chest with the whip. Wordy rocked back in the stall and then gave the wall a sharp kick, leaving a crescent indentation in the glossy paneling. Francesca would love that. The mare's lips were tight and her nostrils wrinkled as she blew her nose hard. Margot then grabbed the chain shank and ran it over the mare's nose, sighing and turning to me.

"Well, now, I had no idea. Please hold the shank while I tack her up. Make sure she gives me space and stands quietly."

I nodded. "Got ya."

Margot handed me the whip and the shank.

The mare suddenly stood up tall and whinnied as if she was in dire straits, a total mood change. I then saw Dennis walking up, as if he were coming to Wordy's rescue. I shanked the mare mildly with the chain to try and get her attention. No luck. Margot looked over her shoulder as she finished picking out a hoof.

She sounded exasperated and said with a down turned mouth. "Great."

Dennis looked at the whip and the chain over his horse's nose and frowned, but thankfully refrained from commenting. Wordy focused on Dennis enough that she stopped trying to kill Margot as she finished picking out her hooves. Margot seemed to be avoiding meeting Dennis' eyes and although they greeted each other normally, there was a palpable chill between them. Margot picked up the four polo wraps and headed to the tack room, saying to me on the way, "I'm putting on galloping boots."

That left me standing with Dennis. He cooed to his mare. "How's my sweet princess?" Then he dug out a peppermint. Wordy saw him unwrap it and said, "Ho-ho-ho-ho" in low soft tones.

When Margot squatted down to put on the boots, Wordy pushed into her, almost knocking her over. I would have sliced her one hard, but had to wait until Margot was safely out of the way, and besides, there stood Dennis, seemingly oblivious to what his mare had just done.

Margot stood up quickly and took the whip from my hand. She said, "Get over" and smacked the mare on the side. Wordy was not stupid. The mare jumped over, Margot nodded to me and handed the whip back to me. Dennis stood by silently but I could tell he was shocked. I could also tell that his shock was angering Margot. And, of course, there was something else that was making Margot angry: Sophie.

I helped get Margot on Wordy, and watched her walk quietly around the indoor one lap, and then Margot said to me, "Darling, I've kept you long enough. Please go get your mare."

Dennis had followed us in and sat on the viewing stand. He said cordially, "Yes, indeed. I'm here, Lizzy, you can go."

Dennis did not seem to have a clue that his presence would be of no use to Margot. But I simply said, "Thanks." I understood. Dennis wanted to see his horse go. I also understood that Margot did not want to be inhibited in how she handled Word Perfect by Dennis' presence. And then of course, I could tell that Margot and Dennis had things hanging between them that needed addressing. I was in the way. So, I lingered a bit over tacking up Winsome.

Twenty minutes had passed, and I was about to get on, when Dennis breezed past me. He didn't say goodbye. I stood silently in the barn aisle, and heard his bike start up, and he was gone. Something had transpired. Whether it was good or bad, I couldn't say. I also did not feel I could ask.

I entered the arena to find a beautiful picture. Sweat had bloomed across Word Perfect's neck. As she passed Winsome and me I saw the white lather between her hind legs, that her ears and eyes were in neutral. I could hear Margot say quietly, "Stay with me, mare; stay with me."

They trotted through the corner and Margot set her up for a half pass that started modestly and then grew and grew, finishing in a big sweeping stride. Margot collected the mare, coming alongside me against the rail and making a few steps of piaffe before halting, doing a rein back and then walking forward. She dropped the reins and Word Perfect, amazingly, whinnied low and soft. Margot and I looked at each other, smiling. I said, "That's the oddest horse I've ever known."

Margot nodded in agreement. She rubbed Wordy's neck and said to the mare, "See, it's not so terrible to work for me. You are a strange girl, but we can be friends. You'll see. But you will respect me. Even if you don't like me just yet, you will respect me."

I tiptoed in my question. "Dennis left without saying goodbye."

Margot pressed her lips together, hesitating to answer. Then she said, "I'm afraid we had words."

I just said, "Oh."

"I regret that you had to see that. I know how to ride and train horses. And I know how to train riders. But, darling, I'm afraid that is the extent of my expertise."

I disagreed. "Margot, anyone who can handle Francesca all these years is pretty good at managing people."

Margot's face nearly lost its graceful composure, something I had never witnessed. She looked terribly sad. She said, "Not true. And I feel terrible about it. You, darling, have had to pay the price. When I found out about Johnny Cash, I selfishly let you carry that burden alone. And still we continue to carry out that charade because I am afraid to face what is surely coming. I told Francesca that the horse was inappropriate for her, and yet, I've left you to try and salvage something out of the wreckage for her. Lizzy, that was my burden to sort through, not yours. I've been a coward. I couldn't face Francesca, and I couldn't bear the thought of trying to coach her through what was surely going to be a disaster. Yet, I let you, with so much less experience go through that torture and humiliation, and I suppose if she fails, you will somehow be blamed. It was wrong of me. Can you ever forgive me?"

I felt myself tearing up. I said, "Margot, I've come to love Johnny. In fact, what I've learned from that horse, and from trying to be help to Francesca, you can't get that in any book, or from any riding lesson. The horse is our most important teacher. You taught me that. So, I'm going to go to that horse show next weekend with Francesca and I'm going to do my best, and whatever happens, happens. Even if it's a disaster, you don't need to apologize for anything. I wouldn't have missed the experience for the world."

Margot said nothing, but I saw something in her eyes, something that warmed me from my toes to my cheeks. I changed the subject. "Word Perfect looked wonderful today."

Margot grimaced. "Well, she still tried to kill me in the beginning.

But, she is giving it up quicker each day. Dennis insisted on watching, and his comment was that the trainer's wife was probably right, that the mare will always wedge herself between her human male owner and any other female."

I said, "Could that be true?"

Margot chuckled ruefully, and then said, "Well, a wedge of some sort is certainly becoming apparent to me."

13. Just A Scratch

When I arrived at the Winstons' barn, Francesca's Mercedes was once again sitting in the lot. It was odd to have Francesca beat me to the barn again. I checked my watch. I wasn't running late.

I found her standing outside of Johnny's stall. He was hanging his big white face out of the stall licking the palms of Francesca's cupped hands. And Francesca was uncharacteristically allowing herself to be slobbered on. I greeted Francesca, but she hardly acknowledged me. So, I left her there while I gathered Johnny's tack. I grabbed a carrot and fetched her horse to groom and tack while Francesca watched.

I tried to chit-chat. "Francesca, you should have come to the show."

She sighed, "Sorry. I couldn't get away."

I tried again. "Deb won the class, and Wild Child never looked so good. They are really peaking."

Francesca looked disinterested. She said in her world-weary way, "I suppose that does increase the horse's value."

I tried to ignore that remark, although it stung considerably under the circumstances. Instead I tried a third time. "Can you come tomorrow night, for freestyles? It's always so much fun."

She shook her head. "I'm aiming to come to Devon. We have a box this year. We had to basically wait for someone to die to get it. All that waiting, at considerable expense, too. I intend to use it, even if it's only once."

I added, "Maybe by then Frank will feel up to joining us. I know he'll want to see Emma and Deb compete at Devon. Won't that be something?"

Francesca pursed her lips before answering, and when she did, she was barely audible, muttering as if to herself. "Yes. Truthfully, I wish it were Margot, but yes. I suppose it's time for the girls to step forward instead of always being in Margot's shadow. I suppose its time for Chess, too. It's time. But I don't want the rocking chair just yet and I won't be forced into it. I won't."

I tightened Johnny's girth one hole, wondering what Francesca meant. I put on my helmet and gloves and then led Johnny out of the grooming stall and toward the arena. No one was trying to put Francesca in a rocking chair that I could see, but I suppose some ambitions of Francesca's did have an expiration date. That I did understand.

Francesca trailed after us. I had lost the fear of being in Francesca's presence, which had been replaced with genuine concern for her. Francesca needed her horse therapy. Johnny was her 'art that moved' and his legs were stronger than hers right now. Francesca needed to become lost in the dance and taken away from her troubles. The quicker she was on her horse, the better.

I aimed for a short and sweet warm up ride on Johnny. I did some posting trot and then some basic canter to trot transitions, getting him past some squirrel antics that took Johnny and me both by surprise, but then I jumped off and changed the stirrups. Francesca did not seem to notice that I had cut the ride time down to a new record, eight minutes, or ten minutes tops. In fact, even as I did so, I regretfully thought to myself, that there was no longer any real need for me to sit on him at all.

I said little as Francesca rode, some small suggestions here and there and as much encouragement as I could honestly find to give. When she got off, Johnny got his lipstick kiss. I thought Francesca looked better. I said, "Are you ready for next weekend?"

She countered with, "Are you?"

I answered with a smile, "Is anyone ever?"

Francesca looked amused, but answered honestly, "I suppose not. No. Not really. How can we be? We only die once."

And with that she walked away with her backward wave. Her remark was just plain weird. Next weekend I gave her a fifty-fifty shot at achieving her goal of a USDF Gold rider medal; but as far as I knew, that wasn't a life or death proposition.

Natalie called me on the cell phone and insisted that I walk up the hill to see what she was working on. She had worked such a long day at the horse show that I was surprised at how perky she sounded. I had not had nearly as long a day, but after I finished the dinner chores in the barn, I trudged up the hill on leaden legs finding both Natalie and Deb behind the barn. Deb was sitting in one of her new lawn chairs, beer in hand, a cat in her lap, and a big grin plastered on her face.

When Natalie spotted me she whistled her ear splitting whistle and waved me over, speaking rapidly. "It's not totally done, but I wanted you to see that I did listen to your idea, and because you said Francesca liked her art to move I thought I would try it for Francesca, y'know, as a thank you. It might work as a garden sculpture. They could put it in one of the flowerbeds around their pool or wherever. God, I hope she likes it. Francesca's not easy to please. So, tell me what you think. Do you think she'll like it?"

It was a marvel, a very realistic and highly detailed rabbit partially sculpted out of what appeared to be baling wire. The large ears and legs and tail were not wire, but instead fashioned from some kind of metal sheeting. The eyes were brown glass bits set in a wire frame, and the whiskers were even finer wire. The rabbit was mounted on a flat bit of metal that sat on a stake that had been pushed into the ground.

I said enthusiastically, "Francesca will love it! It's beautiful, Natalie, but do you ever sleep?"

She winked and picked up a piece of poster board. "Sleep is highly over-rated. Now, watch…wait for it."

Natalie maniacally started fanning the sculpture. The front end gradually rose up, the rabbit's front legs unfolding, its chin lifting as if to sniff the breeze. And then it stayed up, now sitting on its haunches. Natalie stopped fanning.

I said, "Oh Natalie, that is brilliant!"

Then Nat ran around to the back of the sculpture and started fanning again. The rabbit tipped forward, lowering to its original position. I clapped my hands and laughed. "That is the coolest thing ever. Francesca's going to love it."

Natalie jumped up and down like a kid and then twirled around doing her own little victory dance and saying, "Yes, yes, yes!"

Deb applauded from her chair.

Natalie said, "I'm telling you, it was a feat of engineering to get it to do that. I couldn't get it right, but when it finally worked, I felt like I had invented the light bulb or something."

Deb added, "And I had a front row seat. I even got to yell 'Eureka' when it finally worked."

I caught her enthusiasm. "Natalie, you could do a grazing horse! It could have grass in its mouth. You could have it pick up its head and then put it back down in the grass. They would sell."

Natalie was still speaking at machine gun speed, "Yeah, yeah, yeah. I thought of that already. But first let me finish this one. The balance and weight is tricky. And I need to make sure the hinges are going to be sturdy enough to last through windy weather without getting trashed. This one is just a prototype, even though I do want Francesca to have it. The whole thing is really just a glorified whirly-gig."

I was still marveling at it. "I've never seen such a realistic whirly-gig.

Beyond whimsical. It's beautiful. When you're ready to give it to Frank and Francesca, I want to come. I want to see it in their landscape. I think they are both going to love it."

Before I headed to bed, I called Chess to tell him about the beautiful "kinetic sculpture" that Natalie had made for his mother and dad. I did not call it a "whirly-gig." Chess sounded genuinely interested. He and I laughed that Natalie was honing her skills by producing pieces for the Cavelli family. It was true. I had a twinge of jealousy. I certainly did not yet have a sculpture by Nat. I had been to the little shop down the road where they were selling her art, and I had admired the fact that Natalie now had a shelf in the shop devoted to her small pieces. When I turned one over and saw the price I was shocked. My only chance to have one would be if Natalie gave me one. The owner told me she wished Natalie would produce them faster because she kept selling out.

Chess told me to let him know when it was "installed" at his parents' house. He and his dad had been chatting about Natalie, and had thought of someone who needed to see her work. Chess had his piece, his dad had his little rabbit, and they had both been asking around and finally had found the right person who wanted to look at her work. It would be important to add the outdoor piece to their "collection" to showcase.

And to think it wasn't so long ago that Natalie had been jobless and homeless, running away as far as she could get from New Jersey. I had always been amused by Natalie; her wit, her unshakeable sense of right and wrong, her willingness to take chances. She would never be among those "weak and timid souls." Natalie was either headed for greatness or an early grave. I felt relieved and convinced it would be the former.

I decided right then and there, I would ask her for a discounted price on a sculpture, perhaps one of her small rabbits. It would be my talisman, something to show to guests years from now, to prove that I had faith, from this little rabbit, that Natalie was the genuine article, a unique artist of great skill and vision who would be able to make art her life. Natalie's art could quite possibly sustain her in more ways than one. That was something.

I wanted to be able to hold one of her little rabbits in my hand, to be able to mentally take myself back to this place and time. I wanted to remember all those real rabbits of Equus Paradiso Farm, and the days when they nibbled peacefully, securely, in the tall bright spring grass.

***

The next day I woke up early. Natalie's enthusiasm had energized me. Ryder was already gone, and I spent a luxurious amount of time hanging out with Wheezer. I poured her a saucer of half and half and watched her lap it up while I drank my coffee. She had gotten lanky and thin and was constantly eating in an attempt to keep up with her growth spurt. I had gotten her some of those little tins of wet kitten food, but they smelled so rank I found them nauseating. So, instead I was supplementing her dry food with people food, like cream and cheese and bits of my dinner. Unlike most cats, she wasn't finicky at all. She ate what she was given, and now had taken to jumping up on the table and inviting herself to share my plate. She was persistent, too. If you put her on the floor she just jumped back up. In short, I had created a monster, but she was my little monster. I put her on my lap and handed her morsels of my bagel, cooing to her, "I have a busy day today, baby girl." She was purring and meowing at the same time. We both were happy girls this morning.

I was filled with happy anticipation because the Grand Prix musical freestyles were tonight, the highlight of the show. The horses would go in the reverse order of their placing, meaning Deb would show last. By then it would be under the lights. Emma had been third, so she would have a good order, too. Though she had been disappointed in her Grand Prix qualifying ride, her freestyle was fantastic. I hoped she would loosen up and be more focused and in sync with her horse. I was certain that Sophie would still be ringside even though she was a volunteer at the show and surely be assigned a job. And of course, Dennis would be there, too. Emma needed to take a deep breath and let it go. I thought of her talking to Tank on her cell phone. Maybe he was able to reset her emotionally. She could do this.

Margot appeared as I groomed Winsome. I had gotten her tacked up, then slipped the halter on over her bridle and left the girth loose so I could help Margot with Wordy.

Today I went ahead and grabbed a whip and put the chain over Word Perfect's nose before we even got started. Margot looked at me and laughed, saying, "Look at you, darling! Are we tacking up a horse or lion taming today?"

I saluted Margot with the whip and Wordy watched me with ears pricked. I said, "I put a ton of sugar cubes in my pocket, too. I saw her watching me load up. I don't think this mare misses a trick."

Margot addressed the mare in the tones of a guidance counselor at a boarding school. "Now Word Perfect, I know you didn't ask to come here, and you didn't choose me. But, I think you will find, in time, that this was a good place to find yourself with plenty of sugar cubes and peppermints coming your way. In turn, we will try our best to understand you. We will try and make you feel safe, and we will provide sweet grass and fresh air, the best hay, grain, and the softest of beds. But in exchange, we do have expectations. We expect you to be a good student who applies herself to her studies. And you WILL respect me."

The mare seemed to be listening. She actually had a pleasant expression on her face. But, it did not last. As soon as Margot put her hand on the mare's right front cannon bone, asking her to pick up her hoof,

Wordy pinned her ears and shook her head in protest. I hit the whip against the ground with a smack and growled, "Maaaare!"

Word Perfect blew her nose aggressively in response, and the dance began, but we got her tacked up without any actual punishments, just a lot of posturing on both sides.

We got to the arena without any signs of Dennis. I said breezily to Margot, "So, no Dennis today?"

Margot muttered with a down turned mouth. "After yesterday, I'm not sure when we'll see him next."

Though I wanted to ask Margot more questions about Dennis, she seemed to regret even saying that much. She deftly changed the subject. "Darling, are you going to be okay next weekend on your own with Francesca?"

I put on a bit of false bravado, in part to ease her mind. "Piece of cake." And then I laughed, and Margot laughed, too.

Later, when I got to the Winston farm, Francesca was again listless and silent, but workmanlike in her riding. Her ambition and desire that had previously created urgency and tension was gone. She now seemed to be in the ride for the ride. Francesca was different, and although the change somehow worried me, I was fully aware this hard knock she was still reeling from had strangely helped her riding.

Johnny was still Johnny. He still worried about the light and shadows, and now the squirrels had started to gather nuts and foolishly bury them in the arena footing. They worked fast and were absorbed in their work, but then almost played "chicken" with us when they made mad and erratic dashes to leave the arena.

I found Johnny's unplanned movements harmless, but expected Francesca to react negatively. But, Francesca no longer clenched the saddle or swore or complained or blamed the horse or me. She kept her seat and her head in a better place and was able to keep riding without worry. That was real progress. The ride finished in a good place.

I arrived at the horse show later than planned. After finishing the evening chores I just had to have a shower, which I accomplished in record time. I jumped into my truck with wet hair and clothes clinging to my damp body.

I checked in at the stalls, but Margot and Emma and Natalie had already left for the warm up arena. Deb was just getting on Wild Child, with Ryder holding onto her loaded bucket with one hand, and the other hand steadying Wild Child at the mounting block. We exchanged greetings, but it was show time now. Everyone had a job to do. That is, everyone except me.

I felt useless following them down to the arena with empty hands. When I got ringside, I found that even Chess had beaten me there.

He turned and beckoned me to come to his side at the arena rail of the warm up. He looked like he belonged there, standing at Margot's side, chatting amiably with Natalie. I know that Natalie liked to tease him, but I also knew that everyone liked him. He had a sense of humor, and he was willing to laugh at himself and play the clown. But Chess was also serious and cared deeply about what we did because it was important to all of us and because he loved his family. He was also an artist, a musician, a master in the kitchen, and just a good, caring man. There was much to love about Chess.

And I did.

I had called him my boyfriend, had said those words out loud to Sophie, and been surprised at myself for proclaiming it. My reasons at the time were not virtuous. I said them to brag. Sophie had traded her place at the farm for a chance at the brass ring with her grab for Dennis and I was rubbing in what I had gained from her defection. But once I said those words, they were released into the world. The Sophie angle seemed unimportant. I felt bold and strangely brave for saying them, but also lighter, relieved. And now, looking at his relaxed smile and tanned face, well, I felt proud again.

I took my place at his side, and his arm lifted and draped over my shoulder just as naturally as the sound of my name rolled naturally off his lips.

His tone was playful. "Late as usual, Lizzy."

I only mildly defended myself. "I had dinner chores. Glad I didn't miss any of our rides. I feel weird not having a job to do here."

Chess smiled, "No worries, I've kept them all in line for you."

We then got quiet and watched as Emma put Fable through his warm up routine. She looked much looser and calmer. The music and the applause from the main arena were beginning to get to me, making me nervous. There was a good-sized crowd tonight. Freestyle night was exciting for the spectators, and tonight there was a wine and cheese party and tables set out around the sides of the arena for sponsors and competitors. The bleachers looked mostly full. It was good preparation for Devon, which would be much bigger. I did not envy either Emma or Deb when I thought about what show nerves Devon could produce.

I whispered to Chess. "I wish your mom and dad were here."

Chess took his arm off of my shoulders and instead took my hand, lacing his fingers through mine. He said, "Can we go sit in the bleachers?"

I looked at Emma, and then at Margot's back as she focused intently on her student. Then I glanced over at Natalie, her arms crossed over her chest, her bucket of supplies on the ground. Ryder had taken up her post right next to Natalie, while Deb was now walking Wild Child around in the warm up arena. I had to admit, there was no reason why Chess and I couldn't go find seats on the hard bleachers. I nodded. And we quietly slipped away, hand in hand.

Chess and I waited for the horse and rider to finish their test to River Dance music, and then climbed to the top of the bleachers where no one else seemed to want to sit. It was actually a very good seat. I asked to borrow a program from someone sitting in front of us; two more horses to go before Emma. I thanked them and handed it back.

Chess leaned close and whispered. "Was Mother okay today?"

I reflexively answered. "Yeah. Why?"

Chess sighed. "She and Dad have been at war."

I was silent for a moment. "Actually, now that I think of it, she said some strange things. She always kind of ignores me, but she seemed distracted both yesterday and today."

Chess frowned but said nothing. His wheels were turning. I asked. "What is it?"

Chess said, "This is for your ears only, okay?"

I froze in my seat, almost holding my breath. I whispered. "You're scaring me."

He lowered his head and his voice. "I walked into Dad's home office looking for him today. He was sitting behind his desk and Mother was in there, shaking a paper in his face, and she was mad. They both shut up when I came into the room. Dad grabbed the papers from Mother and stuffed them into his desk drawer. Then they changed the subject to talk to me about an upcoming meeting at Cavelli Foods with our lawyer and the 'families.' I didn't ask, and they didn't say what their fight was about."

I latched onto the positive shred from that scene, and did my best rationalization. "I'm so glad that you are getting involved in the problems at Cavelli Foods. Your dad is too, he said as much to me. It's going to make all the difference. But your mother isn't as easy a sell on anything. And I can't even imagine all the 'I told you so's' that your dad has heard. I'm sure there will be lots of tension until things get better. And then of course, your mom hasn't been exactly upfront on what she's done with High Horse Couture's money and all, so he's got his own reasons he could be angry with her."

Chess and I were almost whispering into each other's ears at this point. Another rider had started their freestyle and it seemed rude to talk during the performance. But, I honestly couldn't focus. Chess still frowned in a way that said he didn't agree. He loved his dad, and his relationship with his mother clearly had its problems, but he often took her side.

We watched the rest of a routine to music by the Rolling Stones. The horse and rider unfortunately had let show nerves get to them, so there were too many mistakes despite some great musical arrangement and choreography. At the final salute, we could see Emma at the in-gate, gathering her reins and herself, and then she and Fable bounded into the arena. My heart started thudding in my chest. I could imme-diately tell that Emma was going to go for it tonight. I reached over and grabbed Chess' hand, still staring at Emma and gave it a squeeze, exclaiming, "Doesn't she look great!"

He agreed. "Yes, she does, of course she does."

I glanced at Chess to find that he wasn't looking at Emma, but instead at me. He grabbed my hand back, once again lacing his fingers in mine and squeezing. But I had to pull my hand away, and cross the fingers of both hands, pressing them to my lips and holding them there. The bell rang and Emma halted and lifted her arm. The announcer said, "Emma, your music is rolling."

The music began and Emma passaged into the arena to *Blue Eyes Crying in the Rain* halting squarely and right on the beat with a short and snappy salute. Then she cantered off to *Yellow Rose of Texas*, a killer start.

I still had my fingers crossed and pressed to my lips. I wanted this for Emma. I wanted it badly. I glanced around at the people across the arena, sitting at tables and drinking wine and nibbling on appetizers, all eyes on Emma and Fable. The medley of Texas tunes was seamless and Fable wasn't putting a foot wrong. They finished the canter tour, and walked to *Luchenbach Texas* then went into the trot tour dancing to *Deep in the Heart of Texas*, accented by clapping. And then it happened, the music stopped. And then the clapping began again. And then it stopped, and then the clapping bit replayed once again. I felt the blood drain from my face. Emma soldiered on even after the CD had gone totally silent. She finished in silence with a halt and salute to the judges. The audience was stunned, and there was a long beat of silence before everyone began to applaud.

Emma simply shrugged, looking up into the announcer's booth with a puzzled look on her face. The announcer said; "I am so sorry, Emma. I don't know what happened." Then the judge sitting behind "C" who was always the head of the 'ground jury' waved Emma over. The other judges got out of their boxes and there was a short group discussion. Emma walked out of the arena with a brave face, but I knew she was devastated. There would be no re-ride. How could there be? Fable and Emma had completed the test. I don't think Emma would have wanted one anyway since Fable was spent.

I was eager to get up and check on Emma, but Chess held me back. He touched my elbow and said, "We need to stay to watch Deb. Besides, I know Emma well enough to say she will need some space right now."

Chess was right. I slumped in my seat, elbows on my knees, and chin in my hand. "She has Natalie right now, and Natalie will calm her down. Still, I don't get it. That CD has never skipped before. They even do a sound check at lunch break with all the CDs."

Chess replied, "It's just bad luck. The CD somehow got scratched. I'm not surprised, seeing as it probably has been over-handled by people working in and around horses and barns, you know, with dirty hands."

For some reason Chess' comment rubbed me the wrong way. But all I could say was, "Maybe."

We both spotted Deb and Wild Child at the in gate. They were gathered and attentive, waiting for the moment when they could enter. Chess and I hardly noticed the Canadian rider in the arena, whose music was forgettable, even if his horse was impressive. I found myself impatient for him to finish so Deb and Wild Child could begin.

The arena lights had been on, but were hardly noticeable until now as the sun dropped behind the horizon. It only made Wild Child more impressive. His chestnut coat, always bright orange and shining with health had that special glow that seemed to be part of being a stallion. It flashed an undercoat of gold that moved as he moved, around his taut and flexing and relaxing muscles. He was a vision.

I re-crossed my fingers and placed them back on my lips, but I felt far less nervous. Deb didn't need luck. I felt myself inhale and exhale and let go of the tension in my belly. The bell rang; Deb halted and lifted her arm. The announcer said, "Deb, your music is rolling." And the dance began.

No one over in the peanut gallery made any noise. They were as absorbed as I was. Wild Child was both relaxed and powerful. Deb was deeply focused, but at the same time, I could see a faint smile on her face. She was enjoying herself. That was something. That was Deb. I swear she had the heart and soul of Obi-Wan-Kenobi. I knew that I could never be that mentally and emotionally strong, that relaxed and confident. Deb owned this ride. Every step was hers on this cheeky and lazy stallion that was giving her his best effort.

The audience and the judges held no terror for Deb. Her joy did not depend on their judgments. She was on a wild ride and was damned determined to savor it while it lasted, because nothing in this world could last forever. Horses and humans were mortal, and to do this sport at this level, well, it was a privilege afforded few riders. Deb got it. All those thoughts made me begin to cry. I had tears running down my face. They were partly tears of joy; joy for Deb, joy for Margot, joy for all of Equus Paradiso Farm. But, they were also tears of grief because all of it was fragile and mortal and would be lost, maybe later, or maybe all too soon.

The applause at her final salute was thunderous. Chess felt it too, and gave me a hearty hug, followed by laughter when he saw my tears.

Deb had, of course, won by a good margin and her all-time highest score. There would now be an awards ceremony with lots of fanfare.

All the horses were being gathered outside the gate. Chess and I joined our gang. Margot was holding onto Wild Child while Ryder applied glowing white polo wraps and sparkling white bell boots. Wild Child's bell boots had tiny crystals set along the top, and now under the lights they sparkled. He would literally have "twinkle-toes" for his victory lap of honor.

Emma had pulled herself together, and she and Fable looked beautiful. Fable stood tall and proud as Natalie sweet-talked him and fed him sugar cubes. I walked over to tell Emma how wonderful they both looked and what a great job they had done and was still there when they came to put his ribbon on.

Unfortunately, Sophie was the volunteer putting the ribbons on the horses before they entered for the ceremony. She was accompanied by a child holding the cardboard hanger full of ribbons. Fable had dropped from third to fifth, which in the big scheme of things is simply the color of the ribbon. The real wound was in the regret of what "should have been." But, it was done. Emma had Devon in front of her.

Sophie pinned the ribbon on Fable's brow band, and then carefully wrapped the streamers around his throatlatch. She looked up at Emma and said, "Tough luck, Emma."

Emma looked back at her and said in a cool, matter of fact voice, "Was it?"

I saw color rush into Sophie's face. She said nothing. As if she had not heard, she simply stepped over to the next horse waiting for its ribbon. When she got to Deb, she placed a lovely neck sash around the horse's neck. Sophie reached up and stroked Wild Child on his face, something he would never have allowed had he not been held by Margot and controlled by Deb. Ryder stood slightly aside, scowling. But, then Ryder was often scowling.

247

Margot's face was inscrutable. If Sophie was going to stay in the area, I suppose we would all need to get used to seeing her around. Slow, dramatic music began to play, and the horses, last to first, came in and lined up in the arena. The announcer gave each horse and rider's name, and the "ground jury", consisting of all of the judges, shook the hand of each rider and posed for photos. For the top four horses there were small checks along with the handshakes. Deb not only got a check, but a nice silver platter, and her name would be etched on a beautiful and large perpetual trophy. It made for a photo to hang on the wall in Deb's cottage, with a copy in the office. I wished at that moment to be able to share it with Frank and Francesca. I knew there would be a videoed version. But watching on tape was never the same experience.

The music changed, and Deb led off the line in a fairly controlled gallop. But once the other riders peeled off she gave Wild Child a big kick and they flew down one long side. The announcer changed the music to *The Blacksmith's Song*, a traditional award ceremony piece that featured the sound of a blacksmith's hammer in the background. The audience started to clap along with the rhythmic clanging sound of the smithy's hammer. Wild Child did a barely controlled passage, and a brilliant bit of piaffe. Then Deb let him go into an extended trot that broke into a gallop. They flew past the out gate and now Deb was having trouble pulling him up, but she did finally, laughing and showing off her deep dimples in her cheeks as she waved good-bye and passaged out of the arena. Tonight Deb did not show off Wild Child's one trick of performing a bow. Instead, Ryder literally leapt into their path and grabbed Wild Child by a rein, trotting by his side as they headed back to the barns.

The stands were emptying, but music still played over the PA. I looked up into the announcer's booth and then grabbed Chess by the hand. "We should go pick up the CDs for Deb and Emma from the announcer."

Chess tipped his head and narrowed his eyes. He knew I was still upset about Emma's messed up music. "Should we be the ones to do that?"

I pulled at his hand. "Please. I'll be polite and promise not to embarrass you."

He didn't answer me, but even though he let go of my hand, he followed me. We swam against the tide of exiting spectators to the stairs to the announcer's booth. I started up the airy metal staircase and Chess stopped at the bottom. I turned around and silently gestured for him to follow. He looked uncomfortable, but he followed.

I stopped at the first landing to let Chess catch up to me. Even the floor was metal and had the texture of a cheese-grater. It felt insubstantial. We climbed the second set and stopped at the doorway of the booth. I did a light "knock-knock" on the doorframe. The announcer was busy reading from a printed list, thanking sponsors and volunteers over the soft instrumental background music, but he turned and smiled and held up a finger to show me that he would only be "one moment."

He soon put the list down and swiveled around in his chair, saying brightly, "Hi there!"

I recognized his face and his name popped into my head. "Hi, Jimmy, I've come from Equus Paradiso Farm to pick up Deb's CD for Wild Child, and Emma's CD for Fable."

He spun his chair back around and pulled a CD storage box toward the front of his desk. "Sure, sure. But, listen, I just feel awful for Emma, please let her know that. I don't know how that CD got scratched. I was careful with all of them."

Chess stepped forward. "Do you mind if I take a look at it?"

He shook his head. "No, of course not. Weird thing, I always examine every CD when we do the sound check at noon. It looked fine then as far as I can recall, and there weren't any skips. Then I put it into the storage box along with the rest of them, safe and secure, and don't handle them again until the ride."

He flipped open the box and pulled out two CDs and held them out. They were in their plastic covers. Chess took them, and handed me Deb's. Then he opened the cover and handled Emma's CD carefully by the edges. He held it up to the light, tipped it at an angle, and frowned. He said, "Yeah, there's a fine scratch, it's easy to see in the light. On a CD that fine scratch might as well be as wide as the Grand Canyon."

Jimmy nodded. "I saw it clear as day, too, after I took it out of the player when it messed up."

I said, "And no one comes up here but you?"

He nodded and replied, "No one but me and the volunteers."

Chess said, "That's good to know, right, Lizzy?" He looked at me with eyes that said 'careful.'

I added, "Of course. You wouldn't want a bunch of background noise messing up your announcing."

He added with a smile. "Well, you couldn't hold much of a crowd up here in this bird's nest anyway. But without a volunteer coming up to hand me stuff to announce every so often, I'd get downright lonely."

I smiled, and asked, "Don't they let you out of this booth all weekend?"

Jimmy laughed. "Not for long. I get the same breaks that the show gets, the same ones printed in the program. When the judges get to eat and go to the bathroom, that's when I get to go, too. Though I eat down at the hospitality tent so I won't have to wait in food lines."

I wanted to ask more questions, but Chess had carefully put the CD back in its case and now had his hand lightly cupped around my elbow.

I made my farewells. "Thanks for all your hard work, Jimmy. You really helped keep the energy up."

He seemed pleased. "Sure thing," and started to shut things down.

But he turned and said one more time. "You tell Emma again for me how sorry I am, okay?"

"I will." Chess and I turned and started back down the airy metal staircase. He kept his hand lightly on my elbow on the flimsy feeling stairs all the way to the terra-firma.

We walked silently back to the barns. Alfonso was there and everyone was working to get the horses packed and loaded. I stashed the CDs in my pocketbook, and Chess and I rolled up our sleeves and joined in. Nothing was put in the trailer in any kind of order, we were in 'go' mode and organization could wait. Emma was unhappy at the mess, but she was no longer in control. Ryder and Natalie were running loads out, and their goal was to get the horses home as fast as possible. Deb and Emma were still in their show whites, and Margot fussed over their clothes, trying to get them to change.

Deb was having none of it. She finally put her hands on Margot's shoulders and smiled her great dimpled smile, looking intently into Margot's eyes. "I'm still flying high, Margot. I don't care if these breeches have to soak in bleach for three days to get out the stains, okay? I'm going to help tote and carry and see our hunky stallion safely back to his stall at home. I hope he rests up tomorrow and gets good and dirty and stuffs himself on grass. I may just sit and drink beer all day tomorrow myself."

Deb and Margot hugged for a nice long beat. Margot then shooed her away with shining eyes and turned back to zipping Deb's tailcoat into a bag. She loaded her arms with both the girls' coat bags, and then took both boot bags in her other hand. She then announced to the air. "Okay darlings, I have all of your coats and boots. They're going back in my car. I will see you at the farm."

I got back into the parade to load the trailer. The tack room drapes and banner came down, the little planters with their fake bushes got stowed, hook-eyes were unscrewed from walls. Buckets got dumped and nested.

Muck stuff was thrown into the bed of the truck, still dirty, Emma wrinkling her nose at the sight. Soon it was just the two stallions, braids pulled out, manes standing up in wavy curls, shipping boots on, standing bright eyed and alert. They knew they were done and that they, too, needed to be 'packed.' They had to be tired, but they were both too proud to show it.

Alfonso took Wild Child, and Natalie took Fable. Emma had Uno tucked against her body as we watched the two boys eagerly load up. Once in their spots in the trailer, Wild Child bellowed his farewells, and an assortment of horses answered him from the barns. Fable kept his ears pricked, but stayed silent. The two stallions had worked out a sort of peace between them. It seemed that Fable looked up to the older stallion with deference. He had allowed Wild Child to do all the 'speaking.'

As the ramps came up and Alfonso started up the truck and pulled away, Ryder threw her backpack over her shoulder, "I'm out of here. See you at home."

I said, "Yeah, right behind you, Ryder."

We four watched her walk toward the parking lot. I felt Emma deflate next to me.

My pocket book was now hanging off my shoulder. I pulled out her CD and handed it to her. She opened her mouth. "Oh my God. Thanks for picking this up. I totally forgot."

Then I tapped Deb on the shoulder. "Yeah, here's yours, Deb."

She nodded. "Thanks, Lizzy."

Deb looked at Chess. "So, what do you think happened?"

But Emma interrupted. "Deb and I have a good idea of what happened."

Deb frowned. "Maybe, Blondie. Maybe we're wrong though."

Natalie joined in. "Nah. I think you guys are probably right. The way she's been watching Wild Child all weekend, I could see a little green monster sitting on her shoulder. She's been orbiting around Dennis, too."

Emma exhaled. "Sophie blames me for her not getting Wild Child."

I added, "Uh, Emma, it *was* you, with Frank's help."

"She couldn't have ridden him. She couldn't even have handled him on the ground."

I said, "Emma, when I first met Sophie, you told me she was evil. Is she really that evil?"

Emma almost snorted, "She betrayed Margot! She stole Dennis from Margot. Then she was going to swoop in and take Wild Child from Ben. She's always lurking around waiting for an advantage."

I raised my eyebrows. "Wait, isn't that what we did? We swooped in and got Wild Child, didn't we?"

Emma stared at me, "Totally not the same thing. We *saved* Wild Child. Ben even thanked me for it."

Chess looked appalled. "What are you guys saying here? Do you really think Sophie went into the announcer's booth and purposely scratched Emma's CD for revenge? Isn't that kind of farfetched?"

Natalie raised her eyebrows, "I did see that big diamond ring on her finger. All she'd have to do is make a little swipe. I know her type, yeah, I bet she did it."

Then Emma mumbled. "Bet she hasn't figured out yet that it's not a real diamond. It's CZ for sure."

Deb laughed. "Whoa Blondie, whoa; like that even matters."

We stood rooted to the ground staring at each other, watching as weariness began to take the place of nerves. Finally Nat spoke up.

"Don't you think Alfonso is going to wonder where the hell we are when he's ready to unload the stallions?"

It worked. We dispersed as if hit by an invisible blast of air, scattering us to the parking lot, to start our engines and turn on our headlights, and make a line of vehicles heading to the farm; to our anchor; our home; where the horses were.

14. Weenies And Warriors

It was no secret at the barn that I was showing Winsome at the Hill and Dale show, and that I would be taking Francesca and Johnny Cash. Of course Francesca wasn't to know that, but she hadn't been coming out to ride Lovey so no one had to pretend around her.

The barn felt incomplete without Francesca. Her minions, Chopper and Snapper, were forever causing problems, but I missed them, too. I knew those little guys must have been going stir-crazy cooped up at her house. Those terriers loved to hunt in the fields, startle the horses, and terrorize any cat they could stir up. They also loved to have their tummies rubbed and ears scratched and to curl up in Francesca's expensive upholstered chairs in her office. The smooth coated one, Snapper, seemed to leave his hair everywhere and it had become impossibly woven right into the fabric, as stubborn as the dog it had once been a part of.

Although I had been pleased about Francesca's rides on Johnny Cash, by Thursday Francesca's quiet determination had given way to visible show nerves. When she dismounted, she turned to me, pulled off her gloves, and took a deep breath before speaking. She said, "Did you see the weather forecast?"

I nodded back. "I did."

She frowned. "Non-stop rain beginning tonight. They're even call-ing for thunderstorms."

I replied flippantly. "Well, I guess we'll be getting wet then."

Francesca looked taken aback. Then she muttered, "I do not intend to look like a drowned rat all weekend."

I opened my mouth and my shoulders drooped in exasperation. "Francesca, I'd sure like to know how you plan on arranging that. I mean if the rain comes, we are going to get wet. It happens."

Francesca replied, "Who says I have to ride in those kind of condi-tions? I can always scratch."

I was stunned for a moment, and then my voice rose, despite my wanting to not turn up the volume, "You made Margot ride Hotstuff in those conditions two times!"

Francesca's face was as dark as the gathering thunderclouds above us. All I had done was make her defensive. But then lightning struck, well not real lightning. I stood up taller and giggled. And then I had to work to control my giggle-fit, because I had cracked myself up. Franc-esca's face lightened. If nothing else, at least she was intrigued by my fit. I finally said, "Oh my God, Francesca, I just realized, this is a gift from God. You are about to reject an absolute gift from God!"

Francesca, smoothing down her hair and looking suspicious, said, "Whatever are you cackling about?"

"Francesca, you scratched last time because it was sunny, and the sun was casting shadows. This time there will be NO sun, NO shadows. Now, you want to scratch because you might get wet? God is answering your prayers, even if it isn't exactly how you imagined it. You'd better not reject what He's giving you. Rain is uncomfortable, not life threatening. Deb calls horse showing 'the wild ride.' You get on board and take the ride. It's not life or death, Francesca. It's a horse show. And you want to know what else?"

I could sense she didn't want to ask, but couldn't contain her curi-osity. "What?"

"Rain and mud and muck can screw up even the best rides and riders. It's a no-lose proposition for you. If you do well, then you've overcome bad conditions. And if it doesn't go well . . ." My voice trailed off.

"Then again, the conditions." She finished the sentence and thought for a moment. "You know, maybe a show in the harsh elements would be quite a ride."

I continued, "Francesca, we are going, and we are riding. I don't care if we have to wear scuba masks and floaties."

"That certainly won't be the case." She noted my quizzical expression. "High Horse Couture doesn't carry a line of scuba masks and floaties." She tried to keep her face a mask, but couldn't hold back a thin smile, and for a moment I saw her as an impish teenager. "That was a pretty good one, wasn't it?"

I laughed aloud. "Damn good."

She waited a beat and then asked, "What time can you pick us up tomorrow? We have some riding to do."

I grinned, feeling like I had just won a victory. Francesca wasn't going to weasel out of this. I would get that woman through two Grand Prix tests if it killed me.

"I'll be here no later than noon. I'll pack up Johnny tonight and leave all his stuff in a pile so Winsome won't have to stand on the trailer too long when I pick him up. Remember all your tack has to go in your car. There's no tack room in my trailer."

Francesca, no longer the teenage imp, sniffed, "How could I possibly forget?"

That night I loaded up all of Winsome's tack in my truck. I borrowed the farm's zippered canvas hay bags, but since it was already raining, I didn't put it in the bed of the truck to get wet overnight. The rain started gently enough, and I tossed and turned all through the night, playing out scenes of success and of failure as I listened to the faint sound of the rain on my one bedroom window.

By morning it was coming down steadily. I helped Margot with Word Perfect and rode Lovey, but I felt edgy throughout the morning. I asked Margot's permission to borrow some rubber reins. I was going to have a very wet weekend, and my leather reins would be too slick and difficult to grip.

I had a good raincoat, but just in hooking up the trailer the rain ran down my raincoat and drenched my breeches. Winsome loaded right up, seemingly content to get inside her familiar trailer that was mostly rainproof. There were a few spots where the roofline met the sides where water trickled down the interior walls, but she didn't seem to mind. My truck and trailer were no things of beauty but they were serviceable and I owned them outright. I wondered briefly if I would ever have a shiny new truck and trailer, the kind that graced the parking lots of all the big shows. It was something that other people had, not me. I allowed myself a moment of self-pity and then got back to work.

When I arrived at the Winstons' barn, Francesca's Mercedes was pulled right up to the edge of the barn on the gravel path and she was putting things in the trunk. I was surprised and happy to see her toting anything. Francesca was laboring instead of just supervising. I helped her get the last bits into the car, and then carted her hay and Tupperware tub of grain out into the steady rain, and loaded them into my truck bed. I got Johnny into his shipping boots and then recited Johnny's packing list with Francesca, just to be sure nothing was left behind. It was time.

I led Johnny out to the trailer, the rain sheeting off my raincoat and running down my legs, and even finding its way down into my rubber boots. Francesca followed me out in her Mercedes, and then was forced out into the rain to help load. I recognized the expensive brand names of her glossy floral print rubber boots and her long raincoat with the tailored waistline. She had made a determined effort to dress like a model for rain wear. She had pulled up the hood, but I thought that resistance was futile. She seemed to be afraid of getting wet, but I knew she would be drenched before the day was out. Yet, I wished I had snugger boots and a longer raincoat. The water was beginning to seep down further into my boots, my socks providing a wick that soaked up the moisture.

I made her hold her horse while I lowered the ramp. Winsome, who had been pawing impatiently in the left side of the trailer, twisted her neck and peered out of her right eye to get a good look at her traveling companion. She made an inviting low whinny, a polite "how-de-do." I took Johnny from Francesca and was giving her instructions on putting up the butt-bar and lost focus of Johnny for a moment. Johnny made a fatal error; he shoved his nose into Winsome's private area under her tail, a faux pas for sure but my fault for letting it happen.

Of course, all hell broke out in an instant. Winsome squealed like a stuck pig and lashed out with both hind legs. Luckily those steel clad hooves only met air as Johnny flew backwards as I clung to the lead rope, but he dragged me half way back to the stables before I got him stopped. Winsome had told him off, and he was wary about getting anywhere near her again. I was able to slowly coax him back to the bottom of the ramp of the trailer.

Winsome had made her point. Johnny was now scared to death of getting on the trailer. I had to get a whip out of the truck and have Francesca keep it lightly touching Winsome's butt while I sweet talked Johnny into following me up the ramp. Meanwhile, the rain beat down. I had collected a puddle in the toe box of both rubber boots. Francesca looked annoyed, but I suspect she was still bone dry under all that rain gear.

Francesca followed right behind the trailer on the short drive to Hill and Dale. At every stop sign and light I felt Winsome's pawing rock the trailer. She was not going to forgive and forget, and poor Johnny had nowhere to go to get away from her. Of course, they had a partition between their heads and a partial partition between the two stalls. They also had their legs covered with thick shipping boots. But mentally, I acknowledged that Winsome was likely terrorizing Johnny.

The rain wasn't letting up, and although it was mid day, it was dark as dusk. I pulled as close to the show stabling as I could. We still needed to set up our stalls. I sure could have used Alfonso. But, I also wanted to get the horses off the trailer as soon as I could. I made the executive decision to get the horses off first.

Francesca parked nearby, and then ran to get under the cover of the barn. I put on the brake, and then jumped out to put the ramp down in the relentless rain. The ramp hit the ground with a splash. My boots sank as I stood there. The ground had turned into a liquid slurry of sand and manure and water, mostly water. I had not picked the best spot to unload, that was rapidly becoming clear. The trailer rocked even harder as Winsome pawed vigorously. Johnny was pressed as far away from my tyrant mare as he could get.

Then I realized it was not by choice. Somehow Winsome had un-hooked the partition between their heads and had pushed it over toward Johnny, giving herself all of the head room. I climbed in Johnny's escape door and pushed it back to center. I then saw that Winsome had been grabbing at Johnny's canvas hay bag, tearing it with her teeth. Poor Johnny was trembling.

I stepped back out to yell at Francesca. "I need you to undo the butt bar, but don't do it until I say to, okay? And stay clear of Winsome's heels. I don't want you to get kicked. Catch Johnny on the way out, and then I can get Winsome out by myself. She and I have a routine." I didn't tell Francesca that my mare had been harassing her big weenie for the entire fifteen minute ride.

Francesca stepped up the ramp warily, keeping one eye on Winsome's hind end. The rain pounded the metal roof of my trailer, so I hollered, "Go ahead, Francesca, do it quietly and I'll try and make him wait until you get safely back to the bottom of the ramp."

I was feeling guilty about how I let Johnny get out of my control back at the Winstons'. I was not going to let him rush backwards if I could help it. I wanted Francesca to be safe. She unpinned the butt bar stealthily while I put a hand behind Johnny's eye to keep him from seeing the bar drop. He still flinched, but I managed to make him wait while I watched Francesca position herself at the bottom of the ramp, standing in her glossy floral boots in a deep puddle, a grim expression on her face. I ducked under the chest bar and was able to get the first few steps to stay controlled. Johnny rushed the final steps, but I saw Francesca catch hold of the lead rope as he got all four legs off the ramp. Success! We had made the hand off.

If Johnny had just stopped there, it would have been great. But Winsome squealed and did a little buck, confined by the limited space of her trailer stall. The trailer rocked, and Johnny sat back onto his haunches, startled and afraid, making a modest rear before swiveling and charging into the barns. I couldn't blame him for wanting to put some distance between himself and the angry red headed mare.

Francesca hung on and managed to head into the stables with him, but her glossy floral print rubber boots didn't quite make the trip. There they stood, tipped over and stuck in the mud puddle, the water now finding a new level within the boots. Johnny must have lifted her half way out of her boots with the rear, and then they had tipped over as Francesca had been yanked out of them.

My own horse was now whinnying and demanding my attention. So, I ran the chain over her nose, tied the lead rope around her neck, unclipped the trailer tie, and then walked around the back and undid her butt bar. She very carefully stepped back until her head was clear and then stopped on the ramp to have a look around. I swear I could hear her thoughts. She didn't see Johnny Cash anywhere, and she was thinking, *good, I taught that one to mind his manners.*

I found Francesca standing in her wet and muddy socks, holding Johnny Cash in front of our stalls. She looked pissed, and yet it wasn't about her muddy feet. She said, "Our stalls aren't bedded! What am I supposed to do here?"

Now it was my turn to be annoyed. "Francesca, we just got here. How was I supposed to bed the stalls?"

She looked confused and I realized she had little to no experience taking care of her own horse at a show. I barked at her. "The show management isn't going to bed them for you, Francesca."

I expected her to retort but she was silent.

I put Winsome in her empty stall, even though it still had bags of shavings stacked in the middle of it. She didn't care. She was too busy doing her routine where she reared to look over the top of the stalls to check out her neighbors. Johnny was actually being very good as he stood in the aisle, but I worried about Francesca's unclad toes getting stepped on. And then, typical of Francesca, she said, "Hurry up and take this horse from me. I don't want anyone stealing my boots. They were a limited edition design. You can't find them in the catalogues anymore."

I ripped open the bags of shavings in Johnny's stall and then took Johnny from Francesca, watching her walk daintily in her stocking feet back to the trailer to retrieve her special glossy, limited edition floral print designer rubber boots. This was going to be a long weekend, and I wasn't going to let Francesca preside like a princess with me her serf. No way. I led Johnny into the stall and showed him the mound of shavings. He immediately pawed at them and blew into them, making me rush out of the stall to let him roll. I would need to get the muck fork unloaded to spread them in the stall, but he was getting that project started for me.

It took forever, but I finally got both horses set up, and the contents of our truck and car unloaded into our muck cart and dumped in front of our stalls. I put Francesca in charge of setting up our tack room, and she went to work without resistance. We had kept it to a bare minimum. There would be no rug, no stall curtains or drapes or banners to announce our farm. We had a saddle rack each, a brush box, a laundry bag full of pads and boots, and our hay and grain and a plastic mounting block. We shared one bridle rack. We each had a coat bag and a boot bag. But, still, it was a lot of work.

I went to park the trailer in the field marked for show parking. In all that time, the rain never stopped. It got lighter and darker, heavy and misty-light, but it didn't stop. The outdoor arenas had that sheen across them that indicated saturated footing. Luckily, Hill and Dale had a covered arena, and all the horses at the show today would be crowded inside it to do their warm ups, with the rest of the arenas devoid of a single hoof print of activity.

Francesca picked up our show packets. It was time to start riding, and of course, I was already exhausted. My wet socks had worked their way down into my rubber boots and were clinging to my heel. I peeled them off, squeezed the water out and regretfully put them back on. They were cold and stretched out and immediately started sliding down my ankles.

I made Francesca go first. Johnny got his fake tail put in, but other than that I barely bothered to groom. By the time I walked alongside Francesca to the covered arena, he was soaked and had splashed mud onto his white patent leather boots and shiny bell boots that had crystals inlaid, just like the ones that Wild Child has worn last weekend. Francesca had on her long rain coat with the tailored waist. I realized it had been made for riding, as it fanned stylishly over her thighs, keeping them dry. It was flattering on her slender silhouette.

We joined a large crowd in the covered arena. The show had removed some of the arena boards so that riders could ride in and out of the dressage arena more easily, avoiding a bottleneck. Johnny was up and alert and a little bug-eyed. Francesca looked apprehensive. She looked down at me and said, "Lead me in."

I grabbed a rein, but didn't really need to. I said, "He's going to be fine, Francesca. This is good practice. You have to practice your courage just like anything else if you want to be good at it."

I thought that sounded like great advice, even a bit like Deb. To Francesca it was a presumptuous thing to say. She practically snarled at me, "And what would you know about such things?" But, she put her leg on and marched into the arena without me. I heard her mutter as she moved away, "I've had more than my fair share of courage practice lately."

While Francesca's comment stung, I tried to set it aside, and watch her ride. She was right, and I felt bad about my presumptive comment. She had been through Frank's near-death, and all of the business problems with the farm and Cavelli Foods. What I'd meant was riding-courage.

Francesca's face had an angry expression. But, maybe that wasn't fair. I think she was trying her best to concentrate among the chaos. Francesca was not used to riding with so many horses in the arena at once. Warm up arenas were always challenging when they got crowded, but this was much more crowded than what we were used to handling.

Johnny was nervous. And I was right, in that it was time for Francesca to practice courage as a rider and take that big horse "in hand." She didn't need to let that weenie make the decisions. If she did, his decision would probably be to turn and run all the way back to his stall.

I crossed my arms and kept my eyes on Francesca and Johnny, as if that could help should things go wrong, which of course it couldn't. Francesca had to do the riding.

Each time she went past I gave her a word or two. The first pass I said, "Shorten your reins." The second time I said. "Ride forward."

After a couple of abrupt transitions when someone cut her off, I said. "Claim your line of travel."

The next time I said, "Not so restrained or you'll create a ticking time bomb."

The next time around I said, "Take the outside line and move it."

Francesca's eyes shot me a death ray. She was pissed. I was only trying to channel Deb. The boundary I was supposed to observe had once again been crossed. The next time she came past I said nothing. But, I was smiling inwardly because it appeared that Francesca had actually listened. She was taking charge. She had set her jaw, found a line of travel and claimed it.

I uncrossed my arms and relaxed. Francesca had this. A woman I didn't know came over to me, touched my arm, and said, "Tell Francesca how glad we are to see her. I was so sorry to hear about Frank."

I replied, "He's doing much better;" although, I didn't really believe it myself.

The woman replied. "Well, that's good news." Then she waved at Francesca as she rode past and yelled out, "Francesca, you are riding beautifully, my dear!"

Francesca nodded in acknowledgement and then refocused, and I was happy to see that she no longer looked angry. She had a look of quiet determination. When she finished, she came out into the rain, and we silently marched side by side back to the barns. When she slid off the horse her knees buckled slightly. She looked shaky. I pretended that I hadn't noticed, and said, "You did a great job out there, Francesca."

She nodded, and then sat down on our mounting block, not even checking first to see if it was clean. She pulled off her helmet, then pulled off her gloves. Then she looked directly into my eyes and said, "Now it's your turn to go out there and practice your courage."

She was right. Winsome would be much more of a challenge in there than Johnny Cash, but for different reasons. My mare would not like having all those horses getting into her personal space. I would need to be careful or she could kick out and hurt someone's horse.

Of course I had to put up Johnny with no help from Francesca, then tack up my antsy mare who could hardly stand still. I was wet through and through. I put Margot's rubber reins on my bridle. Francesca had disappeared and I had no one to hang onto Winsome when I mounted. But when I made it down to the arena on my prancing mare, Francesca stood at the gate, holding a large umbrella. She wore totally different clothes, a different raincoat, and a pair of tan slacks tucked into her glossy rubber boots. She had clearly undergone a clean up. She must have packed a change of clothes. Why hadn't I thought of that?

The indoor arena was even more crowded than it had been for Francesca. Rain still came down, though perhaps not quite as hard. I stepped into the covered arena, but Winsome let me know that it was a bad idea. A horse passed us on our left. It cantered by, breathing loudly, a massive animal. Winsome sank toward the ground, her legs trembling, then bounced up and scampered sideways against the railing, lashing out with a hind leg to the side, luckily hitting only air. Not good. I knew she was aggressive only because she was nervous and scared, but I also knew that if she kicked someone's horse I would feel responsible. So, I turned her around and left the crowded warm up arena, heading back out into the rain.

I heard Francesca's voice from behind me. "Where are you going?"

Winsome jigged and balled up underneath me, anxious. I called over my shoulder, "To the warm up arena and then to get her around my outdoor competition ring."

Predictably, the official warm up arena was dead empty and covered in standing water. Francesca, to her credit, followed, umbrella held low over her shoulders. It was now my job to practice what I had been preaching. I knew what my mare needed to do. It did take courage. She felt like she could explode or run away; she was a bundle of discomfort, some of which I shared. It was raining, I was wet through and through, and the ground was soup.

Winsome was still not an experienced show horse. She was nervous and insecure. I could not afford to be either of those things. The answer was just as Deb had told me, to rely on the training. I had to 'move it', just as I had yelled at Francesca.

So, I did. I rode Winsome energetically forward. We splashed grey sandy water as Winsome's hooves made a splash-splash-splash-splash noise in a good steady rhythm. She tossed her head a few times, and snorted like a dragon. But I closed my lower leg around her and took a good firm feeling of her mouth. I had a huge space all to myself, with no need to keep turning. First I did my usual working trot rising, but I gave her some big long lines of lengthened trot in there too, finally deciding to go ahead and sit. It was easier to sit than to rise; she was spending so much time in the air between the diagonal pairs. I was on a Gazelle who was springing across the Savannah. When I asked for canter, she jumped enthusiastically forward. And then something spooked her and she took off. I lost control for a good one hundred feet, but there was nothing in our way and no reason to think it would last. It reminded me of our gallops up our favorite hill, I knew she would tire. After I regained control, I let her walk.

Finally, she calmed and walked flat footed on a long rein even as she was still big eyed and puffing with excitement as much as fatigue. Francesca still stood loyally under her umbrella. Our eyes met for a moment, and she gave me a short nod. I had done my best to channel Deb earlier, but that small nod was Francesca's best effort to give me what Margot would have given me at that moment. Francesca was trying to help me.

I didn't have time to think more about that. I had to pick up my reins and let the training take over, to gather my mare and work through the transitions to bring her into collection, run through the movements and patterns that I would be judged on for the next two days.

The next twenty minutes required my undivided concentration as the rain got heavier and seeped into whatever semi-dry cracks that remained on my body. When I finished my ride and looked up, I was surprised to find Francesca still watching.

Winsome and I exited the still empty warm up arena and I said, "Thank you for staying, Francesca. Please, go get out of the rain. I'm just going to walk her around the arena I have to show in tomorrow. Then I'll be back at the stalls."

When I returned to the stalls, the stalls were clean, the water buckets and hay bags filled. The aisle had even been raked. I didn't mean to sound critical when I exclaimed, "Who did all this? You?"

Francesca looked at me icily and said, "A simple thank you would suffice."

I was immediately remorseful. "I'm sorry. Of course, thank you! Thank you, Francesca."

She sniffed. "Well, I'll be off then. Remember, I'm counting on you to have Johnny braided and ready to go in the morning. I have an early ride." She glanced upward. "Let's hope for better weather. I'd hate to have to warm up in the rain tomorrow, but the radar is not encouraging."

I grinned, "But, no shadows tomorrow for Johnny Cash."

Francesca left, but not before going into Johnny Cash's stall. I couldn't see, but I knew. She was giving him his good night red lipstick kiss.

***

I awakened in the dark, braided Johnny Cash and put in his fake tail, adding an extra layer of tape to secure it. Yesterday it had collected so much arena sand that it had weighed a ton. I didn't want any more "fashion emergencies."

Once that was finished, I cleaned stalls and dumped and refilled water buckets. The rain had stopped, so it was a good time to empty our overfilled muck cart. By that time the concessions trailer was open and I could grab coffee and a hot chicken biscuit.

Francesca arrived as I was brushing biscuit crumbs off my shirt. I sat on the mounting block, my only option since we hadn't packed any chairs. It meant that all weekend long, any time we were at the stalls, only one of us could sit. Francesca looked pale and glassy eyed. She had on her show clothes, wearing a long skirt over her breeches to keep them clean. I greeted her, chirping, "Johnny is braided and groomed. And hey, it stopped raining!"

Francesca drew out her words slowly in a depressing tone. "There's no reason to rejoice, Lizzy. A huge line of storms is moving this way. I may get lucky, but you will certainly be riding in a deluge."

All I could say was what I had been saying. "You've already been given all the luck you need for the weekend, Francesca. No shadows. As for me, well, I saw Margot ride a great test in a deluge, so I know it can be done."

Maybe Francesca had been chastened. She had no comeback. Instead she looked at her watch and remained quiet before saying, "Tack him up in thirty minutes."

Then she did what she usually did. She went shopping to pass the time. It was a small show, but there were still a few vendors.

Francesca's luck held. I got her up on Johnny under heavy clouds, black-bottomed but white on the top. They were fantastic shapes, with blue sky visible above, and their movement, although not fast and furious as in a great storm, was noticeable. Something was afoot for sure, but Francesca might be correct that she would get a pass, and I would not.

I didn't need to tell Francesca to go more forward in the warm up arena. She was coping and much more relaxed today than yesterday. I could have recommended a few things, but I remembered how Margot left us alone as much as she could to focus on the horse and ourselves. Instead, I checked the weather app on my phone and then looked above me.

The clouds seemed to lower themselves on top of us, the dark bottoms now hanging directly over our heads. Thunder rumbled in the distance, and soon fat drops began to fall on my raincoat hood. I pulled my jeans out from my rubber boots, and slid them down on the outside, today preferring wet jeans over water running down my slicker and directly into my boots.

I zipped up my raincoat and waved Francesca out of the warm up arena. We said nothing to each other as I pulled off Johnny's muddy boots. I had no towel or water or brushes, just a bucket in which to drop the dirty stuff. I took one rein and led Francesca to the gate, although she could have ridden him there without assistance. The rain got harder, the drops coming denser. By the time the rider before Francesca had made her final salute, it was coming down hard. I simply said, "Have a great ride," and off she went. It was up to her now.

The rain thundered on the arena's metal roof, so loud that the music could no longer be heard on the loudspeakers, and who knew if the announcer was speaking. Sheets of insulation were now hanging down from the ceiling, apparently from leaks in the metal roof. The insulation had soaked up the water, gotten heavy, and was letting go.

I don't know how or if Francesca had heard the bell; perhaps the judge had spoken to her as she had passed. But, Francesca walked, then picked up the canter and headed down centerline. I was proud of her, proud and nervous, too. I crossed fingers on both hands and pressed them against my mouth, just as I had done for Emma. Johnny looked impressive, on full alert, yet obedient. The rain pounded down, overloading the gutters and making a sort of waterfall curtain around the arena. There would be no outside distractions for Johnny today. The barns disappeared, the warm up arena disappeared. He was the only horse to be seen in the quiet zone in the midst of deafening noise.

Without warning, a large yellow insulation panel let go, landing right in the middle of the dressage arena, but it was behind Francesca so she didn't notice. Soon another panel let go and the focus of the arena audience shifted from horse and rider to the structure's roof. Francesca also missed seeing the second waterlogged panel descend. However, it had landed right on the track. She was somehow going to have to navigate that big square of bright yellow. When she and Johnny came down the long side, he arched his neck and lifted his knees and hocks extra high, but he went right over it!

Francesca flashed me a look as she passed. I nodded vigorously in response. My look said, "Keep going," despite the fact that her show floor was effectively being dive bombed by insulation panels.

And she did. Another panel came down, then another. If the judges blew the whistle, no one could have heard it. So, as each panel descended from above, it made its way into Francesca's test, and Francesca and Johnny trampled right over each one of them blocking their path. Johnny did it with a certain flair, as if the yellow panels were hot coals and he was a firewalker. I couldn't have been more proud, remembering all those towels I had placed in his path back at the home arena. Never in a million years could I have foreseen that those exercises would have prepared him to travel over wet insulation panels.

The finer bits or the obvious mistakes of Francesca's test were a blur. All I knew is that nothing terrible happened, and she made it from salute to salute, straight over an obstacle course of insulation panels in a deafening rain. She approached the judge's booth after her final halt, and I couldn't hear a word of what was said, but could see Francesca grinning and leaning down, petting Johnny Cash enthusiastically.

Then I remembered to check the scoreboard, but it had gone dark. In fact, the entire covered arena was rather dark. They had lost electricity.

Francesca jogged Johnny back to the barns in a driving rain while I jogged behind them. We wouldn't find out for another hour that Francesca had received a 65% or that Johnny Cash had been awarded a 10 for submission. The comment section said, "Your horse must trust you 100 percent to do what he just did for you. Kudos."

I had no desire to show Winsome in this horrible weather. And yet, I put in her braids to the steady rhythm of rain pounding on the stable roof. How could I scratch after Francesca had given her all despite the lousy conditions? The show had not been called because the weather had not yet been deemed "dangerous." So, the judges waited in their little booths. Until the lightning bolts came down alongside the rain, the show would go on. The booths had bus-style windows that could be pulled closed while the judge and her scribe waited. But as soon as a rider entered, the front window was pulled open, and the poor judge and scribe went to work, even if the rain was blowing in their faces.

Winsome and I had a set start time to appear in the arena and perform, but if anyone ahead of us scratched we could move up our time or stay with the scheduled time. Often during open "scratch" times the judges sat, tapping their toes and waiting for the next rider to appear. I decided to go check with the show office to see if I could move up and get this over with as soon as possible. I was told to present myself at my earliest convenience, as multiple riders were scratching because of the weather. It would be only the bold and the foolhardy and those too cheap to forfeit their entry fee who soldiered on.

Francesca came back to the barn aisle in time to see me preparing to mount. She looked confused and said, "Why are you getting on now? You're way early."

I answered much more casually than I felt as I looked out into the unnaturally dark and rainy show grounds. "I'm filling a scratch."

Francesca pointed to Winsome's legs. "You forgot to put on her boots."

I shook my head, "Francesca, I don't want you to have to come stand in the rain, and then peel off muddy boots. She can warm up with bare legs today. I want the shortest warm up possible and then to get this over with."

She looked concerned. "I think it's raining harder, if that's possible."

I agreed. "Yeah, that's why I'm going to go get this done fast. The test is only six minutes long. I'm going to go do a fifteen minute warm up, max."

I swung up and checked my girth as Winsome fidgeted. As I stepped out into the downpour, Winsome tucked her tail and scooted a step. I looked behind me. Francesca had opened her umbrella and was coming, even after I told her she didn't need to. Something welled up inside me, not an emotion I could put a name on. Francesca didn't need to do this. But, maybe neither did I. Or perhaps we both had to.

I stepped into an empty warm up arena that looked like a reflecting pool, the surface water dancing with the rain. The wind gusted and moved the rain in sheets. It reminded me of the dancing bird clouds; the starlings. I had discovered on the internet the clouds of starlings were called a murmuration. The word even sounded like movement. I suddenly saw the moving sheets of rain like the starlings; a murmuration, and one that Winsome and I would now join.

Winsome and I splashed boldly around in trot, buffeted by the gusts of rain. She rounded her neck and flattened her ears, occasionally giving a mighty snort and a toss of her nose, or throwing in an extra high step and strike of a front leg as if to punish the water. She shifted into a medium trot and was strong in my hand. After a few laps in trot, we cantered strongly around each way with a bold flying change. I heard her breathing change into a steady rhythm. She was amazingly focused on me. When I made a transition to walk, she offered her piaffe steps. She was turbo charged, but she was under my control.

I left the warm up arena after ten minutes, passing the place where the warm up steward should have been. I briefly wondered if the show had indeed been "called" and I simply hadn't gotten the notice. The lights were back on, but if the PA system was once again working I couldn't have heard it with the noise of the rain.

I trotted boldly into the show arena, again noticing there was no ring steward at the in-gate. When I got to the judge's box, the judge and the scribe were standing up as if to leave. Suddenly, I really wanted to ride my test. The scribe leaned out of the box and gestured to me. "Number and name? What test are you riding?" I felt relief as I gave her the information, and they both sat back down. Immediately the judge blew the whistle.

I trotted in and made an abrupt halt and salute. When I dropped my head to salute, water fell from the brim of my helmet in a rivulet. The rain blew right into my face in a way that made me squint. The rain wasn't simply coming down, it was coming from every direction and I could barely see the judge and scribe. I realized I could talk to Winsome all I wanted to in this ride without the use of voice earning a penalty. It was kind of funny. So, off we bounded, with me chirping encouragement to my horse. Winsome was a little too round and low in her neck, shielding her flattened ears and eyes from the driving rain. I imagined her eyes were squinting like mine.

A funny emotion came over me; it was giddy and playful. When you remove the fear, when you take away the need to impress, what is left is a sort of childlike glee. Winsome and I were playing in the wind and rain the way I used to love to do as a child. The water was for splashing, and the wind was our playmate that could lift us off the ground and help us fly like Mary Poppins and her umbrella, or it could urge us on, or try and hold us in place or even push us backward. I think Winsome felt my joy and splashed the harder through the standing water.

My first medium trot was really an extended trot as the wind was behind us and seemed to lift us off the ground and push us across the diagonal. I let her go saying, "wheeeeeee" and giving her a pat on her neck, she came back for the corner. My first shoulder in and half passes were cadenced as Winsome and I were now forcing ourselves into the heavy wind, squinting and bracing as we felt battered by the storm. I encouraged her by making clucking noises with my tongue.

Next was the extended trot, which was again pushed along by the strong wind. We got through the walk work, and then when we picked up our left lead canter, the arena began to come apart. The potted ferns went first, and then the tall letters fell like chess pieces knocked over on the board, the letters on one side leaning over the dressage boards and into our rectangle, luckily none blocking our line of travel. Winsome stuttered in place for a stride, unsure.

I closed my legs around Winsome, touching her with my spurs to give her courage, at the same time I took a little stronger hold on her mouth. I sat back and drove on, saying, "Good girl, keep going." I had made a virtual tunnel between my legs and reins, a channel she was not allowed to leave. She seemed to back pedal mid-stride, but I gave her a stout kick to send her through it. She surged forward, staying within that channel, and increasing the impulsion. Once again I could say, "Good Girl" with enthusiasm, knowing no one could hear me.

I made my half pass to my half circle to the single flying change both ways. All I had left in the test was my extended canter down the long side. Winsome did her best as we pushed into the strong wind that seemed to lift us but also slowed us down. There was no problem bringing her back for the corner since as soon as I stopped driving her forward, the wind nearly stopped us completely, as if we had hit an invisible wall.

As I made my transition to trot at C and passed the judge, I noticed that she was already standing. I made my turn at E and my turn at X, and my salute at G. I had done it.

Just then lightning flashed and thunder exploded at nearly the same moment, signaling the end of the day's competition. The door of the judge's booth flew open and the judge came bolting out, soon followed by her scribe. The judge stopped only for a moment as she drew level with me, yelling loud enough that I actually could hear her. She bellowed, "Take cover! Now!" And then she kept running.

Francesca's big umbrella bobbed as she jogged ahead of me back to the stable. I had never seen Francesca jog before. I restrained Winsome to a trot to not mow Francesca down, but Winsome was eager to get out of the storm and overtook Francesca before we reached the stables.

Johnny Cash bellowed out a welcome as we rode into the barn aisle. Winsome wrinkled her nose and pinned her ears in response. Francesca came jogging in behind us and closed her huge umbrella, and then shook herself off, and headed into the tack room for towels.

I put Winsome in her stall and began stripping off her tack. Wet sand covered her chest and stomach, between her hind legs, and even over her blaze. I looked down at myself and realized I looked just as bad. My jacket was not only saturated by the rain, it was sandy. My white breeches would probably never be white again. I looked out into the show grounds to unrelenting rain, punctuated by bolts of lightning. The show was clearly over for the day.

If I had waited for my assigned time, I would have been off the hook. But I was glad that I had gone early. Whatever my score, I was proud of myself, and proud of my horse. We had practiced our courage today, as had Francesca. We had survived the day, and tomorrow, we would be given the privilege to go at it again. Though hopefully in better weather.

I called Margot on the drive home. She was thrilled by my news and we had a good chat. When I got home, Ryder was out. I took a very hot shower and ate a big bowl of cereal, putting the milky bowl on the ground for Wheezer to finish.

At ten p.m., Natalie picked me up and drove me over to the show-grounds for bed check. The rain had stopped and the clouds had been blown away to expose a velvety black sky filled with sparkling stars. We spoke in soft tones, leaning our elbows on the stall ledge and gazing through the bars at the two tired but contented horses, now clean and dry and enjoying their Timothy hay. I felt certain that tomorrow was going to be a good day, a very good day.

15. Shoot For The Moon

I couldn't have asked for better weather for our Sunday rides. The wind and rain had cooled and freshened the air. I had slept the deep and dreamless sleep of the dead.

Although it was important that Francesca break the 60% mark to earn her coveted USDF rider medal, I had no anxiety about it. Yesterday Francesca had surpassed all expectations and had earned that perfect 10 in the collective score for submission. Then Winsome and I had performed in something close to a hurricane. When I finally had received my test I had whooped in joy. I had hit my goal of 70%. The judge's comments consisted of a couple exclamation marks and a smiley face in the comment box, with the one word "brave." The memory made me feel proud as I put in Johnny's braids. Francesca and I both had proven something to ourselves yesterday. We were made of tough stuff, the both of us.

Francesca arrived as I was finishing Johnny's braids. We had just greeted each other when we were called to the office over the PA system. We stood stock still for a moment, staring at each other in disbelief. Were we in trouble? I climbed off the mounting block and turned Johnny loose in his stall. Francesca and I walked side by side in silence to the office.

There was a short line and we joined it. I started to speak, "Do you think…"

Francesca shushed me, then whispered, "All scores stand after an hour."

Incredibly, Francesca and I were both doubting our success, as if it had all been an error. What if we really hadn't earned those scores?

We got to the front of the line and the secretary said, "Hi Francesca, thanks for toughing it out yesterday. So many people have scratched. Most everyone went home after yesterday's weather, which disappoints me since our footing has held up well. It's wet but not slippery. If we can move you and your friend up in the schedule our judges can catch an earlier flight home. But of course, you can still go at your assigned times, no harm no foul."

Francesca looked at her elegant designer wristwatch and then at me. "It would make our schedule tight, but I'm willing if you are."

"Agreed," I said, putting up one open hand to her.

She looked at my hand, then said, "Ah, a high five." She slapped at my hand and for a brief moment held my hand, the closest thing to an embrace I had ever received from her.

I practically jogged back to the barns from the office, finished braiding Johnny and putting in his fake tail, and then tied Winsome up and whipped in her braids and groomed her.

Francesca kindly fussed over my coat. Francesca had a second tailcoat that looked like it had never been worn, but even though I had a fresh pair of breeches and shirt, I had to use yesterday's still soggy show coat. Francesca was trying her best to use towels to press out the dampness and then afterward she brushed it off and tried to reshape it for me.

Francesca and I would be riding for different judges today, as the judges always swapped arenas on the second day. They couldn't know the specifics of our heroic rides yesterday, other than any war stories they might have traded at dinner. We started with clean slates. I was hopeful that no heroics would be required of either of us today, and I was certain there would be no 10's, but that didn't matter.

Francesca was up first, and I got her on quickly and followed her down to the warm up arena. The show had withered to a skeleton staff with only a small cluster of horses and riders, and no spectators. The atmosphere was casual and almost party-like for those of us who had toughed it out and stayed. Even with the sun shining, everything was still sloppy wet. The footing would take days to dry out from its current soupy state.

Francesca was as relaxed as I had ever seen her. The horses too seemed to feel it. Johnny walked to the arena with a long neck and loose reins, his head bobbing up and down in rhythm, his big fake tail swinging, his eyes taking in the environment without fear. I had put on his white patent leather galloping boots, which had cleaned up nicely. Francesca looked like a model in all new threads, no trace of the drowned rat look of yesterday.

I checked in with a bored looking warm up steward, giving him our number, then watched as Francesca put in a very workmanlike warm up. I checked with the steward on the order of go, and was informed that Francesca was the only horse in her class. The others had scratched. She could go as soon as she was ready. I left her alone until I was sure she had prepared enough, but not too much, and then waved her out of the arena. She came out, and I simply asked, "You ready?"

She nodded, so I took off Johnny's sandy wet boots, wiped down Francesca's boots, and then gave her the thumbs up. Francesca walked purposely to the arena, and finding it empty with the judges sitting patiently in their seats, she trotted right in. The whistle blew almost immediately and Francesca cantered Johnny down centerline and did a nice square halt.

I watched Francesca put in a solid test. The sun was shining, and the shadows made a virtual line of cavelletti poles, just as they had at the last horse show. But this time neither Johnny nor Francesca seemed to notice. No, this was the horse who had boldly performed over bright yellow rectangles of insulation panels the day before. This horse and rider were no longer afraid of shadows.

When Francesca finished, the score flashed on the now operational score board. Francesca had scored a 64%. She was now a USDF Gold medal rider. I pushed myself back off the railing, shook a fist in the air, and yelled, "Yes!" I had to wait while the bit checker inspected Johnny's bit and checked Francesca's spurs and then I walked back to the stables alongside Francesca and Johnny. I was still enthusiastic and proud when I said, "You did it, Francesca. Congratulations!"

Francesca, never one to gush, simply said, "Thank you." I realized as I walked beside them that my job was done. Francesca had reached her goal. What did that mean for Johnny Cash? I couldn't allow myself to think beyond that right now. I had to go ride my girl.

Francesca was unusually helpful. She was not idle and anxious, she was in charge, but she was engaged. There was a different energy about her, as if meeting her goal freed her to see me, maybe for the first time. She was present.

She held Johnny while I stripped off his tack and took out his fake tail. We quickly got Johnny settled then switched gears to Winsome. Francesca fetched my tack and helped me into my show clothes. We were in high gear and moving. Francesca was right by my side as I walked to the warm up arena. She went to confer with the steward and then looked at her watch and at me. I got the message. I too could go any time I was ready.

I made sure my horse was in front of my driving aids with a couple medium trots and then a halt rein back. Winsome was good. What else did I need to know before I could go take my test? My little mare was keen and she was listening. I left the arena. Francesca stood with arms crossed and a lifted eyebrow. She said, "Is that all you're going to do?"

I smiled. "I think I warmed up quicker than that yesterday, and it didn't seem to hurt. Can I go now?"

Francesca's lips turned up and she shrugged. She said, "The arena's empty. I expect everyone is eager to finish and go home. As for your preparation, well, the proof of the pudding is in the tasting, isn't it?"

I said, "I don't understand."

She took a towel and gave my boots a wipe, answering, "It means, just go in there and pull off another 70 percent ride. If you do, then that will be the proof that you did the correct warm up."

I gathered my mare and trotted into the show arena in as bold a trot as I could manage without losing control of Winsome. I showed off a little around the outside of the boards while I waited for the whistle, allowing myself to rev my little mare up with a few half steps, fluffing up her trot with cadenced soft passage steps.

When the whistle blew I halted and gave Winsome a scratch on her withers to let her know how proud I was of her. Then I went in and had a blast. The test was now my friend. Winsome and I knew where we were going, we owned each corner and, while little things could still be better, overall it was a smooth test without errors.

When I halted and saluted at the end I felt a wave of relief, like crossing a finish line. I was one tired girl, but it was a happy-tired. Winsome felt the same and walked out of the arena with her nose almost touching the wet sand. Francesca met me at the out gate where the steward quickly checked my bit. I said to Francesca, "How'd you like that pudding?" I saw the confused look on the face of the ring steward.

Francesca smiled and said very slowly, "It was sweet, even sweeter than yesterday."

There was no electronic score board in the outdoor arena, so we had to wait for the test sheet for my score. As we waited, Francesca pulled the Mercedes up to the barn and we put all of her tack in the trunk. We decided to take Johnny home first, alone, and then return for Winsome on a second trip so Johnny wouldn't be terrorized again by my mare. I hooked up the trailer and we packed everything but the horses, leaving one bucket of water in the stall for Winsome. Everything else got heaved into our vehicles and the bed of my truck.

When I finally got my test sheet I had scored an incredible 74%, my best score ever. I made a couple quick phone calls and then it was time to boot up the horses and take Johnny home.

Johnny loaded right up, apparently happy to have the trailer all to himself. I put the ramp up, checked the hitch one more time, and then said a silent prayer as I started up the truck and pulled out. I had left Winsome with a flake of hay on the floor, and on top of that I poured an extra ration of grain and a half dozen carrots broken into pieces to keep her happy. I hope she knew I would be back and wouldn't worry. She had taken a mouthful of grain and pinned her ears at Johnny as we had walked by. I thought she would cope.

Francesca's little black Mercedes pulled in behind the trailer to follow me. I put the radio on the oldies station and was singing along, feeling tired but happy. When I got closer to home, I turned it off and glanced in my tow mirror to check on Francesca. She was still right there behind me. I flew right past the turn off to the Winstons' barn. Francesca flashed her lights at me. I didn't have to count to ten before my cell phone starting playing its ring tone. I let it go to message, making a dicey bet that this would play out as I intended.

When I did pick up my cell phone it was to check in with Margot.

I pointed my remote controller at the farm gates as soon as I knew I was in range, even before I put on my blinker. Francesca was probably cursing me. But, how could she? Margot had strung a banner over the barn door; it read "Congratulations!" The border had little teddy bears and flowers around it, clearly for someone's new baby homecoming. Johnny Cash *was* somebody's baby, even if he wasn't brand-spanking new, and this *was* his homecoming.

And there was the welcoming committee; Margot, and Emma, and Deb, and Natalie, and Ryder, and there, shyly holding a vase full of red roses was Chess. I was glad that Dennis had not shown up. But I was suddenly misty-eyed when I thought of Frank. He should have been here. I had secretly hoped somehow he would make it.

Francesca slowly got out of her car, her face showing real surprise. Margot and company gave her a hearty applause. Francesca looked over at me, but I just shrugged and turned around so I wouldn't have to meet her eyes. I opened Johnny's escape door and he immediately poked his head out, blowing and bobbing. Then I motioned to Ryder, who jumped right in to help. I let her know he was one of those who came out too fast and Ryder nodded and quietly put down the ramp. She said, "Let me know when I can drop the bar."

I unhooked Johnny's head and stepped into the trailer. I threw the rope over his neck and said, "Okay."

Ryder skillfully lowered the bar so stealthily that Johnny was still standing unaware. She put her hand up high on his rump and gave him a pat and said, "Slow now, my man, one step at a time."

The two of us managed to get two quiet steps before he accelerated. It was a vast improvement. Johnny stood at the bottom of the ramp, head held high, looking around with interest at his new digs. The horses in the barn greeted him, and instead of whinnying back, he simply tugged at the lead rope, ready to be lead to his "room."

I glanced over at our group. Francesca's eyes were glued on Johnny. Margot exclaimed, "I'd forgotten how magnificent he is, Francesca!" Emma and Deb and Natalie were all complementing Johnny, and Francesca, despite her usual dry demeanor, could not mask how proud she was of that horse. Margot added, "And now you, too, are a Grand Prix rider. Just think, Francesca, what a journey it has been. I'm so proud of you. And you did it without my help."

Francesca said matter-of-factly, "Margot, you were there every day, whether you realize it or not." The two women smiled warmly at each other and nodded. No explanations were needed or required. It had happened. I felt a huge sense of relief.

Ryder led Johnny Cash into the barn as Margot and Francesca filed in behind them. The rest of us followed en masse to Johnny Cash's stall, deeply bedded with fresh shavings. He was put in the gelding zone next to Lovey, in a stall that had its own banner on the door reading, "Welcome Home!" A card table was set up outside his stall, with plastic champagne glasses and a sheet cake. Chess set his roses on the table and gave his mother a kiss on her cheek. Margot served cake and Natalie poured champagne, while everyone peppered Francesca with questions. I wanted to stay and join the story-telling, but instead pulled Chess aside.

"I have to go get Winsome. I couldn't put her back in the trailer with Johnny Cash. She tried to beat him up on the trip over. Do you have time to come with me?

Chess agreed, and I gave him a quick hug and a peck on his cheek. We turned to go back to the truck, but halfway there I told him to wait. I walked back to the happy group, all talking and laughing as Francesca described the huge sheets of insulation falling from the ceiling during her test. Francesca caught my eye and hesitated. I leaned in and whispered, "I'm not fired, am I?"

Francesca's face went blank, and then she replied in a dry monotone, "Not today, Lizzy, not today."

Francesca turned back to her audience, and resumed her narrative. I returned to Chess, softly laughing. Francesca would always be Francesca. But today, at least, I felt affection toward her, and also pride in both of us. She had chosen the right girl for the job after all. Although Francesca would most likely never say so, we had worked well together and achieved an almost impossible goal. No matter what happened next, that was something. Now, it was time to retrieve my own little superstar mare.

Chess slipped into the passenger seat and buckled up while I put my old truck into gear. He was quiet for a moment, his face serious. He said, "You took a risk back there. Looks like it worked out."

His somber tone worried me. I said, "Chess, I've taken a bunch of risks lately. But, I had to try. If I failed, well, I was going to go down fighting. I guess I'm handing the real burden off to you now."

He turned and looked out the window at the lush New Jersey landscape. The silence started to feel uncomfortable in the truck and I got impatient. Finally I snapped, "For God's sake, tell me what's eating you."

He turned and looked at me and smiled. "Lizzy, just then, when you said 'for God's sake' you sounded just like my mother."

I retorted defensively, "I guess I learned that one from your mother, but that's not all I've learned from her."

Chess was listening intently. I said, "She is actually a magnificent woman, once you get to know her. I mean, her glare used to scare me to death, but I've learned to appreciate some of her other qualities, like the fact that she knows what she wants and she goes for it."

He exhaled and actually shook his head, "Yeah. That's my mother all right. She knows how to fight for what she wants, even though she's short on tact. She's challenging. Thank you for working with her, Lizzy. I know it wasn't easy."

"It wasn't easy. But it was good. Frank was the one who jokingly told me I must suffer for my art, and that working for Francesca I would suffer plenty."

We both laughed at that. Then I asked again, "So, what is it?"

Chess' voice became serious. "All this horse show stuff is fine and good, but tomorrow she and I have a big meeting with the new Cavelli Foods owners and our attorney. I'll be taking Dad's role of good cop, and mother will play her usual role of bad cop. She'll hopefully scare the hell out of them, and if we play our roles well, then they'll be begging to give us what we want."

I said, "You've got to fill in for your dad. Those are big shoes to fill. Is that what's got you worried?"

He shook his head. "No. Well, yes and no. No matter what happens with the company, I've still got Dad's health to worry about. He's started on anti-depressants and I'm hoping they kick in soon, because he's got Mother and me both scared. He's convinced he's going to die and the doctor hasn't been able to convince him that he's not. And Dad cries at the drop of a hat, which is really unsettling, since that is just not like him. When he's not being sentimental and weepy, he is paranoid and fighting with Mother. I snuck into his office and I pulled out that paper he and Mother were fighting over and read it through."

I put on my blinker and pulled into Hill and Dale Farm, pulling up to the show barn, now a ghost town. I felt sorry for my mare who I am sure was anxious. I cut off the engine and shoved the keys in the waistband of my breeches, saying, "I'm listening, but I want to get to Winsome. Keep talking."

I let down the ramp and the butt bar, opened the escape door and then motioned to Chess to follow me. We got to Winsome's stall. She whirled around to the stall front and whinnied loudly. I pulled open the door and slipped on her halter, feeding her a sugar cube that I dug out of my pocket. Chess and I made eye contact and he said, "It was an offer from Dennis for both farms, a "turn-key" offer that included everything on the place, including all the livestock."

Even though I wasn't surprised or shocked, my cheeks still went hot. A written offer made the threat real. Chess continued, "He had a list of all the horses with appraised values next to each name, even that Johnny Cash horse that Mother had hidden away at the Winston place, the horse you brought in today. Dennis even included that one that Emma was supposed to sell, "Romp" out in Texas. Somebody helped him who knew what they were doing. Margot would have all the pieces, would hate to think it was her."

I shook my head. "Not Margot, although I'm sure he's been milking her for information. No, it was Ryder. Dennis promised her some kind of deal on Johnny Cash. Right now, Dennis and Margot appear to be on the outs. I heard some of it. They were fighting over the mare, Wordy."

I pointed at the water bucket on the wall. "Can you grab that, and see if you can bring the hook-eye, too, it's ours."

"Happy to. Got to preserve every asset we have."

It broke a little bit of the somber mood and we both laughed.

Winsome stepped high and lively in her shipping boots as we walked out of the barn, and I could tell she was relieved to see her familiar trailer. I threw the rope over her neck and she eagerly loaded herself, poking her head out of the escape door while snatching a hunk of hay. I hooked the butt bar, and then heaved the ramp up. Chess stood with a bucket in his hand while I clipped the trailer tie to Winsome's halter, gently pushed her head back in and closing the door. I pointed to the bed of the truck. "I have a bungee tie on the side so it won't roll around."

I pulled out on the road, relaxing a bit now that I had my precious mare with me. But I had plenty to fret over. "Chess, you won't let them sell the farm, will you?"

He grimaced. "It's not my farm. Dad's weirdly insistent that it's time for Mother to think of her financial security. He sees himself as no longer able to provide for her, and the farm is just a burden that they can no longer afford. I heard him say to Mother that properties like the two horse farms can take years to sell, that some of the horses are getting old. He said we could guarantee them homes for life if they sold to Dennis, although I don't know how he knows that."

Chess drummed his fingers on the armrest and continued. "The thing is, the properties and livestock are only one part of the problem. We got through the IRS audit, took a little bit of a hit but it could have been a disaster. We still don't have a final signoff, but it's pretty much a done deal. The next problem is that the new owners of Cavelli Foods haven't kept up with the payments to Dad, which kills the cash flow. And without the cash flow, there's no money to pay the ongoing expenses of the properties, livestock, and staff."

I slowed down to negotiate a sharp turn and replied, "And Dennis sweeps in to the rescue, problem solved?"

Chess said, "Dad's listening hard to Dennis's sales pitch. I can understand why Dad wants Mother to stay in their old house on the hill, which they spent a fortune renovating, and that he wants her to keep Marta and the gardener. They are very settled in there. He's thinking that by selling the farms, Mother could still afford to live "in the style to which she has become accustomed.' Dennis has made a lowball offer, but Dad's not thinking straight. Of course, I can't say anything because that contract was not meant for my eyes. Dennis is pretending to be the savior, when in fact he's taking advantage of a bad situation. Personally, I don't like the guy. Never really have."

I nodded in agreement, "Emma practically spits when she says his name. She says he smells blood in the water, and that's why he's back. It's not only that, though. Dennis wanted Wild Child as a trophy, a prize to give to Sophie. Emma and Frank swooped in and bought Wild Child right out from under him. I think this is some weird sort of revenge for an old injury. I know it sounds crazy but I think Dennis thinks if he had been able to buy Wild Child that he and Sophie would still be together. If he can force Frank and Francesca out of the horse business, he'll do it to settle the score, all the while letting the world think it was an act of charity."

Chess nodded his head, "It sounds crazy. You're right about that." Chess looked thoughtful then added, "But what I don't understand is Margot. Emma filled me in on the whole Sophie and Dennis fiasco, so why would Margot give him the time of day after that? I don't understand how Margot can even stand to be around him."

I added, "Let alone getting on the back of his big motorcycle and putting her arms around his waist. It's yucky, I know. But I think I finally figured it out. How do I explain this? Margot isn't interested in Dennis. Margot needs a horse. A horsewoman without a horse is just a pedestrian. And that mare of Dennis' is a problem horse who needs a rider like Margot; Word Perfect is a challenge, a puzzle, but a beautiful puzzle. That horse gives Margot a reason to get up in the morning. That's how she felt about Hotstuff, and he was taken from her. That broke her heart. Losing Dennis to Sophie, although it had to sting her pride, was not a deep wound, but she can't lose another horse right now. She's committed herself to that horse. Word Perfect is just one of the many horses that she has committed herself to... and then there's the rest of us. She's committed to us, too. I think she's willing to do what it takes. She's trying to see a path forward, and just like Frank, she thinks Dennis would keep the whole she-bang intact... for her. Margot aligning herself with Dennis would be a sacrifice, not a selfish act."

Chess was looking thoughtful. I sighed, "But, she's wrong. She's wrong to give up on Frank and Francesca. I'm not sure how we can do it, but we need to get rid of Dennis, and somehow keep Word Perfect for Margot. She deserves that."

Chess sighed and shook his head. "I'm sorry for Margot, but it's a horse. My Dad is more important. Staying financially secure is more important. To do that, we have to get money flowing again from Cavelli Foods. I would prefer to not sell the farm or the horses right now, although we DO have to sell horses. But I especially don't want to sell to Dennis Walker and I think I do understand the nuances of that deal and the personalities and history. At least I think I do. But, don't you think that's a heavy enough load to put on my shoulders without worrying about acquiring another horse?"

I deflated a little. Chess made sense. I was sounding like the crazy horse girl I was. I tried a weak defense. "Is it wrong for me to shoot for the moon?"

"Lizzy, I will do my absolute best to see that Dad and Mother do not sign that contract, and figure out a way for the company to survive and provide for the continued operation of Equus Paradiso, and to provide for both of them. And maybe down the road for me, and for you..." He placed his hand lightly on my leg.

The touch of his hand on my leg and the mention of 'me and you' gave me a small jolt. It was an adrenaline surge, a sensation not unfamiliar to me, but still one that left me weak. I pulled up to the farm gates and pressed the remote. I watched the elegant, the beautiful, the impressive gates swing inward, welcoming us home. I felt exactly the same approaching those gates now as I had when I had been riding a nervous Winsome. There was a good chance I could once again be tossed into the deep mulch outside those gates, forever and permanently on the wrong side of them. If Dennis was the new owner of Equus Paradiso those gates would close me out forever. But there was another possible outcome. Chess had just said something about the farm providing for 'me and...you.'

Chess had been brave to utter those loaded words, and was waiting patiently for my response. I sat there silent for a long moment, and then looked at Chess, who looked back at me, his gaze settling me. I sat there so long, unmoving, that the gates timed out and shut. Winsome, who I was sure was looking through her side window and recognizing she had arrived back at her home, had to wonder why we were stopped. I finally softly echoed him, "Down the road for me and you?"

His voice was equally soft, "Mother and Dad once talked about building up on that hill, up by Deb's barn. It's a spot with a great view. Instead they decided to renovate and stay in their house. I never thought about it much before now. But now I find myself thinking about it a lot. I wouldn't want anything too big or fancy, just a place with a great kitchen and a big front porch looking out over the little widgets playing in the fields. Every time I imagine sitting on that front porch, and cooking in that new kitchen, well, you're there too, right by my side."

I said, "Oh."

Chess held up his finger, "I probably shouldn't have said anything. Even if we get this mess sorted out, well, it might not be affordable or practical. Please don't say anything to anyone."

I smiled. "I am a girl who can keep a secret!" Of course, I hadn't actually kept Francesca's secret after all, so I added, "Um, until I don't."

We laughed and then it was time to get back to work.

I carefully backed Winsome off the trailer and walked her back to her stall. The party had broken up and the place was empty and quiet. Chess followed and watched as I knelt down and pulled off Winsome's shipping boots, and then took off her halter. She was clearly happy to be home. Her mane was still curly from her braids and her blaze silver white from me scrubbing it with blue shampoo. She threw herself down in the clean and deep shavings and moaned as she rubbed her back, getting up and rolling her eyes and shaking like a dog. Then she sighed and wandered over to her hay. She was a relaxed horse who would have a day off tomorrow in the paddock. I felt Chess' arm drape over my shoulders, warm and relaxed and comfortable. I turned to him, "Seeing Winsome content makes me content."

He nodded, "I can see that."

"I think everything will be okay, Chess. Frank had a big scare, but he'll recover and again be the Frank we all love. You and your mother will get Cavelli Foods sorted out one way or another and get the money tap turned back on. Then your mother can keep Johnny Cash, because when you find the horse of a lifetime, you shouldn't let it go. Then we can kick that Dennis creep to the curb, but keep his horse for Margot."

Chess looked incredulous "When you lay it all out like that, Lizzy, it sounds totally impossible, and you sound a little bit nuts."

I nodded. "I know. I've been accused of rainbow and unicorn thinking before."

Chess said, "Uh-huh, and how has that 'rainbow and unicorn' thing worked out for you so far?"

"Well, I wanted my life to be an adventure, one filled with horses; lots of horses and it's been a great adventure so far. Deb calls it taking 'the wild ride' and I have. But, your mother is made of the same stuff, although she would never admit it. She just earned her USDF Gold medal on a horse she was told was unsuitable for her. Worked out for her, didn't it?"

Chess gave me a kiss on the forehead and then pulled his arm off my shoulder. "Is there anything else you want while you're making lists?"

I tipped my head and raised my eyebrows, being coy. "Oh, yes!"

He tipped his head in return, waiting I suppose, to hear what it was. So, I added gleefully, "A dog. I love my Wheezer, but I really want a dog."

He threw both hands in the air, with eyes to heaven in a gesture that somehow made him seem very Italian. He reminded me of his dad. He said, "I am a doomed man." But he was smiling as he left. He would have stayed, but he had a lot to do before his big meeting tomorrow, so it would be Wheezer and me relaxing together tonight.

Wheezer and I greeted each other as if we had been separated for a week. Ryder was stretched out on the sofa watching TV. I scooped up my leggy kitten and Ryder pulled her feet up to make a space for me to sit down on the sofa. Then she hit the mute button on the remote, looking up at me.

She looked bored, with an arm behind her head. She said, "So, you did it."

I smiled and plopped down on the sofa, "Yeah. And you know what? You were right about Francesca."

Now she looked interested. "In what way?"

I scratched Wheezer under the chin. She was purring so loudly and was so ecstatically happy that she was drooling. I looked back at Ryder and I was not kidding when I said, "She's a brave woman. I have new respect for her. You saw something in her that I couldn't see. But, after this weekend, I get it."

Ryder broke our eye contact and got up. She said, "I saved you some of the cake. I know how much you like sweets. I'm going to have coffee. You want some?"

Ryder was being odd. I mean, we had spent so much time being adversarial, and here I was being genuinely complimentary. And, she had saved me cake. I didn't recognize this Ryder, saving me cake and offering to make me a cup of coffee? Who was this? I wrinkled my brow as I struggled to answer. "Sure, coffee and cake sounds good."

I watched Ryder make coffee. Then she opened a cardboard box and cut a piece of cake. I tried to restart the conversation. "Well, Johnny Cash is home, finally."

Ryder put the cake on the table with a napkin and a fork. So, I got up and moved to the table, putting Wheezer on the floor. Wheezer protested with a long sentence of meows. Ryder put mugs on the counter. Then she said, with a frown, "I don't know how you take your coffee."

I thought perhaps, just maybe, there was a hint of regret in her voice. We lived together and I had made myself many cups of coffee in front of her, and yet she had never noticed how I drank it. I knew she took hers black. I replied, "Cream, no sugar."

Ryder was off her game. It was clear to me that she never believed that Francesca and I could pull off what we had pulled off. She had somehow been invested in our failure. But, regardless, what did it matter? Ryder leaned against the counter, waiting for the coffee to finish brewing. She looked so very young. She was not wearing any make up, and her feet were bare. She looked like any American teenager. I suddenly felt a little sorry for her; it had been a disappointing year for her. And when you are a teenager, well, time seems slow, another year of training and waiting for your chance seems forever. The coffee pot beeped, and Ryder turned around and poured our coffee, pouring cream in mine.

She set my coffee in front of me, and sat down with hers. I said, "You're not having cake, I presume?"

She shook her head, "You know I don't eat that stuff."

I took a bite and a sip then said, "Francesca really did earn her scores, you know. The scores were fair, no Santa Claus judging. Not only that, she used Johnny's nerves to channel his power. She really did ride him over sheets of insulation with the rain hammering down on the roof as loud as a hail of gunfire."

Ryder took a sip of her coffee, waiting a beat as if she was deciding on how to respond. Then she said, "Yeah. I was there."

My mouth fell open. "You sly fox! I never saw you."

She answered, "Of course not. You weren't supposed to. Dennis was there, too."

Just hearing his name silenced me. I concentrated on my coffee and cake. My silence wasn't hard to interpret. Ryder was silent, too; I felt her calculating how much more she wanted to say. I was doing the same.

So, here we were once again; adversaries; back in our familiar roles. I didn't need to guess that she had brought Dennis to the show so that he could see Johnny Cash do the Grand Prix. Ryder would have pointed out that if an amateur like Francesca could pull decent scores on Johnny, especially in such drastic conditions, that she, Ryder, would be able to do much, much more. She was trying to whet his appetite to close the deal. He would win back Margot, and get a slew of wonderful horses and Ryder, too, in the bargain; a top up-and-coming star rider.

But Ryder had to have heard; Margot and Dennis had fought. And she had to have heard and noticed, the old girlfriend was back asking questions and placing herself in Dennis' way. I could tell from Ryder's demeanor; she got it. I didn't need to say a word.

So I just said, "Good cake, Ryder. Thanks for saving some for me."

I was exhausted, but I couldn't sleep. I thought about Chess and what he had said. I thought about a house on the top of the hill. I think I knew the spot. It was above Deb's paddocks in a stand of old growth trees. It was the highest point on the farm. I even dared imagine what kind of house. Chess living on the farm would be his full admission to the tribe. He would be part of us; allergy drops probably a part of his life forever. I smiled in the dark.

That house on the top of the hill that Chess had mentioned; it included me in it. That was a brave leap... a mighty leap, the kind of leap that changes everything and changes it forever. I wished Chess hadn't said anything yet. It only gave me one more thing to keep me awake at night. There was still too much uncertainty. I felt sure Francesca would not sign that sales contract yet, but what if Frank insisted? Francesca had said she would sell Johnny Cash after she had earned her Gold medal. Francesca didn't seem to care about Lovey anymore. What would happen to him? What would happen to Word Perfect if Dennis didn't get what he wanted? What would happen to the rest of us if Dennis did get what he wanted? And what would happen to dear Frank if he continued on his downward spiral? I knew that if Frank died, well, Francesca would cease to be the Francesca I knew. And that was, surprisingly, a frightening thought.

That high spot in old growth trees that Chess had mentioned, well, it could be the building site for Dennis and Margot's new house, or maybe a house for Dennis and Sophie.

With that thought I flopped over on my belly and willed my brain to stop whirling. I vowed not to roll over, not to look at my watch or open my eyes, not to get up and go to the bathroom for the umpteenth time. And then I did all of those things.

My last time check that I remember was at three am.

16. Hanging On

I felt like hell in the morning. It was Monday, technically our day off. Still, I had to clean up the sandy wet tack, clean the trailer, do the laundry. And then on Tuesday we would begin the process of getting ready for Devon.

I had never been to Devon, the historic and prestigious show that marked the beginning of fall. Devon was the reason Emma had come all the way from Texas, convincing Lu Ann and Billy that it was important for their stallion to come compete head-to-head with the best East Coast horses. Devon was no longer a rural Pennsylvania location, and the show facilities were tightly bound by commercial and residential development. It had no covered arena, and much of the stabling was old and cramped. However, the atmosphere was festival-like, with a breeding show the first part of the week, like the shows of yesteryear, featuring lanes full of shopping and food where you could spend a great deal of money and keep yourself entertained for hours.

The old grandstand in Devon had a sponsors' section of coveted and expensive box seating. Families had owned certain boxes for generations. Francesca had waited for the opportunity to have a box, and paid handsomely for it. Frank had intended to provide his customary constant flow of food and drink in that box, hosting a continual Equus

Paradiso Farm party. His heart attack had changed everything. Dennis had promised, as usual, to provide, but now I wasn't sure. I hoped Frank could at least make it down for the freestyle night. It might very well be the one and only time he would be the owner of one of the horses in the class, and when would Margot ever again have two of her prized students in the class?

Whatever happened, Emma and Deb were Devon-bound on Wednesday. Natalie would be grooming for Emma, and Ryder grooming for Deb. That left me in charge of things back at the farm, but I had every intention of being at Devon for our rides on Friday and Saturday. Months before, Francesca had booked a block of rooms for all of us at the same hotel. I had invited Chess, but he was unsure if he could make it. Devon was less than a two hour drive, close enough to be possible, but much too far away to come and go.

Ryder was leading Johnny Cash out to the paddock when I finally made my way down to the barn. I fell in beside her, and as usual she had nothing to say to me. I leaned my elbows on the top rail and watched as she unclipped the lead rope and turned him loose. Johnny attentively explored his new territory, sniffing the manure piles he found, and then sampling the grass. Ryder stood at the gate, silently observing. Johnny found a puddle and went right for it, dropping his massive self down with a groan. The first three-quarters of the way he lowered himself carefully, but he last quarter he gave in to gravity and hit the mud with a mighty flop. He rolled all the way over and then moved his neck back and forth, grinding the mud into his mane, rejoicing in having his braids out, of being a free horse, a dirty horse. And that from a horse who had spent the weekend wet and sandy, even with tight braids and a fake tail.

I laughed and looked over at Ryder. "You'd think he'd had enough of the wet and the mud this past weekend."

Ryder said, "Some horses are good mudders, and some aren't. You guys both got lucky in that respect."

"I guess I'll go get Winsome and put her out."

Ryder said, "Alfonso already put her out. She's covered in mud, too."

I replied. "Oh. I guess I'll start tack and laundry then."

And Ryder surprised me by saying, "I put the first load in for you."

All I could think was to say "Thank you, Ryder." And then reflexively get suspicious.

I left the happy mudders to enjoy the sun on their backs and the green grass and headed up the hill towards Deb's. Although it was bright and sunny, the air had changed, feeling lighter, thinner, and somehow cleaner. To me it indicated that summer was over.

Devon would usher in the fall season. It meant USDF Regional and then National Championships were fast approaching. I hoped to ride Winsome in the Regionals, and if I qualified, perhaps I would go on to Nationals. But, all that would depend on what happened next. I still needed to have a place to call home, and an income, too.

Deb and Wild Child should be heading to Florida in November for the High Performance League invitational training sessions, but only if everything worked out. We were all living in uncertainty.

I poked around the barn, petted a few skittish cats, and even knocked on Deb's door to no response. I walked around back and found both Deb and Nat leaning over Natalie's work table, a plywood sheet resting on two sawhorses. They were closely examining something. I called out, "Hey, guys!"

They turned at the same time. They really could have been sisters, both muscled and browned. Although Deb was a head shorter than Natalie and skinnier, they had spent so much time together that they seemed to stand and move the same way, as if their mannerisms and movement were coded into their DNA.

Natalie wore a boy's tee-shirt with the sleeves rolled up and cut-offs with tennis shoes, and Deb had on a tank top, old faded jeans, and paddock boots. Natalie motioned me over. They leaned over drawings of proposed artworks. "Whaddya think?" she asked.

I studied the rough sketches. "I don't know how you do it, Nat. They are mechanical and real all at the same time. You clearly know your rabbits."

She smiled. "Thanks, Lizzy. Now I have to sift through my piles of junk and see what pieces can be molded into these shapes I've drawn. It's like putting together a puzzle, but I've always liked puzzles. Deb helps me sift and sets out possible pieces."

Deb chimed in, "It's fun, a puzzle like she says. We just kind of sing and talk and joke, and then suddenly some little piece of scrap metal you're holding presents itself as something else entirely. When I see the finished product I look over it and find all the little pieces that I found. I kind of get to be part of it, even though I can barely draw stick figures."

Deb turned her attention to me. "And by the way, Lizzy, I don't think I've had a chance to personally congratulate you. I know Francesca's Gold medal is due to you as much as that horse. I can only guess what you've been up to, with all my tarps and rails and stuff. But it must have worked. What I can't figure is how you got Francesca to cooperate. She's always struck me as un-teachable, and because of that I never wanted to work with her. Somehow you got through to her. Nice job."

Nat chimed in. "It's your gift, my friend."

I laughed, recalling the past few weeks. "It was rough at the start. Funny thing though, something finally clicked. I quit being scared of her and once that happened, things began to get better. She's complicated, but weirdly, I've come to appreciate her."

Deb put down the drawing she was holding and said, "Hey, I'll bet my rolls are cool enough to eat now. Let's go eat and drink Earl Grey. It's time we traded information. Natalie's been online, chatting up her new BFF Sophie, and I'm not sure if she's made things better, or if she's screwed things up beyond repair."

I looked over at Natalie, who guffawed loudly and said, "Hah! Yeah, well I guess time will tell. C'mon, Lizzy, let's go drink tea with our pinky fingers stuck out and speak with overdone British accents."

We went inside and Deb put the kettle on for tea, an old fashioned kind that went on the stovetop, and whistled when it boiled. A rack of little buns cooled on the counter, small and round with glossy tops. Natalie put three mugs on the counter and got out a beautiful china teapot I had never seen before. It had a bamboo handle and a painted blue horse on the side. Deb pointed to it. "Isn't it pretty? The little shop where Natalie sells her art sells them. Natalie gave it to me. So, I bought some loose tea since the pot has a strainer built into it. We really are drinking our tea like the English gentry these days."

Nat added, "But the rolls are French. Wait until you bite into one."

I bit carefully into the warm roll to find a dark chocolate center. All I could do initially was make happy noises. I finally said, "Okay Deb, you've outdone yourself this time. These are sinful."

I politely listened to Deb explain how to make chocolate filled French rolls, but it was time to get on a different topic, getting a full report and sharing what I knew.

Nat started. "Sophie must not have many real friends, the way she's opened up to me and as much time as she spends on social media. She knows I work here and that I'm fairly new, so I also assume that what she's told me, even when she asks me to keep it confidential, is most likely meant for me to leak."

Deb and I waited as Natalie took another bite of roll, then continued. "She knows about Frank's heart attack, and she hinted to me that the farm and all the horses were going to be sold. She told me she was giving me a 'heads-up' as a favor, since as my new Internet friend she thought it only fair that I know I would most likely need another job soon. That kind of shocked me, but I didn't let on that it did. One of the good things about chat is that you can think through your response, and the other person can't see your reactions. I mean, we had all suspected, but for her to know about it is a total red flag. It means she's talking to Dennis, right? I just jumped right in and said that I had assumed that Dennis would make an offer, because, y'know, he seemed awfully interested in Margot, and since he was reputed to have deep pockets, I guessed he could easily buy it for Margot, y'know, as a love-offering."

"You said that?" I replied. "Wow, Nat, that's like waving a red cape in front of a bull. I bet she was pissed."

Deb interjected. "I think Nat went a bit too far. She's not heard anything back from Sophie since she dropped that on her, and I predict that Sophie will move heaven and earth to keep that from happening."

Natalie barked out, "Well, duh! Wasn't that my assignment? But, I got in another dig by telling her that her former mare sure was a fantastic horse, and that she must hate losing such a good Grand Prix horse to Margot. I bet she didn't like that one bit. You said she couldn't ride that mare at all, but, c'mon, not that many folks could."

Deb inhaled deeply and said in a low voice, "So, what do you suppose Sophie's going to do about it?"

There was a beat of silence as we all just looked at each other, letting that soak in.

I broke the silence. "Natalie, I can confirm what Sophie said. I heard from Chess that Dennis made a turn-key offer for both farms and everything on them, including livestock. Deb, I'm sorry, but it includes Wild Child. Dennis would be the new owner of Wild Child and Habenero, as well as being our new boss, which won't be a good thing for any of us. Frank is so low right now that he's actually considering it, even though Chess said it's a lousy offer. Dennis, the jerk, is acting like a savior while offering a fire sale price. Frank wants to do the deal, Francesca doesn't. Chess will do his best to block it, but Dennis is taking advantage of Frank's depression. It's such garbage."

Deb put her elbows on the table and her forehead in her palms and groaned, then said, "God bless good old' Chess. There is no way, no way, I would work for Dennis even if he begged me to. And the idea of Margot getting back with him is just sick and puzzling, too. She's smarter than that."

I said, "Okay, I'm going to tell you some other things, but it all stays in this room, okay?"

Deb nodded, and Nat didn't make one of her usual flippant comments, but instead said, "Sure. It all stays here."

"Chess says his parents are financially tapped. Keeping this whole endeavor afloat has eaten up their retirement accounts and maxed out their lines of credits, of which they have plenty for sure, but they still have to pay it all back. That money from selling Hotstuff went directly back to High Horse Couture to pay back the loan Francesca took out of the business to buy Johnny Cash. It's a mess. Chess' deal with the IRS at least means that the vast majority of the back taxes and interest and penalties were erased, which is significant."

Nat said, "Well, at least that sounds encouraging."

"Yes," I said, "But we have to operate like a business going forward and actually be able to show we are legitimate to keep the IRS business designation. If Chess hadn't worked things out with the IRS, well, it would be a total liquidation to pay the IRS debt and the farm would be selling for even less than what Dennis has offered. The IRS can seize assets to settle debts, and real estate has firmer values than horses. The IRS doesn't want livestock; they don't want anything they have to feed. But, we are not in the clear yet. Debts still have to be paid back, and some of the debts are balloon notes, all due at once. Something's got to change and change very soon."

Deb frowned. "I don't understand. They sold Cavelli Foods for a fortune. Where did all that money go?"

"The new owners stopped paying as soon as they started running the company into the ground. The Cavellis barely got any of the money they're owed. Francesca has hired an attorney, someone Francesca knows from the old neighborhood, to renegotiate the sales contract rather than have it go into default. If it goes into default, the Cavellis could take back the company, but Frank can't run it now. Chess has gotten involved, probably to keep his mother from hiring a hit man. They're meeting today with the new owners of Cavelli Foods and the lawyers. Francesca intends to take the company back, Chess thinks that's a terrible idea since neither he or Francesca know what to do to turn the company around. I'll find out tonight from Chess what transpired."

Deb and Natalie sat back in their seats. Natalie blew out her cheeks. She said, "What does Frank have to say about all this?"

My voice choked a little bit when I replied. "Frank doesn't know the half of it. He keeps talking about dying. Chess says he is weirdly detached from life, but he keeps repeating that Francesca has to be provided for before he dies. He keeps talking about the payoff on his life insurance policy. Stuff like that. It's tearing Chess up."

Deb leaned back forward and put her hand on mine. "What do the doctors say?"

"They say that Frank will recover. That depression is not uncommon after bypass surgery. They're treating it with drugs and he's doing his rehab sessions. If Frank can just hang in there he should get better. Chess says when his Dad is at the doctors, Frank puts on a different face, trying to fool the doctors into thinking all is well. But, Chess is worried about what Frank might do. It's that damn life insurance policy hanging out there. It must be really large."

We poured the last of the tea, and silently ate more little rolls. I asked Natalie to bring Emma up to speed because I just couldn't talk about this any more today. I didn't want Emma to feel that we had cut her out in any way.

I walked very slowly back down the hill, taking in the green, green hills of New Jersey. I had come to love these hills and dales. Then I turned and looked at the old growth trees that formed the ridge above

Deb's place, a spot that I looked at a little differently now. The view must be wonderful from that high spot.

I spent the rest of the day cleaning my trailer and then taking my truck to one of those tunnel style car washes, vacuuming out all the dried bits of mud, sand, and hay that were ground into the old floor mats and upholstery. It felt good to focus on uncomplicated tasks. The red paint on my truck was faded and covered with scratches, but I still put elbow grease into rubbing the chrome and hand drying the streaks out of the glass on the windows.

Cleaning the trailer had been even more labor intensive. I pulled out the rubber floor mats and scrubbed the floors clean, inspecting every inch. I even took my hoof pick and an old toothbrush and detailed the edges where horse poop had seeped into the cracks. The rubber trailer mats got scrubbed and sanitized and then I used a pair of pliers to grip the edges and drag the heavy things back into the trailer. It was hard work that strained my back but it absorbed my time so that I couldn't fret too much over Chess and Francesca's meeting with Cavelli Foods.

***

I finished all of Winsome and Johnny's laundry, finding that Ryder had already cleaned Johnny's filthy tack. She seemed to be 'taking ownership' of Johnny, I could see that, but I was still grateful to find his tack beautifully cleaned and put up with care.

I used the last bit of my energy to take a shower and wash my hair. At each stopping point in the day I had checked my phone for messages but found none. Finally, when I got out of the shower and changed into an old tee shirt and drawstring pants, my wet hair twisted on top of my head, I was rewarded by a text message. "Totally exhausted, but encouraged. We meet again at the end of the week after lawyers bat a new contract back and forth. Meanwhile, Mother and I are going to have to run all this by Dad. I can't come over tonight. Need to rest up for tomorrow for when I go see Dad and figure out how to present it."

I read it over several times. End of the week? Deb and Emma and Margot and Natalie and Ryder all left for Devon on Wednesday. The FEI jog was Thursday, and the Grand Prix was Friday. I was glad that Chess was encouraged, but alarm bells rang in my head. I sent a short text, "Miss you so much. Can you come over after you see your dad?"

I think he liked the text. He wrote back, "I like hearing that. See you then, will text you when I leave my meeting with him."

At least that left me with a warm feeling. I shared my dinner with Wheezer, and then got into bed with *Gone with the Wind*. I was absorbed in reading about the flight from a burning Atlanta, but in my exhaustion words began to float on the page and the story took a weird turn. I never felt the book hit the floor.

I followed the story where it led me; a wild buggy ride through leaping flames, with the armory erupting on the skyline behind the wagon like a volcano. Rhett cruelly drove the horse, and Scarlett prattled on like a spoiled brat about getting back to Tara.

Suddenly ahead of the buggy were the gates to Equus Paradiso Farm, and I sat in the buggy with the reins in one hand and the remote control gripped tightly in my other hand.

The farm was no longer my home, it had changed, but I had stealthily kept the remote control. It was like holding the keys to the kingdom. I could still sneak in, and I was going to do so in the dark of night. I could quietly put my tired horse in a stall and tip-toe up into the barn apartment. Maybe no one would notice.

I realized I had clearly left the confines of the novel and now explored the strange forests of my mind, almost comical, though my anxiety was real. I don't know what happened after that, but I woke up with my light still on and a disconnected feeling. I checked my phone. It was Tuesday morning. I felt cheated out on a night of rest, as if I had been riding in that buggy all night fleeing the fires of Atlanta, fleeing the relentless Yankee army.

Another training day was here, and tomorrow Wild Child and Fable would leave for their Devon debut at Grand Prix. Even though I wasn't showing, it felt momentous. I kicked the covers to the floor, disturbing Wheezer, and dragged myself to the bathroom.

I went down at the usual time, mug in hand, and fetched Word Perfect. Ryder and I tacked her up together. Ryder held the lead shank and I kept a pocketful of sugar cubes. We had to tell the mare what was expected of her and reward her for behaving, but let her know the consequences for misbehaving.

I got the impression that she was smart, but she still tested us every second, taking perverse satisfaction in outsmarting us in small ways. For example, if I wanted to put a polo wrap on her left hind, she would back up in the grooming stall until she had left hind pressed against the back wall where I couldn't get to it. When I asked her to move over, she would pin her ears in outrage, then swing over to the other side as if something had stung her. It took lots of patience to get her fully dressed and ready to go. Somehow by the end of the process she looked satisfied with herself, but Ryder and I were tired and pissed off. When Margot arrived, the mare put on a face of innocence, wobbling her nostrils in greeting. This mare knew how to work us and I figured that Sophie got the same treatment Ryder and I were getting, and that Wordy greeted Dennis just like Margot just got greeted. It was hard not to take it personally.

Margot was no longer the one Wordy seemed to hate. When Margot arrived, Word Perfect did her low rumbling whinny. I shook my head in disbelief. "Margot, she's transferred her affection from Dennis to you. Look at that!"

Margot fished a treat from her pocket and handed it to the mare. "Smart girl."

The mare gobbled up her treat and then reached her nose forward like an index finger, wiggling it back and forth, begging for another, which Margot immediately produced.

Ryder led Wordy from the grooming stall, and the mare pinned her ears at Ryder while grimacing.

Margot called her name, and we all laughed as Word Perfect changed her face once again. Margot gave her a sugar cube.

Then I called Wordy's name, and the mare turned her head with another wicked face.

Margot's turn, and the horse's mood immediately changed, cracking us all up. Margot led the mare away, saying, "Now we work, darling. No attempts to take me out today, okay? I'll respect you, and you respect me, and we can get along famously."

Ryder told me we were expecting to see Doc this morning. He needed to make health certificates for Fable and Wild Child to have on board along with their Coggin's test for traveling to Devon. There wasn't much to do except fill out the paperwork.

Ryder and I heard the diesel engine way before we saw Doc. He often took awhile to get out, catching up with his office on his cell phone and organizing his paperwork while sitting in his truck, so it didn't strike us as odd that we heard his truck but didn't see him.

We then heard Dennis' monstrous motorcycle. That meant Dennis would be watching Margot ride his mare. It meant tension in the barn.

Doc and Dennis walked into the barn, side by side, Dennis speaking in low but earnest tones. Doc had the look of thunder on his face, his metal clipboard under his arm, his back upright, and shoulders drawn back like a soldier, his eyes narrowed over his reading glasses. I had never seen him looking like that, but he said nothing, just listened. His brows were drawn together and his lips pressed tight. Dennis' face looked relaxed but serious.

Dennis shook hands with Doc in a way that looked final, seemingly oblivious to the fact that Doc looked like he was about to explode. Then Dennis went to watch Margot ride his mare. Doc stood and watched the back of Dennis. Ryder and I once again exchanged looks. Doc turned around and caught us staring. He put his glasses in a shirt pocket and said, "Do you girls know what the heck is going on around here?"

Ryder saved me from answering. "How 'bout you tell us?"

He took a breath before answering. "Dennis just asked me to make up a health certificate for Word Perfect. The address he gave me was in Florida, but not the Cavellis' place. But he said he preferred I not mention it to Margot today. However, he didn't ask me to keep it from you two."

Ryder's voice sounded stunned. "He's breaking his promises."

I wasn't sure what Ryder meant, nor did Doc, who finally said to Ryder, "Young lady, please explain yourself."

Ryder broke free of her statue-like pose, and she shook her head. "Dennis told me that Frank and Francesca are ready to get out from under all of this, financially, with Frank's poor health and money troubles and all. But Dennis promised, he promised *me* that Margot wouldn't lose any more of her rides the way she lost Hotstuff. He promised a lot of other stuff, too."

I then chimed in, "That was before Sophie showed back up like a bad penny."

That news seemed to surprise Doc. "Sophie's back here? After all of that?"

"Well," I said, "Not back here at the farm, but back in the area. We just saw her at the CDI. She sure seemed interested in watching Deb show Wild Child. She was interested in watching Emma and Fable, too." I almost said more, but I stopped myself. Standing there next to Ryder, I held my tongue.

"I see," Doc replied. "Very interesting." Doc's face lost some of its angry look. He seemed to be processing the information. In fact, his face gradually relaxed, and took on an even more positive expression. "Sheesh, I go on vacation for a week, and all these things happen while I'm gone."

Ryder said, "Doc, you want me to get the Coggins together so you can make up your health certificates?"

He nodded briskly, "Yes, please."

Ryder left and Doc moved closer to me, speaking softly. "Elizabeth," his use of my full name echoing the times when my parents would let me know that I was about to be told something important, "Keep your eyes and ears open, and be vigilant. I don't like what I'm seeing here. And..." he pulled out a card from his shirt pocket and wrote on it, "Here's my cell phone number. Don't hesitate to call me, anytime, if you think you need to. The Cavellis aren't just clients, they're personal friends. Okay?"

"Yes, sir," I answered, noting that he did not mention Margot's name.

He noticed Ryder returning and became happy Doc again. "Excellent, Ryder, thank you. Let's get down to business." Ryder left and went to tack up Wild Child for Deb.

Doc gathered the paperwork and filled out all three sheets. Deb and Nat came in and greeted Doc, then Natalie peeled off to fetch Fable. Emma had arrived and it didn't take long before Deb figured out something was up. She, Emma, and Doc congregated around Doc's truck, as he sat with his driver side door open, the diesel engine loudly rumbling. I smiled, imagining the conversation out there. Doc had now joined our war council. No one could possibly overhear the meeting over that loud engine, and no way was Doc going to have to face either Dennis or Margot, he was ready to hit the road. I always liked Doc, but now more than ever.

But I had other conversations to imagine. When Dennis and Margot came in, no one was speaking, the atmosphere seemed tense. I took

Wordy from Margot with a small nod, leading her into the grooming stall. Word Perfect was tired and sweaty and she bobbed her head, desperately wanting her bridle off. I slipped it off and hung it on a hook and was about to slip her halter on when Dennis reached his hand up to pet her face. She barged forward a step and pinned her ears at him, at Daddy! Then Wordy's nose gave me a shove, her ears still pinned. It was an impatient shove, as if to tell me to get on with my job, slave that I was. But then she looked past me, looking for Margot who had disappeared into the tack room.

Word Perfect's ears swiveled forward when Margot re-emerged, and the mare wobbled her nostrils in her soft begging whinny. Margot produced a carrot, and then scratched behind Wordy's ears. The big ears seemed to loosen in their sockets and the mare yawned. Margot gave a sad little laugh. Dennis sulked, his arms crossed over his chest. His look said it all; he was finished with us, with all of us, including the mare. He left without saying good-bye. In a moment we heard the motorcycle start up. Margot patted her little bun, then examined her cuticles, lost in thought. She said to me in a distracted tone, "Lizzy, please tell Deb I'll be back in twenty minutes. She can start without me. I think I need a cup of coffee."

I wanted to say something comforting, but my instincts said 'not now.' Margot had a day of work to get through, and tomorrow they left for Devon. In fact, for the next four days she needed to do her job. There was no time for barn drama. Margot would have to carry on while wounded, and I knew that she would march forward like a good soldier.

Margot returned and threw herself into her coaching. There were no explanations and no complaints. She patted her bun, sporadically picked up her right hand to gnaw at her cuticles, and enthused during the best parts of our rides with exclamations of, "Beautiful, darling!"

But she didn't fool any of us. Deb and Emma had been updated by Doc about Word Perfect leaving and we could only imagine how

Margot felt about it. It appeared that Natalie may have indeed aided in bringing Sophie back from whatever rock she had been hiding under. While I was happy to see Dennis roar out of here on his giant motorcycle, I hated the thought of Word Perfect leaving. I sensed this could be Sophie's first act of retribution, to deny Margot the pleasure of succeeding where she had failed. Word Perfect would once again be ripped away from a rider who had found a way to get along with her. It wasn't fair or right.

It wasn't hard to figure out that next on Sophie's agenda would be to acquire Wild Child, if not all of Equus Paradiso Farm, both north and south. If that happened, Margot would lose more than a horse. We all would. And would it all be due to Natalie pulling Sophie back in and tipping her off, raising her ire, reignited the feud? Or was Sophie already back in New Jersey for the express purpose of reclaiming Dennis and all the material goodies he could provide?

But as of right now, I still had a job and needed to be like Margot and do it and do it well. I wasn't sure what I should do about Johnny Cash and Lovey. Francesca would not be coming out today. She and Chess had the unenviable task of telling Frank about their goals for Cavelli Foods. The proposed sale of the farms and the horses was bound to come up, and this time Francesca would have Chess there to back her up.

With Johnny Cash now at home I could ask Margot for help. She had gone into the office and shut the door. I was almost afraid to go in, so I knocked and then gently cracked the door, saying, "Margot?"

Margot sat at Francesca's desk, leaning on her elbows, chin resting on her fists. She tipped her head and simply said, "Hmmm?"

I asked, "What do you want me to do with Johnny Cash and Lovey today?"

She nodded back, "Of course. I was just thinking about those two. You and Francesca will have the barn to run and horses to work while the rest of us are at Devon. I'll need you to work Papa and Winsome, and for Francesca to ride Johnny and Lovey. The stallions will be at Devon, and Word Perfect will be leaving."

Just hearing her say those words was painful. I squeezed my eyes shut, almost like bracing for a blow. All I could say was, "That stinks. It's wrong and it's stupid."

Margot looked thoughtful and sad. "It's wrong to give and take animals as enticements and punishments. You hang on to that splendid little mare of yours, Lizzy. You hang on no matter what, because she is yours. But you asked me a question?"

I nodded. "Today, Johnny and Lovey?"

Margot's face remained sad. "You let Ryder ride Johnny Cash today while you ride Lovey. I can't give Ryder what she really wants, but I know she'll enjoy that."

I can't say that the assignment made me happy, or that I fully understood what Margot was saying, but I nodded and said, "Thanks" and then gently shut the door.

Ryder didn't seem all that excited, but she went and fetched Johnny, and I got Lovey and the two of us groomed and tacked up side by side in the grooming stalls in the quiet barn. Margot had left, and Emma and Deb had finished putting up their horses and departed long ago.

The silence between Ryder and me was a normal state of affairs, so I was surprised when she actually initiated conversation. She came out of the tack room with Johnny's saddle over her arm, his full bridle hanging on her shoulder, and stood in front of me while I squatted to put polo wraps on Lovey. She just stood there staring at me before turning away and setting her saddle, girth, and pads on the rack and hanging the bridle on the hook. Then she turned back and in a matter of fact tone asked, "Okay, what's the deal with that woman, Sophie?"

I stood up and began the process of putting on Lovey's saddle, slightly irritated by her tone. Ryder made me tired. I just said, "What do you want to know?"

"Y'know, I shared stuff with you when I didn't have to, and I think you owe me the same." Typical Ryder logic.

I felt my face start to flush, only grunting a non-committal, "Hmmm."

What did I owe Ryder? She had aided and abetted Dennis, expecting a payoff from him for her trouble. She had "shared" with me that I could be losing my job; how generous of her. Was that her idea of kindness? I didn't trust myself to say anything right away. Instead I fussed over the saddle placement on Lovey, pulling the front of the pads up into the gullet of the saddle to prevent binding. I snugged the girth a second time and checked the off side one extra time. When I turned around, Ryder had moved back into the grooming stall and was saddling Johnny.

"The Sophie and Dennis drama was before my time. I was hired to replace Sophie," I said.

Ryder came out of the grooming stall and grabbed Johnny's full bridle off the hook. I picked up Lovey's full bridle. The two of us stood looking at each other like mirror reflections, full bridles in hand.

Ryder frowned, "All Dennis talked about to me was Margot, Margot, Margot, and how great she is. He wouldn't shut up talking to me about her. He had all these grand plans, and today he walked right past me like I was invisible."

I shrugged, "He's moving the mare, sending it to Florida. Bet that's not what he told you he had planned. He clearly has a new plan."

She grimaced, "All because of that woman, Sophie?"

I blurted out, "Guess that's all you need to know about Sophie."

She snorted in disgust, "God, I hate this place."

I felt like I had been slapped. I broke eye contact with her and turned to Lovey, sweet Lovey with the doe-eyes. As I turned I said, almost to myself, but loud enough that she could hear, "I love this place, and the people, and all the horses, too."

I fished a peppermint out of my pocket and handed it to Lovey, and then slipped in his bits listening to the happy crunch as Lovey worked the peppermint back to his molars. I knew that the ride on Johnny Cash that Ryder had so coveted was ruined. There would be no dreams of future glory. Instead, she would go through the ride thinking of what could have been, what she believed should have been, and how she had been cheated out of it.

But how could Ryder have been cheated? Ryder was not entitled, had never had a claim, not to keep the ride on Papa, and certainly not to be handed Johnny Cash. Talent purchased you opportunities and that was all. Opportunities could be gained but also lost. But I supposed the same could be said about Deb and Emma and Margot and the horses they had been given to ride. Word Perfect would be lost to Margot, and if Sophie had her way, Wild Child and every other horse here would be lost to us as well.

Except for Winsome. No one could take away from me my "splendid little mare." I would always do as Margot said and hang on to her. She was mine.

17. Wise Fools

Ryder and I finished the evening chores. It felt odd not to go over to the Winstons', but instead head directly upstairs to take showers. I let Ryder know that Chess was picking me up for dinner. What I didn't tell her was where we were going to eat; Deb's. We were leaving her out of the loop yet again. I tried not to feel guilty about it. Ryder had chosen sides. I thought it was too late to offer her a place back at the table.

Deb called my cell phone to remind me that we would be eating outside, and the evenings were getting cool, so she suggested that I dress accordingly.

Ryder grabbed her purse and left before I did. I waited for Chess, stretching out on the sofa, nose deep into *Gone with the Wind*, Wheezer purring on my stomach.

That is how Chess found me when he knocked lightly and then came in saying,

"Sorry I'm late. You shouldn't have waited for me."

Chess had a sport coat on, his tie pulled down, looking tan and slim and fit, and I was warmed by the thought that he was *my* boyfriend.

I said, "You look sharp."

Chess grinned. "You look like Wheezer did your hair."

I put my hand on top of my head where I had twisted up my ponytail and clipped it in a weak effort of a "do." Most of it had migrated out of the clip and was hanging down. I laughed and said, "Nope, that was all me, Wheezer would have done a better job."

My phone buzzed, and it was Deb. She spoke one sentence. "Move it. Dinner's being served."

I looked up at Chess and said, "We gotta go."

I stood up and unclipped my hair; finger combed my "do," and tried again, missing a strand. Chess turned me around and gathered the strand in his fingers, kissing the nape of my neck, and then managed to bundle it all together and refasten the clip. I turned back around with chills running down my spine and we enjoyed a couple of deep slow kisses, the kind where your lips tingle and your stomach drops and flutters as if you are riding a roller coaster. But, dinner was being served and Deb had summoned us. We pulled ourselves apart and took some deep breaths.

I performed the ritual kitten toss so we could get out of the apartment without losing Wheezer out the door and we headed up the hill on foot. It was cool and the sun was low. The bright green of the grass, the dark green of the trees all illuminated by the low sun seemed to turn even the air a golden green. Before we joined the party, Chess pulled me to a stop and pointed to the top of the hill, to the old growth trees, saying, "There, that's the spot." We silently shared one more embrace.

We gathered once again outside at Deb's around her large table. The Tiki torches were lit, but the breeze kept the bugs at bay anyway. Deb had made multiple quiche's with home made crust, enough that she would surely have leftovers. The spinach salad she served in a huge wooden bowl had fresh strawberries and slivered almonds in it, and was dressed with balsamic vinaigrette. This was Deb's art, beautiful for the briefest of moments before we decimated it.

We had a lot of ground to cover tonight, but first we simply enjoyed our dinner and talked of horses and cats and the end of summer and the upcoming trip to Devon. For at least thirty minutes it seemed that there was nothing to worry us and that no harm could come to us, that we could continue as we were, and at this moment, well, we were kick-ass wonderful. At least that is how I felt. We were mythic knights at Camelot's roundtable. Harmony reigned. Of course, Ryder's chair was empty.

But it was Natalie who finally had the nerve to break the spell. She said, "Chess, we've been fortified, we can take it, man. Is Dennis going to buy this farm or not?"

All of us had turned our eyes towards him. Chess had a heavy burden on his shoulders, but he could take care of himself. He was a Cavelli.

Chess reminded me of his mother when he answered without a hint of emotion. "Mother and I discussed it yesterday. Mother has already spoken to Dennis about it being far too low an offer. Deb's success increased Wild Child's value. Mother has already submitted a request to her insurance carrier for an increased valuation on the horse. Or at least, that is what Mother said. The Florida farm has appreciated more than was reflected in his offer, too. That area has boomed. So, although Dad wanted Mother to sell while we had an offer, Mother has basically taken charge. And as you know, Mother is no pushover."

Deb chuckled. She leaned back in her chair, took a swig at her beer, and after a thoughtful moment added, "Chess, you know there was a day that Francesca and I could barely stand to be within sight of each other. Fortunately we've made peace, but, let me just say this; I'd rather have her on my side in a fight than fight against her. She's tough as they come."

Chess nodded. "Mother is a tough one. Dad..." Chess closed his eyes, took a breath and continued. "Dad is the one with the tender heart. He gives his heart away easily, loves intensely, loyal to the core, and is way too willing to give a totally phony guy like Dennis a second chance. No one can convince Dad that he's not dying. He thinks he is 'putting his affairs in order'."

Chess' answer simply meant more uncertainty. I added a second part to the question that I addressed to no one. "And what if Dennis does buy the farm? It looks pretty clear to me that we won't be allowed to stay. He and Margot are done. Word Perfect is being taken away from her, and if he can finish twisting the knife, this farm and all the horses on it will be his big make-up gift to Sophie."

Emma startled us all by slamming her fist on the table. "No! Not going to happen. No one is buying this farm for Sophie."

Natalie actually laughed. She said, "Blondie, you've been spending too much time down there in Texas, but I love the tough talk."

Emma looked furious. "I'm serious, Natalie. I'll stop the two of them, no matter what I need to do."

The room seemed tense. Deb and I exchanged a worried look. She set her beer down on the table and turned to Emma, leaning on her elbows. "Go on, Em, short of a six-shooter and Texas justice, what are you thinking?"

Natalie answered the question for Emma. "Well, first off, we need the name and number of the farm where Word Perfect is going."

I chimed in, "It's on the health certificate. Doc has a copy." I thought about Doc giving me his card and his numbers. I had entered it all into my cell phone contact list. I fingered my cell phone, hitting the contacts icon.

Natalie looked at Emma. "You may not be able to save the farm, Emma, but maybe you can at least save Word Perfect for Margot."

Chess exhaled deeply and cut his eyes at me with a look that said, 'this again?'

Emma's lower lip trembled, but her voice was clear. "I'm listening."

Natalie continued. "Word Perfect is a Weltmeyer daughter, nothing more valuable out there as a broodmare. They're known for producing FEI horses. Deb says she would cross well with Fable. Your sponsors back in Texas have money, and they're motivated. Get them to buy

Wordy, and a couple of embryo transfer recipient mares. They will get foals from Wordy and Fable, while Margot and you increase the value of the foals by having the mare and the stallion both competing at Grand Prix."

I said, excited, "Natalie, you are brilliant. Oh my God, you are so brilliant!"

Deb added, "But don't you dare let Dennis or Sophie or the agent figure out that the mare is being purchased for Margot to ride. You do, and that Sophie bitch will somehow kill the deal."

Emma's face brightened, her gears were turning. "I can have Tank pose as the buyer. No one would trace him to Margot in a million years. He rides reining horses, for crying out loud."

I had found Doc's contact information. I slid the phone across the table to Emma. A smile spread across her lips. She pulled out her phone and entered the numbers. Then she said, "Will you all excuse me for a few minutes?"

We all nodded in concert, but I could see Chess' right toe tapping the grass as he leaned back in his chair. We chatted away pleasantly for a few moments, and then Chess offered to clear the table. He refused our help. But after he didn't return for the rest of the dishes, I got up and gathered the rest. I came through the kitchen door and was stopped by the sight of Emma and Chess facing each other by the kitchen sink, standing so close. Emma was speaking in low tones, and Chess had his head tipped forward, listening intently.

Their familiarity stung me. I made my presence known by cheerily saying, "This is the last of the dinner plates." But the voice inside my head was grim, it confirmed that 'yes, they had indeed been a couple.'

I returned to the dinner table. Deb gave me an odd look. Natalie looked at me and then at Deb and said, "I'm going to put on the coffee and help wash up the dishes. Then we'll serve dessert. Deb gets a pass since she cooked, and Lizzy, I'll need you to sit and entertain her."

Deb and I were left alone. She was sitting directly across the table from me.

She said, "Hey."

And I said, "Hey."

Deb said, "You're an open book, you know that right?"

I said, "I don't know what you mean."

"Don't be silly. Let them have their talk and stop fretting. Lizzy, there's a lot to worry about right now, but there's one thing you don't need to worry about."

I got her point, feeling embarrassed that I was so easy to read. She smiled again and drained the last of her beer. "Chess looks so much like his mother, but truth is he got the best characteristics of the both of them. He is kind and loyal like his Dad, but he's practical and tough, like his mother. He's always doing nice stuff for others, too, just like his Dad. He's a good guy."

I was still embarrassed and let my eyes drop to examine my rough looking hands and short clipped nails, a laborer's hand. Emma was a glamour girl, and I never would be. Did it matter?

Deb continued, "For example, he's made a connection for Natalie to sell her art. He gave her a prospectus for a commercial job. Some family friend of the Cavellis is a commercial art consultant. This guy's client is a botanical garden looking for a collection of outdoor animal sculptures, all garden animals like frogs and butterflies and rabbits and such. How great is that? He's given her a shot at a big money job. Of course, she has to create a portfolio of drawings of all the sculptures and on a short time schedule, too. But it's a shot, and it's all because of Chess."

I looked up, drawn away from my anxieties. "It's really happening?"

Deb smiled, "She doesn't have the job yet, but yeah, they'd be stupid to pass her up. Her stuff is totally original and beautiful. If she does get the gig, well, there'll be no peace and quiet around here."

Chess soon returned, and then Natalie came back with coffee and home made cream puffs. Emma was missing and Deb raised a questioning eyebrow at him.

He nodded. "Em's got Doc on the line. She waved me away. Maybe we should start without her."

A forced calm returned to our table. We turned to safe topics, like Natalie's art and how the Cavellis' friend had been impressed with what he had been shown.

Emma strode in with her cell phone clutched to her chest, a small smile on her face. She announced, "Doc was very interested in helping us. I did feel badly though about interrupting his dinner. He was in a restaurant and had to excuse himself to take my call. We kept it brief, but he'll text me all the information on Word Perfect's destination first thing in the morning."

Deb said, "Emma, don't feel bad. He's a vet. He's used to taking emergency calls at odd hours."

Chess said, "That's one reason I thought the call could wait. Getting that address wasn't exactly an emergency was it?"

Deb cleared her throat and said, "Well, what's done is done, Chess. Anyway, we've got a lot of other stuff we need to talk about, like tomorrow's schedule."

We ran down the details. Margot and Francesca and I would work horses tomorrow while everyone else loaded and then drove to Devon. Margot would join them later that day. Then it would be just Francesca and me in charge of the farm and the horses left at home, until we joined them on Saturday afternoon to watch the Grand Prix Freestyles. We would stay over Saturday night and return on Sunday.

Emma and Deb described what a grand evening Freestyle night was at Devon, and how Francesca had gone to considerable trouble and expense to secure the farm a box in the grandstands, and reserved the block of rooms at the hotel a whole year in advance.

Chess lounged back in his chair and shook his head in disbelief. He said, "Mother spent all that money. It's like striking up the band while the Titanic is sinking."

Natalie laughed at that. She said, "Chess, my man, all the more reason you need to come. It may be our last hurrah."

Chess was outnumbered. We bugged him until he promised to drive down and join the party.

He reached over and took my hand and gave it a friendly squeeze that made my heart beat a little faster. I glanced over at Emma, but she had lifted her plate and was letting Uno lick off the smear of custard left from her dessert.

Chess and I walked down the hill hand-in-hand. I asked with genuine concern, "Frank doing any better?"

Chess said, "He had a check up this morning. The doctors are still happy with how he's recovering, but Dad's never really been sick before. I can't remember him even having a bad cold. He's always had an iron constitution and endless energy. He's taking this hard, but it could be what he needs to change a lot of bad habits."

"Poor Frank."

Chess continued, "I think those who are blessed with good health are more likely to take it for granted. Dad has always run at full tilt. But, he'll have to figure out for himself what this heart attack means going forward."

I said, "What does he *want* it to mean? To me, that's the question he has to ask himself, because it appears to me that he still has the power to make that decision."

Chess looked thoughtful, then said, "That's where we come in, to steer him toward the decision that we want him to make. Not only to live, but to re-engage in life. He and Mother both thrive on being in charge. This new Dad, I hardly recognize. It's like he's scared of making decisions, he even asks Marta to pick out his socks for him."

The thought made me sad. "I've seen the Cavellis at work, yeah, the both of them, so I know what you mean. I sure do miss the old Frank, and now I have a new appreciation of Francesca. So, what can I do?"

Chess glanced at his watch and back at me, as if he were seriously considering my question. He finally said, "It's not too late, so why don't we go sneak Dad a shot of whiskey?"

My mouth fell open. "Whiskey? Now?"

He grinned back. "Marta gathered up all the booze and hid it. But, I know where. Poor Dad feels deprived of all his little pleasures, and Mother said the doctor said one drink a day would be fine, no more than a shot, but Marta's been denying him even that. So both Mother and I have been sneaking it to him. It's a game, and I'm guessing Marta knows, but all the same, stolen fruit is all the sweeter. Anyway, it will cheer him up to see you."

Chess was including me. It wasn't just a "Cavelli family problem" after all. I just said, "Okay, let's go."

Chess and I walked to his car. If sneaking Frank a little shot of forbidden bourbon gave him a reason to live, then I was happy to lose a little sleep to do it.

Chess and I made the short drive, and went through the electric gate, winding our way up the dark and silent drive. Chess used his key to open the front door and we walked right in to the dark house, and Chess held a finger up to his lips. Of course with Chopper and Snapper in the house it was useless to think we could get away with such stealth. They charged down the stairs, barking their heads off, but when they saw us they did their happy terrier acrobatics as we squatted down and greeted them.

The light came on at the top of the stairs, and there stood Francesca glaring down at us. She wore floral pajamas. I felt awkward and intrusive, suddenly thinking this was a very bad idea. But, Chess stood up, and made a motion to his mother of tipping a drink into his mouth.

She frowned and then called, "Chopper, Snapper...come!"

The dogs ran up the stairs, and then the light went off.

I followed Chess down a dimly lit hallway to the back of the house and into a laundry room. He opened a cabinet over the washer, and there stood a half dozen bottles of booze. He winked at me and whispered, "Dad would never look in the laundry room. He's never done a load of laundry in his life."

From there we stepped into a huge gourmet kitchen. For a moment I imagined Chess in here, cooking alongside his Nonna. But, I didn't know if she'd lived to see this kitchen. Chess picked up a shot glass, and then motioned me back into the shadowy hall. We stepped into another hall that ran under the grand staircase, and stepped down one step into the other wing of the addition. We stopped outside a door that had a strip of light shining under it. Chess seemed to have known for certain that his dad would still be awake. He knocked on the door and Frank's grumpy voice replied, "What?"

Chess opened the door a little wider, handed me the bottle and the glass, and gave me a gentle shove. I started by just putting my hand inside, the one clutching the bottle.

Frank said, his voice raspy but optimistic, "Sweet mother-of-God, have I died and gone to heaven?"

That made me giggle in relief; it sounded like the Frank I knew and loved. I stepped into the dim light of his room. Frank exclaimed, "I *have* died, and God has sent an angel to carry me home."

Frank was propped up in bed in what clearly was a guest room, his reading glasses askew and his bedside light was on. His latest read was opened in front of him, face-down on the bedspread. I stepped forward and Chess came in quietly behind me.

Chess said, "Lizzy here has been desperate to see you."

I added, "I come bearing libations." And I clicked the shot glass against the bottle, and then leaned forward and kissed his whiskered cheek. Chess took the bottle and glass from me and poured the drink, handing it to his dad. "Sip it slowly, Pop, it's the only one you get tonight."

Frank nodded with a serious expression, and then said, "I dream of whiskey." He spent time smelling the drink before taking a small sip. Then he smacked his lips and said, "Bliss. And good for your health. I think I read that somewhere."

Chess pulled a squat blue tufted chair up to the bedside and motioned for me to sit. Then he addressed his dad.

"Dad, you and I had a good talk today didn't we? And Lizzy and I had a good talk today, too. It was a good day all around because today I felt good for you and Mother and Cavelli Foods, and the future."

Frank took another sip and then leaned back into his pillows and sighed. He grumbled, "Well, *I* had a crappy day. I still have my damn days and nights mixed up, you know. I try to read, but I can't concentrate worth a damn. So, I worry. I worry all damn night, and then sleep all damn day. And awake or asleep I think about how much I want a drink. And pasta. Your Nonna's pasta."

Chess shot me a sideward glance. I suddenly thought about how weary Francesca must be dealing with Frank. How stressful this had been for Chess, and then how important Marta was in the scheme of things. We at the farm had been worried and stressed, but this was the front line and from this, we at the farm had all been spared.

Chess cleared his throat. Then he said, "Dad, I want to say something to you with Lizzy sitting right here. And I don't want to talk about it too much because it feels too early and everything is uncertain, but I want you to hear it now in hopes it makes a difference."

That perked Frank up. He was intrigued.

Chess smiled and looked at me. I smiled back. "I've gotten kind of attached to this girl here."

Frank blinked. "So, are you telling me that you have some kind of announcement?"

"No, no," Chess said, looking at me, "At least, not right now. But . . ."

I smiled at him and reached out my hand. Deb was right. This was a good man.

"You know, son," Frank said, "Good things don't come around all that often. Time's shorter than you think. Just sayin'."

I said, "Frank, you have to recover and get strong again. And you will."

He gave my other hand a firm squeeze back. It was not the grip of a dying man. It dawned on me, with conviction, that his doctors were right. He would recover. Frank just needed to decide to get better. This was a new level of suffering for him, perhaps greater than he had ever known before, but it was not the end. I had a strange moment of insight; that life never got easier in the way that you imagined it would when you were young. We needed greater and greater courage as life went on, not less.

I said, "I hate it that you have suffered. I can tell it's been a shock and that you feel that it's changed everything. But, does it really have to? You are not alone, you know. There's a whole bunch of us over at the farm, plus Chess. We've got your back."

A tear slid slowly down Frank's cheek, which he didn't bother to wipe away. Instead, he knocked back what was left in his shot glass and handed it to Chess. He said, "I think I'll sleep now. And Chess?""

"Yes, Pop?"

"Like I say, life is shorter than you think. Don't waste it."

I stood up and gave him another kiss on his cheek. Then Chess did the same, putting the blue chair back while I held the bottle and the glass. As I shut the door he called out, "By the way, I think I read somewhere that lemon squares really help on recovery from heart attacks."

Chess and I giggled, happy to hear a bit of the old Frank Cavelli.

It was almost 11:00 when Chess and I pulled in the barn. Doc's truck was parked in front of the barn and the aisle lights were on. Immediately adrenaline hit my veins. No one ever wants to see the vet truck at that hour, it was never good. Chess saw the frightened look on my face. Silently he got out of the car and trailed after me as I rushed into the barn.

Doc and Margot stood in front of Word Perfect's stall. They looked as surprised to see Chess and me as I was to see them.

I drew even with them, breathless with worry, and I said, "Is she okay?"

Doc looked down and answered calmly, "Oh, she's fine, just fine. All the horses seem to be fine."

I weakly said, "Oh." Then I took in the scene. Margot wore a dress, and Doc had on a sport coat. Margot had a bag of carrots in her hand, and was slowly feeding them through the bars of the stall front to Word Perfect. Doc stood next to her, watching.

Chess stepped up behind me, placing his hands on my shoulders and the four of us stood there and watched as Word Perfect happily munched her carrots with relaxed ears and a contented expression.

It came to me then it had been Doc and Margot's dinner that Emma's call had interrupted. And here they were together still while Margot said her good-byes to Wordy. I didn't ask when Word Perfect was being picked up, but assumed Doc knew and had shared it with Margot. I assumed with some certainty that when Margot returned from Devon, Wordy would be gone. It looked like Doc had realized how hard this would be for Margot and taken her out for the evening, but their evening was ending on a sad note. I felt that our presence was intrusive. I turned and looked at Chess and he understood immediately.

Chess said, "Well, it's a school night for me." He gave me a chaste peck on my cheek. "Goodnight all." With a wave, he walked back out to his car.

I was going to just say goodnight like Chess, and give Margot her space to say her good-byes, but unplanned words tumbled out of my mouth. "I can't believe he would do this."

Margot sounded sad but calm. "It's no surprise really. Tigers don't change their stripes. Liars will lie; cheaters will cheat, thieves will steal. And they will do it without remorse, convincing themselves that whatever they do is righteous."

Doc nodded. "Well put, Margot."

Margot sniffed, "Not wise at all, darling. In fact, I'm the biggest fool ever."

Doc said, "Stop being so hard on yourself."

Margot sighed again. "I feel so sorry for the mare though, truly I do."

I wanted to say something about Natalie's plan, but if that could be pulled off, it would be Emma's gift to give to Margot, not mine. Instead, I simply said, "Margot, if I had the money, I would buy that horse for you. I would."

I looked directly at Doc when I said it. But, he showed no sign of understanding.

Margot said, "Darling, that is so sweet of you to say. You get some rest. Tomorrow is a busy day for all of us."

I said goodnight and headed up the stairs. Without particularly knowing why, I had a buzzing feeling about seeing Doc and Margot together. Maybe it was the after effect of the adrenaline surge. But maybe it was something else, like a realization hitting me like a thunderbolt. We all depended on Doc, trusted him, felt his solid protection like a sturdily built house, and somehow in that role he took care of all of us. He was indeed "our" Doc, a good, solid man like Chess and like Frank Cavelli.

Seeing him standing next to Margot, dressed from a night out at a nice restaurant, well, why hadn't it occurred to me before? Doc and Margot fit together in a natural way that seemed almost pre-ordained. I smiled all the way up the stairs, and then into the apartment. I scooped up my chatty Wheezer and just kept smiling as I got ready for bed. I had the most peaceful feeling and could barely read a chapter before I had to close GWTW, and turn off the light. I fell into a deep and dreamless sleep.

18. Shipping Out

Francesca arrived early, flanked by her lieutenants, Chopper and Snapper. She carried herself like a general inspecting her troops, nose held high. The trailer was parked in front of the barn, the ramp down. Alfonso and Ryder and Natalie huddled in front of the open trailer tack room, conferring over the laminated packing list, but dropped their arms and stopped talking as Francesca approached. Ryder had assumed what used to be Emma's role, white board marker in hand, checking off the items on the laminated list.

This was no ordinary horse show they were shipping out to, this was Dressage at Devon and Equus Paradiso Farm would be on full display with two entries in the Grand Prix. DAD was a special fixture on the competition calendar. The dressage and sport horse breeding show was over forty years old, but the show grounds were much older, and the annual "Country Fair" Devon Horse Show was first held in 1896. The place had prestige, it had history, and the Dixon Oval, the main arena, had its own special charm and aura.

Francesca passed her critical eyes over each inch and then had a few words with "staff." Alfonso had the truck and trailer sparkling; freshly waxed, the tire sidewalls gleaming, the chrome polished, the tack room compartment vacuumed. It passed inspection with flying colors.

Fable and Wild Child would travel together in the farm rig. Alfonso would be driving, helping with set up, and then coming home until Sunday when he went back down to pick them up. Emma would follow the trailer in her big truck, the bed loaded down with hay and feed and mucking equipment.

Francesca called Natalie over to the open trunk of her Mercedes, pointing to a stack of thin and mysterious boxes that Nat loaded into Emma's back seat.

Margot would not be riding Word Perfect today, or maybe ever again. I was instructed to turn her out each day until she shipped out, whenever that was. That left four horses to work: Lovey and Johnny Cash for Francesca, and Winsome and Papa for me. Francesca and I were to ride together for the next four days, check on the mares and foals, and direct Alfonso's crew while he was away. We two were being left in charge, together.

The idea of spending all that time alone with Francesca was not as dreaded as it once would have been. I did worry that Word Perfect would be leaving us, leaving Margot, and I had no idea if any of us would see the big black mare again. I could only hope that Emma, loyal and tenacious, was on it, and wouldn't give up until she was successful in getting the mare back for Margot. But of course, Emma had a lot on her plate this weekend. Her first duty was to her sponsors. She had to ride better than last weekend and get through her freestyle without disasters.

Margot was extraordinarily late. In fact, she pulled in just as Alfonso finished putting up the ramp, the horses loaded. Deb and Emma's vehicles were lined up and ready to go. Margot jumped out of her car and pulled her sunglasses to the top of her head, peering down the barn aisle. She said something to Alfonso and he got into the truck and closed the door and started up the noisy diesel. Then Margot walked down the aisle toward Francesca and me to give us her parting directions.

"Darlings, I am so sorry to be late. Lizzy, please do have fun with my Papa. I know he looks and feels a little intimidating, but remember he's a pussycat. Just leave the piaffe and one-tempis alone, but the rest is there for your education and pleasure. Enjoy."

Then she turned to Francesca, "It feels so strange to drive off without you. But, no matter what is going on here, I want to see you there on Saturday for the freestyles. After all you've put into this Devon, you must come. Promise you'll be there. Promise." Margot reached forward and took hold of Francesca's hand.

Francesca did not promise, but patted Margot on the arm reassuringly.

Margot leaned close and whispered something in her ear. Francesca smiled a wicked little smile and whispered back. I wondered what that was about. I got a hug from Margot, but no whispered secret.

Francesca and I watched Margot walk past Word Perfect's stall without a glance, even though Wordy tried to call her over with a soft wobbly whinny that tore at my heart. Tears sprang up in my eyes and my lower lip trembled. Francesca cut a sideward glance my way. Then we both looked back down the aisle at Margot's departing back.

Margot had the erect posture of a dancer, lithe and long limbed. I felt sure she would carry herself like that the rest of her life. She always struck me as calm, assured, self-contained, and oh so accomplished. But she was not made of stone, she had to be heartsick, so distressed at the turn of affairs, yet there she strode, the picture of confidence. She had a job to do and she intended to do it well. She had her "girls" to see through this very important weekend. She would see them through with style and pride.

Last night when I had seen her with Doc, I saw for the first time that he was her perfect counterpart. Good old Doc had been here, quietly observing the ups and downs of the farm and its people for years. And I had observed Margot so often standing out at Doc's truck or by his side in long, comfortable conversations. They were old friends. Why not more? What had stopped them? I wondered if I should mention it to Francesca, but decided not to. That conversation would wait until I could see Emma and Deb, and they did not need that distraction now.

Francesca asked me to put Lovey in the grooming stall, and to set out his tack, informing me she would groom and tack him up herself. That was a first. I smiled, thinking that she still needed me to set out his tack because I'm certain she couldn't have located it herself.

Francesca had not mentioned seeing Chess and me at her house the previous evening. I snapped Lovey in, and offered to pick out his hooves, an offer Francesca accepted. Then I went for Winsome and things got quiet while we worked side by side. Finally I said, "Um, Chess said you and he are speaking, uh, with the attorney, and, uh, the new guys over at Cavelli Foods."

Francesca stepped out of her grooming stall and said, "Please tighten the girth for me. I have to put on my boots and spurs and fetch my helmet and gloves."

Which left me wondering if she had even heard me? I finished putting on Winsome's saddle, then stepped over to Lovey and repositioned his saddle and pads and then tightened his girth. While I was at it, I figured I might as well bridle him too, since Francesca had disappeared.

I bridled Lovey and, since Francesca was still in the tack room, went ahead and pulled him out into the aisle, ran down her stirrups, and snugged up the girth one last time. I could hear her on her cell phone coming out of the tack room. She finished her call, pulled on her gloves and simply said, "Thank you, Lizzy."

Yeah, Francesca and I were going to finally get a chance to chum around. I felt distracted as I turned back to Winsome. This time alone with Francesca wasn't exactly new. I'd been spending one-on-one time with Francesca every day with Johnny Cash. But, this felt different. Our mission before had been clear, even if it had felt impossible. And we had done it. But, what now? Francesca could make my life easier by throwing me a little bone, a bit of encouragement, reassurance that all would be well in time, or barring that, she could at least make small talk.

However, Francesca had never been about making me feel comfortable. No, just the opposite, she seemed to thrive on causing me discomfort and unease. From the very first day that I arrived, she had made me feel unwanted, a burden, a distraction for Margot. And then when I had thought she cared for me, that I had won her over when she had given me Wheezer as a thank you gift, I learned instead that my feline gift was a tactic to keep her son from visiting me in the apartment.

I had done right by Francesca, kept her secret, gone the extra mile to help her achieve her dreams. I *had* been the right girl for the job. It also appeared I was the right girl for her son, too; at least, her son seemed to think so. All I wanted was to hear something like that from her lips, and to hear it without a sneer. The fact was I had put myself on track to possibly become her daughter-in-law.

I wasn't sure she would allow that to happen without a battle. Did I want to win that battle?

I finished tacking up Winsome, and took a moment to feed her sugar cubes, to bury my nose in her neck and inhale her sweet smells, part horse dander and part fly spray and coat polish, aroma therapy that immediately reduced my stress levels, and made me smile. It would have sent Chess into a fit of sneezing, even with his new prescriptions. I recalibrated my emotional state. How self-defeating, to work myself up while Francesca blithely rode around on Lovey not giving my feelings or me a thought. That in itself was a survival trait of hers worth emulating.

We rode Winsome and Lovey in silence, then we showered them and I helped her with tacking up Johnny Cash. Since he was over seventeen hands, she couldn't lift his saddle high enough because it was too heavy for her. In some ways Francesca was quite helpless, and I was not. When it came to the horses, I was self-sufficient. Maybe Francesca resented that, but it didn't make her cold-shoulder easier to take. Not today.

After we finished, Francesca helped me shower and put up Johnny and Papa, while hardly saying a word, and not surprisingly she left me all the tack to clean and put away.

I finished my day early, going upstairs to read and eat my frozen dinner alone in peace. Peace would not come. Instead I felt lonely and anxious, despite my purring kitten. So much for a recalibrated emotional state. I was too tired to go back down for more horse therapy. Wheezer would have to do; I mindlessly stroked her under the chin and brooded about my relationship with Francesca. I had softened toward Francesca. I had. Why couldn't she soften more toward me?

I had three more days alone with Francesca, three days with the silent ice-queen who shut me out and made me feel like nothing but a lowly servant. Did she not understand that I was more than that now? What if I did figure in to Chess' future? Would Francesca spend the rest of her days marginalizing my very existence?

Chess called and broke my self-absorbed state. I asked hopefully, "Any good news on the negotiations with Cavelli Foods?"

There was a prolonged silence at the other end. "Mother wants me to stay quiet about it for now. But, she and Dad have been fighting. Even though Dad had disengaged from the problems of Cavelli Foods, he blew up when he heard how Mother had engaged a lawyer and gone at the new owners. He knows she's an attack dog."

I said, "That's bad, isn't it?"

Chess' resigned sigh was audible. "Maybe, but the more I think about it, Lizzy, the more I think it's actually not a bad thing. It was pretty uncomfortable to witness. I can tell you that. But, now, Dad's coming to the meeting on Thursday. The fact that he is rousing himself to leave the house for anything other than a doctor's visit is encouraging."

I could see his point. The news dawned on me as possibly pivotal. I said with cautious enthusiasm, "Frank is back. Oh Chess, this is wonderful news."

He answered softly, "Yeah. I think so, too. Dad's angry, but I see a change. I can take his anger much better than I can take his depression and weird detachment. Dad was about to throw in the towel, and now, now he's going to march into the next meeting and make it all work. I just know it. That's what Dad does best. He did say he was proud and happy that I wanted in at Cavelli Foods, and part of what he wants is to make a good place for me in the company, one where I can find my 'highest and best use'."

I considered my next words, then spoke them earnestly. "I know that's what your father wants, but what do you want? I mean, you got involved in this to work on the audit, and then had to do more when Frank had the heart attack. And if you're in, that means you'll have to deal with your mother. As hard as she treats her employees, I expect she's even harder on her own son."

There was a long silence, so long that I was afraid that my call had dropped, but then I heard Chess exhale long and slow. He said, "It's been tough, but good in some ways. I sort of see my parents from a new perspective. In the past, I wanted to be like my brother, to put some distance between myself and Mother and Dad, well, especially Mother, and make my own way in the world. Mother made it impossible for me to feel competent and mature, no matter how I struggled to prove that I was grown up, that I was competent. And Dad, though he is kind, can be larger than life. When Dad is in the room, he owns the room. He is a commanding presence. So, even working alongside Dad is tough."

"Lots of challenges," I offered.

"Definitely," he answered, "But now, unlike my brother, I think I can make it work, because now those two are not simply Mother and Dad. They are two very complicated but good people I admire and love, even if I don't understand them sometimes. They built an empire from almost nothing, and they have a lot to teach me, as an adult now and not as a child. And I don't know how much longer they'll be around for that. Almost losing Dad made me realize that right here, right now, I want to be near them. What scared me the most was to see the fight go out of Dad. I thought for sure he was finished."

There was another gap of silence, which I filled. "Frank is not finished."

That encouraged Chess to go on. "So, Lizzy, in this battle for the survival of Cavelli Foods, while I am trying to help and support Mother in this, in the end, it will come down to more than just lawyers and re-negotiating a new contract with the new guys. It will come down to Mother and Dad negotiating a new future together; one in which Dad lives and regains his health and makes more sensible choices. I have to stay out of that part because that is a private thing between the two of them, and I think he's the only one who truly understands her, and vice-versa."

My eyes had grown moist. I had my own problems to work out with Francesca. I needed both tact and courage. Francesca needed to become more than the person who wrote my skimpy paychecks, the person who gave orders. She needed to see me as a person of worth, the person who loved and was loved by her son. I had to have a higher value than that of her lowly groom. Without that, I didn't see a future here with Chess, at least not one that was tolerable. But, I wasn't going to burden Chess with that, not now.

We finished the call by confirming our own plans for Devon. Chess was coming to see what all the fuss was about and offered to drive me down. Since I wasn't grooming this show, it was going to be a date of sorts. I was looking forward to it. We exchanged sweet good nights.

***

The next morning, Francesca was so late that I had both Lovey and Winsome completely groomed and tacked up. I was in the tack room and had pulled a warm dryer load of polo wraps and towels and saddle pads out onto the floor to put away when Chopper and Snapper rushed in. I squatted down to pet their squirming bodies. Before I could prevent it, smooth-coated "Snapper" had grabbed a freshly washed tangled ball of new polo wraps. He looked up at me with the devil in his eyes.

I said indignantly, "Hey!" And at that he took off out the door and down the barn aisle, wad held high, one polo unraveling from the ball and trailing behind him. Chopper sprinted after him, barking frantically. I joined the chase, passing Francesca who walked toward me, talking on her cell phone and pulling off her sunglasses with raised brows. She stopped and frowned, waving her sunglasses in the direction of her naughty dogs and saying angrily, "I just bought those!"

Once Chopper caught up with his demonic partner, he grabbed a trailing polo, digging in his feet and whipping his brother around to face him. Intense growling commenced as the two dogs stretched out the fabric, tugging. It gave me a chance. I stomped on an end and crowed in victory as it pulled free of the wad, but when it let loose the boys were off, running out of the barn.

Francesca watched me chase them around the barnyard in my heavy riding boots, yelling at her dogs. It was a noisy game as the dogs' added sound effects, growls and yips and yaps. I stomped on another bit and it turned loose. I held it up like I had won some kind of prize.

Chopper and Snapper both stopped to watch me celebrate. They wagged their stumpy tails slowly, grinning but keeping the polos in their mouths. But of course, as soon as I twitched a muscle to move, they were off again, this time holding the flattened wad side by side, tucking their butts and charging around the parking area. But as they zigged and zagged teasingly close, I tagged another polo with my toe and nearly flipped them over, this time I reeled the little monsters in like fish. They leaned back against the pull, growling and snarling. Francesca made horrified noises behind me as she examined over the captured polos, saying, "They've ruined them. Lizzy, they've overstretched the fabric and poked them full of holes."

I lifted the boys off the ground and toted them like that back to the tack room with Francesca at my heels. They came by their names honestly; Chopper had chops, and Snapper's jaws were snapped shut. I lectured them as I walked, fully aware that I would be receiving the next lecture on my careless laundry habits.

Once I had them in the tack room, I shut the door and set them on the ground. They still held onto their prize. Francesca came in, closing the door behind her. She watched with narrowed eyes, one hand on her hip, the other twirling her sunglasses as I conducted an exchange; one German-style molasses horse cookie dangled in front of each twitching nose, for the return of the remaining bundle of ruined polo wraps.

They looked at each other intently and then seemed to agree to the deal, spitting out the polo wraps in unison. Francesca said, "Hand those to me. I don't want Margot to see these. She catalogues Chopper and Snapper's sins, and after a glass of wine I get to hear them recited ad nauseam."

Francesca pointed her sunglasses at me. "Lizzy, you will have no idea what happened to those new wraps."

I giggled stupidly, mostly in relief. "It will be our secret, Francesca."

Francesca said, "Hmmm." And I saw her face soften, the anger replaced with amusement.

Francesca made her tight-lipped smile and I pulled an imaginary zipper across my lips, awash in relief, not only that Francesca hadn't yelled at me, but that she had lost the vacant look in her eye.

She said, "Let's ride, shall we?" Francesca bundled up the ruined wraps and said, "Let me put these in my car so I don't forget. I'll be right back." Then she pointed at her terriers who wagged stumpy tails, looking self-satisfied. She said, "Don't test my patience further. Do you understand?"

***

I wasn't going to ask Francesca any direct questions about Cavelli Foods today; instead I tried a polite question about Chess. Now was a good time while she was warmed up and seemed friendly. I said, "I've really enjoyed getting to know Chess. He's such a great guy."

Francesca didn't answer. She knew I was reaching, but at least she appeared amused or perhaps curious about where I was going rather than dismissive. I continued. "It's unusual to meet someone who has talents both in math and the arts. People usually tend to be more one or the other, don't you think?"

We led our horses to the mounting block and got on, walking companionably enough to the indoor arena. Francesca didn't answer right away, but this time she couldn't just leave me standing in the grooming stall. The question was not open ended. Winsome was about a hand taller than Lovey, so for once I was looking down on Francesca. Even though Winsome and I had the rail, I still had to check Winsome's stride to stay abreast of Francesca and Lovey, but I made sure that Francesca and I were shoulder-to-shoulder. She would have to talk to me.

Finally Francesca spoke, and as she did I could see that she had drawn inward, like she was watching old family movies in her mind. It wasn't an unpleasant expression, more like absorbed. She said, "Chess

343

is like me, and always has been. Do you know that he was christened Anthony?"

She was talking! I wanted to keep her going. I nodded enthusiastically, "When I first met Chess he introduced himself as Anthony! But that was it. He's been Chess ever since. Deb refused to call him anything else."

She continued in a thoughtful tone, "Because he is my little clone. Everyone could see it the moment he could crawl. If he had been a girl, he would have been named after me, but Chess was what we ended up calling him anyway, and it stuck. Chess, after FranCHESSca." She emphasized the second syllable and it clicked. The older brother named for Frank, the younger brother nicknamed for Francesca,

Well, that was a revelation. My surprise was genuine. "I had no idea. He never said."

Francesca began to gather her reins as if to indicate that the discussion was over. But she added matter-of-factly, "Well, there is a time when children need to separate themselves from their parents. It was quite natural that he would not want anyone to think he was nicknamed after his mother. It's rather emasculating when you think of it that way. But, he looks like me, has my business sense, and is able to be clear-headed and practical, at the same time he is creative and artistic, although he mostly hides that fact. But, down deep he knows that he's his mother's child. I'm a dancer, and he played tennis like a dancer, light on his feet and fast as blazes. And his dexterity on the piano was something his teachers used to rave about. He got all of those things from me, not from Frank."

Francesca peeled off, changing direction with a walk pirouette and picking up the trot to begin her work session.

I tried hard not to smile. Typical of Francesca, she wanted to claim Chess' talents as her own. He did have her looks, but he was not Francesca. He was not cold or dismissive. Francesca was wrong as I saw it, but at least she was showing some maternal feelings when she talked about Chess...her Chess...my Chess.

Francesca and I had uneventful rides on Papa and Johnny. She showered off her own horses, and left me the mounds of tack to clean. I didn't mind. Before she left she whistled up her dogs who had been flying around the pastures, probably exercising our adolescent bunnies, keeping them lean and wary. Luckily, they didn't seem to catch any, which relieved me. I considered our wild bunnies my pets.

Francesca's parting words to me disturbed my relaxed state. "Word Perfect will be picked up tonight between ten and twelve. She is shipping bare-legged. Her health certificate is on my desk, and you will need to send her saddle and bridle with her. You can just put them in a large trash bag with her name written on masking tape and stuck on the bag. Dennis Walker will not be in attendance."

I was able to only silently mouth the words "okay" as I thought, "So that's the way it will end." Francesca had turned and walked away without waiting for me to respond. Francesca knew how to avoid meaningful discussions.

Chess called a few minutes later, sounding tired but confident. He said, "I'm beat and can't come over, but I'll be ready for our trip to Devon."

I answered, "I can't wait." Then added, "Hey, I had a good day with your mother. It never occurred to me that your nickname, 'Chess' came from 'Francesca.'"

I could imagine a grimace on his face. "Busted. Yeah. It's felt like a curse or something. It got imbedded from the time I was born."

I shook my head slightly even though he couldn't see me. "No, Chess, don't think of it that way. The way she spoke of you today, well, she is proud of you. I learned a couple of things about your mother today. She can be sharp tongued and intimidating, but she's very guarded. It's hard to get her to tell me anything about herself or what she's thinking. And every time she says a tiny little bit, I see a little more. She doesn't want me to see who she is, but when I do, I don't dislike her so much. There's someone in there that I want to know better."

Chess sounded very tired when he answered, "Yeah. It's hard sometimes to love a porcupine. I've been trying all my life. It's finally getting a little easier. And, Lizzy?"

I softly said, "Yes?"

He continued, "Thanks for trying. Keep trying. I'll work her from my side, and you keep working from your side, and we'll win her over. Mother's not a very trusting person, but she's very loyal. You hang in there and once you're in, you're in. I promise you." Then he laughed, "You don't need to worry about Dad though, you've had him from the get-go."

I wanted to ask more questions about the meetings, about his dad, but I could hear the exhaustion in his voice so I let him go. Plus, it was my final night with Word Perfect, and my thoughts drifted toward what I had in front of me.

I went to Francesca's office and carefully copied all the pertinent information from the health certificate, gathered Wordy's saddle and bridle, and put it into a big black plastic trash bag. It was a terrible way to wrap up a custom saddle and fancy full bridle; the saddle alone probably had cost over five thousand dollars, even if Margot had hated it.

I searched for a couple of old saddle pads for padding, then put it into another bag to create a handle. I wrote the name of the horse and the name and address of the farm where it needed to be delivered on the bag on masking tape with a felt tip marker. After setting it all outside her stall, then I got her out and gave her a bubble bath while she pinned her ears, gnashed her teeth, and periodically kicked the back wall of the wash stall. She relaxed after I gave her some carrots and then I hand grazed her on lush grass while she dried off.

Word Perfect was a stunning horse. She may be surly but she was a sight and she needed to stay here and be Margot's horse. The mare had suffered for her beauty. She had aroused jealousy and greed and ambition from her owners all along the way; dangled as bait; snatched away as punishment. It needed to stop. This place needed to be her forever home. I watched as she happily tore at the grass and swatted at flies. Evidently, it was not to be.

The sun was sinking behind the horizon, the air was cooling, and the sounds of birds were being replaced by night sounds. From the woods came the low-toned "wooh-wooh" of owls. It was time to go in.

Wheezer sat in my lap and nuzzled under my chin as I watched TV in my sweat pants. I finished my microwave frozen dinner straight from the box, then let Wheezer lick it clean. We did the same routine with a bowl of ice cream. Still no call from the shipper. I fell asleep on the sofa. My phone woke me up. The driver was at the gate asking for the gate code. I let him in, glancing at my watch. Two a.m. I felt like I had been zapped with an electric charge, up and alert and strangely vibrating under my skin.

I gave the driver the paperwork and the tack-filled garbage bag. Then I signed for Dennis Walker, which felt wrong. But nothing felt worse than handing Wordy her final carrot and slipping on her halter to lead her out to the trailer. I was a traitor. When I handed the man her lead rope I had to stifle a sob that burned in my throat and nose. I handed her to him bare-legged, as per my instructions.

She followed him up the ramp and he backed her into a space next to another horse. Wordy pinned her ears at her traveling companion and bellowed in indignation. A chest bar was quickly set in place. The man shook his head and said, "Mares," then hung a huge hay net high between her nose and the nose of her trailer-mate. I walked up the ramp for a final good-bye, digging a peppermint out of my pocket. I could not speak, but I offered it to her. She blew her nose disdainfully, refusing to take it. Her rejection cut me to the quick. I was no different than all those who had come before me. We had all let her down, or so it appeared.

Once I was back in my bed, curled on my side with Wheezer tucked against my chest, I allowed myself to cry. The tears ran down my cheeks, my nose dripped and I unceremoniously wiped it with my nightshirt. Putting Word Perfect on the trailer seemed somehow worse than when we sold Hotstuff. As terrible as it was to see Hotstuff leave the only home he had ever known, and for Margot to lose her favorite horse, he was going to someone who loved him, would care for him, and would ride him well.

Without Margot, what chance did Word Perfect have for a future with those guarantees? That thought brought more tears. I needed to stop thinking of Wordy and Margot or I would never get back to sleep. I tossed and turned, and when I finally slept had an awful dream about looking for Word Perfect in South Florida and finding her in a run-down weedy pasture, her jet black coat burned to red, all her ribs showing and her legs covered with fungus. I was telling some person that she was a Grand Prix dressage horse, a valuable animal, and they were laughing at me. I woke up long enough to relive the scene in my mind and had trouble falling back asleep.

I was late getting down to the barn, but still beat Francesca. It was Friday, and I felt nervous and excited and wished I was at Devon today for Emma and Deb's Grand Prix rides. They had good draw times, toward the end of the class. I pictured them, mulling around the stables, hand grazing the stallions, sipping coffee, Emma pacing, and Deb lounging. Nat and Ryder would be grooming and braiding and fussing over the tack and clothes and stable chores with hours to kill.

Waiting was the hardest part. If Francesca had been there, she would be taking them shopping and buying little gifts. She had told me that Devon shopping was better than any dressage show in America, but not quite up to European horse show standards. It must be nice to think of horse shows as shopping opportunities. I knew that Francesca would be there already if she felt that she could. With everything going on, I was glad she at least would make it down tomorrow.

Chopper and Snapper flew into the barn and delivered their usual frenetic greeting. They jumped all over my legs with happy smiles, twisted their heads around, searching for an opportunity to make trouble. Today I had everything off the ground. Chopper made long eye contact with me, and then barked in frustration. They had enjoyed yesterday immensely.

I fetched them each a carrot, handing a carrot to each dog like awarding trophies. Chopper and Snapper, like most dogs, loved carrots. They held their prizes high and trotted proudly down the barn aisle and out toward the paddocks to settle somewhere dirty and gnaw on their treats.

Francesca made her way toward me slowly, stopping briefly outside of Word Perfect's empty stall. When she got to me, her voice was flat. "Were there any difficulties?"

I knew she meant Word Perfect's departure. "Yeah, but not from her. I hated putting her on the trailer. It nearly killed me."

Francesca crossed her arms. "I warned Margot it would end like this."

I felt frustrated. "Dennis wormed his way back in with that horse, and Margot took the bait. It's sick what he did. It's not fair to Margot, but it's especially cruel to the horse. You can't explain things to a horse."

Francesca leaned back, tipping her head slightly and narrowing her eyes, studying my face. "Dennis won't get anything he wants. I am certain of that. He may think he wants that Sophie creature, but he'll regret that decision in time, although we won't know that until after Sophie is officially his next ex-wife. I have no doubt that will ultimately occur."

A slow smile spread across my face as her words took full meaning. "Oh my God. Dennis isn't getting *anything* he wants?"

Francesca's face was a mask, but she didn't correct me.

I had a million questions, and I blurted out, "Are you telling me that Frank's not going to sell him either of the farms? That you're not selling Wild Child?"

Francesca looked affronted. "For heaven's sake, no. Deb is doing so well with Wild Child that the press would kill us for selling her ride. That would be terrible for business, too. And Deb and Emma need our Florida farm as HQ for the High Performance training sessions that start in November and the Florida qualifiers. I have a feeling there will be European tours for both of them. While Emma will be well-financed from her people in Texas, Wild Child is our responsibility and training grants won't cover all of Wild Child's expenses."

I stared at Francesca and said, "That's going to be very expensive."

She shrugged, "Well then, Frank needs to get back to work as soon as he is able, and so do I. Chess will need to work the hardest of all of us, as the new CFO of Cavelli Foods."

I took a moment to process what she was saying then hugged Francesca. "Frank is going back to work? Chess is CFO? Oh Francesca, that's great news!"

Francesca did not return my embrace so I didn't prolong it but stepped back and collected myself. "So, things here will be pretty much the same?"

She arched an eyebrow. "Who led you to believe otherwise?"

I suddenly felt cautious. As much as Ryder and I had chafed against each other, I was not going to rat her out now. Ryder had backed the wrong horse, but I didn't want to sic Francesca after her. Then there was Chess, who had shared so much with me about the offer from Dennis.

So, I hedged, "Um, well, it's just, I mean, we've *all* been anxious since Frank's heart attack."

That seemed to satisfy her for now. But her eyebrow was still raised and her head tilted examining me, "Why do I get the impression that even now plots are being hatched behind my back? Is there anything you want to tell me?"

I laughed uncomfortably. "Which ones do you want to know about?"

I braced for the worst but Francesca surprised me. Her smile was not catty or cruel but amused. She narrowed her eyes, her eyebrow relaxed and she lowered her voice conspiratorially, "If you're worried about Margot, don't. There are top-notch people hard at work on that project."

Francesca gave my arm a condescending pat-pat-pat, her lips turned up in the corners, looking pleased with herself. "Now, that job you love so much, let's see you do it."

I said, with real enthusiasm, "Yes, ma'am."

I began gathering up bridles and saddles and running back and forth to the grooming stalls to set out the tack for Lovey and Winsome while Francesca went to get her horse. Francesca was not going to give me any details, but her few words and her tone and expression made me feel a surge of confidence. I supposed that Chess would want to give me the good news himself later. Would I act surprised, or let him know first that Francesca had spilled the beans? Chess was the new CFO! I wondered if he was going to be anxious or excited. The important thing though, for all of us that depended on the Cavellis, was that things were going to be the same, at least as much the same as possible. Wild Child would never be Sophie's, and Johnny Cash appeared to be staying put. I felt energized and hopeful. Even though we had lost Word Perfect, things were going to be okay, maybe even better than okay.

19. Back On A High Horse

I called Chess as soon as I could. When he answered I said, "Congratu-
lations!"

He said, "So, Mother told you."

He sounded more resigned than excited. My doubts came back in a
wave. I said, "Chess, are you okay with all of this?"

He paused before answering. "I don't know. I'm being put in to
oversee what the new guys are doing, and I suspect they think this is
simple nepotism, and I'm afraid they'll resent me. The best I can hope
for is that they'll be reserving judgment based on my performance. I
don't want to disappoint anyone."

I tried to sound reassuring, "I think a company called Cavelli Foods
should have an actual Cavelli around. Otherwise it seems inauthentic."

Chess laughed. "No. Family businesses have to grow, Lizzy. Most
companies, if they grow, will lose the original family connection. It happens. In this case, the new guys intended to retain the name Cavelli
without retaining any members of the Cavelli family. Now, because they
screwed things up so bad and can't pay us, they are getting saddled with
not just one Cavelli, but two. Dad's back."

My spirits lifted. "Really? That's the best news of all."

Chess laughed, "Yeah, I think there's been a 'laying on of hands' or something. It's miraculous. The new guys at the company seemed happy to have Dad on board, too. They willingly put him on the payroll to placate Mother. Hiring me wasn't as easy to sell, but Mother wasn't going to allow Dad back to work under any other terms. So, basically they wanted Dad and I'm a throw-in."

I nodded into the phone, "Francesca has Frank play the good cop, while she takes the role of the bad cop. I've seen her at work. She's a good bad cop, scary really."

Chess sounded amused. "Mother never was in the running for Miss Congeniality. The point is, Mother and Dad have put me in the thick of things and expectations are high. If I make one wrong step, those guys will rub my nose in it. I'll have to work hard and deliver results."

I said, "I hope you won't come to resent, um, you know, the things, and um, the people that forced you out of the life you had made for yourself; that forced you back to the family business and the stress of supporting this farm."

I could imagine Chess rolling his eyes and staring at the ceiling when he answered. "I am unsure about a lot of things, but I don't think my judgment has been off, so no one forced me to do anything. This is not just about me anymore and that's not a bad thing. I told you that I wanted to have this time with my folks. I wasn't ready before now, but I am now. You'll have to be patient with me, though, as I find my feet in this new role and if I share my fears with you it doesn't mean I want out, or that I resent anyone."

He changed the subject, taking the focus off himself. "Hey, I understand that our friend Dennis Walker has disappeared. Hopefully, we've seen the last of him. I know you've got to be happy about that."

I hesitated. "Well, I'm happy that Dennis is gone. But, Word Perfect shipped out to Florida, so she's gone, too. So we're not really done yet."

There was a long pause, then, "What do you mean 'not done'? I personally put his sales contract through our shredder and had a few parting words with Dennis myself. As far as I'm concerned, the Cavellis are done."

I thought of Margot walking stoically past Word Perfect while the mare called softly to her. The image choked me up. "Chess, Word Perfect is gone, but we have to get her back. That mare needs Margot. She deserves Margot. Margot needs that horse; she earned that horse. I don't know how to explain how important it is for Margot to get that horse back, and unfortunately, the mare still belongs to Dennis."

Chess made a sound like "Hmmmm" into the phone. It was a tired sound.

I spoke quietly, trying hard to sound reasonable, "Margot risked life and limb to ride through that horse's defenses, and has earned the mare's trust. Anyway, we know Sophie doesn't want Word Perfect because she blames the horse for her break up with Dennis."

Chess sounded doubtful. "Whatever is going on between Sophie and Dennis isn't our problem. We are free of him, Lizzy. Dredging up all this emotional horse stuff just pulls him back into our lives. Let the horse go."

"It's not about Dennis. It's about Word Perfect, and Margot. We can pull this off, Chess. It's going to take some strategy though. Dennis sent the horse to a dealer in Florida to sell. And I promise you, that mare won't be an easy sell, she'll raise holy-hell when they are showcasing her, and could even hurt someone. And horses like that, well, sometimes they fall through the cracks. Sometimes they end up on the trash heap, neglected or abused."

A strong image, strong as the memory of a photograph, appeared in my mind's eye. It was my dream image of a sun-bleached and ribby Wordy.

Chess said, "Okay, if this horse is such a nut-job, why would we want her back?"

I answered firmly, "We do want her back. Margot wants her back.

Margot needs her back. And Word Perfect needs Margot as much or more than Margot needs her."

Chess whistled into the phone. "Lizzy, I don't think…" his voice trailed off. "The horse belongs to Dennis, not us, and money is still very tight."

I broke in, "Of course I realize it won't be your parents coming up with the cash this time. Emma is working on it. Her sponsors have money. But, if Dennis gets wind that the horse is being purchased for Margot, he would block the sale. This needs to be handled *covertly*."

Chess audibly sighed, "At times, with you and your friends, I feel like I'm in a spy movie."

I glanced down at my watch. "Oh, I've got to go. The Grand Prix class at Devon is being broadcast live stream, and Deb and Emma are showing pretty soon."

Chess said briskly. "Right, Mother mentioned that she and Dad will be watching that. I'll be on my laptop, too, Lizzy, but not watching the horse show. I'm looking at financial reports from Cavelli Foods."

We made plans for Chess to pick me up tomorrow to drive to Devon, and then I settled in with my laptop to watch Deb and Emma perform the Grand Prix test that would qualify them to do their freestyles tomorrow night. I put aside any thought of the conflict with Chess over Word Perfect, because this was Devon!

The famous Dixon Oval looked bigger than I had imagined, with every camera angle filled with bright yellow mums. They adorned the tops of every arena letter, and were mounded around the judge's boxes. Sponsor banners adorned the interior of the fence line and the camera panned slowly over them as the commentator read ad copy.

It was raining steadily with what looked like a stiff breeze. The overcast skies only made the bright yellow color of the mums "pop." Rain had been lucky for me and for Francesca. I didn't wish my buddies a hurricane-type storm like the one Winsome and I rode in, but I did wish them the same luck. I had begun to acquire my own superstitions.

The horses would enter the Dixon Oval from the designated FEI warm up arena by coming up a fenced lane set in the middle of the long side of the show arena. This lane connected the warm up to the competition arena. The commentator pointed out in a smooth and professional voice that grooms and trainers stood at the edge to watch, sending riders off to be tested and receiving them after the test. They stood ready to embrace their students and reward the horses, regardless of the outcome. He stated that it was a physical space embedded with emotion.

I thought he had stated it poetically, if a little over-dramatically. The professional voice then introduced the expert commentator. It was a well-known judge, who simply said a few words as they waited for the first horse to enter. Soft music played in the background. Even with the music playing I could hear birds chirping. I leaned in toward my laptop screen, frustrated not to be there and searching the screen for a familiar face.

The camera was focused on the lane as the first rider blasted into view in a flamboyant trot. I could barely focus on the ride on the screen or each successive pair. Rider after rider went, with tactful expert commentary from the judge being added to the voice of the sportscaster. The rain lightened up, and then miraculously, the sun came out. A rider from Canada on a large grey had the best ride so far with some moments of brilliance. Her score was the first to break 70 percent.

The camera panned around the arena, and my heart started to pound when I saw a flash of Deb and Wild Child in the warm up arena. Deb would be first after the break. I worried that the judges would still be getting settled in their booths and not fully focused. But I needn't have worried.

Wild Child trotted boldly into the arena, and I got a brief glimpse of Margot and Ryder walking behind him before the camera followed Deb around the outside of the dressage boards. The sun was glinting off his brilliant chestnut coat, and he was stunningly beautiful. My heart was pounding and I had a moment of light-headedness. There was something about seeing Wild Child and Deb "on TV" that made me giddy. It was odd; here was a horse and rider that I saw every day, whose talent I knew intimately. Heck, I had even had the pleasure of sitting on Wild Child, but now that they were being broadcast live, well, they seemed like a celebrity and larger than life. I had a premonition that Deb and Wild Child would become known throughout the US dressage scene after this broadcast.

The sportscaster was going over Deb's last competitive results and mentioned that the horse was owned by Frank and Francesca Cavelli, and that Deb was a long-time student of Margot Fanning's.

Once the whistle blew, Deb halted, and picked up the canter for her entry. At this point the sportscaster fell silent, and the expert commentator began her whispered analysis. Typical of Deb, she did not hold back in her riding or show the least bit of nerves. Deb might have been short, but she was mighty. I knew her spurs were sharp and her kicks had concentrated power. I was probably one of only a handful who saw Deb remind Wild Child just how much she expected as they came through the first corner with a quick tap of her spurs.

It was a threat and Wild Child heard it. No lolly-gagging, no girl-watching was allowed. Wild Child lowered his croup and rose mightily in his shoulders out of the corner into his first extended trot. Deb looked relaxed and tall but she made sure Wild Child didn't flag in his energy before the diagonal was finished and the corner was prepared. What a start! Of course, the trot work was Wild Child's strong suit. Deb wasn't going to let a single point go in the portion of the test she knew she could ace. The judge doing the commentary expressed her approval with the word "wow," but what really had her reaching for superlatives was Wild Child's strong piaffe and passage. She enthused that we would probably not see any other horses today who could match Wild Child's piaffe in technical correctness and in power.

Wild Child also had a wonderful walk, and Deb rode for those points, too. But, the tough part of the test was ahead; the canter tour. Deb rode through it correctly, managing the dreaded zigzags so that she made the correct count and fit in her last flying change early enough to set up the turn at the letter C, but it couldn't match the dramatic flair of her trot work. The commentator got enthusiastic again when Deb turned down her last centerline and delivered an incredibly powerful final passage to piaffe to passage to halt.

The crowd gave her a wonderful loud and enthusiastic applause, and from somewhere I registered Natalie's whistle, which made me grin at my screen. Oh how I longed to be there to greet Deb as she left the arena. I watched her walk out on a tired but content looking Wild Child. He was puffing, but his ears were pricked, studying the crowd with bright eyes. The camera panned to the scoreboard: Deb was the new leader with a score of 74% and change. The camera then panned to the lane as the next horse trotted in, and caught a bit of Deb having her bit checked by the steward while Margot and Ryder waited to receive their horse and rider. I felt exhilarated but wistful. I should be there. I would be there. Tomorrow couldn't come too soon.

I had to run to the bathroom, get a drink, and be ready to watch Emma and Fable. I knew that Emma was warming up, even if I couldn't see her. Natalie would have done her best to help Emma find her groove. Emma needed to impress the judges, not just for herself, but so that her sponsors; LuAnn and Billy, would be in a mind to do her a favor; a very large and expensive favor, not for herself exactly, not for Fable, exactly, but for Margot... exactly.

Deb had done an incredible job, and I now had confidence that her "wild ride" was not over. She would go to Florida for the High Performance League Training sessions where she would be observed by the

United States Equestrian Team coaches. From there, who knew what was possible? Just riding in the training sessions would be a crowning achievement of this crazy year. Whatever happened next, I knew Deb would be fine. She was competitive, but her strength was that she was as constant as the northern star, and would continue to shine regardless of the turnings of the world of competitive dressage.

Emma was far more brittle. She had all the talent and drive; she had Fable; she had the financial backing. But, she had her nerves, and under her veneer of perfection, I had seen deep insecurity. The woman who arranged her clothes in her closet by colors; whose collection of clogs were organized and displayed like the crown jewels of England, well, she fought to keep the rest of her life as well-ordered and it was an exhausting job that frayed at her emotional stability. Deb understood, and had taught me that all our training, all our time "practicing courage" was for those moments, certain as death, that we had absolutely no control over, moments that no person alive could evade. Emma was not there yet. Emma was still at war with her fears.

It was soon Emma's turn to enter the famous Dixon Oval and although the camera was focused on the lane, it was empty. The commentator was already going over Emma and Fable's bio and competition results, while the camera stayed focused on an empty lane. Margot and Natalie came walking up the lane, and trailing behind them I saw Emma and Fable walking tentatively. I actually gasped out loud when I recognized a cowboy-hatted and booted man walking beside them: Tank!

Tank was walking at her side, a hand on her knee. He was looking up at her and speaking. Emma was looking down at Tank and nodding. He stopped walking and Emma continued on. As Fable walked past him, he gave the stallion a friendly slap on the butt.

The camera followed Emma into the arena, and almost immediately the whistle blew. I was smiling as I watched. Seeing Tank slap that stallion on the butt, seeing Emma and Tank looking at each other in that moment; well, I had a revelation. Margot had always been Emma's rock. Tank, God bless him, was Emma's rock now. As Emma cantered down centerline I could see a difference. She was focused today. Emma had pulled herself together. She made her salute and began her test.

As impressive as Wild Child was, Fable had something equally special. Fable was the future of dressage sport, light and elegant. He was tall and long-legged and danced over the ground. Emma, too, had the look of a ballerina; equally long-legged with a delicate sort of beauty...."Blondie" looked good.

I wondered how the judges would compare the two tests, because Fable also had a good piaffe and passage and very flashy trot style, but different. The expert commentator said, "This is a new combination to me." Then exclaimed, "I need to get down to Texas more often!"

Fable and Emma were in complete harmony today as they flowed through the patterns. The doubt was gone. I began to smile and feel a wave of something run through my body. I think it was relief.

Fable had a better quality canter than Wild Child, and that could work for Emma in the scores for canter. I rode through the zigzags with her, and I counted out all her changes, too. Perhaps her pirouettes traveled too much off centerline. But it was hard to fault her ride.

When she made her final salute, the crowd went wild, and I heard Natalie's wolf whistle clearly this time. The camera followed Emma out of the arena as she rubbed Fable's withers and smiled. The cameraman pulled in for a close up of Emma's face. He hadn't done that for any of the other riders. I knew why; Emma was exceptionally pretty. She was still on camera while the steward did the bit check, and we waited for the final score to come up on the electronic scoreboard. The cameraman must have liked what he had seen. I watched her walk over to her group, which contained Margot and Natalie, and the solid form of Tank in his iconic cowboy hat.

The cameraman had to redirect to the scoreboard as the crowd applauded. Emma had a 75%. She had beaten Deb by less than a percentage point. And then all my gang disappeared from the screen, leaving me feeling lonely and drained.

I did watch the awards ceremony, and with only Wheezer to see my tears, I cried without restraint. Emma led the parade and then took her solo lap of honor. The lane was now crowded with trainers and grooms and I could still pick out Tank's cowboy hat as the camera followed the riders around. Emma and Deb looked amazing with beautiful award sashes around the necks of the horses. I knew that if Frank had been there, what a celebration they would have had tonight. I cried some more, but not with sadness and fear, instead with hope.

Tomorrow I would be there and regardless of the outcome of the Grand Prix Freestyle, I just knew I would have plenty to celebrate with my team.

I tried to start reading a new novel, but I had another story playing in my mind. It included everyone at the farm, and all the horses, too. I didn't know how it ended, but it was enthralling.

I tacked up Winsome and Lovey early the next morning and waited for Francesca. I was still on a high from watching Deb and Emma ride last night. I stood in front of the grooming stall watching the video clips that were popping up all over my Facebook feed when the terriers came zooming down the barn aisle, skidding hard into my legs, their toe nails getting a free filing down against the concrete as they slid "into home." I tucked my phone into my waistband and knelt down to give them some rubbing and baby talk.

Francesca caught up with her dogs, and got straight to business. "We have a full day and night ahead of us, Lizzy. Pull Lovey out. I just need to put on my boots and gloves and helmet."

I enthused, "Did you watch! Weren't they great?"

Francesca didn't answer but ducked into the tack room. Francesca was not going to rain on my parade. This was exciting stuff. I led Lovey to the mounting block and waited. Francesca came out ready to ride, whip in hand, looking like a military commander ready to review the troops. I barely suppressed a smile, which was not lost on Francesca.

She weighed in on yesterday's performance, "I would have reversed the placing, but no matter, tonight will be a shoot-out between our girls."

I was still smiling when I asked, "Did you notice that Tank was there?"

Francesca nodded. "Margot is quite astute when it comes to knowing what her students need."

"Margot arranged that?" I was surprised.

Francesca raised one of her perfectly shaped and arched brows. "More like sent out an SOS call. Tank was in Oklahoma chasing cows around, which I understand, unlike dressage competitions, pays real prize money. But he gave the ride to his assistant so he could come."

I laughed. "For him to leave a competition really says something. I'm beginning to think he might be in love."

Francesca dryly responded, "Astute observation," and rode away. I wasn't sure if Francesca was being sarcastic, or simply honest, but it didn't matter.

I got on Winsome, but had a hard time concentrating. After about twenty minutes I dismounted, and stuffed her with carrots, and gave her a cursory "lick and a promise" grooming. Then I got the next two horses groomed and was able to hand Francesca Johnny while I put away Lovey and then jumped on Papa for another brief ride, getting off of Papa before Francesca finished her ride on Johnny.

When Francesca returned with Johnny, I was just putting Papa back in his stall. She handed off Johnny and planted her customary kiss on his white nose. Then she turned and commanded sternly, "Don't tarry." And off she sauntered with her backward wave.

I ran around the apartment at high speed and set Wheezer up with food and fresh litter, then called Alfonso to go over feeding and turn out. He was in charge tonight and tomorrow, and he was patient with me even though I could tell he thought I needed a tranquilizer.

I packed a small bag, and although I was only staying over one night still managed to stuff it full to bursting for every weather possibility. I couldn't remember being so excited to go anywhere.

When Chess arrived, my hair was wet and hung down my back, soaking my shirt. I had a toothbrush stuck in my mint-frothy mouth, but at least I was dressed. I held up a finger and mumbled "one sec" as he kissed me on my cheek.

I thought about drying my hair, but instead twisted it into a knot and used a butterfly clip to secure it. I glanced in the mirror and had the strangest feeling. I did not recognize the girl, no, the woman, who looked back at me; she was glowing: happy, confident, attractive. She looked like someone I would like to know; like someone I would like to be. I laughed out loud and walked briskly back to Chess, my bulging overnight bag slung over my shoulder and my sunglasses propped on my head.

We picked up coffee for the road and headed for Devon. I stretched out my legs and gave Chess a recap of Emma and Deb's Grand Prix rides. He smiled while I babbled, occasionally turning his head to look at me full on. Whenever he did I scolded him with, "Eyes on the road, please!"

When I stopped to draw a breath, he said, "One of the things I love about you is your capacity to be joyful for others."

I didn't quite follow. "What?"

He followed instructions and kept his eyes on the road. "I've been around a lot of competitive people, and not everyone is secure enough to really be happy for others' success."

I pondered that for about a second, then shook my head. "But these are my teammates, they're my best friends, they're the people I love.

We've all been under this weird, dark cloud. And now that cloud is lifting, and I can't imagine feeling any other way but totally happy about what Deb and Emma have accomplished. They deserve it."

He flexed his fingers on the steering wheel and said, "Do you think Ryder feels the same way?"

I drew a deep breath and a sense of unease replaced my euphoria. "I don't understand Ryder. We're not that much different in age, but she seems like she's from a different generation. Maybe I didn't try hard enough, or maybe I tried too hard. She always shut me out. The one thing I do know is that Ryder is totally laser focused on Ryder. I don't think she wants the distraction of caring about anyone. So no, I don't think she feels like I do about what Emma and Deb just did."

Chess said, "Mother says she is gifted on a horse."

Chess' words stung a bit. But he was right. I said, "She's talented and focused and she works hard, too. But, she's always kept herself outside the circle. I've worked hard to step inside that circle, to feel the comfort of belonging. I feel sorry for her in a way."

We drove in silence for a few moments, and then I realized had forgotten to tell Chess about seeing Tank on the live stream video. So, I told him how Margot had sent for him. "Francesca said something about how astute Margot is about knowing just what her students need."

Chess agreed. "That's her job. She knows what you guys need to succeed. You and her horses, well, that's her life, isn't it?"

"Well, that's probably too much to put on all of us. I mean, we all try hard to ride up to the standards she sets for us, but Margot deserves more than just us in her life."

Chess sighed, glanced at me sideways, then said, "Is this about that horse of Dennis' again?"

I actually hadn't been thinking of Word Perfect at all. I had been thinking of Doc. But Chess had given me an opening. "Word Perfect is her name. And yes, we need to see that Wordy comes back to Margot."

Chess bit his lower lip. "Lizzy, you made that horse sound very dangerous. Unless you were exaggerating, I still say good-riddance. No horse is worth that sort of risk."

I realized I was pushing and adjusted my tone. "Of course horses can be dangerous. But you don't need to protect Margot. She knows how to set herself up for success, just like she knows what her students need to succeed. Besides, she's come through the tough part already with Wordy. I know, I was there to witness it."

Chess looked doubtful.

I mulled things over in my mind, trying to find a way to explain the risk and rewards of a horse like Word Perfect. "Do you know how Harry Houdini died?"

I had his interest. He said, "Houdini the escape artist? No, I don't know how he died."

I nodded, "I read somewhere that he used to let people come up to him in his shows and punch him in the stomach. He knew how to prepare his super-strong abs to block the blow."

Chess tipped his head, curious. "Okay."

"But one day a college boy came into his dressing room while he was resting on a couch and before Houdini could prepare, the kid punched him four times in the stomach."

Chess said, "And that killed him?"

I nodded, "It ruptured his appendix, and he died two weeks later from peritonitis since it happened in the days before antibiotics."

Chess looked puzzled. "And this would be about Margot and Word Perfect, how?"

I grinned, "Okay, so maybe it wasn't a perfect analogy, but my point is that preparation and knowledge is everything. Wordy could certainly hurt someone if it was the wrong someone. If that happens, she could end up on a downward trajectory, neglected, and often that's the path that ends with being sold for horsemeat. But, that won't happen with Margot."

Chess was silent for a long time. I looked out the window and watched the world go by while Chess kept his eyes on the road. Finally he said, "I trust your judgment, and I love Margot, too. If I can help in any way, I will."

I grinned at my own reflection before turning around to smile at Chess. There was no way to do more while driving than reach over and squeeze his arm before saying, "I feel right now like anything is possible."

Chess added, "But, remember, preparation is everything."

I laughed, "In life, as in dressage, you have to train, train, train, but in the end, you just have to summon the courage to take the wild ride."

He glanced at me with a puzzled look, then looked back at the road. I said, "Just quoting a famous philosopher."

I got another glance, and I smiled at him as I said, "Deb."

***

Devon wasn't anything like I imagined, even after seeing it live streamed on my computer screen. We drove down a road in a commercially developed area, past a commuter train station and various small shops, then turned down a side street following signs for the Devon Horse Show. Chess pulled around a line of cars waiting to park in a muddy grass and gravel parking lot. He wheeled into a VIP gate and pulled out a parking pass from his shirt pocket.

"You have a VIP parking pass?" I asked.

"Preparation, right?" He handed the pass and a five-dollar bill to the attendant, who checked his clipboard. "Yes, Mr. Cavelli, welcome to Devon. Please follow the signs and the folks in the blue shorts will show you where to park."

"Thank you," Chess replied.

"Okay," I said, "But what about…"

"Tickets?" he replied, pulling another envelope from the car's console.

I laughed.

We parked close to the VIP entrance gate and walked through an ancient looking turnstile and there it was: the famous Dixon Oval show arena, heavily decorated with banks of mums. Live evergreen trees were set inside the arena, along with two luxury automobiles with advertising banners on their doors.

Everything struck me as smaller and more intimate than the impression from my laptop screen. To our left was a path leading to the shopping "village." Even from this distance I could see there were a lot of shops. The air was scented with cooking foods coming from a lane of food stalls. In front of me was a vendor tent of custom boots set close to the arena and grandstand seating. I brightened when I realized it was the same vendor that Natalie and I had made friends with in Chicago! I even waved at her like an old friend, and she politely waved back.

Next to the boot vendor I was stunned to see a vendor tent featuring a gigantic blown up image of Ryder Anderson standing beside two gorgeous English Setters. It was a photo from her modeling session she had done earlier for Francesca's company. The tent was emblazoned with the banner "High Horse Couture." Under that, another banner read "Custom tailored and designed technical riding jackets and breeches."

Chess whistled in amazement. He said, "Did you know about this?"

I shook my head and whispered, "Nope. Francesca unloaded a bunch of boxes into the trailer, but I know nothing about this."

Chess whispered in my ear, "I sure hope Mother can sell some product to at least cover the booth rental. Can't be cheap."

I walked over to the tent, Chess in tow, and a salesperson greeted me. She began her spiel. She said, "Can I show you the most comfortable and high-tech breeches and jackets ever made? They are all custom-made so the fit is unparalleled. And with the choice of fabric, lining, piping and collars, you can design a distinctive look for yourself, even color coordinating with your horse."

I stuttered my reply. "I, I, I work for the Cavellis but I haven't seen the jackets yet."

She enthused, "How wonderful! Well, I understand that both Deb and Emma are wearing High Horse Couture coats and breeches to-night. Have a look at the fabric choices. It's just astounding the variety that is now allowed since the rules have been relaxed."

Some real customers came into the tent and the salesperson politely excused herself. I briefly opened a few fabric sample books, and then examined the sample racks of jackets and breeches. The Cavellis had just come through tough financial times, and in that time, Francesca had shifted money around to buy and hide Johnny Cash, keeping him secret from almost everyone. At the same time she had expanded High Horse Couture, adding custom jackets to her line of custom breeches, all "under the radar." How she did it I suppose no one would ever know. I noted that the saleswoman had gotten out her measuring tape. A cus-tomer was making an order. Chess pulled me reluctantly away from the tent. We were supposed to locate the Cavelli "box" and join the party.

There was a cowboy in the arena doing a liberty show that included three horses. Chess and I both stopped for a moment to watch him stand on the back of one of the horses, barebacked and bridle-less, cracking a bullwhip in each hand. The whips were loud as gunfire, but all three horses looked bored. Across the arena I saw another cow-boy-hatted figure leaning on the rail. He was watching intently and applauding the cowboy's acrobatic moves. I smiled to myself. It was Tank. Kindred spirits.

I tugged at Chess' arm to pull him along while we looked for our "box." There was already a large crowd, the grandstands full, and the noise level such that I guessed the crowd was already tippling while having appetizers. Chess and I continued to scan the stands without spotting any of our crew. Then I heard a loud, "Yo!" We looked up to see a wildly waving Frank Cavelli.

Chess yelled, "Dad! You made it!" Chess and I exchanged glances and broke out in wide grins. Not only was Frank sitting in the stands, there sitting beside him was another surprise. Doc.

Chess took my hand and we climbed the stairs then slid in behind a narrow small trestle style folding table loaded down with food and drink to sit in a cramped space that had six folding chairs.

I giggled with glee when I greeted Frank with a kiss and shook Doc's hand crazily. Doc and Frank were well dressed with blazers sporting High Horse Couture logo patches on the breast pockets. Frank even had a rose bud in his lapel. But the best part was the twinkle in his eye. Frank was Frank once again. I said, "Frank, you and Doc look so handsome." I leaned over toward Doc and said, "Doc, I had no idea you were coming."

Doc shrugged. "Usually when I come to one of these I'm working the event. It's kind of nice to just be a spectator. Though," he pulled out his cell phone, "I'm on standby with the vet to assist if needed."

Frank said, "Poor Doc got drafted to baby sit the old man since Francesca is flitting around in the main office like she owns the place. Her little company is sponsoring all the freestyle classes. Every Freestyle champion gets a custom jacket, and every reserve champion gets a pair of custom breeches. And hey, what do you think of the jackets?" As if anticipating Chess' objection he said, "Marketing, my boy. Totally tax deductible. I can get you one if you want. No charge."

Chess and Frank both laughed. "I'll pass, Dad. Thanks."

I enthused, "Well, I had no idea. But, what a great way to promote her clothes. I saw the store, it's beautiful. I don't know how she does it all."

Frank nodded, "Franny is still empire-building. I was ready to be done, but Franscesa won't hear of it. Now she's putting me back to work, so back to work I go. I wouldn't dare disobey my beautiful empress." He whispered in my ear. "I got a real good checkup yesterday."

I gave him a long hug and felt myself tearing up. "That's so terrific. I'm just . . . just so happy."

"Yeah," he said, "Yeah, me, too. It's been a long road."

Doc reached into an inner pocket and handed Chess and me wristbands, different colors than our VIP bands. "Francesca said you and Chess could borrow her owner's wrist bands to go visit the crew in the barns."

Frank pulled a cigar out of his inner pocket and leaned back. My eyes widened and Frank smiled a naughty smile, then added, "No worries. I only smell them and hold them in my mouth. Scout's honor."

Chess looked doubtful. Doc said, "I'm under strict orders to beat the pulp out of him if he pulls out a lighter or heads toward the food booths. Not only that, his flask is loaded with only one bullet. He has to decide when to use it."

The two men guffawed. Frank said, "I only get one drink per day of liquor. It's a hardship for sure, but at least there's wine. I brought some lovely wine to go with our dinner. You guys be sure to have some of this food. These are just the appetizers. Francesca is allowing me to partake of the real food tonight."

"In reasonable amounts," Doc said.

"Ah, what do you know about it?" Frank replied.

"Well, I've done my share of horse nutrition plans." The looked at each other and laughed like a couple of schoolboys.

I stood and put the wristband on and at the same time gave Chess permission to stay with the boys. "Chess, you enjoy. These two guys need a chaperone. After I see my team in the barns I promise to sample the food, because I know no one packs a picnic basket like Frank Cavelli."

"Damn right," Frank replied. "Frank Cavelli is back."

I gave Frank a hug and another kiss, and then just stared into his eyes for a moment, smiling at him while he fingered his cigar and almost looked a little bashful. I felt myself begin to crack once again, so I dropped his hand and headed for the stables before my emotions totally got away from me.

20. Let's Dance

I wandered through the barn feeling like an outsider. The barns were old, with narrow aisles crowded with trunks and tables and chairs. I didn't recognize anyone. Finally, I spotted Deb leaning against an open stall door and talking to whoever was inside the stall. Our hostess table was set against the same wall with a vase full of red roses as a centerpiece. I called out, "Deb, oh my God, you and Wild Child were awesome yesterday! I watched it all."

I sounded like I was twelve years old. Deb looked amused, her dimples deep, her eyes bright. She said, "Lizzy, it's about time you showed up."

"I would have gotten to the barns sooner but stopped to visit up in the Cavelli box." I pointed to the roses. "Wow, these are beautiful. Who sent them?"

Deb dimpled up coyly, "I have a fan."

We hadn't spoken about her on again, off again romance for a long time, but I hadn't forgotten Pali, and it appeared Pali hadn't forgotten Deb. I prodded playfully, "Would this fan have an eastern European accent?"

Deb nodded. "That would be my fan. Good job, Lizzy. Pali is busy on tour at the moment, but he managed to watch my ride yesterday on the live feed. It was good to hear from him, and the flowers were a nice touch."

I started to ask more, but Deb had turned her attention back to the stall.

Natalie stood on a step-stool braiding Fable, who looked tranquilized, his head hanging low, ears drooped to the sides.

I said, "Is he okay?"

Nat laughed. "Yup, Fable saves his energy for the ring. The rest of the time he's practically in a coma, except when he's begging for treats. He'll eat anything, but bananas are one of his favorites."

I asked, "Where's Emma? I want to congratulate her. I was floored at how she pulled herself together last night after her last show. That was some test."

Deb and Natalie exchanged a look. I said, "What?"

Deb said, "Well, we think Tank deserved that ribbon as much as Emma. She had a little 'come-apart' when we got down here. It had nothing to do with Fable. He's the best stallion ever. Emma got stage fright. Margot did her best to talk her off the ledge, but then Margot called in Tank for backup. I got to say, that guy is the genuine deal. He dropped everything and came. Just like that." And Deb snapped her fingers.

I nodded. "Yeah, just now I spotted him watching the cowboy doing the liberty act in the main arena, but I was too far away to talk to him."

Deb said, "Tank and that cowboy happen to know each other from back in Texas. When they talk to each other it's like listening to a foreign language."

Natalie added, "You should have seen Emma when she spotted Tank. Pretty impressive how he helped her find her backbone. That girl's made of tougher stuff than she knows. Tank reminds her of that. Good dude."

I nodded. "But, she won't totally believe it until she is tested more than a few times. None of us can believe it about ourselves until we keep sticking the landing."

Deb slapped me on the back. "Lizzy, you are becoming a dressage guru."

"Nope, you're the guru, Deb. I'm your 'guru-in-training'."

Margot came down the aisle with a clothing bag in one hand and a boot bag in the other. "Lizzy, darling! I'm so glad you're here."

She handed Deb the bags and then gave me a hug and a kiss on my cheek. I bubbled, "What an incredible show. I rode every step with Deb and Emma yesterday and was dying I was so excited."

Margot smiled broadly, "It was something. Emma is finding her courage, and Deb, well the world is finally discovering our Deb."

I said, "I couldn't believe it when I saw the High Horse Couture tent. Francesca has added jackets."

Natalie added slyly, "And Ryder is literally eight feet tall. Larger than life."

Deb shot Natalie a look that said, 'careful,' then Deb added, "Y'know, the kid looks great in the ad. I doubt if anyone here has noticed it's the same teenager who's hanging on to Wild Child and cleaning my stall and my tack. I'm wondering if she'll stick this out. I'm going to go out on a limb and guess the pay for modeling beats what she's earning as a groom."

It was Natalie's turn to return the warning glance to Deb, but it wasn't lost on either Margot or me. Margot purposefully changed the subject, turning to me, "Darling, did everything go smoothly at home?"

I nodded, then got excited again, "Margot, did you know that Frank is here?"

All three women made surprised and happy sounds that showed they clearly did not know it. Margot asked, "How does he look?"

"Well, thinner, but he looks more like our old Frank. He and Doc and Chess are sitting in the stands in Francesca's reserved box, and they

375

have a great spread of food and drink, and everything is going to be okay again. By the way, Doc and Frank are wearing High Horse blazers with logo patches."

Margot bit her lower lip and smiled. "Doc is here? Oh, dear. And wearing a High Horse Couture blazer? Will wonders never cease?" Margot shook her head, amused. "Why am I not surprised they've been enlisted as walking advertisements for Francesca's business?"

I cleared my throat respectfully before continuing. "Um, and when I say everything is going to be okay, I mean everything." I lowered my voice. "Chess and Frank are back at Cavelli Foods and Equus Paradiso Farms is NOT for sale. The horses are NOT for sale. Chess said he and Dennis had some choice parting words, and then Chess tore up Dennis' contract."

Margot grabbed me by the shoulders with excitement, her fingers gripping me hard. She said, "What?"

"Francesca didn't tell you?" For a moment I felt panic, like I had shared information I wasn't supposed to.

Natalie frowned, "What is wrong with that woman?"

Margot had me repeat my words, slowly and carefully.

Deb shook her head and said, "Any other tidbits to throw our way? You're a valuable informant now, y'know, with you and Chess being an item."

That embarrassed me, and Natalie saw it. She said, "Lizzy, come on and own it, sister. He's a good man. We all know it."

The three women stared at me and I shifted a bit left and right, and then said, "Okay. Yeah. I own it."

Margot laughed out loud, shaking her head. "Darling, you are absolutely adorable, and thank you for delivering such good news. I can't for the world understand why Doc is here, though. He never mentioned it to me and he's not working the show, unless maybe they called him in at the last minute."

I said, "Oh, no, that's not it. He's here as a guest of the Cavellis. Doc and Chess and Frank are sitting together in the grandstand, in the farm's reserved box."

Margot rocked back on her feet, shaking her head almost in disbelief. "Well, well, that IS a surprise."

I added, "Frank called him his 'babysitter' but I think that was just a joke."

Our conversation was cut short when Emma and Tank arrived, holding hands and involved in an intense conversation carried on in low tones. I could sense that her voice was anxious and Tank's soothing. Then Ryder joined the group and things got into high drive. Chit-chat time was over. I needed to get out of the way and let the grooms do their jobs, while Deb and Emma began the process of detaching themselves from the social aspect of the show and focusing on their own mental preparation. Tank stayed within arm's length of Emma, silent now but present.

I walked with Margot to the warm up arena. We stood side by side, leaned on the fence and watched a few competitors begin to warm up. Margot put her arm around my shoulders and tipped her head until it touched mine. She whispered, "Thank you, darling Lizzy."

I said, "For what?"

She dropped her arm and turned to look at me full in the face. "For all the little kindnesses that I don't even know about."

I smiled but felt a knot form in the pit of my stomach. I needed to talk to Tank and Emma something fierce since there was still one 'kindness' left to perform, and it was out of my hands. The image of a ribby, sunburned Word Perfect flashed in my mind like a warning, reminding me we must not fail. I would have to wait, though. I turned my attention back to the arena.

Because the horses were going in the class in reverse order of the previous day's standings, Deb and then Emma would be the last to go.

Margot and I still had time to lean on the fence of the warm up and observe the other riders in the class go through their warm up routines. We did that for a few minutes, only horse talk quietly passing between the two of us. Margot constantly checked her watch and finally sent me back to the stands to keep the guys company, although I was sure Francesca would be taking her seat shortly.

The sun was dipping below the horizon, the large arena lights humming as they came on.

It was time for the Grand Prix Freestyles to begin.

When I arrived back at the Cavelli seats, it was dark enough that the lights made a halo at the top of each post and the air temp had dropped, making it chilly. The rain had thankfully moved out, ushering in crisp air. Summer had come and gone. Fall was officially here in Pennsylvania.

Dressage at Devon was a boisterous party on freestyle night, with spectators' moods limbered by alcohol and happy anticipation. I was so keyed up with nerves that I could barely appreciate the rides that were going on inside the arena, or participate with the enthusiastic applause as each finished. The freestyle music was loud and clear and the stands were packed, with additional spectators crowding the railings.

Francesca had to raise her voice and lean in to explain Dressage at Devon to Chess who, unlike Doc and Frank, had never been to a competition of this size. But really, she was explaining things about Devon to me, too. She said, "Dressage at Devon, this atmosphere here tonight, well, so many of the European shows have this exact feel to them. Frank and I have gone to watch many of the big shows in Europe and we both think this is exactly what we need more of to increase both spectators and prize money in the US."

I watched the next rider come in, the grey horse from Canada. That meant that Deb was up next. I peered through the stands across from us to see if I could catch a glimpse of Wild Child, but the stands were packed tonight and I had no luck.

Two girls in official DAD staff matching shirts and slacks were standing like soldiers waiting for the rider to enter, when they would step forward in unison and put the section of arena back in place.

The judge at "C" rang his bell, and the rider came to a halt outside of the competition arena, raising her arm. The announcer said, "Jackie, your music is rolling." The boisterous crowd instantly fell silent.

She cantered smoothly up centerline, making a good and square halt. The DAD girls marched forward with the section of little white dressage boards, and closed up the entrance gap at "A."

It was a wonderful freestyle. The Canadian rider was good, very good. The music was emotionally moving and dramatic, rising and falling with the beat of the trot and canter. The canter music was especially powerful, and the ride closed even stronger than it had begun.

The gauntlet had been thrown down to both Deb and Emma. I had sudden doubts about their musical choices. Deb, and especially Emma, had music that was excellent, and matched the horses well, but neither had music that packed the same emotional punch as what the Canadian had done.

When the score went up I got worried. The judges had been moved. They received over 76%, with very high scores in the boxes for artistry. This was not going to be simply a shoot-out between Deb and Emma.

Chess leaned over to me and said, "That's a really good score, isn't it?"

I had tears in my eyes from being so moved by the ride that I could only nod enthusiastically. "And totally deserved. One of the best I've ever seen. She might just win it."

I leaned forward and gripped poor Chess' leg because next came our stunning Wild Child. Margot and Ryder stood at the gate. Even across the arena I could see that Margot was chewing her cuticles without taking her eyes off of Deb.

Deb had on a new coat. Silly how I noticed such a thing, but it was brown instead of black, with black velvet on the collar with bronze piping and bronze points on the front. Under the lights, the bronze gave off a metallic sheen that matched the sheen of Wild Child's coat. I knew that Francesca was watching for my reaction. She had color coordinated the fabric to match the horse. Francesca had a gift for design. I leaned over and whispered, "Now that's a sharp jacket, Francesca."

Typical Francesca, she said nothing in return, but I knew she was lapping up my compliment like Wheezer lapped up cream. I could almost bet that jacket would show up on social media tonight even if it was placed there by Francesca herself.

Even though I was used to Wild Child, and the way the light reflected ripples of bronze undertones in his sleek chestnut coat, he still had an effect on me. Even without dramatic music, he was dramatic.

Most people in the stands had never seen Wild Child under the lights. There was a hushing in the stands, with a low murmuring. The bell rang, and Deb made a few steps of breathtaking piaffe, showcasing his talent before the judging had begun. And then she stopped and raised her arm. The announcer said, "Deb, your music is rolling."

When Wild Child's music came on loud over the speakers, he turned into a ball of fire, like a rock star on stage. Deb would not need to kick him in the corners tonight. When he heard his swing music start, the arched crest of his neck seemed to inflate, rising up high in front of Deb, his ears went up and pointed straight ahead, his eyes grew large and his nostrils flared.

Wild Child looked ready for danger. He was not a spooky horse, but I had seen him bolt twice; once when the pistol-style sprinklers had suddenly come on in the warm up arena, and then in an awards ceremony. Like all horses, Wild Child used flight as the first line of defense, but if flight was not available, he would go to battle. He would never fight with Deb, not after all they had accomplished together, but he would fight alongside Deb, shoulder to shoulder.

I glanced at Francesca and then at Doc. They both had on their poker faces, but Doc blinked a couple of times. He had seen a lot of horse shows. Wild Child fidgeted in his halt, never attaining immobility, and when his music started back up he jumped forward ready to throw himself at this with all his heart and soul and all the substantial muscle power he could muster. Deb had to hold him back, to tell him only with her small aids of leg, rein, and weight that 110 percent was too much, to wait on her seat, to trust her. I sat on the edge of my flimsy folding chair focused on Wild Child and Deb with crossed-fingers on both hands and I sent Wild Child this message telepathically, "Remember your training big guy, and all will be well."

I swear I saw him visibly settle. But I knew it had nothing to do with me. Deb managed each step, feeling that Wild Child's engine was revving on too high an idle, she had to ease the clutch out ever so gently and smoothly.

I barely registered Deb's music; I was so focused on the technical aspects of the ride I could barely breathe. But I could see in my periphery Chess nodding in time to the music. The canter always went smoother in the freestyle than the Grand Prix since Deb and Margot had cleverly worked the choreography to highlight his strengths and mask his weaknesses.

When Deb headed down centerline for her final piece, loaded with piaffe and passage transitions, I had real tears in my eyes. They were tears of joy, but also tears of relief. Whatever scores the judges awarded Deb and Wild Child; they were champions to me. Wild Child had been one of the most difficult horses I had known in my life, but he would forever remain in my mind and heart as the most magnificent creature on God's green earth.

I drew a deep breath and was able to sit back more securely in my folding chair, while applauding and cheering and watching the ring steward do the bit and spur check and then Margot and Deb embracing and, along with Ryder, staring at the scoreboard.

"What do you think?" Chess asked.

"It's going to be close," I replied.

It seemed a long moment where we all held our collective breaths, but then there it was...77.750%. Deb was the new leader. Now it was Emma's turn.

Emma and Fable danced into the arena in a light-footed and lofty trot. Margot and Natalie and Tank took up their positions at the gate. The arena lights reflected on Fable's blue-black coat. He was certainly as impressive as Wild Child, but a totally different character. Fable was tall but narrow, with extraordinarily long legs, like a fashion model. Emma matched his looks, lean and equally long legged. She, too, was wearing a new creation of Francesca's. Emma's coat was the traditional color of black with pale blue corduroy on the collar and shadbelly points, and the collar had a fine row of rhinestone crystals. Fable's brow band was also set with crystals that flashed under the lights. For Francesca, this was relatively understated styling, but the effect was elegant, like the horse and the rider.

The bell rang, and Emma halted. She arranged her tails on her shadbelly, licked her lips, and then raised her arm. The announcer said, "Emma, your music is rolling."

As the first familiar strains of Emma's Texas-themed music filled the famous Dixon Oval, I could tell that the crowd had immediately fallen for Emma's music. People were making the sorts of noises of approval that caught hold and began to echo through the seating.

Emma and Fable seemed to feel it, too. Fable did not show the fire and power of Wild Child, but instead showed incredible confidence and ease, showcasing his lightness. This was Emma at her finest, the best I had ever seen her perform. This was her moment, and this was her horse of a lifetime. "Blondie" who was from the northeast, was now and would forever be, the "Yellow Rose of Texas." It was our inside joke that this person who hated country music, cows (and supposedly) cowboys, was now branded as a full- fledged Texan.

And "Blondie" now had herself a genuine cowboy. I sure hoped she understood what a lucky girl she was. I glanced across the arena again at Tank, black hat pulled low over his brows. He watched intently while Emma had what he called her "run," although, no cows or running was involved in the Grand Prix Dressage Freestyle. I wondered if he understood that Emma was having the "run" of her life.

Tank began to clap in time with Emma's music, and then Margot and Natalie joined in. I took their cue and began to clap in time, and then people around us joined in. Soon the entire stands seemed to be clapping with us. It was exhilarating. I felt like the audience rode stride for stride with Emma's last piaffe and passage tour. Fable seemed to lift his legs higher in time to our clapping. We in the audience rode with Emma, bringing her safely down that last centerline. At the final salute, the applause was deafening. Emma looked stunned after her salute. She gazed around the arena with one gloved hand over her mouth. People stood up in their seats. Fable walked out of the arena on loose reins; head bobbing, unfazed by the night lights and audience and noise. He was one cool customer.

Fable stood quietly puffing for his bit and spur check, white foamy sweat showing against his black coat under the reins and between his legs. Again, it seemed a long time for the scores to come up, but when they did there was a collective gasp from the crowd. 77.750%.

Deb and Emma had tied.

The announcer exclaimed, "Well, I never have seen this before. What happens now? Let me get my expert commentator here from the live stream booth to educate both me and any of you in our audience who are wondering the same thing."

There was some rustling around and static in the booth; soft background music began to play. Emma and Fable left the arena, and the top eight horses were being called to the warm up arena to be pinned for the awards ceremony. We knew for certain that Deb and Emma would be the top two horses; how it shook down at this point was not really important in the big picture.

Finally another voice came on the PA system, the voice of the judge who had done the expert commentating of the Grand Prix test yesterday. She said, "The FEI rules state that in the case of a tie, the higher artistic mark breaks the tie. If those artistic marks are the same, then the higher mark for harmony breaks the tie, if those marks are the same then the higher mark for choreography breaks the tie. So, now we just watch the scoreboard to see how the judges ranked our class."

The announcer came back on and thanked the judge, then said, "However our judges rank this class, we have certainly had an evening to remember." Then the scoreboard, which had been blank, lit up, and the announcer's voice grew excited as he read off the results. Emma, our golden girl, our "Yellow Rose," was on top and Deb was second. The crowd roared their approval.

The horses were quickly pinned in the adjoining warm up arena with colorful neck sashes and Fable and Wild Child also were dressed in their award blankets.

We were all on our feet now, even Frank stood as the eight top horses filed into the arena for the ceremony. The judges walked from horse to horse, shaking hands with the riders as the announcer called out names and places. Horses were photographed with trophies, and then it was time for the victory gallop. The third place Canadian, who on most other nights would have won, gave a nod and tip of the hat to Deb and Emma.

Fable led off quite conservatively, and Deb had to rein in Wild Child who clearly saw this as a challenge to his masculinity and wanted desperately to "overtake." Deb was grinning and had no trouble barking at Emma to, "Step up the pace, Blondie!"

Emma gave Fable a bit of gas and Deb brought Wild Child into a trot, letting him show off his gigantic extended trot that still looked like it would catch Fable's canter. But then Deb and the rest of the field left the arena, and Emma came into trot to enjoy her solo lap of honor.

The announcer put on Emma's music, and let her linger a bit with *Yellow Rose of Texas* while we stood on our feet and clapped along while she passaged. Emma was grinning now and petting Fable. It was time to leave, and she waved at the crowd, stopping inside the gate where Tank, still wearing his cowboy hat, stepped forward to hand her a bouquet of yellow roses, which delighted the crowd. Natalie was there to take Fable, so Emma slid off her horse. Tank took off his cowboy hat and threw his arm around her, and they kissed. It was a kiss that we all watched, and was most likely shown on the live coverage. No denying it now. Not sure how you could make a more public statement than that.

The music got louder, and the announcer exclaimed: "And now, for one of our most treasured traditions of Freestyle night at Dressage at Devon. The horses have danced all evening in our beloved Dixon Oval, and now it's time for the humans to dance. So, everyone, come on in! Then he surprised me even more, he said, "Emma, why don't you and your beau start the party? You certainly have reason to celebrate."

Emma looked frozen in place, but Tank put his Stetson back on and broke off one yellow rose, handing the bouquet to Nat. Then, he slipped the single yellow rose through a buttonhole on her jacket, and gave her hand a tug. They walked right into the middle of the arena, and Tank took her by the waist and grabbed her hand. She looked mortified, and beckoned at the stands in a "come on, please!" gesture. Chess grabbed my hand and said, "Come on, let's help them out."

We needn't have worried. The arena quickly was flooded with euphoric dancers. Soon there was a crush of us dancing away and laughing. Chess was trying his best to twirl me around. He knew how to dance better than I did. From time to time I caught a flash of Tank's black hat. Then I saw that Doc was there with Margot. I stopped long enough to grab Margot and give her a hug. Then I saw Frank and Francesca, Frank standing tall over his petite wife, both her arms around his neck. He was smiling broadly as she laughed. The sight of them looking light-hearted and happy made my eyes fill with tears. Things turned a bit more raucous when Natalie stood up on the judge's platform and led the crowd in a boisterous rendition of "YMCA." I did wonder how she had put Fable up so quickly. Natalie did love a party.

Exhausted from dancing, we finally made our way back to our box. It was getting late and the crowd had thinned, but Frank still had wine that he insisted needed drinking. He claimed there was no reason for us to carry any bottles home, and I expected Francesca to argue with him. He was "glowing," perhaps a bit too much. But tonight, on this night, she let it go. Besides, we needed to wait for Ryder and Natalie who had gone back to the barn to attend to the horses. Nat told me they had quickly taken care of their horses earlier, but left the barn a total wreck to join the party, so they had a lot left to do. In addition, tonight they would be getting the horses legs set up with support wraps, and the stalls would be bedded deeply so the horses would at some quiet point in the night get some much deserved rest. I offered to help, but Natalie insisted that I stay put.

So, I sat in the box and watched the crowds thin out and a self-satisfied quiet settle among us. We had extended our "box" with chairs set on the stairs, probably a strict violation of fire codes, but no matter. We were extending our happiness. Emma still had on her boots and spurs and shadbelly coat. She didn't care; she simply unbuttoned her jacket and pulled the zippers on her boots down a couple inches.

Finally, Ryder and Natalie and Deb joined our circle and Frank upended the last wine bottle into two healthy glassfuls and pushed platters of our leftover feast at them.

Margot stood up and said, "Well, team, this has been the most perfect night I can remember." She raised her glass. "I want to raise a glass and toast our wonderful horses who were both valiant and brilliant tonight. I want to toast my two lovely girls who demonstrated the highest standard of the classical art of dressage tonight. I am so proud. I also want to toast my dearest friends, Frank and Francesca Cavelli, who have come through rings of fire to be here and remain here as the body, the heart, and the soul of Equus Paradiso Dressage....Salut!"

We echoed Margot with raised glasses, "Salut!"

Margot sat down, and we all turned our attention to Tank. He had taken off his hat, set it on his chair, and stood. Without his hat he looked younger, and even a bit bashful. Then he looked at Emma and said, in his deep Texas drawl, "Emma, hon, maybe you should do this." But she shook her head. So, he continued. "Margot, when you called me, you were concerned about Emma. But, what you didn't know was she was concerned about you."

Margot looked uncomfortable and confused. Tank continued. "It wasn't just Emma. I heard from Emma but you had an entire circle here lookin' out for you, and I understand that things weren't looking so good for a bit."

Tank looked around at each of us. "Lizzy there, and Deb there, along with Emma, and then we pulled in Doc there, and then I came into the concern and got LuAnn and Billy on board. And all the while, Frank there and Francesca, they both stayed apprised of the situation."

Margot was looking even more confused. "Tank, darling, I have no idea what you are talking about, but the suspense is killing me."

Tank said, "Well, LuAnn and Billy just bought, sight unseen, some crazy black mare down in Florida." He nodded toward our collective group. "Just on the strength of what all your friends had to say."

Margot's hand flew to her mouth, and Doc put his arm around her shoulder. She fought back sobs and her eyes filled with tears. Doc tightened his grip, and said, "I had a nice talk with both LuAnn and Billy, and here's what they were planning. They have some frozen semen from Fable, and I have a vet buddy in Florida who specializes in embryo transfers. We've already shipped Word Perfect to his clinic. They'll keep her there as long as it takes to flush an embryo. They'll lease us a recipient mare, and that way LuAnn and Billy get Fable foals from Word Perfect. Once they're done, you get Wordy back to ride and show. They'd love to get one foal a year if that's possible, the rest of the time, she's all yours. They still own her, but you have kind of a permanent ride, if you want."

Margot sputtered, "How did you manage? Dennis would never knowingly let her come back to me."

Natalie blurted out, "Got that right. But, Dennis thinks the horse is going to Midland, Texas to be a broodmare, and that Tank here was the buyer. He thinks the buyer is a retired pro-football player."

Tank pointed to Chess. "And this one, he came up with just the right paperwork to make it happen."

Chess shrugged modestly. "All in a day's work, pardner." He and Tank exchanged high fives and toasted each other with a Texas-brand beer.

Francesca added, "Honestly, Margot, I'm not sure how you can love that mare, she's so terribly difficult."

But Frank waggled his finger at his wife accusingly. "Ah, ah, ah...the best ones always are my love, the best ones always are."

And we all burst out laughing.

Epilogue

Chess and I wandered around, feeling slightly disoriented from jet lag.
I kept saying, "Guten Morgen" and smiling at everyone we passed, receiving friendly *Guten Morgen*s in reply. Finally someone answered, "Good morning" in an American accent.

I quickly asked, "Can you please direct us to the show office?"

We waited in line to speak to a show official. When we got to the front of the line, I considered attempting my high school German, but the woman behind the desk took one look at us and initiated the conversation in British accented English. "How can I help you?"

I answered, "We were told to pick up our security passes here before going to the stabling area."

She nodded, "You are with the Americans?"

"Yes, the dressage team."

"In what capacity?" Her voice was clipped, efficient.

For the life of me I couldn't think of an answer, but Chess stepped forward, "Owners. We own the dressage horse, Wild Child."

The woman put on framed tortoise shell reading glasses and began to look through a file box. She pulled out a large envelope and said, "Yes, I have them right here. You would be Mr. and Mrs. Cavelli?"

Chess had the good sense to answer for both of us, because in my mind, Mr. and Mrs. Cavelli were back in Peapack, New Jersey. He said, "Yes."

She said, "You will need to show me your ID's and sign for them."

Chess and I pulled out our passports, flipping them open on the counter top. We signed a paper saying that we had picked up our passes and I signed my name: Elizabeth Cavelli. It still felt awkward. We hung our security passes around our necks and were directed to the stables.

The stabling area was ringed by a chain link fence with thick shrubbery. We passed through security to find a block of stabling and a warm up arena full of horses and riders training. Beyond the stables sprawled a huge parking area with seemingly endless rows of horse vans. Chess and I drifted over to the arena, listening to several languages among the railbirds. I scanned my eyes over the horses and riders in the arena, not recognizing anyone.

Then I heard a familiar laugh followed by the word "Darling" somewhere to my right. My eyes followed my ears, and there she was.

Margot and Emma and Deb had been on the road two solid months, and I had missed them all terribly; but most especially Margot. She stood with several other coaches, switching comfortably between German and English, the group laughing. She was wearing slacks and a tailored jacket, her hair in its typical bun, sunglasses tipped up on her head, still an elegant standout among a small knot of her peers.

I tugged on Chess's sleeve and tipped my head in her direction. She hadn't yet seen us. I suddenly felt inexplicably shy. Chess took my hand in his as we walked over to her. Coming up behind Margot, he touched her on her arm saying, "Excuse us for interrupting, ma'am, but we heard you speaking English and thought you might help us."

She pivoted around, eyes wide, and threw her arms around both of us exclaiming, "Oh my darlings, you made it. Just look at you two! You have that newlywed glow. I haven't seen you since the wedding reception, what a night that was!" She waved good-bye to her friends and led us away from the warmup toward the stable block.

I said, "Don't look too close, Margot, I'm wearing the same clothes as yesterday and I couldn't sleep on the plane. I'm exhausted."

Margot wagged her finger at us. "You must stay awake though, darlings. You must not give in to the exhaustion. You can sleep tonight. Otherwise, it will take you three days to adjust and we simply don't have time for that."

We walked through the stables until we got to a large American flag and red white and blue drapes. Deb yelled my name and then Wild Child whinnied. Emma popped out of the tack room followed by Tank, who, as always, wore a cowboy hat. We had a happy greeting. I gave carrots and scratchies to Fable and Wild Child, and then was introduced to our new "traveling grooms." Deb looked at us and said, "Margot, I think those two need some good strong German coffee."

Our group left the chain link inner-sanctum and found our way to the shopping and eating "district" of the large showground, leaving the grooms in charge of the horses. We stood around a tall table drinking dark roast coffee with heavy cream and eating fresh baked "brotchen," taking in the sights and sounds and breakfast aromas.

Margot pulled a German magazine out of her tote bag. The cover photo was of Emma on Fable, and standing next to her was Tank, wearing his best black cowboy hat. Emma was a "cover girl."

Deb started to laugh. "Blondie and Fable have been shaking things up, but who knew that the Germans would be so cowboy crazy? They can't get enough of Tank. They love the guy."

Tank looked embarrassed. "That magazine lady kept asking *me* questions."

Deb said, "They don't see too many guys in Germany wearing cowboy hats, Tank."

"But," he replied, "I'd feel plain odd without it."

Deb teased again, "You need it, you might get a sunburn."

Emma added, "Hah! Sunburn? I've never been so cold in June! I had to buy a new jacket."

I looked at Emma and noticed something different about the way she looked at Tank. Germany had given her a new way to look at her adoring cowboy. Tank's stock was still on the rise and I couldn't help but wonder when they would finally make it official.

Deb changed the subject, "I know Nat has her hands full, but she claims she's got it all under control. You think she's doing alright?"

I said, "Yeah she's doing fine. She is working her tail off what with riding all three of the bambinos and handling the others youngsters. She's good about spending time with the new babies. When you get back you'll be amazed how much Wordy's foals have grown in just two months. They are all pistols, but those draft mares are incredibly patient with them. If Wordy had raised her foals herself she would have killed all three of them by now."

Margot said, "I still can't believe they got three embryos from Wordy. It does make me feel better about their investment." Margot paused, looking at Tank. "I will be eternally grateful for what Billy and LuAnn have done for us."

Tank nodded. "They're good folks."

Deb changed the subject back to Natalie. "So, how do you think Nat's enjoying being a horse owner?"

I grinned, "Deb, Natalie is spending all her money on stuff for Boingo. She just bought him a custom saddle. That photo spread of her garden sculptures brought in a new commission, but I think she's already run through the down payment. You might have to reel her in when you get home."

Deb and Margot exchanged glances. Deb said, "I wish I could go back home now, but Wild Child's been the anchor ride for the team and they still need me. I won't be sad, though, when they tell me to pack my bags, but it looks like I've got another month to go."

"But, Deb," I replied, "It's been one heck of a wild ride, hasn't it?"

The dimples came back and she nodded back. "I'm still taking the wild ride, Lizzy. But I admit I've been homesick."

Emma added, "Deb hasn't been able to save any feral cats since she's been here and it's killing her."

Everyone grinned, but Margot changed the subject, "Darling, I hope Word Perfect is behaving."

I was still grinning when I answered. "Wordy and I have an understanding. I don't ask her to work too hard, and she doesn't try to kill me. She really needs you in the tack to bring out her best, but you should see Doc and her. Wordy has a total crush on him. He puts his arms around her neck and calls her "Mama" and she whinnies whenever she sees him."

Emma sniffed, "Word Perfect certainly has better taste in men these days."

We sipped our coffees and left our thoughts unspoken for a beat.

Margot turned to Chess. "And how is Frank?"

Chess said, "Dad looks great! He's lost more weight, and Mother has him going to ballroom dancing classes. He complains, but they are actually pretty good. Well, Mother is better than good with her dance background, but the two of them are having a lot of fun. Good news on the drinking, too. He's stuck to only one glass of wine at dinner. Mother and I know he still occasionally sneaks a shot of whiskey but we're turning a blind eye to it. It makes him happy to think he's getting away with it."

Margot put her hand over his. "That's wonderful news, Chess. And how are you doing?"

He turned his hand and curled his fingers around Margot's and said, "Never been better. I actually like working at Cavelli Foods. I've finally finished my feasibility study on the Nona Cavelli frozen entrées. It looks like I'm getting a green light on it. We've never done frozen foods, it's a whole different market, but the research and marketing people think it will be a hit."

Everyone around the table offered congratulations. Chess had done it, along with Frank and Francesca. Cavelli Foods was back on its feet.

Then I realized I had news to share. "Hey, you guys, I forget to tell you that Ryder came by the barn."

Emma frowned. "Hah, I thought I'd never hear her name again. She's not still scheming about buying Johnny Cash, is she?"

"Nope," I replied, "But she did look into his stall and said, 'What a waste.'"

Margot mused, "I wonder why she stopped by. She left pretty abruptly, saying she was going to take a break from riding."

"Break must be over. She came by for a pair of spare riding boots she left at the back of our hall closet in the apartment."

Margot said, "Good for her."

I added, "She did say that she has a new plan. She's been modeling and taking courses at NYU. She says she will still make it to the Olympics, but it will be on her own horse, bought with her own money from her modeling career."

Emma rolled her eyes and said, "She's delusional. Competition is brutal."

"Emma, darling," Margot replied, "Don't count that one out. I have a feeling she could do it." Then Margot looked at me, amused. "Lizzy, what say you?"

I said without hesitation, "I never liked Ryder, but to her credit she's not afraid of anything. She's as tough as they come and she can ride. I could see her in the Olympics one day."

Margot smiled broader. "Me, too."

We finished our coffee, and Margot linked her arm through mine and we led the way back to the stables. She drew me close, giving my arm a squeeze. "I'm so glad that you're here. It's always good to have the family together."

All I could do is return the squeeze, marveling that Margot had called me 'family'.

Margot continued, her head bent toward mine, her voice lowered. "You girls have made me so proud. It's not an easy life we've chosen, but for us, it's the only life we would choose."

I smiled back, "You're right, Margot. I never considered leaving. Even when I hurt in every part of my body. Even when I was so sad my legs wouldn't hold me up. Even when I was really afraid of being injured or worse."

"And why is that, do you think?"

I had to think about that a moment. I said softly, "Because of you. Because of Deb. And Emma, and Frank, and if I'm honest, because of Francesca, too. I made those leaps through rings of fire on faith. I always knew you would be on the landing side."

Margot gave my arm another squeeze, and we were welcomed into the stable by a sweet chorus of whinnies; home.

Karen McGoldrick rides, teaches, and trains dressage at her own Prospect Hill Farm in Alpharetta, Georgia.

She is a United States Dressage Federation certified instructor/trainer; earned her USDF Bronze, Silver, and Gold medal rider awards, all on horses she trained; and she graduated "With Distinction" from the USDF "L" program.

Karen got her first "working student" job by answering an ad in her community newspaper at the age of 12. Before, during, and after college, she worked on and off for a variety of trainers until she and her husband bought their first farm in 1992.

Karen feels that the best part of being a dressage instructor is sharing the insights, joys, and sorrows that riding, training, and loving horses have brought to her life. Writing a novel is one more way to do this.

The *Dressage Chronicles* books come straight from her heart.

Author photograph courtesy of Alicia Frese

CPSIA information can be obtained
at www.ICGtesting.com
Printed in the USA
FSOW01n0201310317
32518FS